ABOUT THE BOOK:

Hot steamy New Orleans, is laced with pure Southern sexiness. Main characters Celia DuBois and Jeffrey Jackson are going through the ups and downs of love and are experiencing the consequences of past relationships where there was a lack of self-love.

Relationship issues, skin color bias, domestic violence, distrust, self-doubt and irresponsible sexual behavior are just a few of the issues that is placed under a microscope and then enlarged for the reader to absorb as both characters "speak" in first person, giving the reader an up close and personal view of the story being told.

Benny's Place, a Coffee House/Café located in the French Quarters of New Orleans; charming and visually nostalgic embodying the ambiance of a 1940's juke joint, is where Celia and Jeff meet. Benny Thibodeaux, the proprietor (or as Benny pronounces, pro pie ta) of the café is a New Orleans native who's wisdom and clairvoyance is the motivational balm that both Celia DuBois and Jeffrey Jackson are in desperate need of.

PRAISES FOR "COFFEE-COLORED DREAMS":

"I really enjoyed reading "Coffee-Colored Dreams"! It is VERY good....an absolutely delightful gem! You have your unique style. It's real...it's honest and provides authentic characters everyone can relate to. The main characters, Celia and Jeffrey, have texture and depth, speaking in the first person...bridge the narratives so that they create moving pictures of themselves and the love story so that we are never lost. I especially liked the healthy attitudes around being true to oneself...goals & purpose in life. Congratulations on your debut novel. I know we are going to hear more from you. Wishing you continued success! You go girl"
--Anelle Williams, aka Sistah Anelle, Co-Host The Women's Collective KPFT 90.1 FM Houston Pacifica Radio

"Coffee-Colored Dreams has a strong and clear voice driving it. The dialogue is clear. You have a good book here!"
--William July, Author, BROTHERS LUST & LOVE, UNDERSTANDING THE TIN MAN and THE HIDDEN LOVER

"I received a renewed belief in the concept of "falling in love" and see that romance is beautiful when it's genuine. I would suggest this novel to any lover of fiction as it not only tells a great story but can also draw you in to learn about yourself"
--Asar, Moca Suite Magazine

"Wonderfully written and so full of life, each page brings you into each character completely and beautifully. I am now a huge fan of Pamela Davis-Noland!!!! A true talent! I loved each word, from the first to the last........"
--Michele T (Houston, TX)

"I was very fortunate to meet Mrs. Noland and I must say that her book was outstanding! It made me feel like there are other people in this world who go through the same issues. Celia's dream came true. She found her Prince Charming in the form of Jeffrey. I am anxiously awaiting a sequel. I have to know what happens to Benny and especially if Laura will come back into the picture. This book was just REAL. Pick it up. You won't be disappointed."
--Erika R. Malveaux "Avid Book Reader" (Houston, TX)

COFFEE-COLORED DREAMS

by pamela davis-noland

KEEN-AMITY PUBLISHING
New Orleans, LA
keenamity@yahoo.com

Contact Author:
info@coffeecoloreddreams.com

All Rights Reserved
Copyright © 2003 by Pamela Davis-Noland
No part of this book may be reproduced or transmitted
in any form or by any means, electronic or mechanical,
including photocopying, recording, or by any information
storage and retrieval system without permission in
writing from the author.

Printed in the United States of America

First Printing

To Ryan —

May all of your dreams come true, sweetie.

— Mama

ACKNOWLEDGEMENTS

First off, I would like to thank the Father, the Son (Jesus Christ) and the Holy Spirit for blessing me and giving me this opportunity to share the gift He's given me.

Now, I'm going to riddle off a few names and these people are the one's who listened to me talk about this book for YEARS! Thanks guys for always believing in me: Peace aNd Love... ;pamela

Mama - (You taught me that prayers work! Thank you Mama!)

Daddy - (I finally did it "Old Man", although I can't place it in your hands, I know you are proud of your little girl and you are smiling down from heaven. I love you, Daddy...)

Garrett Noland - (G-Money, words cannot describe how grateful I am for all your sacrifices and your unending encouragement. I love you. Always...)

Jeannie, Clifton Jr., Carol, Cynthia, Donald, Danny, Patricia & Geraldine – (My wonderful siblings I grew up with. I couldn't have asked for a better childhood with you guys! Thanks for accepting my strangeness. (smile) And to Joyce, my long lost sister, I am glad you were found.)

Angie Patterson-Edwards – (I did it, girl! Can you believe it?!)

Phillman Bellow – (You are a great listener. Thanks a million!)

Tanya Wardlow - (You were the first one to encourage me to keep writing, thank you so very much. You were also the first one who ever heard me utter the words, "Coffee-Colored Dreams" when I was afraid to tell anyone else. I am forever grateful to you.)

Veronica Bell- (My #1 fan! I'll never forget those afternoons when you listened to me read my book to you. You have no idea how much you inspired me to go on.)

Carrington Lei – (You are such a talented writer, I look forward to the day when your books will be on display for all the world to read. KEEP WRITING!!!)

Carless Grays - (I love you, man! Thanks for all your kind words.)

Lidia Pedraza – (You are a great lawyer and an even better friend! Get ready, there are more books to come.)

William July II – (You have been my inspiration through this long tough road. I am forever grateful! You are an awesome Black Man!)

BEULAH LAND COMMUNITY CHURCH - (I absolutely love being a part of the rag-tag team! You see what God can do? (smile)

COFFEE-COLORED DREAMS

*For Jazz...
All My love,
Aunt Pam*

1/2020

Introduction

Celia DuBois

When I was just a little girl, about 8 or 9 years old, I already had big hopes and dreams about my life as an adult. I knew exactly what I wanted out of life and what I would give back in return. I knew I wanted to be a teacher since I was in the second grade. I was always an exceptional student who loved to go to school more than anyone I knew, and it thrilled me to help others in my class who were not as smart as I was. Secondly, I knew I had a special gift with words. I knew how to spell them and how to use them in sentences. Thus, my writing career began at the age of thirteen when I wrote my autobiography and Sister LaSalle told me that I had a gift.

I teach creative writing at St. Theresa's High School on Chenevre St. in the upper eastside of New Orleans, Louisiana where crime is low and eminence is high. Mainly because of the priests and nuns who live in this area. They are greatly respected by the many Catholics in this community who fear the wrath of God. They rule these streets with folded hands, sharp tongues and judgmental glares. I know because I grew up right here in this neighborhood.

I am also a part-time, working on being a full-time, writer. I have a few short stories that have already been published in magazines, a published book of poems proficiently entitled *"Black Girl Blues"* and I am currently writing a novel that I started seven years ago. I would have finished by now if I could stay focused. I seem to get sidetracked every time I meet a new "Mr. Right."

The first thing I thought I would do as an adult was to get married to a wonderful man who treats me like a queen. Just like my father treats my mother, after forty plus glorious years of their somewhat sickening, blissfully happy marriage. As a matter of fact, my mother and all her sisters (six of them) have good husbands. I don't know what my grandmother taught them but whatever it was, they learned it at a young age because all of them have been married to the same man for years.

I have one sister and one brother and they are both married with children. My aunts must have passed their joie de vivre down to their daughters because all of them seem happy as ever with life and their husbands. They are all mar-

pamela davis-noland

ried to halfway decent men and unless they are putting up a front, they all seem happy too. And then there's me: Celia DuBois. I am the youngest daughter of Clifton Ellis DuBois and Mary Leora DuBois. I am the mother of none and wife to no one, and no real prospects to speak of! I have enough bridesmaids' dresses to open up my own ugly-bridesmaid-dress boutique. I feel like the proverbial spinster schoolteacher, and going to *any* family function makes me physically ill.

The good fortune of being a sadistically happy wife and mother, like my mother, my sister, my aunts and their daughters, has not yet smiled on me. Nor was I blessed with their perfect butternut-colored skin, or their long, shoulder-length, fine, brown hair. No. I look just like dear old Dad and his people – dark skin, big dark eyes and hair the color of crude oil.

"Lil' Bull," that's what everyone in my family calls me because I look just like "Big Bull," my father. I found out when I was about twelve years old why my father was given the name "Bull," and I was floored. I assumed it had something to do with his tenacity and his incredible strength but that wasn't it, although he is both tenacious and strong. No, my father acquired his nickname from his mother, who on several occasions out of sheer anger toward him for looking just like his father, used to curse at him and tell him that he was as black as a bull and twice as ugly. Just like his father, she would say. Someone should have told Nana about verbal abuse. The name was meant to harm but God sure turned it around for my father's good because he is definitely a strong man. The name has stuck with him all these years and so it stuck with me too. Especially when I was a little girl and my siblings wanted to get even with me for whatever mortal sin I had committed. "Ol' black bull," they would say. I wish I had a dime for every time I was called that. The only thing that saved me from being totally ugly in their sight was my wavy, easy to manage hair. I distinctly remember my mother thanking the Lord that I "at least" have some decent hair.

I'm thirty years old now and I'm starting to get really depressed about my life. I consider myself truly blessed in most aspects but I can't help but feel a little less than adequate whenever I go to any family function and get asked the same question over and over, "Chile, when you gone put that pen down and pick you up a man?" Or, "Hey, Cee, what happen to the last dude you was wit?" Or my favorite one, "Now dis' here one would make some pretty babies, girl. You gone keep dis' one, right?"

Ugghh! Anyway, this is my story....

Introduction

Jeffrey Jackson

I knew I had made a mistake the minute the preacher began to utter the words, "I now pronounce you…". I remember thinking to myself "This woman is not my soul mate," and man, was I ever right. Six years have passed since then and I've finally come to the realization that I need to make some changes in my life… soon…real soon! And then she came home from work one night and informed me that she realized that we had possibly made a mistake. I could have leaped for joy right where I was standing. I had practiced saying those exact words to her countless times but had chickened out every time. I knew if I had said something in the first place, we wouldn't have gotten so caught up in both our mothers' joy for us *and* we would have taken some time and thought this thing through a little bit more maturely. Every time I would begin to say anything remotely close to "I want a divorce," a pain of guilt would shoot straight to heart and I would brush it off and pray that someday things would just work themselves out.

I knew this woman was not for me because during our entire marriage (and I use the word "marriage" very loosely) I had a recurring dream about another woman. Another woman who is the complete opposite of the one lying next to me every night. This woman, I believe, is my soul mate and as soon as I find her I'm going to make her mine, as corny as that may sound.

I dreamed about her again the night before I was to go to Court to end my six years of hell, i.e. my marriage. I dreamed she was standing near a huge picture window wearing a long flowing gown and the sun was shining brightly through the window. I could see right through her gown and she was stark naked underneath and her skin was the color of mocha and as smooth as silk. She was staring at me wide-eyed and innocent as though she was waiting for some sign from me that I wanted her. I reached out my hand to her and she moved forward just a little. But when I took a step toward her, she retreated. I could tell she was afraid of me so I folded my arms and waited for her to make the next move. She smiled sweetly and then turned and began to walk away. I ran after her but no matter how hard I tried, I couldn't catch up with her. I felt a tug on my shirt and

pamela davis-noland

turned around and several people, mainly my family members and a few close friends, were holding on to me... I woke up in a cold sweat.

I couldn't go back to sleep so I decided to get up and start my day. I did my usual morning ritual: thirty-minute workout, eat two bowls of cereal, shave and cuss for having to shave and shower. The minute I turned on the water in the shower and stepped in, I started weeping uncontrollably, so much so that I couldn't tell the water coming from the showerhead from my tears. It was trippin' me out 'cuz I couldn't put my finger on the reason for *so many* tears. Were they happy or sad tears? *Maaannn*... I don't know. Maybe both.

For the majority of my life I have let other people tell me what is best for me. What I *should* do or *shouldn't* do whom I *should* or *shouldn't* hang out with, whom I *should* or *shouldn't* date. I've even allowed my mother to talk me into being an accountant instead of following my dreams of being a singer. Oh, I still sing, but only part time and only as a backup 'cuz I've never really had the nerve or the self-esteem to be a lead singer but I've been told I have a great voice and I should. I've been writing songs for years but I haven't done anything with them except sing when I'm by myself, which has been quite a bit since the divorce. I'm cool with that, though. I need some time alone anyway 'cuz my life is about to change tremendously.

I don't know if it's the fact that I'm finally free from my marriage or if it was the dream I had the night before the divorce was final but whatever it was that clicked the light bulb on, I couldn't be any happier.

This is my story...

POOR, POOR PITIFUL ME

Celia DuBois

The minute I walked into Calvin's apartment and saw the painfully attractive, Mulatto woman sitting on the sofa, my heart fluttered exactly four times. I know because I counted. And if I'm not mistaken, I think I heard it. Maybe it was just my imagination but the look I saw on his face wasn't. He looked guilty to me, but in a cool kind of way. I quickly dismissed the look and mentally assured myself that she must be his sister or a very close relative, with them having the same urine-yellow color and all, but mainly because neither of them seemed to look the least bit worried about my unannounced visit. Or so it seemed...

Calvin ushered me in with all the charm of a Southern Creole gentleman and she sat upright, arms crossed over her chest and gave me what I thought to be a genuine smile. And then came the slap in the face; he introduced me as his "good friend" Celia. Not my "girlfriend, Celia" not my "lover, Celia," not "the one who I made passionate love to last night," not "my future wife, Celia," just, "My good friend, Celia."

When the hot flash of embarrassment subsided and my vision came back into focus, I noticed that smile of hers again. It was then that I realized I'd seen it a million times before from so many light-skinned, silky-haired "sistas" here in this majority Creole populated State of Louisiana. That "Oh, you poor lil' black thang" look, that "You know you too black for him anyway" look, that "Now you know he can't take you over to his grandmama house" look. The same "look" that I get from so many of my pigment-deprived "sistas" when the dating competition begins. The "look" that is as familiar to me as my reflection.

I could have slapped them fake blue contacts out of her eyes. It's bad enough that she was only a set of full lips and a big ass away from being a white girl; she did not have to go there with them fake blue eyes. And the tossing of her silky, shoulder length *real* hair when she stood to greet me was also her way of saying, "Bitch, I'm better than you." I could have choked the life out of Calvin for making me go through this.

She reminded me of all the little light-skinned girls I went to school with who, when they felt like being mean to me, would remind me that my hair was nappier and my skin, darker than theirs, but then smile and say "But you not *that*

pamela davis-noland

ugly." That's how she acted when she extended her perfectly manicured little skinny hand to me and barely touched it for fear of a maybe getting an instant tan or something, said hello, stood and walked to the kitchen calling over her shoulders asking if someone wanted something to drink. Calvin said no and then looked at me with pleading eyes, begging me not to trip. I guess he saw the steam coming from my ears. But I was not about to give either one of them the satisfaction, especially my new enemy. She could have his yella' ass, they could get married and have a thousand yella' babies for all I care. At least that's what I told myself so that I wouldn't break down and make a *complete* ass of myself. I made up some excuse about having to borrow his car the next day, smiled a little *too* big when she sashayed back in the living room with a glass of wine in one hand and a steaming hot plate of food in the other, and left. But I *did* slam the door behind me for an extra effect, and I haven't talked to him since.

That was two weeks ago and now here I am sitting in my living room feeling sorry for myself –*again*. I am so sick of these so-called relationships. I don't know when I'm gonna learn to just take my time. I am the worst hopeless romantic I know. No matter how hard I try to just go out on dates and leave the romance out, I always seem to get involved somehow. Now I'm doing the same thing I always do – *trip*. I've even resorted to my old smoking habit and I haven't smoked herb this much in almost a year. This man has completely blown my mind and I wasn't even prepared. That's what I get for not focusing. I should have known he was too good to be true. But I really wanted it to be true this time. He treated me just like my father treats my mother: very attentive. And he acted like I was the only woman for him.

Now here I am staring out of the window at my neighbors, Liz and her crazy ass husband, arguing as usual. Those two make me so sick with all of their drama. At least once a week, he'll pop up unexpected and demand that she let him in because he has "a right to see his child." At least that's what he screams at her every time she puts him out. She put him out this time because he's been sleeping with some other woman and she caught him in the act. And now he has the nerve to tell her that if he ever came over and found another man in the house, he'd kill her and him. *Men* - I swear I'll never understand them. I just feel sorry for that precious little girl. I've never seen him so much as speak to her, but she's suppose to be the reason he drops by every other day.

Now there are a million things I could be doing right now instead of sitting here getting emotional gratification from someone else's misery. Like for instance, I can finish my novel instead of tossin' it aside every time I meet a new man. And tossin' it even further when we break up. But it feels plenty good to know that there is somebody as miserable as I am at the exact time that I am. I know that's pretty triflin' but right now I don't care. I'm feeling selfish. And this high is putting me in one of my moods.

I cannot believe I'm going through this crap again after I specifically told myself that I wasn't going to let it happen. I had had just about enough of this

COFFEE-COLORED DREAMS

when I broke up with my so-called fiancé, Stephen, and now here I am again. But this is totally different, I mean this man was like a dream come true and I wasn't looking when he appeared out of the clear blue. And just like all the others, we got real deep - *too* deep - too fast.

I don't know what it is about me, but sometimes I feel like that little puppy in the window with the big sad eyes waiting for someone to come along and take me home and love me. I become loyal and at his beck and call. And then he does something dumb to piss me off and I turn on him like a rabid Doberman.

Calvin was so sweet, nothing at all like Stephen, with his angry black ass. Stephen had issues. He was always mad about something, and his pleasant days came about as often as a snowstorm in New Orleans. To this very day, I can't for the life of me figure out why I got so deep with him. That is one of my problems: taking on someone else's. I knew from day one this man wasn't for me but I had to try and make it work, as if it was my duty as an American or something. We argued about everything. I put up with him for as long I could stand it. I even went so far as to let that fool put a ring on my finger only because I wanted to show my mother, my aunts, my sister and everybody else who gave a damn that I was in fact worthy of a marriage proposal. But after that knock-down-drag-out fight we had, when he accused me of messing around with one of his friends; I said "see ya." He took back his funky ring and I vowed that this would be the last man I put up with. I know exactly how I want to be treated and I thought Calvin was the one. Well, he was for a season, a really short season. Until he showed me that I was right about all my fears I had in the beginning of our short-lived love affair. He's not the first light-skinned brotha who's kicked me to the curb for someone that their family might approve of more. But I guess I just thought he was different.

I was feeling about as low as I'm feeling right now when I met him. I was still pissed at myself for wasting so much of my time with Stephen. And all I was doing was getting high with my best friend, Maria or hanging out at my favorite bookstore in the Old French Market. I literally ran into Calvin in the Social Science section. I had my head down because my eyes were red and I had left my Visine in my backpack at home. He looked up at me with this big silly grin, like he knew I was high, and said something extremely corny like, "Hey if you wanted to get to know me…" or something of that nature. Anyway, I wasn't in the mood for conversation so I just smiled and kept right on walking. Next thing I knew, he was standing behind me talking ninety miles an hour about a writer named E. Lynn Harris and how tripped out his books were. I looked up and acknowledged that I had in fact read all of his books and politely dismissed him with another smile. But the brotha was persistent. He started a whole'notha' conversation about the magazine I was reading. So against my better judgment, only because I thought he was so cute with his crooked smile, I let my guard down just a little. Next thing I knew; we were exchanging phone numbers, calling each other every night, going to Dragon's Den to listen to the poets every Friday,

pamela davis-noland

spending Saturdays in bed talking about the night before. Watching cartoons between lovemaking, taking off from work just to hang out and go to Jackson Square or the Riverwalk, and finishing each other's sentences. For five-and-a-half months I was on cloud ninety-nine. *Now* you would think a sista like myself would have picked up on the oh-so-slight-hints. Like for instance how he had me on some sort of schedule. He made it a point to plan our meetings down to the exact second but I never put much thought into it until two weeks ago when I defied the silent rule. Now the memories of past conversations when he said he wasn't ready to settle down with one woman yet are rushing in like a mighty wave. *Still* - I was shocked to see some other female in his house. Of all places! A pretty, well built, mulatto female, at that. I was never too keen on sharing, so here I am again, back to square one. Right where I was when I met him - high and mad at myself.

Just as I was about to open my window so that I could hear what Liz and her psychotic mate were arguing about this time, the phone starts ringing. I almost let the answering machine pick up the call, but I decided to answer it instead, hoping it's Calvin because I feel like cussin'.

"Hello." I said dryly.

"Hey, girl, whatcha' doin'?" Maria asked.

"Hey, Black, what's up?"

"Nuttin' girl, just chillin' tryin'ta figure out what I'm gonna do with this nappy-ass hair. I done fired my so-called beautician, Sissy. You know she chopped off my shit and then charged me full price. After I specifically told her dense ass that I hated it. Not to mention she always so busy since she hired that fag."

Now I know I should have let this phone ring. I'm not in the mood for Black today. "I thought it looked nice," I said, as if I was really interested.

"Girl puuh-leeze. Anyway, I thought maybe my best friend might fix it for me."

"I don't know, Black. I'm in a funky mood today. I doubt you want me to do it."

"Cee, don't tell me you still trippin' over Calvin? Girl, I ain't never seen you trip this long after breaking up with nobody. That brotha' wasn't takin' no hair out'cha brush, was he?"

"No, Miss Rudolph, contrary to you and your whole voodoo practicin' family, not everybody in New Orleans believes in that shit."

"Forget you, Cee. My family ain't even practicin' no voodoo. At least nobody but my crazy Aunt Mauchin. But, everybody knows she crazy. Anyway, don't be tryin' to change the subject. Why you still trippin'?"

"I'm just tired of the same old tired relationships. I mean one day I'm the queen on the throne, the next day, nothin'. Just like that."

"Which is why I keep me a spare at all times. I never know when I'm gonna have a blow out. As a matta'a'fact, I got me a hot date tonight with a fine spare,

COFFEE-COLORED DREAMS

which is why I need you to do somethin' with my hair. Please Cee, this is important."

"Important?!!" Damn, this girl is pissin' me off.

"Yeah, I mean come on girl, you can't just stop livin' just because of a few bad choices. Hell, you know I done made me a few, but still and all you can't just give up and become a hermit with a million books to read and a ounce of weed to smoke. And I *know* you been smokin'. You just gon' say the hell with the rest of the world? Come on, girl. I done told you once, if not a thousand times to be careful. You fall in love too fast, Cee. Always, holdin' out on the drawers until neither one of y'all can take it no more and when you finally do get some, the shit feel so good you think you in love. And that fool, too, but he just happy you finally gave him some and now he thinks he special. Girl, will you ever learn?"

Now although Maria isn't exactly poetic, she does have a point. She just described me to a "T." I can't even deny it. I'm very careful whom I let get that close to me. Besides my Mudear always said that the quickest way to lose a man is to give him the drawls too soon. And several past experiences led me to believe that I was right in thinking Mudear knew everything. Case in point: Calvin. I gave in to Calvin way too soon. If I had had so much as the slightest inkling that he was seeing other people, he would have never gotten any.

Maria Antoinette LeVine, whose nickname is Black, because of her dark-roast coffee color, has been my best friend for the last thirteen years. We used to tell people that we were sisters. She's a half shade darker than I am and about three inches taller, but people just assume we're related because of our skin color.

I have big round eyes and hers are slanted. I'm a little below average height for a woman and she's tall. I have full lips and she has thin lips. I have a low round butt and hers damn near sits in the middle of her back. I have thick coarse, wavy hair that I keep braided and she has naturally long, thin hair that she "can't ever do a thing with." And our personalities are totally different. I sometimes wonder how we even managed to stay as close as we are. Lord knows that girl can work a nerve.

Maria and I have both had our share of disappointments in the dating game. Living here in New Orleans is hard on a dark-skinned sista. We both grew up being referred to as "that pretty dark-skinned girl," with just a little bit of an extra emphasis on "dark." Maria's mother once told her that society seems to associate pretty with anything remotely close to women of the Caucasian-persuasion and people are just shocked at how pretty she is "despite" her dark skin. This shit really pisses us off. I know damn well I look better than a whole bushel of light-skinned women, but our brain-washed, color-struck people are still livin' by massah's rules; the closer you are to looking like them, the higher you are on the "status ladder." Pretty lame, I think. And so does Maria. That's one of the reasons we became such good friends. We have a common bond when it comes to "taking the backseat," sort to speak, when in a room full of lighter-skinned women.

Maria and I have totally different taste in men though. She seems to pick

pamela davis-noland

men according to how well they fill out a pair of jeans. I, on the other hand, prefer a man with intelligence and a decent conversation. If I can't be intellectually stimulated, a man might not have a chance at stimulating me in any other way.

And this girl knows she can spot a broke brotha a mile away. I'm no gold digger or anything, but I'm not about to pay for everything. There have been times when that girl borrowed money from me to go out on dates with a brotha who was a little "down on his luck." And she has the nerve to lecture me about my relationships. Well, I guess we're both ignorant in that department. The difference being that Maria got married once. I have no idea what this girl was thinking though. She had only known him for approximately four months. Four months and eight paychecks. The brotha' damn near sent her to the poor house. He had champagne taste and forty-ounce money but she married him anyway because he had the finest, mouthwatering ass, teeth the color of bleached snow and all the charm a woman could ever want.

She bought and paid for that man from the time she met him, to the time she said "I do," to the time she walked out on him because all of her utilities were about to be turned off and her furniture was about to be repossessed. But of course, he was too pretty to work at just any job. And then, like always, who bailed her out? Me. Like I wasn't the one who warned her in the first place. Maria doesn't have any shame, though. At least not when it comes to depending on me. She is spoiled rotten. And truth be known, I'm guilty of spoiling her. All she has to do is shed one tear and there I am, just like that. No questions asked and no "I told you so."

"What are you doing home today, anyway?" I finally asked.

"I took the day off to do somethin' with this hair."

"How did you know I was home?"

"I called your school and no one answered, so I figured it was one of those so-called holidays that y'all use as an excuse to take the day off. So which one is it this time?"

"Actually, it's not. We're having an In-service meeting today."

"Why you didn't go?"

"Didn't feel up to it today. I got other things on my mind. I've been feeling pretty creative lately, Black. I think I'm finally going to finish this novel."

"Yeah. Okay."

"Why you say it like that?" I pouted.

"Girl please. Anyway. Is Mr. Fine-Ass Lee still yo' boss? Girl, why you ain't never thought about dating him?"

"Oh please, Black. Mr. Lee gets on my nerves. Walkin' round like some old playa' playa'. And what do you mean, 'girl, please?'"

"Girl, what you talkin' bout? That man looks good for his age. And, ooh...the color of them eyes. That brotha' look just like Smokey. And you know damn well as soon as you get over Calvin's ass and meet somebody else, you gonna forget all about that book. That's why I said, 'girl, please.'"

COFFEE-COLORED DREAMS

"That's not fair, Maria. I mean I'll admit, it has been a long time since I've actually done anything with my book, but this time I'm sincere." I placed my hands together and said a silent prayer. "Anyway. Smokey who? Smokey on *'Friday'*?"

"Robinson, fool! That's who he reminds me of. I mean come on, Cee, you work with the man every day, why don't you go out with him?"

"Cause, I am not into old two-timing' flirts. And besides that, he's obnoxious and a borderline pervert. I swear that man shouldn't be 'round young girls. So why haven't you commented on what I said? You really don't think I'm gonna do it this time, do you?"

"Look Cee. Don't get me wrong. I would love to see you finish your book. Hell I want to see it finished more than you do! Shiiit! I'm tired of talkin' 'bout my friend the soon-to-be-famous writer who is writing a bestseller that she never talks about. It's a good thing I've kept all the magazine articles and short stories you've written. At least I have proof that you do exist. And if one more mothafucka ax me what that book is about, I'ma scream. Girl, what is that damn book about anyway?"

"You bitch. It's all about your life as a cheap whore." I laughed.

"Yeah alright. Don't fool around and get sued, Ms. Secretive. Now tell me again why you won't go out with Mr. Lee?"

"Girl that man ain't tryin' to have no relationship with nobody. He still thinks he the Mack."

"Well, all he probably need is a good woman to change him."

"Black, that man is forty-nine years old. If he hasn't changed by now, he's not going to."

"Girl, what you got against attractive men?"

"I don't have anything against attractive men. I just have other qualifications in mind when I decide to go out with someone. And besides, Mr. Lee ain't hardly attractive."

"Yeah, well anyway, you 'gon do my hair, or what?"

Typical Maria, always more interested in what she wants, not what I'm going through. "What time are you going to be here, Maria?" I asked with plenty of attitude.

"Give me an hour. And be ready to talk about that book."

I rush back to the window only to find my entertainment for the evening was That damn Maria!

Jeffrey Jackson

Maaann...I love New Orleans. I couldn't have picked a better place to start my new life. It's about ten times smaller than Chicago is and there is no snow or barely even a winter but I love it just the same. Truth is, I've wanted to live here

pamela davis-noland

for a long time.

When I finally came to the realization that I was truly an unhappy man and that I was only one disappointment away from a damn shrink and two disappointments away from puttin' a gun to my freakin' head; I decided a change of scenery and a new life was by far overdue. So exactly one month after the divorce became final, I packed my shit and hauled ass like a free slave with a bus pass and decided for once in my life I'm going to do what makes me happy.

I decided that I wanted to live again, be happy again and I definitely wanted to sing again. So one day on one of my long rides home from my homeboy Miles' studio, after another non-productive "jam session" with a bunch of hard head lil' niggahs he had been trying to get me to sing backup for, the thought hit me like a lightning bolt - I had to get out of Chicago as soon as possible before I snapped.

I've visited New Orleans several times as a kid to see my pops' family and his gravesite. Pops died when I was eight. My mother insisted that he be buried in the family plot with all of the other great Jackson men, and just like when he was alive, Mama got anything she wanted. So once every two or so years, we'd take our family trip "down south" right around Father's Day and come to this eclectic lil' city and hobnob with all of my French speakin', borderline Negro, bourgeois relatives. You know, I was infatuated with my relatives. The way they spoke and the way they carried themselves with that southern, snobbish charm. My pop's people were the epitome of the upper class New Orleans high society rich and somewhat famous back in the day. I used to daydream about living here and singing in one of the cafés in the French Quarters, like my grandfather did, but I kept that dream to myself for years. The old man wasn't exactly one of the more prominent Jackson men. He was the youngest son of five boys and the family drunk who sang in juke joints to make a scarce living. All of my pops' uncles did really well for themselves and my grandfather was an embarrassment to everybody in the family except me. I was infatuated with a man I'd never met.

My grandfather's father, my great-grandfather, was a preacher and his wife, my great-grandmother worked in every white woman's house who needed a "pretty black gal" to serve the gentlemen at fancy balls and sleazy poker games. Now how's that for an odd couple. She was the backbone of the Jackson family, though, the main provider and the second contributor of all of the old money; her white daddy was the first. When I would look at the old beat up torn photos and flyers of my grandfather wearing snazzy clothes, standing in front of a microphone or just coolin' it at some New Orleans juke joint I would pretend he was me. Normally, he had a drink in his hand and a cigarette hanging out of his mouth.

I knew one day I would live here, it was just a matter of time. I love everything about New Orleans, Louisiana. It is one of the most festive cities in the world with its beautiful French colonial architecture and it's non-stop celebrations. But I guess what I love about it most is the music. New Orleans is the birth-

COFFEE-COLORED DREAMS

place of some of the best traditional jazz in the world. I fully understand why it's always been such a popular tourist town with its wonderful cuisine and the traditional laid back southern charm of its entire being, not to mention the unique architecture and the jazz. I love the essence, man…the sheer essence. It's just me. It's who I am. The real me, not the man I've pretended to be for far too long.

I spent the last six years of my life married to a woman I was not passionately in love with. I also spent the last six years working full time at an accounting firm run by a bunch of old white dudes that I hated. And believe me when I tell you that they weren't too fond of my black ass either. They signed that transfer I asked for in writing and had that bitch mailed to their Louisiana office before the ink was even dry on the paper. Humph! Suited me just fine being that my choices had come down to a transfer or a murder. Those white men had tried my patience just that much. And because I was so busy there, (you know a brotha gotta work overtime just to be noticed), I had to keep my singing career on the back burner. I *had* to keep the job, though. As long as I was with Laura and her expensive ways, the job was definitely a necessity.

Laura and I have known each other all of our lives and I must say it's been a trip for the most part. Our parents were friends for years; they got married together, blah, blah, blah… anyway, my mother gave birth to me on the exact day Laura's mother, who will swear to this on a stack of Bibles, says that Laura was conceived. Now how the hell she knows that is pretty sad to me. Laura's pops was definitely on a schedule. My grandmother, Mama Ella, said that it was an omen and then she convinced everybody that the two of us were going to someday get married and give them the most beautiful light skinned black grandbabies in the world. Well she was half-right; we did get married but neither one of us wanted children. I don't know what *her* reasons were, nor did I really care. I just knew that I could not bring a child into a loveless home. Oh, we do love each other, but it's not the same kind of love a couple should have, you know, to be trying to have a family and spending fifty glorious years together.

I guess the reason we were able to stay together as long as we did was because we were both married to our jobs. Laura was definitely married to her job. She's a buyer for a very expensive boutique and she's always out of town doing her buying I guess. I was so busy most of the time, I barely stopped to ask her. Couldn't. Didn't have time with being an accountant by day and a part-time back up singer by night. There just wasn't enough hours in the day to pacify Laura.

I also believe that the love we do feel for each other is another reason we were able to stick it out for so long. We love each other like family. You know? I mean we we're already family, there was no need to get married. There was never any passion. Lust maybe, but no passion. It seems like we'd been having sex forever. We started with playing doctor, then graduated to "let me see yours first" and then "touch it." Although, the older we got the less interested I got. We went all the way on her sixteenth birthday only because she begged me too.

pamela davis-noland

I had a girlfriend and I was in love with her and I didn't want to cheat on her but man, Laura insisted. That was the only thing she wanted for her sweet sixteenth and she wanted me to teach her. So being the gentleman that I am, I had to oblige her that night. And any other night she wanted to. Sometimes I would feel bad afterwards, but then she would remind me that we were friends and that friends helped each other out, so I should just think of it like that. And far be it from me to not be the best friend I can be. So from then on I figured if that line of bullshit was okay with her, it was just fine with my teenage hormones and me. Only thing was that same attitude carried over into our marriage, "What's love got to do with it?"

I do believe out of all my so-called relationships I've only been in love once. I was head over heels in love with my first girlfriend whose trust I lost when she found out Laura and I slept together. I found out about a year later that Laura was the one who told her even though she denies it to this very day. I wouldn't put it past Laura though; she hated her. Said she was too dark for me and our kids were going to have nappy hair. And my colorstruck pod'na, Miles, who doesn't even look at ladies darker than a paper bag, thought she was ugly and I should marry someone who looks more like Laura, if not Laura herself. But against everyone's wishes, marrying her was the first thing I was going to do as soon as I graduated from college. Like I gave a damn what they, or any of my colorstruck relatives down south, for that matter, said. Lettie Smalls was the most beautiful chocolate sista I had ever laid eyes on and I wanted her to be my wife.

My mother and my sisters seemed to be the only ones who really liked Lettie. Although, my mother was probably more than relieved when we broke up. She couldn't help the way that she felt though, it was just the way she was raised. But her good Christian heart would never allow her to act on her deeply tucked away, true feelings about the issue of skin color. And I appreciated her for that. Moms loved me enough to see pass that.

I tried explaining to Lettie that Laura and I were more like family and what happened was just a mistake. I told her that we were not in love or sexually involved by *no* means. But she wouldn't hear of it. She went away to college at NYU and I never saw her again. And that, my friends, is what a brotha get for listening to his smaller head.

Every time I close my eyes and get a vision of those nights that we'd laid in bed and talk about our future together after we made love *maaann*…those cocoa brown thighs glistening from sweat, my nature rises to its full potential. And every time I think how close I was to spending the rest of my life with them thighs wrapped around me every night, I could just kick my own ass.

And now here I am, thirty-four years old and I'm starting my life over. But that's a'ight, this time I plan on doing it right. No more pity parties. This Jackson man is about to follow in his grandfather's footsteps and live my life according to *my* own rules, and not the rules of the Jackson men. Just the way I always dreamed I would.

HOPELESSLY DEVOTED

Celia DuBois

I called my agent last night and informed her that I have given myself one year in which to complete my novel. I got the same reaction from her that I got from Maria but at least Brianna was a little more sympathetic. She knows what type of stress I've been under for the past few years. Maria is not a writer so she has no idea how hard it is to try and create when your mind is clogged. And dealing with these last two relationships, among all of life's other little stresses, has kept my mind clogged indeed.

I really feel as though I'm ready to concentrate on my writing now more than ever. I tend to write better when I'm a little blue anyway. Besides I can actually look myself in the mirror and say, "I've learned my lesson," and really feel it in my soul. No man and I do mean *no* man is going to cloud my mind now because I fully intend on taking a sabbatical from men. Well… at least until I've finished my book.

I've come to the realization that maybe the reason I am not fully able to find my soul mate is because *I* am not yet complete. I've been so busy trying to find someone to complete me when in fact all I need is me. I don't have to have a man to complete me. Contrary to what every female in my family has told me in actions as well as words. I'm just fine the way that I am and it's high time I started acting like it.

I believe that there is a season for everything and this is my season to write, not marry. And the sooner I come to grips with that, the better off I'll be. I've also come to the conclusion that in order for me to be complete, I have to care more about myself and not feel worthy only when a man is lying on top of me and whispering in my ears that he loves me. Because men can toss those words around like horseshoes and they definitely have the mentality that close is good enough for us.

Maria is so right about me. I really do equate lust with love. Whenever I give in to my current mate, I give in because I usually believe I'm in love, or very close to it. And I assume he feels the same way otherwise we wouldn't be "making love." But time and many a failed relationship has proven that theory to be

pamela davis-noland

dead wrong. I feel like a complete ass for being so naïve for so long in thinking that when I give my body to a man that that means he considers me to be special.

Five days after the breakup with Calvin and the tears finally stopped flowing; I made two huge commitments that I fully intend to keep. I have totally committed myself to the completion of my novel, and I've totally committed myself to a life of celibacy. I figure the latter may just help the former. I am no longer allowing a man to get into that space, neither physically or emotionally, until I am absolutely, positively sure that it is love. And by that I mean at least a ring and talks of saying some vows together. My days of fooling myself in believing that sex will help me to keep a man are over.

Being that I'll be focusing more on my writing anyway, I probably won't have any trouble with the celibacy vow. It's not as if I have a gang of men waiting to take me out or anything anyway. So sex for me is going to be nothing more than a memory until I get myself together.

My biggest fear about making this decision is going back on it. This is not the first time I've decided to make such a life change like this. As a matter of fact, this is the second time I've decided to become celibate. The first time was when I was twenty years old and still practicing Catholicism. I thought I wanted to be a nun. Or at least I thought it was my calling because one – I knew that I loved to teach and two – it didn't seem as though God wanted me to have a husband anyway. Twenty was the age, or so it seemed to be the age when all of the women in my family and a few of my close friends decided whom they would marry and the majority had carried out that plan with no apparent problem. I, on the other hand, hadn't had a steady boyfriend since I was a senior in high school. At the time I was cool with the decision I had made and had convinced everyone around me that this was to be so. That is until I went to a retreat with a few other young women who felt like they had received the calling also.

I remember meeting this one girl named, Carla. Carla helped me to see that I was only fooling myself. She cried every night that we were there because it was not *her* choice to become a nun but it was her mother's choice for her. She said that she loved men and had a current boyfriend who she was madly in love with, although dear old mom had no idea he even existed. Carla shared with me that she was not a virgin and had no intentions of ever being one again. She said the thought of not ever having sex again sent shivers down her spine.

Later that night when she finally calmed down and went to sleep, I lied in that top bunk and stared at the ceiling as if to find my answer. I questioned myself over and over. Why was I there? Why did I think I wanted to become a nun? And after tasting of the forbidden fruit a few times myself, what made me think I could live without it? After much thought and consideration, I realized that it wasn't the actual act of sex that I'd miss. I felt as though it was the closeness of a man, the smell of a man and the security I felt when I was in love with a man that I'd miss more than anything. So on the last day of the retreat when Sister Mary Katherine asked if there was anyone present who had changed their

COFFEE-COLORED DREAMS

minds and decided that they were not actually called, I was the first to raise my hand. And the second to walk out of those big, heavy, wooden convent doors; my new friend, Carla was the first. She and her boyfriend gave me a ride home and we smoked a big fat joint on the way. All three of us were happier than pigs in slop.

    This time my head is together and I don't think there is a "Carla" in the world that would make me think twice about my decision. I'm absolutely sure this is what I want to do. Besides, it is the way I was raised anyway. The majority of the women in my family were virgins when they got married or at least the man they married was the only man they'd been with. I, on the other hand, have had too many partners to have had been raised in such a Catholic home. And although I don't practice Catholicism anymore, some of beliefs and customs have stuck with me even now at the "ripe old age" of thirty. So celibate I am now, and celibate I plan to stay. I don't need any man clouding my mind right now.

    I guess you can say that I'm hopelessly devoted to me...

Jeffrey Jackson

I've decided since I've moved to Louisiana where no one really knows me, including my estranged relatives, I can feel free to concentrate on my career as a singer without the hassles from certain family members and an ex-wife who I believe deep down inside despised my singing career. I also decided that I no longer want to hide behind some diva sista or some talentless brotha. I want to stand out in the forefront where my voice can actually be heard. I'm not being conceited or anything, but I do believe that all of these boy groups and quartets and Lenny Kravitz wannabes that are popping up like bad weeds are really taking a toll on the art of singing and I could sing circles around quite a few of them. I've just let my insecurities overshadow my full potential as an artist. But those days are long gone or at least I hope they are because Jeffrey Jackson is about to reinvent himself and fame and fortune are the very least of my worries. I still have a little money saved up and I've made a few good investments that I think are going to pay off one day. And I don't have to worry about catering to Laura's expensive taste anymore, so I'm not really looking to make a whole lot of money. I just want to sing. So whatever happens - *happens*. And eventually I'll stop working for a firm and start my own business 'cuz I've got the skills; all I needs is a few loyal clients. I have no intentions of quitting my day job just yet, though. But I do plan on spending every other waking hour singing something somewhere. My buddy Miles says he has some connects here and he'd see what he could do, but in the meantime, I'm just gonna have to do this myself. Which is probably what I need to do anyway. I mean I appreciate everything Miles has done for me back in Chicago but it's time that I cut the cord.

    I have a talent I've been pretty much sitting on for too long and my plan is

pamela davis-noland

to do a complete 360° turn. I'm going to learn how to be laid back and really comfortable when I make some type of decision and not look over my shoulders waiting for someone to be standing there with some "constructive" criticism. Hell, now that I look back on it, most of the advice I took was destructive to me. I'm a grown man and the time has come for me to go ahead and jump in with both feet instead of one toe at a time.

The morning before I boarded the plane heading for Louisiana I went to church. Well, let's say, I parked in front of a church. I hadn't stepped foot inside of a church in many years so I wasn't exactly feeling worthy, ya' know. Anyway, I parked in front of the church and began to pray. I first asked the Lord to forgive me for not talking to him in such a long time and then I asked Him for some wisdom and guidance on my new journey. I sat there until a calm feeling came over me, said "Amen," and then I drove off and left every doubt and worry right where I'd prayed.

I've decided to devote myself to my art. I'm going to let it lead me and I am more than ready to follow.

MONDAY MONDAY

Celia DuBois

I love my job, and I love to teach. But I hate Mondays! I especially hate Monday morning meetings with Mr. Lee. I miss Sister Theresa so much. I wept the day she left New Orleans and moved back to Ireland. I wept even louder when I realized that her assistant vice-principal, Roosevelt Andrew Lee, would be taking her place.

I am in no mood to face Mr. Lee today. I hate the way he looks at me with that sneaky grin. And those eyes. I swear I don't know what Maria sees in him. He looks like a snake. *Ugh!* And that laugh, he sounds so creepy. Just looking at him sometimes makes my stomach hurt.

"Good morning, Mr. Lee." I tried my best to look as though I was still feeling under the weather.

"Well, good morning to you, Miss DuBois. How are you this fine Monday morning?"

There goes that damn grin again. Damn, I feel like I'm gonna puke. "Oh, I'm fine." I lied.

"Feeling any better?"

"Well, I was. But I think I feel a relapse coming on."

"Do you think you'll be okay? If you feel the need to go home I can have the secretary call in a substitute."

"No, that's quite alright. I'm sure I'll feel much better once I get to my class." This man doesn't have a clue. He thinks so highly of himself that he can't possibly recognize a sly insult.

"Have a seat, Miss DuBois. You know for a woman who's not feeling well, you sure look beautiful this morning. How in the world do you stay so fit? Do you exercise?"

"Mr. Lee, I think we're here to talk about my agenda." *Always tryin' to mack. He makes me sick!*

"You're right. But I don't see any reason why we can't have a friendly conversation. You know you really need to loosen up a bit. You seem to be so serious all the time."

pamela davis-noland

Is that a booger in his nose? Yuck!!! "No, I'm not serious all the time. As a matter of fact, my students think that I'm quite the comedienne. I just know that there's a time and a place for everything." *Oh, that's a big-ass clump of nose hairs. Doesn't this man own a pair of scissors? Somebody ought to really tell him that from a certain light that looks just like a booger. What the hell does Black see in this man?*

"So what would be a good time for us to have a nice friendly conversation? You know maybe go out for drinks after work or something?"

Or something?! Brotha' please! "How about February 30th?"

"My, my, you are quite the comedienne, aren't you?" He laughed.

"Can we get started, Mr. Lee?"

"You're wish is my command, my lady."

Whatever.

To my surprise, the day went quick and easy. My mind wandered from time to time, though. I couldn't stop thinking about Calvin. My students had to call my name a few times, because I was in a total trance.

We had quite an interesting day. I wasn't in the mood for lecturing so I let the kids decide what they wanted to do provided they didn't get too loud. One of the students suggested that we have a talent show. Everyone agreed, so each student had ten minutes to display whatever talent they were best at. I am always amazed at how talented and gifted some of these kids are. Some sang or rapped; others read poetry or did scenes from a favorite play. Some of them may be future stars. If they could only focus more on their art and not succumb to the gangster life so many of the young black men and women in New Orleans have adopted. If they could only be more like Jennifer Guidry, one of my most gifted students who seems to know what she wants in life and concentrates more on her gift of writing and not what everyone else is doing. Sort of like I should have been doing these last past failed relationships, concentrating on my gift.

She usually comes by to visit me after school so I didn't look up when she walked in.

"Uh-um, excuse me Miss DuBois, but can I talk to you?"

"One second baby." *Why do I always lose my keys?*

"Well, if you busy right now, I can talk to ya' lata'." Her voice quivered.

"What's the matter, Jenny. Here, have a seat."

"Miss DuBois, I don't know what to do!" she cried.

"Well, I don't know what you should do either. You might want to tell me what's going on." *Lord, I hope this chile ain't pregnant.*

She looked up at me with the saddest puppy dog eyes I've ever seen. "It's just that…that…. that Jimmy broke up wit'me and …" She started sobbing.

"And what baby?" I sat down and braced myself.

"And he won't give me a reason why." She squeaked.

Now I gotta admit, that lil' boy is a future hunk with his French-dark skin,

COFFEE-COLORED DREAMS

coal black wavy hair, doe eyes and a newly brace-free set of pearly whites. He was just a little bit too cocky, though. Every little hot mama on campus either has, or contemplates "knockin' boots" in the back of his raggedy Dodge Daytona. He's the star quarterback as well as the star center on the basketball team. He has calmed down since he started dating Jennifer, though. He even signed up to be in my class next semester. Jenny has sort of refined him. She's a classy little lady and from what she has told me, she is very much a young lady. Which is probably the reason he broke up with her.

I haven't the heart to tell her that just because he's not getting any from her, doesn't mean he isn't getting any. And all those little so-called new "friends" she has now that she's dating the big man on campus is the same one's givin' it to him. They sure start young, don't they?

Now, isn't this ironic, young lady? I'm going through the same shit. Too bad there isn't a limit to this madness. This is only your first of many disappointments. "So how long have you two been dating?" I finally asked.

"About four months."

"Well, that's not too long."

"I know Miss DuBois, but I ain't never felt like this 'bout nobody. Jimmy is my first real boyfriend. Well, he wuz."

This poor chile, she looks so pitiful. I know exactly what we both can use. A cup of hot café'au lait, and some cool blues at Benny's Place. "Jenny, do you ride the bus home?"

"No, I walk. I just live up the street."

"Why don't you go to the office and call your mother and ask her if it's okay to have dinner with me."

"Ooh…okay. I know she 'gonna say yeah. She really like you, Miss DuBois. Where we goin?"

"To my favorite unwind spot. A little café' in the Quarters. You're going to like it."

Jeffrey Jackson

I don't know whose bright idea it was for us to take a couple's vacation last year. But whoever came up with the idea should have waited for that second thought. Miles. It was Miles who insisted on coming to New Orleans with Laura and I during the Essence Festival. Being that he was the one who gave us the tickets, how could we say no? But why he insisted on bringing his new freak of the moment, I have no idea. He should have followed his first mind and brought his son. The entire weekend was a disaster. The two women acted like high school rivals at a football game. Miles and I were the referees for the entire trip. They were at each other's throats from the time we boarded the plane heading for New Orleans until we landed back in Chicago. The only good thing that came out of

pamela davis-noland

the trip was that Miles hipped us to this joint called Benny's Place. He knew a couple of guys in a band that performed there frequently and he wanted me to hear them play.

When we stepped in from the ever-crowded Rampart Street into the doors of Benny's Place; I'd felt like I'd been there a thousand times before. The smells were even familiar. It was the eeriest shit I ever felt in my life. It swept through me with a force that made me sway and I almost lost my footing. And then this lil' old bow-legged man with pupils as gray as his hair and his ashy hands, grabbed my arm in an effort to save me. He smiled, tipped his beret and led us to a table directly in front of the tiny stage. He introduced himself as Benny Thibodeaux, the proprietor. Or as he said, "pro pie ta".

As I sat there and watched that old man hobble up onto that stage, sit on that beat up old wooden stool and blow that saxophone with all the passion only a true musician could muster, I knew I'd be back.

After I settled into my new apartment and everything was squared away at my new job, I went back to Benny's Place and asked the old man if he knew of any bands that were looking for a back up singer. He riddled off a few names and then he looked at me sideways and asked me if I could really sing. I told him yeah, and then he handed me a sheet of paper.

"Dis' here a song I wrote myself." He said. "Need me somebody to sing it fo' me. Ol' Benny ain't no singer. I'm a sax playa."

So I took the sheet of paper and started practicing with him that very evening. He says if I can get it right he'll hire me to sing. "And it won't be no backup," he said. So how was a brotha going to say no? As bad as I want to sing lead. We've been practicing every Monday evening because it's his slowest night at the Place and I'm having the time of my life.

As a matter of fact, I look forward to Mondays now. It used to be the worst day of my week back in Chicago. To have to endure the Monday morning ritual of white men talking about their *wonderful* weekends was more than I could stomach sometimes. At least I work with a few brothas now. We don't hang out too tough after work because they are all married with children, but we do get together at lunch and talk about basketball and other sports instead of deep-sea fishing and golf. They're all married except for this one dude. But I think he's gay. Not that I'm homophobic or anything, I just don't see the point in hangin' out with a brotha I have absolutely nothing in common with. So after five o'clock, my evening belongs to my art. And Mondays are now my favorite day of the week instead of the day I dread the most.

STRUMMIN' MY PAIN

Celia DuBois

Benny's Place has all the nostalgia and charm of a French Quarter establishment with the ambiance of a 1940's juke joint. I fell in love with it the first afternoon I walked in by accident trying to find some other bar. I was walking along the streets in the Quarters being bombarded by drunk tourists wanting me to take their picture with throw-away cameras and lil' black boys with bottle caps tacked to the bottoms of their shoes tap dancing for some change. I hadn't hung out in those streets in so long so needless to say I had loss all sense of direction. I was looking for a bar called Famous Door, it was Maria's new hangout. Maria, the "Happy Hour 'Ho." That girl loves her some happy hour.

When I walked in the doors Benny was sitting on a barstool in the middle of the tiny dais playing the most hypnotic rendition of Amazing Grace. I had chill bumps all over. He had his eyes closed so he didn't see me pull up a chair and sit down. I was trippin'. I love the saxophone, and this little gray-haired man with the black beret tilted sideways on his head sure knew how to blow.

When I finally did meet up with Maria, she asked me where I had been. I lied. I told her that I got stuck in traffic. I didn't dare tell her about Benny's Place. It had suddenly become sacred to me and I didn't want her going in there trying to pick up men. It wasn't *that* kind of café'. Besides, from what I could see, the kind of brothas that hung out at Benny's were on a totally different level, a level she's knows nothing about. Highly intellectual, down to earth, jazz lovin', Miles Davis worshipin', poem writin', classy men. They were the kind of men Black despised. So Benny's Place has been my little secret getaway. I've never invited anyone to come here with me...until today.

"You come here a lot Miss DuBois?" Jenny asked.

"Every time I feel the need to unwind. And as uptight as I feel most of the time lately, I guess the answer to your question would be yes."

"Yeah, I know what'chamean, I'm always uptight."

Now what does this chile think she knows about being uptight? Boy, is she in for a rude awakening. She hasn't been introduced to up, much less tight. "You know Jenny, you're a very bright girl. I know you've probably heard this a million times, but one day you'll look back on this and laugh. I know you're hurt right now, and you think that the pain will never end. But believe me, lil' sista', it does. Take it from a woman who's been there and done that."

"Why you ain't never got married, Miss DuBois?" Jenny looked down at her hands as if she hoped she hadn't overstepped her boundaries by asking such a personal question.

"Well, to be honest, uh… I have no idea. It's not like I haven't wanted to. I'm just one of those people with a low tolerance for bullshit, if you'll pardon my French. I can give and give and give until the lies start, and believe me, they all lie, and then I'm outta there, like yesterday. I don't stick around and try and fool myself that things will get better. Take for instance your situation. Now, you and Jimmy have been dating for how long?"

"Four months."

"Well, that's not too long, have you two had any major problems?"

"No. Nothin' major. Sometimes I get upset at him cuz he always in some other girl face, and when I say somethin' he say I'm trippin'. He say he don't care about nobody but me. And all them hoochies love to try and make a play for him right in my face." She looked over her shoulders to make sure no one heard her whisper, "and he get mad at me cuz I won't do it."

Still a virgin; now how many teenagers can say that. Hell, some of them got two baby daddies. I know what he's thinking. He broke up with her thinking she'll beg him not to, and then he'll give her an ultimatum – put up or shut up. I sure hope this young lady is smarter than I was at her age, I fell for the same trick. But then again, she is a teenager, a walking hormone.

"Did he ever try to force you, Jenny?"

"No ma'am, he just be talkin' about all the time. Talkin'bout we'll have a stronger love for one another. Sometimes I wanna do it just to shut him up, but I'm too scared. My mama had me when she was sixteen years old and she quit school. My daddy skipped out so she had to get a job. My daddy skipped out just like her daddy did. I don't wanna be a third generation single black mother. And my mama and my big mama sacrificed so much for me; I wanna make'em proud. I ain't even thinkin' bout Jimmy. I love him an'er thang, but I ain't ready."

Oh this young lady is wise beyond her years. Hell, you could probably teach me a thing or two. "That's music to my ears, Jenny."

"Yeah but I wish Jimmy understood."

"Well, Jenny, I think you've made a great decision. You've already figured out what you don't want to do, now it's time to figure out exactly what it is that you do want to do, and do not stray away from that, no matter how difficult it may be sometimes. And believe me, it will get difficult. But you see you're already getting off to a good start. By standing your ground and not giving in to your weakness, which happens to be Jimmy right now, then you'll become stronger and able to handle situations like this and even harder ones. And pretty soon you'll realize that you are an attractive and incredibly smart young lady

COFFEE-COLORED DREAMS

who doesn't let trivial things like temporary love affairs with cocky quarterbacks get in the way of your dreams of a better life for yourself. See, you already know how to eliminate the BS."

"I like talking to you, Miss DuBois. You remind me of my big mama. She is wild. She be tellin' me stories 'bout how she use'ta dog men out before she met my pawpaw. She say he was the only man who could tame her. She fell in love with him the first time she laid eyes on him, she said. I think she still love him."

"Oh, look, here comes Benny. You're gonna love Benny."

Benny Thibodeaux is the most interesting old man I have ever met. He's like a living breathing character out of a Zora Neale Hurston story. He is the color of coffee that sat on the stove all day. His hair looks like cotton balls, carefully placed around the black beret he wears, religiously, and his legs resemble a "C" and its reflection. He sort of rocks from side to side when he walks. He wears a crisp white shirt and his loud vest of many colors every single day. He always has a story to tell, and because of his low raspy voice, his stories sound more like secrets.

"Well, well, well, look who'da Lord done blessed me wit' today. Two beautiful young ladies with smiles as refreshin' as sunshine afta a week a rain." Benny versed. He is also a self-proclaimed poet.

"Hi Benny, how've you been?" He always makes me smile.

"Well, Doll, there ain't too much Ol' Benny can complain 'bout. Lord jest be blessin' me everyday. I guess he not quite ready for me. But when he do call, I sho wanna ax him 'bout bein' in that band up there so's I can bring my sax."

"I'm sure he will, Benny. But I hope he knows how much you're still needed down here. Some of us can't get through one week without your coffee and some of the finest saxophone playin' this side of heaven."

"Who's dis'here lovely angel I see before me?" Benny asked smiling at Jenny.

"Benny this is Jennifer Guidry, one of my favorite students and my new friend. Jennifer, this is Benny Thibodeaux. He owns this place."

"Well, sho as I tell ya'. You must be a real good friend too. Cuz as long as I've known dis'here young lady, she ain't never brung nobody in here. She come by hu'self, sit by hu'self, and leave by hu'self. Won't give none a these young fellas the time a day. I know she got plenty already, though. Too pretty not to."

Benny is always teasing me about the men I'm supposed to have. Chile, if he only knew. And the reason I don't talk to anybody when I come here is because Benny sits with me most of the time telling me stories and before I know it, it's time for me to go. I'm not complaining, I love talking to Benny. He always knows exactly what to say and when to say it. Sometimes it's scary. It's like he's reading my mind or something.

The day that I showed up at Calvin's house and found that woman there, I came straight here. Benny "rocked" over to my table with a cup of coffee and an oyster poboy. He sat them down in front of me, smiled and "rocked" away. He

25

pamela davis-noland

left me alone the entire evening. I don't know who told him, but he knew two things about me. One - I didn't feel like holding a friendly conversation. And two - I had the munchies - bad.

"Nice to meet you, Mr. Thibodeaux."

Benny took off his beret and leaned over and kissed her hand. "The names Benny, lil' angel. Ain't no need for formalities here at my place. Now what can I git for ya? You two look hungry."

"I'm not really hung…"

"Save your breath, Jennifer, Benny will bring you something anyway. That's his way of getting you hooked. Once you've had a cup of his coffee and one of his poboys, there ain't no turning back."

"Okay, then I'm a have a shrimp poboy, a large onion ring, and a side of jambalaya." She looked over at me and smiled. "Oh, and a coke."

"And whattabout'choo, doll? How hungry are you?" Benny giggled.

"Just coffee for me, Benny."

"Be right back." He winked and smiled, and "rocked" away.

"Do Benny know your real name, Miss DuBois?"

"You know, I told Benny my name the first day I met him, but he always calls me Doll. He doesn't call anybody by his or her real name. Your new name is Angel."

"I kinda like it here."

"Oh, it gets better. You haven't heard Benny play his sax, yet." I paused and took a deep breath. "So, do you feel like talking about how you're feeling right now?"

"Yeah, I guess so. I mean, I'm just sad cuz I know Jimmy don't really want to break up. He just tryin' to prove somethin'. He just think he 'gon make me give in. And I ain't dumb as he think I am. I know he be messin' around wit them same girls who be smilin' all up in my face, like I'm stupid or somethin'. But I ain't the stupid one, I ain't bein' used for my body. He don't care 'bout none of them hoe's. Oh, excuse me Miss DuBois."

"Quite alright."

"Anyway, they don't even get to see the other side of Jimmy."

"What side is that?"

"The sweet side." She looked away smiling like she was having a wonderful flashback. "When we go places together, he treat me just like a queen. He opens the door for me, pull out my chair for me when we go to McDonalds, and he always hold my hand when we cross the street. He always be tellin' me how pretty I am, too. He say I don't never need to wear makeup, cause I have a natural beauty. And when we alone he be hisself. He don't be tryin' to front like he do when he wit his boys. He is such a nicer person one-on-one. I love that side of Jimmy. The other side ain't nuttin' but a dog. And them girls he be sleepin' wit ain't 'gon never see that side of him. I'm the only one he show it to, and I don't wanna lose him, cause he scared to be himself."

COFFEE-COLORED DREAMS

"Yeah, I know what you mean. I guess that's what makes it hurt so bad. How in the world can they treat you so special and then turn around and just break your heart? How are they able to switch it on and off? It makes me wonder whether they ever cared to begin with, or if it was some kind of act." *Damn, I know I better not start cryin' over Calvin's ass. He is not worth another tear of mine. I was hoodwinked. It's a simple as that. Ain't no need to cry now. But damn, I loved his ass.*

"Are you okay, Miss DuBois?"

"I'm fine. We're here to talk about you, not me."

"Yeah, I know, but you lookin' kinda sad. You sho you alright?"

"Well, lil' sista, to tell you the truth, I'm going through the exact same sh… crap, you're going through right now. I know exactly how you're feeling. I just broke up with a man that treated me the same way that Jimmy treats you."

"Oh, I'm sorry, Miss DuBois. This might not be a good time to talk about my lil' old problems, huh? Yours is worse. I still have plenty of time to find my mista' right. I mean… not that you're out of time, it's just that…"

"You might want to stop sometime soon, Jenny, cause no matter how hard you try, you can't save that one." I nudged her and she giggled. I was crying on the inside. Even *she* knows that I'm too old to still be single with no apparent prospects.

"Well, we don't have to talk about it no more. I'm ready to eat."

"Actually, I'd love to talk about it. Maybe if I hear it aloud, I'll feel better."

"Well, I feel funny tryin' to get all up in my teacher's bizness."

By all means, please get all up in my "bizness." I need to release this shit and I can't afford a therapist.

I tried talking it out with Black but that poor chile doesn't have a clue. When she breaks up with a man she just keeps right on rollin' like nothing happened. That girl seems to think that the best remedy for a broken heart is a good stiff one, and I ain't talkin' about no drink.

Just as I was about to tell her my story, Benny was bringing the food and drinks. "Alright ladies, here we go. A cup of hot coffee for you, Doll, and the rest is for the lil' angel. Can I get you anything else?"

Jennifer was too busy trying to stuff onion rings in her mouth, adding to her already mouth full of shrimp poboy, so I answered for both of us, "I don't think we'll need anything else except to hear you play, Benny."

"Well, you're in luck. I been workin' on somethin' new. Song I wrote, too. I got me a young man by the name of Jeffrey Jackson to sing for me. He ought-ta be here soon, we got some more practicin' to do. If you two beautiful ladies are still here when he comes we'll sing it for ya."

"Benny, are you married?"

"Well Doll, the wife passed on 'bout seven years ago."

"You looking for a new wife?"

"Now, doll, if I didn't know any betta', I'd think you tryin' to get fresh with

pamela davis-noland

Ol' Benny. Girl as pretty as you shouldn't have no troubles findin' a husband. Pickin's must be pretty bad, huh?"

"Pickins are almost non-existent, Benny."

"Put it in the Lord hands, honey. He'll provide. He'll provide betta'n what you could wish or think. I'll remember you at prayer time. Got me some good connections up there."

"You do that, Benny."

"He's so sweet." Jenny managed to say with her mouth full of onion rings.

"Yeah, and I bet he thought I was joking when I asked him if he was looking for a wife."

Jenny laughed at first, but then when it had dawned on her that I wasn't laughing with her she looked at me wide-eyed. The look on her face, with her jaws full of food, made me spit out my coffee with laughter. We laughed so loud people started staring.

"You girls alright?" Benny yelled from across the room.

"We're fine Benny. Just fine." I yelled back.

I told Jennifer all about Calvin as she guzzled down her food like only a teenager can. I told her all about our first meeting, our first date, but was careful about not telling her that he stayed all night. I didn't think it would be appropriate to tell her that I slept with a man on our first date. That was a rule I had never broken before and I haven't shared that with anyone, not even Maria. It was one of those proverbial "it just happened" things. I think he was just as shocked as I was. I was so horny that night, and I really didn't think anything would become of us, nor did I care at the time, but I must have done something right, because he never stopped coming by or calling.

I told her all about our short love affair. I must admit, we did have some wonderful times together, but somewhere tucked away in the corner of my mind, I knew it wasn't going to last forever. I just tried to ignore it. Maybe I felt that way because he used to always say that he had not yet accomplished everything he wanted in life, and because he was getting so old, (he's only twenty-five), that settling down with one woman was not in his immediate plans until he had more to offer. Boy, was I in some serious denial. I should have picked up that "settling down with one woman" thing, if nothing else.

I can honestly say that I do not regret one single moment that we shared together, though. I guess that's why I decided to never see him again. I only want to remember the good times. I don't want to start hating him for lying to me. I know if I was to ask anyone, they'd say that I was overreacting, but I have a built-in bullshit detector, and the minute I walked in that apartment and saw him and that woman, the sonuvabitch went off like a siren.

"Man, Miss DuBois, you just stop seeing him just like that. He didn't beg you to take him back, or nothin'?"

"Yeah, he's called and left a thousand messages, but I haven't returned any of his calls. I've been too busy focusing on more important things. Like my writ-

COFFEE-COLORED DREAMS

ing. I really don't want to hear what he has to say. In the words of my mother, "Mais, he done tow hiz drawls wit me, *sha*."

"My big mama say the same thing."

"You know Jenny, there's gonna be a time when you'll get tired. Hopefully, you'll find your 'mista' right' sooner than I have, and you won't have to go around kissing as many frogs as I have, but if you don't find him right away, please do not settle. Do not settle for second best. Don't fall for any man who is not true to himself because if he's not, he will never be true to you. And if he cheats on you while you are dating, chances are he'll cheat on you after the wedding. Some men's morals don't get any better just because they say I do."

"Men. They can sho be some dogs, huh?"

"Yep. So try and avoid relationships that involves too much drama. You might end up with a hard heart."

"Is yours hard?"

"Well it's a little toasted, but I've been praying about it. Sista done been through some drama, you knowwhatImean." I winked at her. "Well anyway, look at the time, I better get you home, lil' lady."

"I'm not ready to go, yet. Can I go call my big mama and ask her if its okay if I stay a lil' bit longer. My mama at work, anyway, so big mama might have some company, she keep her a boyfriend. Anyway, I wanted to hear Benny play. She 'gon say yeah, please Miss DuBois."

"Well, I guess it wouldn't be right to bring you here and not let you hear Benny play his sax. There's a payphone right around the corner, I'll go call your big mama and ask her if it's okay. What's your phone number?"

Jeffrey Jackson

The generous beam of sunlight that shone through the window she was standing in front of illuminated her silky smooth fudgesicle-brown skin. Her runners legs are slightly bow and I can see them clear as a bell despite that knee length silky skirt she's wearing. Thanks to that same beam of sunlight. *Damn!* I love a pair of sexy legs. And her mouth watering ass was definitely giving the rest of her fine body a run for its money the way it demanded attention from my eyes. Man, I tell you what, there is nothing more beautiful than a fine black sista, when she is fine. And the woman standing there with her back to me laughing and talking on the payphone across the room is the finest specimen of a fine black sista, when she is fine, that I have *ever* seen.

Her hair is neatly braided in a thousand braids that hang oh-so-seductively just past her shoulders. She looks like a goddess. When she turned around and I caught a glimpse of her face, I knew I wanted to see it a little closer. I had to, man. She was the woman in my dreams. I blinked several times to make sure that my eyes weren't playing tricks on me. They weren't. And the fact that I had just smoked some killa' had nothing to do with it either. It was she in all of her glory. My heart began to pound and my palms were drenched with sweat. I don't know how long I had been standing there staring at her before Benny finally called out my name. Time had stood still for a moment. I walked away thinking in the back of my mind, *"She is not going to walk out of here until I know her name."*

Celia DuBois

While I was on the phone listening to Big Mama gossip about one of her neighbors, I noticed Benny smiling at me and he was pointing toward the dais. His friend had finally showed up, and from where I was standing, he was a rather nice looking friend. I hurried Big Mama off of the phone and quickly returned to my seat. Benny "rocked" over to our table with his fine-as-wine, gorgeous, café au lait smooth colored friend he had been waiting on. The brotha' has a smile only seen in magazines. I quickly chastised myself for allowing myself to exercise the same practice of sizing up a potential mate the way I've always done when meeting an attractive man. *"Is he single? Naw, he's too fine to be single. I'm probably not his type anyway. He looks like he's into "music video" sistas. I'm probably too dark for his ass."*

"Doll and Angel, this'here Mr. Dimples Jackson."

The name spoke for itself, okay. Now I know how his regular patrons acquire their nicknames. When I first met Benny, he said that I have eyes like a baby doll. I guess he can sense Jennifer's angelic innocence. And as I said before, Mr. Jackson's name speaks for itself. He has the most incredible dimples, and he isn't even smiling.

"Nice to meet you ladies. I see Benny has changed your names as well?" He smiled.

Ohmygod! This man is gorgeous. Where in the hell has he been? Okay Celia, now before you start trippin' too hard, remember the commitment you've made. Please don't let anyone come in and trip you up. "Hi, nice to meet you." I managed to say.

He is definitely not from New Orleans. He's got a northern accent and he dresses like a buppie. He has "good hair" and a nose like a white man, but all the rest of him is all brotha. Definitely Creole.

I reached out my sweaty hand, just like the proper southern girl that I am; he gave me a firm handshake and a sexy smile.

"Hi." Jennifer said.

"Well, come on here boy, let's show these here beautiful women what I taught'cha."

"Be right there, Benny." He waited until he thought Benny was out of hearing range. "My real name is Jeffrey Jackson, but everyone calls me Jeff, well, everyone except Benny. What are your real names?"

COFFEE-COLORED DREAMS

"As long as you in my café your name is Dimples, boy, now get over here, we got some practicin' to do. Them ladies been waitin' long enough, they ain't got all evenin'." Benny yelled from across the room.

Jenny laughed. Jeffrey Jackson just shrugged his shoulders and walked away shaking his head.

Benny began playing this slow bluesy type music. He played at least five minutes before Jeffrey Jackson started to sing. His voice, so deep and mellow, cuts right to the soul and makes you feel like crying, no matter what the words are. He could sing "patty cake" and it would sound wonderful.

I tripped out when I heard the words that he was singing, the words that were cutting into *my* very soul…

>There was a time when you thrilled me
>There was a time when I couldn't let go
>There was a time when you convinced me
>That I was the only one you loved…
>And now that time is gone.
>You took my heart and broke it in two…
>Now all I have is coffee-colored dreams of you
>You taught me how to love
>You taught me how to hate
>You took away my peaceful times
>Now all I do is cry.
>You took my heart and broke it in two…
>Now all I have is coffee-colored dreams of you.
>I'm not gonna stop livin'
>I'm not gonna die
>I'm gonna find that true love
>Someday I'll be able to smile again.
>You took my heart and broke it in two….
>Now all I have is coffee-colored dreams of you.

Before Benny could finish playing the last stanza, Jenny excused herself from the table and damn near ran to the ladies room. I, on the other hand, was so mesmerized by the way Jeffrey Jackson was staring at me, I couldn't move. Every part of my body was numb. I couldn't even bring my hands together to clap.

I've had men stare at me countless times, but never like this. He stared at me in a different way. As though he was trying to read my mind or as if he knew something about me that *I* didn't even know. His eyes held questions that I so wanted to answer but I knew this was not the right time. I have to stay focused. And a man as fine as he would definitely deter me from my goals. So I just smiled sweetly and attempted to stand and go and check on Jennifer. But before

pamela davis-noland

I could will my eyes to look away, Benny tapped me on my shoulder.

"Well honey, how'd you like it?" Benny asked.

"Beautiful. Just beautiful." I answered Benny *and* Jeffrey Jackson, whose eyes were still looking into mine.

"Are you sure? I didn't see you clappin' And where's Angel? I know that boy can't sing all that good, but I didn't think he was that bad."

"Benny?" I asked when I was finally able to look away from Dimples Jackson.

"Yes, Doll?"

I did not know quite how to word it, but I swear sometimes that Benny is some sort of angel. He always knows what to say and when to say it, but this is too much - a song! A song that *he* wrote. How in the world can this little man know so much about me? I suddenly have the urge to start singing "Killing Me Softly."

"Benny, are you some kind of angel or something?" I felt stupid for asking, but I didn't know of any other way to go about finding out.

"No Doll. Not yet." He said this with a straight face. "Why don't you go over to the restroom and see if your lil' friend is doin' a'right, she may need you."

"Benny, how do you do it? I mean how…?"

"Go on honey," he interrupted, "go on and see 'bout yo lil' friend. I'll get you a fresh cup of coffee."

When I walked into the ladies room, Jenny was standing with her face against the wall, crying her little eyes out. Poor little thing has no idea that this is just one of many heartaches. I had to wipe a tear that had welled up in my right eye. I walked up behind her and touched her shoulder and she spun around and hugged me and started to sob. Another tear welled up.

"I hate Jimmy." She sobbed.

"No you don't, you're just hurt."

I held her in my arms and let her cry until she ran out of tears. It was good therapy for me too. I was beginning to think that I had forgotten how to feel anything except anger.

Jeffrey Jackson

Damn. She left before I could even talk to her again. I feel like a fool for staring at her the way that I did but she is so beautiful and the way she was staring back paralyzed me.

I was just about to muster up enough nerve to join them at their table when I saw her coming from the ladies room. The little girl looked upset. I didn't want to interrupt so I watched them as they grabbed their things and stood at the door talking with Benny for a while. Benny hugged them both and they left. But she

COFFEE-COLORED DREAMS

did look over her shoulder at me once more and smiled. That was enough to let me know she was at least pleased with my singing. I'm not really sure if she liked my voice or not. She didn't even clap.

I decided to get the scoop about "Doll" from my boy, Benny. He seems to know her pretty well. I wonder why I've never seen her before today. *Damn! I hope she's not married.*

"Hey Benny." I called out just as he made his way pass me.

He slowly turned around and smiled, "Yeah boy?"

I nodded toward the window as they walked by it trying to make their way through the crowded sidewalk. "Who is she?" I asked.

"Why, she's Doll." He answered.

"I know that old man. You introduced us remember? Is Doll single?"

"That's what I hear tell. But a girl pretty as that one ain't gonna be for very long."

No shit! Damn, she probably has a man. "She gotta a man Benny?"

"I ain't never seen her wit one. Mattafact, I ain't never seen her wit nobody. Today the furst time she brung anybody wit her."

"So what do you know about her Benny?"

"What I know don't matta boy. If you wanna know 'bout a woman you gotta ax her." And with that he wobbled his way toward the kitchen, yelling out, "She probably left cuz a yo' sangin'. Brush up boy."

"Yeah. Thanks for the boost of confidence old man." I yelled back.

Benny chuckled and shook his head as he pushed open the swinging kitchen door and left me there with my doubts. I haven't pursued a woman in such a long time, man, I don't even remember how to do it anymore.

I'm gonna have to call Miles when I get home. Naw… forget that. The first thing Miles is going to ask is what she look like and when I tell him, he's gonna piss me off. I could just hear him saying, "Man you moved yo' ass all the way to Louisiana and you got the hots for some dark-skin chick? You in Louisiana, niggah! You know the state with all the sexy ass yellow-bones. Niggah what is it wit you and them nappy head sistas?" Naw… if I'm gonna start my new life, the first thing I'm gonna do is quit listening to Miles. Like that niggah know anything about women of any color. Miles is too wrapped up in himself to take the time to find out what a woman is all about. I've never known him to say he loved anybody but Miles.

I'm going to see Doll again. I can feel it in my bones. She seemed a little bit interested in me. Hell, I wasn't the only one staring. I just hope she doesn't have a man. If she does have a man, he must not be a good one. Benny says he has never seen her with anybody. Hell, I wouldn't let that woman out of my sight.

But it's all good, man. I can wait. I know she hangs out here, so chances are she'll be back. And next time I'm not wasting a second.

FRIENDS. HOW MANY OF US HAVE 'EM?

Celia DuBois

I jumped when the phone rang. I was in such a deep sleep. I looked at my caller I.D. It was Maria.

"What?" I hate it when she calls me so early.

"What? Girl, is that any way to answer the damn phone? Git yo ass up. It's nine-fifteen, it's Saturday, and it's time to get our shop on."

"Not today, Black. I got about a week's worth of laundry to do and I have to clean out that nasty refrigerator. I have shit in there that I don't even recognize. And after I do all that, I have a date with my book."

"Ooh…how exciting, let me get this right, you have some dirty drawls, a dirty refrigerator, and a date with a non-dirty book. Girl, you need some dick in your life. Fake or otherwise."

"You so nasty, Maria." I laughed.

"Yep. Sho is. And my nasty ass 'bout to go to the mall and find me a nasty new outfit. Ooh…let's go to The Rink. You know how much you like that bourgeoisie Garden District. Let's go there and look around first."

"Don't tell me? You have a hot date tonight, and you don't have a thing to wear." I said, rolling my eyes.

"Chile, it's scary how well you know me. So you comin' or what? You know I need your opinion, Cee." She begged.

"No, seriously Black, I'm really not in the mood. And I've already told you; I'm committed to my book. I have to keep my priorities straight this time, Black."

"I got a blunt." She was doing her best to entice me.

"I don't feel like going to The Rink today. If I do go we're gonna have to go somewhere closer. And it's too early to be getting high, Maria. You know how lazy I get if I smoke this early in the morning. Besides, I don't like blunts anyway. And I ain't even tryin' to go to no mall all fucked up."

"Since when?"

"Since I'm tryin' to turn over a new leaf."

"Oh shit, not again." Maria laughed. "Now how many times have I heard

COFFEE-COLORED DREAMS

you say that?"

"Probably too many to count but the fact still remains. I have other things to do."

"Well didn't you tell me that Brianna says that you should learn how to enjoy life and not completely shut down when you're writing. Didn't she say that that's probably the reason why you put it down anyway? Because you become so cynical of yourself if you don't write twenty-four seven to the point where you just toss it aside because you can't take the pressure. Now if you gonna turn over a new leaf, I suggest you turn that one over too."

"Fuck you, Black. What time you pickin' me up?"

"Aww come on Cee, you know the mall is closer to my house."

"Well, you and your blunt have fun. Call me when you get back."

"Okay, okay, damn! I'll be there at 11:00."

"And don't be late."

"Whatever. And you betta not wear them damn sweats either. Put on somethin' cute, please. Ain't no tellin' who we might meet today."

That girl always wins. But at least I can honestly say that she's right this time. I've got to learn how to enjoy life when I'm in the middle of a creative period. I just hate it when she just dismisses anything I say. If I had told her I got into a car accident last night and my leg was in a cast, she would have reminded me that there are wheel chairs at the mall. She takes this best friend shit to a whole 'notha level.

She showed up at about 11:30, blowing her horn. It's bad enough that she talked me into going and now she's late and rushing me like I'm holding her up.

"You could have at least come in for a minute, Black!" I said, slamming her car door so that she'd know I was pissed.

"Don't be slammin' my door, girl." She said while handing me the already lit and halfway smoked blunt. She turned the music up real loud and bobbed her head just like the kids do in all those rap videos.

"You high as a kite already, huh?"

"Yep, and this some good shit, too." She snorted. "I got it from that lil' gangsta' niggah over in the *Nolia*. That lil' gold tooth brotha know he be havin' some good shit. You look good girl. I like them shoes."

"The *Nolia?!*" I laughed. "Girl you been hangin' out in the projects? Since when?"

"Girl I ain't even hangin' out in no projects. This lil' niggah I work with get it fo' me. I mean don't get me wrong, ain't nothin' wrong with datin' a niggah from the Magnolia Projects, but I ain't hardly gon' hang out there."

"You a stone trip, Maria."

"Stoned is right, *sha*." She giggled.

We rode in silence, smoking all the way to the mall. Of course Maria took all the back streets. She likes to flirt with the brothas that hang out on the corners drinkin' forties sportin' more gold teeth than Master P *and* the whole No Limit Soldier crew. When we finally made it to the mall we went straight to the cosmetics department in Macys and sprayed perfume on our smoky clothes. I kept my shades on because I didn't want to risk running into one of my students with my eyes as red as my shirt.

"Well?" I asked Maria.

"Well, what?"

"Well, who's the new victim… I mean boyfriend?"

"Ha Ha. You so damn funny. Don't be hatin' just cuz you don't get dates. If you wasn't so damn stuck up all the time, you'd get dates too."

"I am not stuck up, Maria. I just think I'm a little too damn old to be dating around like I did in college. That's done played out for me."

"Damn, Celia, you're only thirty years old, and you look all of twenty-five. Them teenagers you teach must be messin' with your head, *sha*. You need to find you another job where people who look as old as you ain't callin' you Miss DuBois. Them kids got you thinkin' that you old or something."

"It has absolutely nothing to do with the kids that I teach. It's just that I'm not where I wanna be right now, Black."

"Well, hell girl, who is? You think I like being single? I liked being married. The bastard was no good, but it was still nice to have someone lying next to me every night. We had some wonderful moments."

"Yep. Right there in that bed y'all slept in every night."

Maria laughed because she knows it's true. That man had her whipped, and she can't even deny it. "Girl, you got that right!" She said.

"So, who is the new guy?"

"Well, his name is Jaye. We met at Tonya's party. You know the one you wouldn't go to with me. And you sure should have cuz they had some of the finest brothas there. Anyway, he's kinda cute."

"Girl, get outta here!" I said sarcastically.

"Fuck you, Cee. He's got a lot of other good qualities, too."

"Such as?"

"Such as, he's a reporter and he's never been married and he don't have no babies, which means no babies' mamas, and he don't know any other women 'round here because he just moved here from Houston, 'bout two months ago."

"Aahh… qualities to make any mother proud."

"You such a smart ass, Celia. And you wonder why you don't have a man. You're that cold-fish type men don't understand."

"I don't have a man, cuz I choose not to have a man. If I wanted to have any man, I'd still be with Calvin. I refuse to settle Black. Besides my main goal right now is to get in touch with myself. I ain't worried about a man right now."

"Who said anything about settling? Just get out and live a little. You think that good men are just gonna fall out of the sky?"

"No I don't, but I do know what I don't want. I don't want any more empty relationships that are based on sex and nothing else. I've had just about enough of those to last me a lifetime. Which is why I've decided to take a vow of celibacy." I didn't want to tell Maria about my new vow but it slipped out of my mouth before I could catch it. The look on her face made me burst into laughter.

"I hope you're laughing because you're joking," she said with a look of concern.

"No, I'm not. I'm totally serious. I want to get to know a brotha for who he is and not what he can do in bed. Maybe this will teach me how to slow down. And not to mention, that is the way I was raised, anyway. My Mudear and my mama and all of my aunts were virgins when they got married."

"That's the key word, chick - virgins. It's a little too late for that don't you think?"

"I reclaimed my virginity when I made my vow."

Now I know I must sound crazy because by this time Maria is clutching her stomach and laughing so hard that people are starting to stare. It just may sound crazy because we're stoned. But then again…

"You (ha, ha, ha)… reclaimed…(ha, ha)… your what!" she yelled.

By this time I had to grab her loud ass and walk her to the nearest ladies room. I was getting paranoid. I hate being around so many people when I'm high.

When we walked in the ladies room, she stopped laughing and looked at me sideways. She tilted her head to the left and to the right.

"What?" I asked.

"You know you have got to be one of the most unique people I know. I swear, sometimes I wonder if you were meant to live such an ordinary life. You have such a good aura about you. I need to take you to see my Aunt Mauchin."

"See, I knew you was into that voodoo shit!" I accused her.

"No I'm not. I just know that there's something special about you. I can't quite put my finger on it, but whatever it is, it's something really good. Anyway, whatever man, do what you think is best for you." She gave me a hug and kissed me on the cheek. "But my nasty ass 'gon get me some tonight, so come help me find something to wear."

I love Maria.

Jeffrey Jackson

Against my better judgment, but for lack of anything else to do, I picked up the phone and dialed Miles' number. I guess I kinda miss that brotha. We used to hang out on Saturdays and smoke herb all day, shoot ball or maybe play a couple'a rounds of golf. Lately the only person I've been hangin' out with is Benny. But Benny doesn't smoke herb, he for damn sure can't play no ball and he hasn't ever played golf in his life. He's cool as hell to talk to though. But there are some things that I can't talk over with Benny. So I called my boy instead.

pamela davis-noland

The first thing that niggah asked me was, "Man you got'choo some pussy yet?" Then he went on some rampage about this freak he used to mess with from Louisiana who told him how the women here practice voodoo and to be careful not to get "trapped". He said he still falls on his knees every time he sees that woman. "And you know a niggah like myself don't have to fall on his knees very often?" He said. That's one conceited niggah.

Miles has been bed-hoppin' ever since high school. He's never had a steady girlfriend any longer than two or three months. I try to tell him it's time for him to stop playing Russian roulette with this jimmy but that niggah ain't even tryin' to hear it. He says he never goes in uncovered but I know that brotha Miles, man, he a damn lie.

When I told him I wasn't even looking for a quick lay right now, Miles laughed. Then he asked me if I had moved all the way across the country to come out of the closet. Or as he so eloquently inquired, "You ain't lookin' for no pussy? Hey niggah, is there somethin' you want to tell a brotha'? Yo' ass ain't been hangin' 'round at them gay bars on Bourbon have you?"

I cussed that niggah out. That Miles is a trip, man. I tried explaining that my goal is to find one special lady to kick it with. But of course, true to his nature, he just changed the subject and started talking about his new freak he just finished bangin' ten minutes before I called. Again... I have no idea why I dialed his number.

Miles never understood my willpower when it came to women. His one-track mind cannot allow him to comprehend how I'm able to turn down the drawers when some skeezer all but lifts her skirt and bends over in front of me. I just can't stand an easy woman. There is no excitement to an easy woman. No chase at all is boring as hell to me. I love a good chase. I love it when a woman makes me wait. At least I know I ain't sleepin' with a ho. Or should I say the chances are better that I might not be sleeping with a ho? Anyway, women come on to me all the time, but that doesn't do a thing for me. Don't get me wrong, though. Sometimes a brotha' had to hit it in order to prove he wasn't no punk. But you better believe she never heard from me again.

I didn't tell him about Doll. Although I was dying to tell somebody how when I close my eyes at night, I get a vision of that sunlight hitting that skirt just so. Enabling me to see those sexy thighs right through it. I've thought about that woman every waking hour since that moment. She's no longer a dream. She's flesh and blood now. And I can't wait to see her again.

After the one-sided conversation with Miles, I decided to get out and get some fresh air. I had walked through that mall at least three times and was just about to leave when I looked over to my right and saw her. Doll and another sista were standing in line at the food court laughing and talking. I blinked twice just to make sure my eyes weren't deceiving me. I was afraid my imagination was getting just a little out of hand. I didn't want to walk up on someone who just looks like her. And then her friend said something that must have been really funny and she threw her head back and laughed just like she did when she was talking on that payphone.

I made my way through the crowd and was standing right behind her before I even realized what I was doing. I couldn't let them get away without at least finding out the *real* name of my fantasy woman.

Celia DuBois

We walked around the mall acting like two schoolgirls. We tried on everything from jeans to evening gowns. We flirted with salesmen and gave out phony phone numbers. Maria even flirted with a lesbian. I wonder about that girl sometimes. She's never admitted it, but I know she's bisexual. Or she could just be a nympho. Who knows?

We were standing in line at the Cookie Factory when someone tapped me on the shoulder. "You think I could get your real name now that Benny's not around?" He asked.

Oh my god, it's him. Damn, he is cute. "Hi Jeff, how are you?" I handed the girl behind the counter my money and shook his hand.

"Just fine. How are you, Miss..." He made a gesture with his hand for me to finish the sentence.

"Miss DuBois. But you can call me Celia."

"Now that's a name you don't hear too often. So where's Angel?"

"She's not with me today."

"Is she your little sister?"

"No, my daughter."

"What?!"

I laughed. "Just kidding, she's one of my students."

He smiled - I melted.

"You look like a student yourself."

"Well, thank you, but I haven't been a student in years."

"So have you been by Benny's Place, lately. I haven't seen you there since the first time we met. My singing didn't scare you away did it?"

"I don't get to the Quarters often, but no, you're singing did not scare me away. You sing beautifully. I had to get Angel home, though, it was a school night."

"She looked pretty upset when you guys left, Benny said it was my singing."

"No, it definitely was not that." I laughed at the thought of Benny saying something so untrue.

Maria finally became restless and a little agitated that I had not introduced her. She poked me in the side with her elbow. I got a kick out of it. I knew she was dying to flirt with this one, but somebody done told her wrong. He strikes me as the slow moving type - my type. Too bad I've decided not to date right

pamela davis-noland

now. Me and my rotten luck.

After the third poke, I finally introduced her. "Oh, Jeff, this is my friend, Maria. Maria, this is Jeffrey Jackson."

"Nice to meet you, Maria."

"Nice to meet you, too, Jeff. Why do you look so familiar?"

Oh no! Not that line again. Jesus Maria, you know you need to give that one a rest. Maria is famous for that line. Whenever she sets out to conquer a fine brotha and make him her very own, she uses this very same line.

"Well, I don't know. You don't look familiar to me at all." He answered.

Way to go, Jeff, finally someone can see straight through that line.

"Oh well, maybe you just look like somebody I know." Maria was embarrassed. He is probably the first fish that didn't bite that hook.

"So when are going back to see Benny?" He turned his attention back towards me.

"Oh, I don't know."

"Well, maybe I'll see you there soon." He winked and tugged at my sleeve. "You ladies have a good day."

"Okay, bye Jeff." I blushed and chastised myself all at the same time.

"Goodbye. Oh, and it was nice meeting you…um…"

"Maria." She said flatly.

"Yeah. It was nice meeting you. Bye Celia DuBois."

We stood there and watched him walk away. Damn! There ain't nothing finer than a brotha who knows how to carry his fineness. He even walks sexy. I finally looked over at Maria, whose eyes were fixated on Jeff, and giggled. It was about time for someone to put her in her place. And he did it with such style. She is so used to getting what she wants. I knew he was more my type.

"What'choo gigglin' at?" She asked.

"Black, you just got dissed, girl. He dissed you with class."

"Ain't nobody got dissed Miss Thang. He just don't know when a woman is tryin' to pay him a compliment. It must not happen very often."

"Yeah, right. And I guess tellin' him he looks familiar is a compliment?"

"Yep. It's letting him know that he's cute enough for me to remember his face. And it opens the door for further conversation."

"Oh please, Maria. Well, anyway, it doesn't seem like he was very interested in having a conversation with you. In fact, he didn't even notice you until you decided to bruise my ribs."

"Forget all that girl, who the hell is he? And who is Benny and this Angel person? You got friends I don't even know about, Cee? I share everything with you. How can you keep someone like that to yourself? You're not leading some double life are you, girl?" She asked all of this in one breath.

"No Black, I am not leading a double life. You want to go to JC Penny?"

"Hell no, I hate their clothes. And don't be tryin' to change the subject. I want to know why I don't know these people. You tell me all you do is sit at

COFFEE-COLORED DREAMS

home and read and write that damn book of yours. When did you meet him? That brotha is fine."

"Yeah, he is. I'm hungry, let's go to the food court. I want some fried crawfish."

"Dammit, Cee! I thought I was your best friend? Why you keepin' secrets from me?"

"Oh, Maria, stop pouting. Let's go get something to eat and I'll tell you all about him. And why you gotta refer to my art as 'that damn book'?"

"*Tsk.* Come on, girl." She grabbed my arm and led me to the food court. She was dying to hear about Jeff.

I told Maria all about Benny's Place. I told her about the kind of crowd that hung out there and how Benny gave everyone nicknames. I told her about how I had come across his place by accident, the same day that I was suppose to meet her at Famous Door for drinks after work. I told her how I'd go there whenever I felt sad or uptight, and the reason I had taken one of my students there was because she was very upset. I told her all about Benny and his saxophone. I told her everything except how I met Jeff.

"Well?" she asked.

"Well what?"

"Well what? How did you meet Jeff, fool?"

"Oh, well, to be honest with you, I really don't know Jeff. Benny introduced him to me as "Dimples" Jackson. He sang a song with Benny and I left." I waved my hand in the air as if Jeff was not a significant part of the story. I knew better than to tell her too much. If she knew how good he sang, she would talk me into taking her there.

"Can he sing?"

"You know, I was so busy tryin' to console Jennifer, that I didn't even notice." I lied.

"Well, honey, I tell you what. Anybody that fine would be on somebody's radio or TV if he could sing. He must not be that good."

If you only knew.

"So when are you going back?"

"I don't know. Benny's is in the Quarters. You know I don't hang out there much."

"Well, you better start. Hell, just to see *that* man, if for no other reason. Don't be no fool, Celia DuBois. That man is very interested. A blind man can see that."

"What makes you say that?"

"You saw the way he ignored me didn't you?"

"See, I told you. You got dissed!" I laughed.

"Aww, shut up. Let's go girl. I got a date to get ready for. And I still ain't got nothin' to wear. I think I'll just wear what I have."

Good idea. "Are you sure, girl?"

"Yeah, let's go."

pamela davis-noland

Jeffrey Jackson

Celia DuBois. Odd name, but that is one fine sista. I wish she were by herself. I would've asked her for her phone number at least. But the way her girl was sizing me up, I figured this was not a good time. But I did let her know I'd been looking for her at Benny's. I hoped she picked up on the hint. Hell I hoped she picked up on all my hints.

And speaking of hints. Her girl was a trip! Talkin' about why do I look so familiar? Knowing good and damn well she has never laid eyes on me in her life. I wanted to tell her that after sleeping with about a hundred or so, we all start to look alike. I can't stand tricks like that. Always throwin' the panties. Won't give a brotha time to even decide if he really want to hit that. She was lickin' her lips and shit when she shook my hand. Man, she is definitely Miles' type.

But her girl Celia, on the other hand, now she's got class. She didn't even get pissed when her friend tried to push up on a niggah when it was obvious I was interested in her girl. I like that in a woman: confidence. Hell, she sure got a lot of reasons to be confident. *Damn!*

LIVE A LITTLE

Celia DuBois

I am having another boring Friday night. I've been sitting at my computer ever since I came home from work and I've yet to get inspired. Being that I have no date, this is the perfect opportunity to concentrate on my novel but my mind keeps wandering. I guess the fact that Calvin has called two times and left sickening messages has something to do with my lack of concentration. He just can't seem to get the hint. I almost picked up the phone the last time but I still care about him too much and I'm not exactly strong enough yet to fight any urges. One kind word from him and the next thing you know my clothes are crumpled on the floor.

    I should just get up and put on some clothes and get the hell outta' here before I do something stupid but I don't feel like being around people. I hate that I'm so anti-social at times. I'm getting more and more like my mother everyday. She's happy just staying home and talking on the phone with one of her crazy sisters. There have been times when she would stay home for weeks at a time and never step foot out of the front door.

    I was just about to pick up the phone and call Maria when someone knocked on my door. My mind started racing thinking about what I'm going to say if it's Calvin. I was so relieved when I looked through the peephole and saw my neighbor, Liz. She was holding her sleeping little girl over her shoulder.

"Come in Liz." I whispered.

"I'm sorry to bother you, Celia, but can I please use the phone?" She asked.

"Yeah sure. Is everything okay?"

"Yeah. I just saw Bobby's car parked out in front of my apartment. He didn't see us so I turned the car around and parked behind your building. I'm glad he wasn't looking through his rearview mirrors."

"Has he been harassing you?"

"No more than usual, chile. I can handle him though. I'm just not in the mood for his shit today. I just want to call my mama and see if she's home before I drive all the way to Chalmette. I'll just spend the night there."

"Here, give me the baby. The phone is over there."

pamela davis-noland

"Thanks, girl. I'll just be a minute."

"Take your time."

Liz called her mother and thanked me for using the phone. And then she asked the same question everyone always asks me, "So how's your book coming along? You know I've told everyone in my bookclub about you. They can't wait until it comes out. What's it about?"

"It's a love story. But that's all the info I'm giving out right now." I smiled but I was crying on the inside. I feel like such a failure for not being able to concentrate on my book and I am so tired of repeating myself.

"So girl, you don't have you a hot date tonight? It must be nice to be single and free."

Well that's easy for you to say. "No. Not tonight." I pointed toward my computer. "Kinda busy, you know."

"Yeah I guess writing must keep you pretty busy. But girl you ain't dead! You betta enjoy this single life while you still can. Don't get stuck like me." She smiled although I could see the pain behind those last five words she had just uttered.

I offered to walk down with her but she said no. She insisted that she was going to be okay. She told me that Bobby was probably drunk and may have passed out in the car anyway. She thanked me again and left.

"Poor woman. How can someone as nice as she get hooked up with that asshole?" I said aloud to no one, "Oh well, it happens to the best of us."

Liz's words hung over me like a cloud. She's right. I am pretty lucky to not have to be dealing with any drama right now. I shouldn't be sitting here alone on a Friday night. I'm young, intelligent, attractive and single. I could pretty much be doing anything I want. I could just go out dancing or maybe go to Preservation Hall and listen to some jazz and maybe get a few free drinks or something. Guys come on to me all the time. Although they're the wrong guys! They're either gold-tooth, dope slangin' brothas or old pimps, like Mr. Lee. The only compliments I get are about my ass and my slightly bow, smooth as a babies' bottom, legs. Why oh why doesn't anyone see me as the intelligent black woman that I am? I have so much to offer a brotha. I love to love. I can treat a man like royalty, wait on him hand and foot and give him all the lovin' he needs. I can be supportive of anything positive that he does. I can really appreciate a good man. Hell, I've done all that and I'm still alone. What's the deal? Am I giving too much of myself and when I don't get it in return, I tell him to kiss my ass and then walk away? Yep, that's me. Maybe Maria is right. Maybe I am a cold fish that men don't understand. I can be turned on and off just like a faucet.

Well, I'm going to take her advice and Liz's too. I'm going to live a little. I have a new little cream colored catsuit that I've only worn once, because I got a little too much attention. I'm going to wear it, pin up my braids, put on my new earth toned makeup, and get out and make a few heads turn.

COFFEE-COLORED DREAMS

Jeffrey Jackson

Well, tonight's the night. Tonight my dreams of singing in a smoke filled, dimly lit café in front of a crowd of jazz lovers in the French Quarters come true.

I called Miles, my mother and Laura, in that order, and told each of them my good news. Miles was happy for me and said he'd try and come down and catch my next show, although I'm not gonna hold my breath. Miles is always so caught up in Miles to give any kind of real support. But he my niggah though, and I know he is probably the only one that is truly happy for me.

My mother took me on a long journey with her down memory lane. She told me all about my father and how he so yearned to have a successful career as a singer (a story I've only heard maybe 200 times) and how he gave it all up to raise a family and provide them a decent home. She also reminded me that I am a successful accountant and that I shouldn't throw all that away after all of my years of hard work.

And then there was Laura's comment, "Just because everybody tells you that you look, act and sound like your grandfather does not mean you have to try and be him Jeff. I mean come on baby. You are an accountant, a very successful accountant for a very prestigious firm. You've even talked about opening your own firm one day and you said you were going to concentrate on doing *that* in New Orleans not singing on Bourbon Street or whatever sleazy street in the French Quarters. This is just a hobby, right?" This is why I keep my business to myself. I can't stand for someone to give me a negative vibe and unsolicited advice about my life.

I blew Laura and my mother's comments off just like I should have done years ago. I was nervous enough. I didn't need to hold on to that vibe. Instead I went to my full-length mirror to check my gear for the tenth time. Loose fitting black slacks, black patent leather Stacey's and a long-sleeved, loose-fitting, crushed-velvet, burnt orange shirt buttoned down just enough to show a chest hair or two (that the lil' salesgirl with the dirty blond hair sittin' a mile high on her head and a gold tooth, with a open face in the shape of a star, swore was "the bomb shit"), is what I decided to wear. After trying on several others, the salesgirl said it was sexy and would look good if I were going to be singing on stage in front of a bunch of ladies. I don't know if there are going to be a bunch of ladies there tonight but I sure hope Celia shows up. Benny informed me that she would be. Which is another reason I bought this outfit. I wanna look my best when I try to Mack... oh and believe me... a brotha' has every intention of Mackin' on Celia DuBois tonight.

One more look in the mirror. *Damn I hope she shows up.*

pamela davis-noland

Celia DuBois

I rode up and down Canal Street for what seemed like hours before I decided to go to the Quarters. I parked about a block away from Benny's and sat in my jeep contemplating. I know I have an ulterior motive for dressing like this. And his name is Jeff. I hate it when I fall for a man so soon. And right now is not the time to be getting caught up. I know nothing about him except that he can sing and he is fine as all hell. I just saw him at the mall last week and I don't want him to think I'm desperate. *Desperate? Am I? Oh, shit, I don't need this in my life. I should just carry my confused ass right back home and finish working on my book. Well, what's the chances of him being there anyway? I'll just pop in and say hello to Benny and leave.*

    I walked in the door and was surprised to see Benny's Place jam-packed. Benny had asked me to pop in on a Friday or Saturday night but I never imagined that it would be so many people in here. Benny's isn't your normal New Orleans' hangout. He doesn't sell liquor and if you're drunk, you're not even allowed in. His doorman is big, black and scary looking. No one has ever questioned his authority. Benny doesn't consider his place to be a haven for drunken tourists. It is a place for natives such as myself to enjoy the Quarters without having to deal with all of the camaraderie. It is really laid back. Laid back for the Quarters, that is.

    Benny was standing in the very middle of the dais introducing a local band when I walked in. I was so busy looking for a place to sit that I didn't see Jeffrey Jackson walk up behind me. But I was hearing his voice again.

    "I'm so glad you took the hint the other day. I'll admit I'm not as good at throwing hints like your friend Maria but I really tried."

    I laughed but didn't turn around. I figured I'd let him enjoy the view from behind for just a little while.

    "Can I help you find a seat, Doll?"

    "Well, Dimples, if you think you can. I would love to sit down. These high heels are new and my feet are killin' me." I laughed but still had not turned around and looked at him yet.

    "Right this way my lady."

    I immediately thought of Mr. Lee when he said that but it sounds much cuter coming from him. He found an empty table in the far-left corner of the café. I could barely see the band.

    "Is this okay?" he asked.

    "Sure. This is just fine. Thank you." I finally looked at him.

    "You look beautiful. I hope you don't mind me saying so."

    "No, I don't mind at all. Thank you, you look nice yourself."

    "Yeah, well, I don't normally dress like this. But I wanted to look good for my debut. Besides, Benny said that you were coming here tonight to hear me sing

COFFEE-COLORED DREAMS

so I'm dressed in my Mack Daddy gear. " He stood and posed. "So what do you think?"

"I think you look quite handsome." He makes me laugh. I love a man with a sense of humor. But my smile turned into a frown when I realized what he'd just said. "Benny said what? I don't know why he told you that. I had no idea that you were singing tonight. Hell, I've never even been here on a Friday night. Did you tell him that you saw me last week?"

"No I didn't. After practice the other night, he told me to make sure I wore something decent because Doll was coming for my debut. I thought that he may have spoken to you about it."

"Not me. Are you sure he was talking about me? He could have been talking about someone else."

"No. I asked him if you were bringing Angel and he said no. So I'm sure he was talking about you."

"Now that's scary. I never talk to Benny unless I come here. In fact, I didn't even know I was coming here until a few hours ago. I was on my way to Preservation Hall. I just decided to get out of the house because I was so bored. Now how do you think Benny knew?"

"Well, that I can't explain. But he does say he has some good connections." He pointed to the ceiling and smiled that wonderful smile. The whole corner lit up.

"He's got the kind of connections I would love to have."

"Would you like something to drink?"

"Yeah, I'd like a cup of café'au lait."

"Don't you just love this place. I mean how many places can you go to on a Friday night and listen to a good band and leave just as sober as you were when you walked in."

"None in the French Quarters, except this one. Must be those connections."

"Must be. I'll be right back."

I have never seen so many people in Benny's before. I wonder if they all have nicknames too. I have a hard enough time remembering real names. I guess it must be easy for Benny, though. Being that he uses physical attributes as his basis.

Benny even has waiters and waitresses. I had no idea that anybody else worked here. Whenever I've come all I see is Benny and the dude at the door where he always is. The big dude that has now acquired the name, "Big Man" because neither of us faithful patrons know his name nor do we have the guts to ask him. He's not what you'd consider a talker. He's more of a grunter. And who is this man with the dirty apron on yelling at that waitress? He must be the one hookin' up those poboys and that awesome jambalaya. That brotha can cook!

I looked up to see Benny and Jeff looking at me and talking at the same time. I know they're talking about me by the way Jeff keeps smiling. Benny must sense my uneasiness because he's "rocking" toward me grinning from ear to ear.

pamela davis-noland

"Hi ya'there Doll. Don't you look like'a vision this evenin'. I wasn't sho if it wuz you or the Lord had done took me home and I wuz lookin' at an angel."

"Benny, do you mind if I start jotting down some of the compliments you give me?"

"Want somethin' to rememba' ol' Benny by, huh?"

"No, I've just never heard such poetry before. I need some new material and I'd love to use some of your words."

"Feel free, Doll."

"Benny can I ask you a question?"

"Sure honey, anything?"

"How did you know that I was coming here tonight?"

Benny suddenly noticed a nice looking couple walk through the doors. He waved. "Gotta go see if I can find another' table. You enjoy yu'self, now Doll. Benny'll be back to talk to ya' lata'. That's if that boy don't keep you too bizzy." He winked and "rocked" away.

"Here's your café' au lait, ma'am." Jeff said.

"Jeff, what do you think about Benny? I mean, do you find him a bit uh, what's the word…uh…. psychic maybe?"

"Did you ask him how he knew that you were coming tonight?"

"Yes."

"He didn't answer you did he?"

"Nope. He went to find that couple over there a table."

Jeff shook his head. "Yeah, when I asked him, he said he'd seem to have caught the attention of a lovely woman in the corner and he walked over here to you."

"I love this place."

"When did you start coming here?"

"A little over a year ago. I found Benny's totally by accident. And you?"

"A friend of mine back in Chicago hipped me to it when we came one summer for a little vacation. We came to see this band, some friends of my boy. When I moved here, I came back. Now it's my favorite hang out spot."

"Mine too."

"I've never dreamed that I'd have become so close to Benny, though. I mean, he's like a father figure in my life now. My father died when I was eight years old and my mother never remarried. My dad was in a band and he played tenor sax and sang lead. My mother was in the band too. Until she started having babies, then they both quit the band, got married and my father got a real job, as my mother puts it. She does all of her singing in church now."

"I guess that's why you sing so beautifully, huh, because of your parents?"

"Yeah, well, I guess that you can say I am doubly blessed."

Hmmm, I'll say.

"What about your parents? Are they both still alive?"

"Yes. And still happily married. Forty-one years next month."

COFFEE-COLORED DREAMS

"How nice. You guys pretty close?"

"Yeah, I guess. My father and I get along a lot better than my mother and I. But I think that's because we are too much alike, her and I, although she says I'm just like my father. But the older I get, the more I understand her."

"How old are you, if you don't mind me asking?"

"Thirty. And you?"

"Thirty-four."

We talked for about an hour before Benny came back. He "rocked" over to our table with a big smile on his face. "Let's go boy. It's time fo' yo' debut."

"Are you two going to do that song you wrote, Benny?" I asked.

"Yep. Now don't you go and choke up on me, boy, ya'here me. Just close yo' eyez and pretend that this'here doll is the only one in the place and you'll do jest fine."

"Wish me luck." Jeff whispered.

"Break a leg." I whispered back.

The crowd became as quiet as Sunday Mass when Benny walked up on the tiny dais. It was as though they were about to hear a word from God instead of an old man about to play his favorite instrument. I watched the faces of four women at a nearby table. Their mouths flew open when Jeff stepped up on stage next to Benny. One of them bit her bottom lip and sank down in her chair. I smiled. And to think he had been sitting here with me all night.

I couldn't believe my ears. He sounded better than he did the first time I heard him. He sang with his eyes closed and I wondered if he was taking Benny's advice.

When they were finished, everyone in the café' stood and applauded. Myself included. The four women were going wild. The one who bit her lip couldn't control herself. She started screaming like she'd just won the lottery. Now she would have gotten away with it if she was drunk, but being that Benny didn't serve liquor, she looked like a fool. But then again, she could have been high. Benny's crowd didn't drink, but I can spot a pot-head a mile away. And believe me, there are plenty of us that hang out at Benny's Place.

As Jeff was trying to make his way back to my table, the woman with the lip problem approached him. He talked to her for a minute and turned again to get through the crowd when the other three women stopped him. He just smiled and nodded. Pretty soon he had a crowd of people around him. I could barely see him anymore. I decided to go home. I sure didn't want to come off like I was some damn groupie. Besides, I had done what I set out to do, anyway. I lived a little. And I had a wonderful time. I sat at the table with a sexy brotha and talked. Not one time did he show any signs of trying to Mack on me or fill my head up with meaningless promises. He was a perfect gentleman. I found Benny, kissed him on the cheek and said goodnight.

I was making my way through the crowded streets when I heard him yell out my name. I stopped and turned around. Jeff was walking toward me looking pissed off. "You hate my singing?" He asked when he got close enough for me to hear him. He was practically out of breath.

"No Dimples, I just love yo' sangin'" I used my fake southern accent.

"Then why do you always leave right after I sing?" He got right in my face and he looked genuinely hurt.

"Well, you were pretty busy and it is getting late. I didn't know how long your new fans were going to keep you."

"You're definitely not a fan."

"And why would you say that? Is it because I didn't run up to you and tell you how wonderful you are?" I batted my eyes dramatically.

"Well, I don't expect you to do all that. But you can give a brotha' some kind of an opinion." He pouted.

"You want my opinion?"

"Yes I do."

I took a step closer to him and whispered, "I think you had better stop looking so sexy when you sing. I saw a woman in there who was going to need a paramedic if she would have bitten her lip any harder."

He laughed a hearty laugh, "You're so crazy, Celia." He said.

"So I've been told." *Many times.*

"So, when are you coming back?"

"I don't know. When are you singing again?"

"Whenever Benny asks me to. But if it'll get you here sooner, I'll sing tomorrow."

"My day is pretty much booked tomorrow. I have a project that I'm working on, some papers to grade and I have to visit my parents. They haven't seen me in weeks."

"Well, some other time then." He looked at me curiously.

"Why are you looking at me like that?"

"No reason. Why? Does it bother you when people stare at you?"

"No, not really. I get that look all the time. I'm kind of used to it."

"I'll bet you are." He looked me up and down. "So did you have a nice time tonight?"

"I had a wonderful time. You?"

"Yes. Yes I did. May I walk you to your car?"

"Sure." I turned and began walking a few steps in front of him. I wanted to give him a little "somethin' somethin'" to look at to cap off his night. I may be celibate but I'm still human. A girl needs to know that she's still got it.

We walked to my jeep laughing and talking like two old friends. I drove off humming his song. I looked in my rearview mirror and saw him waving. I laughed. He knew I was looking back at him.

Although I'm not allowing myself to even think about what he would be like to date, I at least feel alive again. "Thank you Lord." I whispered.

SURPRISE:
TO COME UPON AND ATTACK UNEXPECTEDLY

Jeffrey Jackson

I miss the smell of a woman. That was one of the things I actually liked about being married. Every night when Laura would finally come to bed, if I weren't feigning sleep, I'd reach over and pull her close to me just so that I could smell her. The scent of a woman is the only aphrodisiac I need sometimes. It's a good thing too. Because if it wasn't, I don't think Laura would have gotten as much as she did.

 Celia DuBois smells sexy, if there is such a smell. I don't know how to describe it but when I was sitting across the table from her at Benny's, I found myself inhaling excessively every few minutes or so. The smell made me a little light-headed. I love the way it made me swoon. Between her scent and the way her big eyes mesmerized me,(they all but glowed in the dark) I thought I was going to have trouble standing because my jimmy seemed to have a mind of its own and a damn good memory. If she only knew what was going on in my mind. Damn!!

 When she walked in with that ass-huggin' outfit on, time stood still for just a second. And then I saw every brotha in Benny's Place, with a pulse, turn their attention toward her. I made my move so fast I surprised myself. I wanted to let every brotha in the place know that she was there for me. Or at least that's what Benny had told me. He'd said she was coming although we still don't know how he knew. That Benny be trippin' a niggah out on a regular.

 I would have loved it if Celia had stuck around a little longer instead of skippin' out after I sang. Again! Well, at least she complimented me on my singing this time. Man, and the way she complimented me. Oooowee!!! Sista know she got it goin' on. Showing off her ass and getting all up on me whisperin' and shit. Just teasin' a brotha the way a brotha like me loves to be teased.

 When I returned to Benny's after making sure she made it to her car safely, I got stuck the rest of the night trying to fight off three horny-ass-beauty-deprived-freaks that are now my new self-proclaimed fan club. They were cool though. Well, at least until one of them asked me to leave and go kick it with them. There wasn't a chance in hell that I was going anywhere with them. Hell,

pamela davis-noland

I wasn't even a hundred percent sure about their gender. I mean I usually don't like to call a woman ugly because I believe all women have their own special beauty. But these women were butt-ugly! That's why the gender thang was questionable.

I pretended that I saw Benny trying to get my attention across the room and then I snuck off to the office in back to lay down. I picked up Benny's cordless and called Laura. The smell of Celia made me miss her.

Celia DuBois

My horoscope says that I'm in for a wonderful weekend. I normally don't believe in that stuff but I woke up in such a good mood that it seemed to be some sort of a sign. Or at least that's what I'm hoping. At least I had a decent conversation with my mother when she called to remind me that I owed her money. At five-thirty in the morning she calls to give me that little reminder, mind you. I was looking forward to having an exciting day anyway.

I was preparing for my first class when Jennifer walked in. She had both hands behind her back and she was grinning from ear to ear. "Good morning, Miss DuBois?" she sang.

"Well, hey, good morning to you, Jennifer. I thought I wasn't going to see much of you this semester."

"Oh I'ma still come by and see my favorite teacher. I came by to give you this." She revealed what she was hiding behind her back. "It's not much, but I wanted to give you somethin' to let you know how much I appreciate you."

She handed me a pink envelope and a little white box.

"You didn't have to get me anything, Jennifer."

"I know. But I'ma never forget how nice you was to me that day me and Jimmy broke up. I was trippin'."

"No you weren't trippin', you were hurt. Besides, I knew exactly how you were feeling. What ever happened with you two anyway. I've been so busy that I haven't had the time to ask you if everything is okay."

"Oh, I'm a'ight. I just ignore Jimmy. I ain't even got time for his mess. I'm tryin'ta get ready to graduate and go to college. My mama and me decided that I should go to LSU. I can't wait to get away from here, I 'bout had enough of Jimmy and his hoochies."

"Well, good for you. I knew you'd bounce back. All you needed was a little time."

"What 'bout you? You talk to your friend yet?"

"No, not yet. But guess who I did talk to?"

"Who?"

"Do you remember the guy that sang at Benny's?"

"Dimples?!" She yelled so loud I had to get up and go close the door.

COFFEE-COLORED DREAMS

"I'm sorry I didn't mean to yell," she apologized.

I laughed. "Anyway, I met him at the mall a couple of weeks ago and we talked. He even asked about you."

"He did?!" She was having a hard time controlling her excitement.

"And then I went back to Benny's and I heard him sing again and we sat and talked for hours. He's very nice. I really enjoyed spending time with him."

"Nice? Miss DuBois that man is *fiiiinne*! If I was olda', I'd be tryin'ta git wit'im." She snapped her finger and rolled her neck.

I blushed. I have to admit the man is fine as hell but I am still just a little leery. And I'm more afraid of myself than I am of him. He is just a little too damn fine not to be attached anyway. I'm sure he didn't go home alone that night. "Yeah he is fine, but I need a little bit more than that to get my attention." I said.

"He sang that song again?"

"Yes he did!" I mimicked her by snapping my fingers and rolling my neck.

"I still can't get over that. It sho' seem like somebody planned that huh?"

"Yeah, that happens a lot at Benny's."

"You seen him again?"

"No, I haven't been back yet."

"Why Miss DuBois?!" she yelled. "You trippin', you should go back."

"I will. I'm just trying to be a little cautious, that's all."

"Well, don't be too cautious. You don't know when that mistah right 'gon show up. You don't wanna be too busy being cautious and miss out."

"Are you giving me advice, Miss Guidry? I mean you've only had to deal with one broken heart. I have lots of experience in that department."

She laughed. "You 'gon open your present Miss DuBois? The bell 'bout to ring."

I opened the envelope first. Inside was a lovely pink card with a picture of a spring bouquet of flowers and the words "Thank you." I opened it to find a hand written letter. It read:

> *Thank you for being you. Thank you for not being the typical high school teacher. You know how to relate to us. You know how to make us smile. Thank you for comforting me.*
>
> *But above all, thank you for sharing a little bit of yourself with me. You're wonderful, Doll. (smile)*
>
> *P.S. Don't forget my signed copy of your book. And send me a shout out when you make it to Oprah.*

I smiled, hugged her and kissed her cheek. I was just about to open my the little box when the bell rang and my students barged through the door.

"Open it lata'," Jennifer whispered. "I'm gonna go."

My horoscope may be right after all. So far I'm having a wonderful day. I

pamela davis-noland

love it when I touch someone's life in a positive way. Sometimes I think I missed my calling. I should've been a therapist or a counselor or something of that nature. I'm so good at giving advice. Now taking it is something I haven't quite mastered. I can be stubborn sometimes. Even if I know that someone is giving me some helpful advice, I still do what I want. I surprise myself sometimes. But that's the way life is for a free-spirited person. We love to live life on the edge. We do things that normal people won't do no matter how crazy it may be. If our minds are made up, that's it, there ain't no turning back.

I was in the middle of a lecture about sixteenth-century writers when Mrs. Jenkins, the school secretary, called over the loud speaker. "Miss DuBois?" she sang.

"Yes Mrs. Jenkins."

"Miss DuBois, there is a gentleman here to see you. He wants to walk over to your class. Are you pretty busy?"

Oh shit! It better not be Calvin. This is just like him with his persistent ass. "I'm in the middle of a lecture, Miss Jenkins. May I ask who it is?"

There was silence for a minute. Now, I don't know what he told her, but when she spoke again, she was cheery and giggling when she informed me that he was already on his way to my class.

I immediately became suspicious. For one thing, Miss Jenkins is never happy or cheery, and it damn near takes an act of Congress for anyone to walk into *her* school and think that they're going to walk down *her* halls to see anybody.

A few minutes later my classroom door opened and an arm with a long stemmed rose in hand came in. The students went wild. The girls howled and the boys barked like dogs, pumpin' their fist in the air. I, on the other hand, was pissed. I was not in the mood for Calvin and his bullshit. The first thing I'm going to do is cuss Mrs. Jenkins out for letting this fool come to my class.

"Okay class, calm down." I said. "Turn to page 87 in your handbooks and begin reading. Jamal, can you please stand here and read aloud. There will be a pop quiz when I return and believe me I'll only be gone for a minute." *Calvin is about to get cussed out and he don't even know it. I'm no longer missing him.*

I was flustered, flabbergasted, awe-stricken and all that when I walked out of my door and saw him and his incredible dimples standing before me. My knees weakened and my eyes wouldn't focus.

"Hi Doll." He said.

Now I know that I've seen some incredible smiles before but this man can put Tyson (not Mike) out of business for good. His teeth are perfect and his lips are delicious. His goatee: impeccable. His dimples would make a perfect circle if they were to magically remove themselves and become one. The way they danced on his face, they seemed to have a personality of their own. His smile sang to me.

I know he must think I'm crazy for standing here staring at him with my

COFFEE-COLORED DREAMS

mouth wide open. "How, um, how did you know where I worked?" I finally asked. My mind was racing. I know Benny didn't tell him because I never told Benny where I worked. Like that has anything to do with Benny knowing all of my business. He seems to know a lot about me whether I tell him or not. But I asked anyway, "Did Benny tell you?"

"No, not this time. You get all the credit for this." He said, handing me the rose.

"Me? I didn't tell you where I work."

"No you didn't. But you did tell me that you were a teacher. I've been to just about every school in New Orleans asking for a Miss Celia DuBois. You wouldn't believe how long I've been looking for you, man. It's been three days now and I haven't eaten or changed clothes or slept, I've just been walking up and down the streets of New Orleans with this rose in my hand...."

"Oh shut up," I interrupted. He almost had me going until he put on that sad puppydog face and started talking about not eating or sleeping. "Now tell me the truth, how did you find me? You're starting to make me think I better start carrying my nine with me to school." I laughed.

"Okay, okay, the truth is I saw you this morning. I was right across the street getting my morning paper when I saw you getting out of your car. That's when I remembered you telling me that you were a school teacher."

"Do you live around here?"

"Well, yeah, over on Claire Street, 'bout four blocks away."

"Oh. Um… how in the world did you get by Miss Jenkins? She's not an easy woman to deal with. Exactly what did you tell her?"

"Well, let me just put it this way - you had six roses." He smiled and my heart fluttered. About five times.

"So, why haven't you been back to Benny's yet?" He asked, somewhat concerned. "Benny is even wondering. He mentions your name every chance he gets you know. We can be in the middle of a simple conversation and he'll look at me and say out of the clear blue, "I wonder where Doll is?" and then he'll just keep right on doing whatever he was doing. That Benny is a trip."

"Well, you tell Benny that as soon as school is out he'll be seeing me a whole lot more. I usually teach a class or two during the summer, but I decided not too this year so I'll be as free as a bird."

"You flyin' solo?"

He makes me blush too much and I hate it. I didn't even answer him.

"Celia, I know you have to get back to your class. But can I ask you one question?"

"Yeah. But just one." I pointed my index finger at him.

"Am I ugly?"

"What?!" My laugh echoed down the halls.

He took a step closer to me. "No, I'm serious. Am I ugly?"

"No Jeff, you know very well that you – are – not - ugly."

pamela davis-noland

He took another step closer and said, "Do I stink?"

"No, you don't stink." I giggled.

"Do I have bad breath?" He took another step closer.

By this time, my underarms were itching and my giggling became nervous laughter. "You said one question, Jeff." I tried to sound firm.

"Oh so that's it, huh? My breath stinks!"

"No, Jeff, your breath does not stink." I took a step back and smiled.

Brotha, please back up. The vow, girl. Remember the vow.

Jeff came as close to me as possible without touching me. He looked directly into my eyes as if they were mirrors. I became even more nervous and my palms were soaking wet. I had to wipe them on my pant legs and prayed that he didn't see me do it. I swear this man is turning me on and I just made this drastic decision. This might be a little harder than I thought. But then again, would it be any other way? That just seems to be the norm for me.

He stepped up to me and said once more but in a sexier voice, "Are you sure my breath doesn't stink?"

I swallowed hard. I had a lump in my throat as big as an apple.

"Are you sure?" he asked again, a little sexier.

"I'm sure." I managed to whisper.

He leaned forward close enough so that his lips were nearly touching mine. He studied my face a little longer and whispered, "Good."

He winked at me and walked away backwards. When he came to the end of the hall, he waved and walked out of the doors.

Damn!!!

Jeffrey Jackson

Every morning on my way to work I stop at the 7-11 and get a Times-Picayune, a cup of strong black coffee, two beignets and if I've smoked before I left the house, a pack of Big Red. Now I've done this religiously since I moved here but I've never noticed the school directly across street. I noticed the old cathedral and the big plantation lookin' house on the corner where all the nuns live. And I've seen the kids in uniforms but I never noticed the school. Well I guess I noticed. But this morning I really noticed.

I recognized the royal blue Jeep Cherokee with the well-tinted windows first. She had the two front windows rolled down and she was bobbin' her head and singing along with the music that was blasting from her speakers. To see her smiling like she was already having a wonderful day at 7:05 in the freakin' morning tripped me out. I shook my head in disbelief of just how much she reminded me of that sweet innocent goddess in my dreams.

Hers was the second car in the left turn only lane waiting for the light to change. I stood next to my car for a minute hoping she'd look my way but some-

COFFEE-COLORED DREAMS

one pulled up next to her and caught her attention and then the light changed. I watched as she pulled into the school parking lot and then it dawned on me that she was going to work.

When and why I decided to try and be Prince Charming I don't know. I don't think I put much thought into it at all really. I had just decided right there as I saw her walking up the walkway at St. Theresa's High School that I was going to come back and see her. It was just that simple and felt just as natural. I mean there was no pondering, no plan, no nothing. I just took a late lunch and told my boy in the next office that I was going to be gone a little longer because I had to run an errand if anyone asks. I stopped at the first florist I saw and drove back to the upper east side like a man on a mission. I must say I was pretty pleased with her reaction though. At least I made her blush. I guess I might still have it after all.

I just hope she doesn't think I'm some kind of desperate stalker. I mean I don't think men even do the kind of shit I did today anymore. Maybe more of us should.

Damn this woman is making me crazy!

THE CLOSER I GET TO YOU.......

Celia DuBois

The minute I walked in my apartment I realized that I had left Jennifer's gift in my desk drawer. After Jeff startled me, my day was pretty much shot. I didn't want to wait until Monday to see what it was so I decided to go back and get it.

    I took a quick shower, threw on my favorite Bob Marley T-shirt and my most worn-out, comfortable jeans. I opened the sunroof and rolled down all the windows of my dirty jeep and cruised the long way back to school enjoying the sights and sounds of New Orleans at dusk. Dusk is always so colorful. The time when there is a parade of street vendors with umbrella-covered carts, mimes in every size, shape and color, well dressed waiters and waitresses, dingy little boys with torn up Converse, street musicians, fortune tellers, strippers, not to mention the tourists with all of their beads and festive clothing. They fill the streets, buses and streetcars heading in the same direction with the same hungry look in their eyes and same pep in their step, all knowing that the tourists never fail them. I admire them for their tenacity. It must take a whole lot of dedication to go to a job every day where you know that your wages depend on the kindness of others. My Mudear used to call them beggars. "Common street trash begga's! Dey need'ta git dem'selves some real jobs." She would say. But I've always admired them for not being ashamed to express their art for the world to see. And getting paid to do it. Sounds like it could be a fun job.

When I walked in my class, Mr. Hollier, the school custodian was sweeping the floor.
    "Excuse me, Mr. Hollier, but if you don't mind me walking across your floor, I'd like to get something out of my desk drawer."
    He looked up and nodded toward my desk with a frown. He didn't say anything and I was glad. I can't understand him anyway. His French accent is a little too thick and Mr. Hollier hates repeating himself.
    I tiptoed to my desk and smiled at him but he didn't smile back. I sat at my desk and opened the little box. Inside was a beautiful silver pendant in the shape

COFFEE-COLORED DREAMS

of a pen and pad and the words, "Write On!" was skillfully inscribed on it. I held it to my heart and smiled. It was a beautiful gift and it further encouraged me to do just that. I thanked Mr. Hollier for letting me interrupt his work and quickly left before he decided to have a conversation with me.

Just as I was walking toward the exit doors, I heard Mr. Lee's sickening voice. The first thing I thought was to keep walking like I didn't hear him but his voice echoed through the quiet halls so loudly, I had no choice but to turn around.

"I wasn't sure it was you. You look like one of the students." Mr. Lee yelled.

"Hello Mr. Lee. I was just on my way out. I just came to get something out of my desk." I quickly let him know that I was in a hurry. I turned around and headed for the door.

"Wait, I'll walk you to your car."

Shit!

"So, what do you have planned for this evening, Miss DuBois? I'm sure you must have a date."

"No, as a matter of fact, I don't. I have other things on my mind right now. Dating is not one of them. Well, here's my jeep. Thank you."

"So how is your book coming along?"

Ughh! "Just fine. Thanks." I fake smiled.

"Say, uh, which way are you going? Maybe we could go and find a good happy hour or something. You know you can't bury yourself in work all the time."

What is it with his "or something"? I hope this Niggah ain't tryin' to drop no subtle hints. Damn, didn't he learn shit from Anita and Clarence?!

"Thanks but no thanks, Mr. Lee." I said as politely as I could.

"Well, what about taking in a movie or a bite to eat? It is almost dinner time and I know a lovely place, "Court of Two Sisters," it's deep in the heart of the Quarters. Have you ever been? It's one of the more exquisite courtyards."

"No, I haven't. And it sounds lovely. But like I said before, no thanks."

"So what do you suggest?"

Why does this shit always happen to me? Do I even look like his type? I mean, damn, I'm tryin' to be polite niggah but you're startin' to piss me off.
"Well, I suggest that you walk over to your big stankin' lankin' over there, start it up and go and find you a happy hour *or something*. I'm gonna start my little jeep here and go home. I've had a really long week, Mr. Lee. Thank you for all your offers but I gotta go."

"You're a difficult one, Miss DuBois. If you're worried about the fact that we work together, please don't. Believe me I am very discreet."

"Yeah, I know. That's what Miss Crane, the science teacher says, not to mention, Miss Gray, the cook, and oh yeah, the librarian who substituted for Miss Quibodeaux when she was out on maternity leave. They all told me just how discreet you are. Goodbye Mr. Lee."

And with that I drove off and left him standing right there looking like the

pamela davis-noland

punk he is. Old high-yella' playa', he makes me sick. He may be able to turn them old ladies on but he don't do shit for me.

"What a jackass!" I yelled and giggled at the same time as soon as I thought he was out of hearing range.

I was sitting at the red light when I looked over and saw Jeff at a Texaco pumping gas in his car. Of all days to be driving in the left lane. I know damn well I always drive in the right lane. I turned on my blinker and prayed the old man sitting behind me on the right would have a little mercy. He did.

I pulled up next to Jeff's car as soon as he was getting ready to back out. I pretended like the meeting was totally coincidental. I looked over at him and he was already smiling.

He pulled up next to me. "Hey," he yelled out, "what are you doing, following me? Am I gonna have to go get *my* nine?" He laughed a hearty laugh.

"Naw… don't worry, I'm just stoppin' in to get some Gatorade."

"Where you headed? You're just going home from work?"

"No, I had to go back and get something."

"Where you headed now?"

"Back home. What about you?"

"Actually, I'm starving. I was thinking about ordering pizza and maybe rentin' some movies."

"Oh, that's nice." *Damn, now I know I could have said something better than that!* I wish he would ask me to join him. Then again… maybe it'd be better if he didn't. I really don't know if I want to hang out with him too much. I just want to be asked as crazy as that may sound.

"You hungry?" He asked.

I didn't answer.

"Hey, Celia, you hungry?" He asked again.

"I'm thinking."

"Thinking about what? You're either hungry or you're not. So, you hungry or what?"

"Will you quit asking me that." I snapped.

"Well, will you answer me. My stomach is starting to growl."

"No." Now I know damn well I want to say yes. I mean what could it hurt. Besides, I am absolutely sure that I'm not going to sleep with him anyway.

"No, you're not hungry, or no you don't want to eat with me?"

I just looked at him and smiled.

"Say, can you follow me across the street for a second?"

"Alright, but let me just run in and get my Gatorade." I had to make it look authentic.

"Okay, I'll be right over there in that Blockbuster parking lot."

When I pulled up he was standing next to his car with both his legs and arms folded. He jumped in my jeep, uninvited, before I could even stop the engine.

"Jump in. Have a seat." I said.

COFFEE-COLORED DREAMS

He ignored me and started rummaging through my cassette case. He found my Best of Miles Davis cassette, popped it in, and preceded to pick out a few and lay them on the dashboard as if he planned on listening to all of them. "So when did you guys break up?" He said without looking up.

"Oh you have been hanging out with Benny *waaay* too long." I laughed.

"So am I right?" He smiled.

"Maybe. Maybe not." I shrugged my shoulders.

"Well if I was a bettin' man," he finally looked at me, "I'd bet all my money on that maybe." He smiled even bigger.

"So what makes you so sure?"

"Well, I wasn't at first, but so far all the answers you've given me point in that direction. If you hadn't just broke up with someone you would have just said so from the start. So, how long did you guys date?"

"Not long."

Well what was I to say? He was right.

"How long is 'not long'?"

"You sure do ask a lot of questions, Jeff? What's that all about?"

"Well, why don't you just tell me the story and then I won't have any more questions."

"Okay. Let's see. The story huh? Okay. Well…we met, we dated, we shared, we, no I, fell in love, he cheated, I split. The end. Anything else you wanna know?"

"Do you still love him?"

"My my. We sure are getting a little personal aren't we?"

"Are we? I'm sorry. I didn't mean to make you uncomfortable. I have a habit of thinking out loud. Sorry. But since I already asked, do you?"

"No. At least I don't think so. I don't think about it much anymore. It's just that the breakup happened so fast. I wasn't really prepared. Normally, there are some warning signs. But this brotha' was good. I had no idea. Up until I actually saw it for myself."

"You caught him in the act?! Damn!" He laughed.

"No. I did not! And if I did, what would be so damn funny?" I asked, trying to sound hurt.

"Oh I'm sorry, man, I didn't mean to laugh. But when you said you saw it… I mean I didn't know what you were talking about. So what did you see?"

"I popped up at his apartment, unannounced, and he had some other woman there."

"What were they doing?"

"Well when I walked in she was sitting on the couch."

"He let you in?"

"Yes. Let me finish. He was real cool about it. The woman didn't seem to be upset but I was embarrassed. They were a little bit too cool. You know."

"So did she have clothes on?"

pamela davis-noland

"Jeff, will you be quiet! Anyway he introduced me as his "good friend" Celia. Not his girlfriend, his "good" friend. I got the hint."

"Ooh."

"Yeah, ooh! I walked out and haven't talked to him since."

"So why not give him a chance to explain? There could have been a good explanation."

"That – is – such – a – man answer. I swear." I laughed.

He laughed even louder. "It was, huh? But you never know. Maybe she was just an ex. Well anyway, I guess that doesn't really matter much now. Now does it?" He winked at me for the hundredth time since I first met him.

"So what about you?" I asked, "Do you have a girlfriend, a wife, a "good friend", or all of the above?"

"None of the above. I haven't had a girlfriend in years."

Ohmygod, he's gay! "Years?"

"Yeah. I was married for six and a half years. I've recently divorced."

"Oh." *Whew!*

We sat in total silence except for low sounds of Miles' trumpet in the background. I sat there pretending to be interested in the posters in the Blockbuster window and he continued rummaging through my cassettes.

"So what's your story?" I finally break the silence.

"My story? Well, let's see. I have known my ex-wife all of my life. Our parents were all best friends. Her father was in the band with my parents. We were suppose to be a match made in heaven. Well, at least that's what everyone told us. Anyway, we were more like brother and sister but both of us did what was expected of us anyway. I was the only boy her parents let her go out with. Sometimes I was just a cover up so that she could date someone else. We did that a lot. They finally let her date other people when I went off to college. When I graduated, I went back home and she had just broke up with some dude and we sort of consoled one another because I had had my share of disappointments during my time away from home. The next thing you know everyone was caught up, man. Her parents, my mother, my sisters and brothers, friends, cousins, everybody. They started planning shit before I knew what was going on. And then *she* got all caught up. Everyone had convinced her that it was meant to be because when we were babies we held hands in the crib together…or some shit like that. Anyway, we did it. We got married. At least we were smart enough not to bring kids in and fuck their heads up. Laura, that's her name, she's a buyer for a very expensive boutique that caters to some of Chicago's finest so therefore she has to travel a lot. We didn't spend much time together because we were both married to our jobs. And I was definitely married to my music. That's why after the divorce was final, I packed my shit and left runnin'. And here I am in this little eclectic city of sin following my dreams of singing the blues in a New Orleans café. Just like my grandfather did. The end."

"So how do you like it so far?"

COFFEE-COLORED DREAMS

"It just keeps getting better and better." He smiled and looked me up and down.

"Are you going to stay long. I mean what else do you do besides sing at Benny's?"

"I'm an accountant. And I'm not going back to Chicago to live. Ever. I should have been born here. I love this laid back lazy shit. My mother always told me I moved too slow. The Big Easy. Yep. That's me alright."

"You don't think you'll miss the snow?"

"Yeah, maybe. But I'm going to always go home and visit. Now, enough about me, I have to ask you a question."

"No you are not ugly. No, your breath doesn't stink. No, you don't stink." I answered.

He laughed. "That's not what I wanted to ask you. I wanted to ask you how long are you going to keep this guard up?"

"Excuse me? What guard?"

"The one I see and hear."

"Oh. It shows that bad, huh?"

"Yeah man, why are you trying so hard *not* to like me? I'll admit, I'm no prince charming but I am a nice guy. If you'll just give a brotha' a chance."

"I'm just trying to be cautious, Jeff. I just got out of a relationship. And besides, how do I know that you don't have two or three women hiding somewhere."

"You heard her?"

"Did I hear who?"

"The woman I have locked in the trunk of my car. I told that 'ho to keep her mouth shut. Damn!"

I laughed. He has such a cute sense of humor. I love a man who can make me laugh.

"Look, man, I don't have two or three or even one woman. I just moved here a few months ago and I haven't had time to socialize much. I'm either at the café' with Benny or at work or asleep. My plate is pretty full right now. But I would like to have a social life. At least I'm trying to have one. But there's this sista who won't give me the time of day for some reason. I mean I used to think I was quite charming back in my college days. I must be rusty. Hell, to be honest with you, I never really had to work hard on getting attention. Women, like the one's at the café' the other night, seem to think I'm only tryin' to hit it. But, man, that ain't even my style. Never has been and never will be. Hell, I figure if a woman will give it up that easy, then she ain't worth tryin' to get wit. 'Cause if she'll give it to me, she'll give it the next brotha' just that easy. You knowwhatImean?"

"Yeah. I imagine you do get a lot of attention. I saw that for myself the other night."

"Man, did you see those women? You see what I mean? Man, one of them looked like a dude. I swear. Man, when I walked back into the café' after I

pamela davis-noland

walked you to your jeep, they begged me to sit at their table. I sat down for a little while, 'til the one who look like a dude asked me if I wanted to go back to her, his, or whatever, place and smoke some herb."

"Did you go?" I laughed.

He looked at me and rolled his eyes. "Man, hell no! I went to Benny's office and fell asleep on the couch 'til everybody left. I was so tired. I sang again the other night. I was hoping you'd show up. My lil' fan club was there again."

"I'm sure they'll become regulars."

"Yeah, I know. But that pisses me off. They're not there for my art. They act like I'm on stage takin' off my clothes. All that screamin' and shit ain't even necessary. You smoke herb?"

Do I smoke herb? Does a bear shit in the woods? "Occasionally," I lied. "What about you?"

"Yeah, man, especially since I moved here. I tell you what. I'm going to run in here," he said pointing to Blockbuster, "and pick up a few movies. You like comedies? Anyway, I'll pick out something funny. Here," he jumped out of my jeep and handed me his cell phone, "call that pizza joint around the corner and order a large whatever, and we'll pick it up on the way to my crib. I have some herb. Maybe we can just chill and blaze out for a little while? I'll be right back."

A man who knows how to take charge...unh! "Hold up. Wait a minute. Aren't you even going to ask?"

"Oh yeah. You want popcorn?" He smiled and winked. "Don't worry I'll get butter flavored. I don't know the number to that pizza joint. Call information." And with that, he pigeon-toed his fine ass right into Blockbuster.

I called information.

His apartment is nice. A little junky, but nice. I like a man who's neat but an anal brotha' makes me a little nervous. I dated this one guy who kept the food in his pantry in alphabetical order! Now that brotha' had issues. Hell, I was afraid to touch anything in his house. It looked more like a damn museum. I was waiting to see a fat security guard come out from the back the first time I visited him.

Jeff has good taste. I like his plants. They sure look a whole lot better than mine. I swear I wish I had a green thumb like my mama. Man, and look at all the books. Thank you Jesus. The man reads, too. And from the look of all these photographs, he's pretty good with a camera too.

"Have a seat. Just move those things to one side. It's nothing important. Just some old letters, bills and stuff. I just have to pop upstairs for a minute."

The entire upstairs loft is his bedroom. I can see the big four-post bed from where I'm standing. *My, my what a big bed we have. I hope he doesn't try to push up on me tonight. So far he's acted like a gentleman, I hope he doesn't change now that I'm on his turf.*

"Hey, look in that wooden box on the floor. Roll one." He yelled.

By the time he came back downstairs, I was already on my second slice of

COFFEE-COLORED DREAMS

pizza. I always eat when I get nervous and he is really making me hungry.

"Hey, you want something to drink? A beer or a Coke?"

"Do you have any iced tea?"

"One Coke, comin' up."

"Jeff, I love your pictures. You're a photographer too?"

"I dabble. But of lot of the older looking black and whites are old photos of my grandfather that I had refinished. Hey come here. Do you know who this is?" He pointed to a 8x10 black and white old photograph of a man playing a saxophone.

"No who is it?"

"I want you to guess. You don't have to guess now, though, I'll ask you again later. Let's play chess."

"What makes you think I know how to play chess?"

He lit the joint, took a long steady puff, and handed it to me. "Well, if you can't play, that'll just make it better for me. Now won't it?" He winked.

"Well we'll just have to see. Now won't we?" I winked back at him and took a longer, steadier puff.

We played chess, smoked herb, ate more pizza, laughed and had a wonderful time. The last time I had this much fun was with Calvin. Which may explain why I'm, all of sudden, paranoid. I feel the need to break out running. Well, maybe it's the herb. It is definitely some killa'. Then again, maybe it's this framed picture of this pretty woman that's been staring at me all night. I've been dying to ask who she is. This looks like a picture he took himself. It doesn't look like the other black and whites. Hell, all I have to do is ask.

"That is a pretty pearl necklace that lady has on." I said.

"Yeah it's antique. You need something else to drink?"

"No, I'm fine. Did you take that picture?"

"Yeah, I did." He answered.

Yeah you did?! Well, who is she? Damn, I hate it when men feel guilty about nothing. I don't even know him. So why is he trippin?

"She's pretty."

"I think she's beautiful. She taught me how to play chess."

Well, la - dee - da. "That's nice. Did you buy that antique necklace?"

He looked over at me and grinned. "Getting a little personal, aren't we?"

"Oh, I'm sorry. Are we?"

"Hey, if you want to know who she is why don't you just ask? I'm not shy."

"Okay, then who is she?"

"None of your business." He winked.

I wish you would stop winking at me. Instead of teaching your ass how to play chess, she should've taught you that tryin' to make a woman jealous on your first date, is not gonna guarantee your ass a second date. I really don't give a fuck who she is!

"She's my mother, Celia."

pamela davis-noland

"I knew that." I lied.

We laughed and laughed and laughed and laughed. He knew I was full of shit.

"Now who is the brotha' playing the saxophone?"

"Guess?"

"Your mother?" I laughed, "I'm just kidding. I don't know."

"Go over there, pick it up and tell me who it is."

He is so bossy. I love it.

I picked up the photo and stared at it for a while. But I still have no idea who it is.

"Bring it here."

"Just tell me who it is. What's with all the guessing games?"

"Sit down. Now look closely. Look at the shoes and the shirt."

"Nothin'."

"Okay, look at how he's holding his sax."

"Benny!" I yelled. "It's Benny. Damn, Benny was fine back in his day! Where did you get this from?"

"My grandfather."

"Were they friends?"

"Naw, my grandfather didn't know him personally, he just admired him. Benny used to be top billing back in his day. My grandfather was born and raised right here in New Orleans. He used to sing in juke joints, like he called them, from here to the Mississippi, and even in Atlanta. He opened for Benny a few times. But he never really got to know him personally. He would have given anything to have worked closely with Benny. And now two generations later, here I am. My body; my grandfather's spirit. My mother says I sing just like him."

"That's pretty neat. Does Benny know this story?"

"Does Benny know this story? Hell, he told it to me. I didn't know who this man was in the picture until I met Benny. He told me all about this man who had a wonderful voice, and who used to open some nights for him. He said that he would have given anything to work with him, but because of his drinking problem, he never kept a steady gig. Benny says the last time he saw my grandfather sing he told him how much he admired Benny and that he would love it if they could work together sometime. But my grandfather got put out of the club the same night. Benny never saw him again. But he'll never forget that voice. Talk about some creepy shit. You see my grandfather had a drinking problem and he never fulfilled his dream of being top biller because he wasn't very reliable and people got tired of him. He was a good old dude, though. He just drank too much. He's one of the reasons I have never drunk anything harder than beer or wine in my whole life. People always told me that I was my grandfather reincarnated, so I was scared if I drank, I may become the same drunkard he was."

"So can you get to the part when you figured out that this was Benny?"

COFFEE-COLORED DREAMS

"Yeah, so anyway, after he told me that story, I came home and was unpacking some more of my things and this picture was at the bottom of one of my boxes. I had seen it a thousand times, but for some reason, I decided to take it out of its old frame and reframe it. That's when I read the back. It says, 'To Smooth. Keep singing. Benjamin Thibodeaux, New Orleans - Mardi Gras 1948. Man I tripped."

"What! So Benny was talking about your grandfather?"

"Yep. I took this picture of my grandfather with me," he pulled a small beat up photo of a man standing in the same background as in the picture of Benny, "read the back."

"New Orleans – Mardi Gras 1948." Damn. This is a trip."

"Yeah man, anyway when I showed it to Benny, he looked at it and said "Smooth Jackson." He told me all these stories about my grandfather that I'd never heard.

"So you are Creole. I thought you might be. You just don't act like your typical Creole man."

"And what might that be?" He looked truly offended.

"What might what be?"

"A typical Creole man? What might that be?"

"I didn't mean anything about that Jeff. Did I offend you?"

"I don't know. Were you trying to?" He folded his arms and glared at me.

"Never mind. Hey, look, I gotta be going." I guess I hit a nerve.

"Okay, but can I ask you a question?"

"Oh Lord!"

"Naw, it's not like that. I'm serious. Please, can I ask just one?"

"Hell, you're gonna ask anyway. What?"

"Will you dance with me?"

"What?" *Oh shit, here we go. I knew you wasn't gonna let me up outta here without tryin' to feel up all over me.*

"Well, as corny as this may sound, I miss dancing. I haven't danced in so long, I might have forgotten. Man, I don't think I've danced in the last three years."

"Are you serious?"

"Very."

"Alright. But wait…. Fast or slow?"

"Um, I don't have a whole lot of rhythm, so we betta make it slow. I promise not to grind." He laughed that wonderful laugh.

"You betta' not!"

He grabbed me by the hand and pulled me into the middle of the floor. He pressed his remote control and D'Angelo's "Cruisin'" came blaring through the speakers.

He moves with such smoothness and grace. I wonder if he got that from his grandfather too. For someone with no rhythm, he sure knows how to slow dance.

pamela davis-noland

I normally hate it when a man hums in my ear, but he sounds so cute. He's so much broader than I am, I can barely clasp my hands together without getting too close. I hope "it" doesn't get hard. I looked up and he was staring at me.

"Why do you stare at me so much? Do I remind you of somebody?"

"Yep. As a matter of fact you do."

"Oh yeah, who?"

He stopped smiling, "The lady in my dreams." He said this like he was dead serious.

If you make me blush one more time, I'm going to have to run up outta here. The vow girl, remember the vow. I know I should have gone home.

"Do you mind?" he asked.

"Do I mind wha....?"

He kissed me hard and he kissed me long. He kissed me just like he danced, slow, methodically, and with a whole lot of passion.

Now I've been kissed more than a few times before, but I ain't hardly exaggerating when I say that this man can *KISS*! He can kiss better than my high school sweetheart, David Andrews can. I compare every man I kiss to David. Until tonight, David was the shit. No one could compare. Move over David, you've finally been bumped to the #2 spot!

When the song was over, he grabbed me by the hand again and walked me back over to the couch where he sat, legs open, with one leg in the couch and one on the floor and sat me down in between them so that he could kiss my neck. He was moving a little fast, but it wasn't sexual. It was more sensual, than sexual. He wasn't tryin' to get the drawls. Yet. If I'm not mistaken, I think he's tryin' to tease me. And it's working!

He leaned his head back and invited me to do the same and we stayed that way, listening to D'Angelo while sharing a peaceful moment until the last song finished. I did feel him get a little hard once but I ignored it and it went away.

He walked me out to my jeep and kissed me again. I was weak as hell, but I did a good job of not showing it. If he was as weak as I was, I couldn't tell. We exchanged phone numbers and said goodnight.

I can't believe this is happening again so soon. Especially after I've made these commitments. Brianna would kill me if she found out that I was on a date instead of at my computer. I'm gonna have to chill. A few more nights like this and I'll be right back where I started. And I am definitely not going back there.

I'm not too sure I'd want to get involved with Jeff anyway. I mean I can hardly believe that someone as handsome as he would not have a woman. He might just have the hots for some dark meat. He's probably rebelling since his family isn't here. I can look at that picture of his mother and tell she ain't hardly gonna approve of her baby dating such a dark skin woman. I bet they are all stuck up and bourgeois. I wonder what Miss "Buyer for the Bigtime Boutique" look like? I'd bet a whole paycheck that she don't look a thing like me.

Well, I had a nice time but that's all it was - a nice time. I've got other things

COFFEE-COLORED DREAMS

to do right now and by no means am I gonna let this man, I don't care how nice he is, cloud my mind.

Jesus keep me near the cross. Amen.

I'M NOT 'GON CRY

Jeffrey Jackson

I had a terrible night's sleep. I tossed and turned all night long so when the phone rang, it was a welcome sound. Anything to free me from my thoughts.
"Hello."
"Hi baby. How are you?"
"What's up L? How you doin'?"
"So Miles says you got the hots for some dark skin chick."
That sonovabitch Miles makes me sick. That niggah cannot keep a promise to save his life. I told him, no - I *begged* him not to tell Laura anything we talked about.

I called him the other day at 2:00 in the morning. I woke up feeling lonely as hell and I needed someone to talk to. I figured he would probably still be up being that he usually slept until noon anyway and I was right. He was wide-awake and ready to talk.

I don't know what possessed me but I just got tired of him asking me the same question every five minutes, "Niggah you ain't even *tryin*' to get no pussy?" After the fourth time he asked this, I dropped Celia's name. I told him how cool she is and how we just talk on the phone and kick it just a lil' bit, but nothing serious. I told him that she's a nice lady. I made sure and told him that she is a writer, hoping that that would deter the skin color issue. I also told him about her best friend that he'd probably love (provided she was the right shade for him that is).

The conversation went well and then Miles changed the subject. He started talking about this new chick he's thinking about producing. He said she's half-Black and half-Asian and she's gorgeous and has coal black hair that flowed down her back. Like I gave a damn! Hell, she'd be gone next month and replaced with one he thought was prettier. Miles can care less about talent.

I was just about to end the conversation when my luck ran out. He asked the dreaded question, "So, ole girl a yellow bone?"

"Naw Miles. She's a fine ass chocolate sista." I said it like I needed that niggah's approval and I immediately got mad at myself. What difference does it

COFFEE-COLORED DREAMS

make anyway? We all Black! Damn! And now here comes Laura callin' to talk shit. She hates the fact that I find dark-skinned women so attractive. She told me it was an insult to her. Whatever man, I ain't even tryin' to insult nobody. I just know what turns me on and I'll be damn if Celia DuBois ain't got it all and then some. And not just in looks either. Sista got it goin' on in every way. She's intelligent, fine, strong and spiritual. I love a strong black woman. A brotha like me need a strong black woman in his life. I guess that's why I stayed with Laura. At least she wasn't always sweatin' me.

"So you called me at," I reached over and picked up the clock, "6:30 in the morning to ask me about something Miles told you?"

"Well?"

"Well what?"

"Well do you?"

"Laura. I ain't even about to talk to you about any woman I got the hots for okay? Let's get that straight first. I don't want to discuss my relationships with you and I don't want to hear about yours, baby. Okay? Come on now Laura, we said we were going to remain friends for life. We can't remain friends if we try and get involved with each other's love life."

"Relationship? Love life? Damn! Oh it's like that. It was that easy for you to move on. It's enough you ran away to that lil' hot ass country ass State but now you're telling me that you're already seeing one of those country skeezers?"

"Look! I'm gonna say it once more real nice this second time, but if I have to say it a third time, you're not going to appreciate the tone or the cuss words."

"Okay okay."

"Hey?"

"What?" She was pouting.

"I'm not having a relationship with anyone but I do like someone and I'm sure you do too so don't even trip. Miles tells me about you too."

She laughed. "I'm not seeing anyone baby."

"Yeah okay. Anyway I gotta go. I'll talk to you later."

"Bye."

I know she's trippin' and she's gonna call everyone in my family and tell them something she knows nothing about. Man, who cares, all I know is I'm sick and tired of dealing with my folks on any aspect of my life. I'm not like them. Therefore, I have to stop trying to please them so much.

I'm crazy about Celia DuBois and I hope like hell she picks up that phone and dials my number before my pride kicks in and I have to ignore her next time I see her. I was up late last night thinking about that damn see-through skirt again and I picked up my pen and wrote a poem. Man this woman has got me trippin' for real. Anyway, you wanna hear it, here it goes…

pamela davis-noland

The smell of Jasmine
the sound of rain
the feel of silk
the look of pain
Oh, and the smell of you
the sound of your voice
the feel of your skin
the look of it
Smooth, Cocoa-brown
shimmering in the day, gleaming at night
The true Black woman in all of her glory
no pretenses, no additives
pure as snow
darkened glow
Oh, to feel you close to me
Miss Cocoa-Brown
Oh, how you thrill me.

Celia DuBois

The weatherman was wrong again. Everyday it's a 50% chance of rain and all we keep getting is these gloomy, misty days. I hate New Orleans when it rains. It becomes such a soggy, smelly city.

    I don't know why I'm sitting out here on this balcony instead of inside where it's cool like everyone else with some sense, but I kind of like days like this when I'm feelin' blue. Sometimes I like to be blue. I seem to write better when I'm a little sad. And by the way I'm feeling today, I may just complete my novel. I came out here to try and get inspired. I figure the gloomy mist might send me in a deeper funk as sadistic as that may sound. But hey, whatever works. I'm on a roll and I want to stay there.

    I've been thinking about Jeff, lately. I guess he stopped calling because I was so cold to him the last few times and I haven't called *him* at all. It's not like I haven't wanted to. He just makes me so nervous. And if I'm nervous, than that makes me weak. And he's so damn fine. I might not be able to stay strong if I spend too much time with him. He's the type of brotha' every woman dreams about sleeping with. Long hands, long legs and long feet. Ooh, chile, them feet! And then I'd sleep with him and then what? I pop up to visit him and he's got some other chick in there. *Uhn Uhn*, I ain't even trippin'. I'm sorry Jeff, but if I don't protect myself, who will. I've had enough bullshit with men to last me a lifetime, especially Creole men. So far the ones I've dated seem to have the same motto: Good enough to lay with, not good enough to stay with.

COFFEE-COLORED DREAMS

I decided to go inside and take a shower when I heard a soft knock on the door. I tiptoed over and looked through the peephole. My first reaction was to smile; my second was to cry. I was wondering when he'd show up. I leaned against the door and contemplated whether or not to open it.

"Celia. I can hear you. If you want me to leave just say so." He spoke quietly.

I opened the door slowly. He walked in and I didn't even look at him. I just stood there a few minutes staring at the door trying not to cry. I hate that I'm so damn emotional. The last thing I want to do is let this man see me cry. I had no idea how much I had fallen in love with him until this very moment.

"You look good, Cee Cee, you 'gon turn 'round so I can see the rest'a ya'?"

"What do you want, Calvin?" I turned around and rolled my eyes. "And how you 'gon just walk up in my house and not call first? I may have had company." *Yeah right.*

"I called. Lots of times. You won't return my calls. Why you trippin' so hard, Cee Cee? You won't even give a brotha' a chance?"

"Look Calvin, umm…I'm kind of busy right now. I just took a break from my book to take a quick shower, okay. You got about two minutes to say whatever you came here to say. Go."

"I need more than two minutes, so if I take longer, you 'gon call the cops on me?"

Don't get smart niggah, you lucky I let you in the door. "I might."

"Look, don't let me stop you from taking your shower. You got some iced tea? I'll just sit here 'til you finish."

"Excuse me? I don't think so."

He walked up to me and kissed me on the forehead. "Please Cee Cee," he pleaded, "I promise not to stay long, and I'll never come back if you don't want me too. But just let me stay and talk to ya' for a lil' while. Okay."

Damn, he looks good! Now I know why I dismissed all those subtle hints. "The iced tea is in the refrigerator." I said it like I was pissed. But the truth is I am really happy to see him again. I miss the smell of a man in my house.

I wish I knew why I always fall for the wrong man. I'm getting too old for this. I should know better by now. I should be able to go to family reunions and actually have a family get out of the car with me. I hate going to family reunions! Every other year I have a new date. And every other year my drunk-ass Uncle Charles will ask me if I finally got married.

I just hope Calvin doesn't get any crazy ideas and try to come in this bathroom. I'd probably give him some, but he'd know I hated his ass by the time we finished. The way I feel right now, I could just scratch his eyes out. I hate it when a man knows he has the upper hand. He knew I wouldn't have another man in here. And if I did, he would've expected me to ask him to leave. He has so much nerve. So why do I love him? Hell if I know.

I walked back in the living room and he was gone. He wasn't in the kitchen

pamela davis-noland

either. I saw his glass on the coffee table so I assumed he left. I picked it up and put it to my nose to see if I could smell him.

"Hey, I'm out here, Cee Cee," he called from the balcony. He was standing looking over the edge. "You still like to sit out here and write?"

"Yeah. That's what I was doing earlier."

"Hey do tourists still walk by and yell, 'throw me somethin',' like it's Mardi Gras year 'round?"

"Yep. I keep a bag of beads just in case."

"So how's your book coming, baby?" He asked as he walked up to me and pulled my hair. Something he used to do all the time when we were together.

"It's coming along wonderfully. As a matter of fact, I think I'll be finished by the end of summer."

"Oh yeah. So what's it about?"

I just looked at him. He knows I don't ever talk about my writings until they're published and sometimes not even then. It's a part of me I don't share with a whole lot of people. My students are even amazed when they read my work. I never talk about it; I just let them read it. I guess to many people I may seem strange in that aspect but my writing is my therapy. My dream is to one day afford to focus on my writing full time and that's exactly what I intend to do as soon as I get married. Whenever the hell that's gonna be. I guess that's why I don't discuss my work with anyone. Deep down in the pit of my stomach I'm somewhat ashamed that I don't try harder to accomplish my goal to be a famous writer instead of my goal to be a wife.

"Oh yeah, I forgot, Celia's Secret." He rolled his eyes. "I don't know what the big secret is. Everyone knows about your book anyway."

"Okay, Calvin, enough small talk. Why did you come here today? To explain? Because if that's the reason, I really don't want to hear an explanation."

"I came because I missed you Celia. I mean I know you're upset wit'me and er'thang but please baby believe me, I didn't set out to hurt you. I'm sorry. I just thought I wasn't ready to settle with one woman at that time."

"So what? You think you're ready now? Is that what you came over here to tell me?"

"Well, I don't know if I'm ready, but I'd like to give it a try. I really miss you, Cee Cee. Will you just give me a chance to show you that I wanna try? I mean, that's all I'm askin'."

Negro are you serious? Is that suppose to make me fall at your feet and say, "Ooh, yeah, daddy, I'll take you back"? Brotha' please. I wonder how heavy this Niggah is? 'Cause I swear if one of them damn tourists pass by and ask me to throw 'em somethin', his ass is going over. He has more nerve than I thought.

"Calvin. Do you realize how weak that shit is? First of all, you come here without callin' like you just know I didn't have company. And then you insist on staying here even after I specifically told you that I was about to get in the shower. But I let all that slide. But now you tell me that you don't know, but you're will-

COFFEE-COLORED DREAMS

ing to *try* and have a relationship with me. You're going to *try* to be faithful to me and not ho' around. You gon' *try* to be wit' me? Are you crazy? And I'm supposed to just say yeah come on back into my life? And then show up at your house again and you say, oops, my bad, I'm still trying? Damn Calvin, give me some credit! What about the times you said 'I love you?' What about the times you didn't want to go home because you said you would miss me too much? What about the times when we laid in bed and talked about the future? What was that? You were already getting the pussy so there was no need to pretend. And then you go and introduce me as your 'good friend' to some high-yellow bitch who looked at me like she felt sorry for me! And then walk me to the door and close it behind me without even coming out to explain! Calvin, you lucky I let your ass in my house! You led me on the whole time and now you think I'm just going to forget that and let you back in? Niggah, you got me fucked up! You better leave, Calvin! One heartbreak per man is more than a woman should have to take."

He walked up to me and kissed me in the mouth, and no matter how hard I tried I couldn't stop the tears from welling up in my eyes. Not because I still love him but because I still love love. I'm going to miss those feelings. I'm thirty years old and I'm still at the same place I was 10 years ago: cryin' over another failed relationship.

He left.

The phone rang. I looked up at the clock and saw that I had been asleep for two hours. I had cried myself to sleep and now I have a splitting headache. I was scared to pick up the phone. The caller I.D. is in the bedroom and I have no idea who this might be. After the seventh ring though, I knew it had to be Maria. She's the only one who lets the phone ring that many times.

"Hello." My voice was hoarse.

"Girl, what's wrong wit'choo? You sound like shit?"

I started crying the minute I heard her voice.

"What's the matter, Cee? Why you cryin'?"

I didn't answer.

"Come on girl, I can't read yo' mind, no. What happened? Don't tell me it's that Jeff person? Girl, didn't I tell you to be careful of that niggah? I told you he look sneaky. Chile, when you 'gon ever learn? "

"This has nothing to do with Jeff, Black. Calvin came by today."

"What?! Girl, you *still* trippin' over that yellow boy? I didn't know it was like that! You were in love with that fool, huh? Damn, the niggah had a gold tip at the end of his shit or what? *Tsk*. I thought you had *been* got over his ass. What happened with Jeff?"

"Nothin'."

"Nothin'? Why not? I thought you said he could kiss?"

"Black? When you gonna learn that that is not the basis of a good relationship?"

pamela davis-noland

"Fuck that! It may not be number one, but it's for damn sho' in the top ten. Girl let it go. He was not all of that, okay! I'm mean we can't help who we fall in love with but we sure can decide if we want to stay in love or move on. And I think what you really want to do is move on but you scared. Hell, I don't blame you. If my family gave me as much hell about getting married as yours does I'd be tryin' to shut they ass up too." She laughed.

"It's not that, Maria. I'm just tired that's all. I was just hoping Calvin would be different."

"Different from what?"

"Different from all the other niggahs that I broke up with because they made me feel like I wasn't good enough or light enough for them. Or should I say, good enough to lay with, but…"

"Not good enough to stay with, yeah, yeah." She interrupted. "But not all men are like that. You just need to get that chip off your shoulder about men not liking you because of your skin color. A whole lot of brothas like that dark berry girl. Quit trippin'. If you just tried to have some fun and not even think about having a relationship you might be a happier person. I know damn well I'm happy. Hell, I met me another one girl. A tall, chocolate-black ass man with snow-white teeth, and girl he has a washboard stomach and you can bounce a silver dollar on that ass. Girl, when I say fine, I mean fine. Chile, he put the F in that motherfucker. He's a construction worker. He's working on that new pediatrics wing at the hospital. Girl, the first day I saw him I was lookin' out my office window when low and behold that black man was on a scaffold right in front of my window. He smiled and asked me for my phone number right then. Girl, he called me that same night and we been fuckin' ever since."

And to think, this is my girlfriend's idea of romance. Well, at least she's having more fun than me.

"But anyway, enough about me. You better pick up that phone and call that Jeff person. Have some fun, girl. You deserve it. Fuck your Uncle Charles wit' his drunk ass. Girl, did I tell you every time I see him he ask to eat my pussy? See girl, just 'cause every woman in yo' family married doesn't mean they happy. You 'gon find your prince charmin'. All in due time. Call that man, girl. Have some fun in the meantime."

"Yeah, I guess you're right. Maybe I will. Thanks Black. You always know what to say. You say it in a helluva way but I understand."

"You 'gon be a'right?"

"Yep. At least those are my intentions."

"Call him, Cee."

"Okay, Black, I'll call. Goodbye."

"Bye." She paused, "Cee?"

"What?"

"I love you, man."

"I love you, too, Black. Bye."

GUESS WHOSE COMIN' TO DINNER?

Celia DuBois

>The smells of food, flowers
>And romance
>The music for listening and maybe a
>Dance
>Gots'ta make sure to look my best,
>Got on my new perfume and my
>Favorite dress
>Everything's perfect
>According to plan
>Now all I need is to invite a
>Good Man…

I wrote that poem about 7years ago and it still plays over in my mind when I'm getting ready for a big date. I am so nervous. I don't know why I let Maria talk me into doing this. I would have been more comfortable at a restaurant or at Benny's or something but she insisted that I should invite him over because it was my turn. I just hope he don't get the wrong idea and think that I want anything more than a friendship with him right now. He ain't even about to get no drawls. I don't care how fine he is. I've made my vow and I intend on keeping it.

He loves the food here in New Orleans so I prepared a Cajun dish to impress him. I cooked sausage jambalaya, baked catfish, with shrimp stuffing, a nice dinner salad and French bread. I bought a bottle of wine, too, just in case I need something stronger than iced tea. And right now I have a feeling I might.

Maria also insisted that I borrow her grandmother's white lace tablecloth and crystal candleholders. She says that it's time I learn how to be a little romantic and a little less "hard". Now, I've considered myself to be a lot of things, but "hard"? I don't exactly know what she meant by that, but that really offended me. So I borrowed her things and even went out and bought a fresh bouquet of flowers and I even treated myself to that whimsically decorated set of dishes that I had had my eyes on since last year. I thought about having our meal out on the

pamela davis-noland

balcony but between the mosquitoes and the humidity we would have been too miserable to enjoy it.

I went out and bought new CD's and new plants. My CD collection is outdated and my plants look like shit. I have no idea why I'm trying so hard. I guess I'm just trying to convince Maria and myself that I am not "hard" and I am not that much of a cold fish. I really know what it takes to please a man. I just don't have much luck in finding the right man to please.

When he knocked on the door my heart pounded.

Lord, why do I listen to Maria of all people? I always let this girl talk me into doing something that I don't want to do. She has no idea how hard this is for me. Although I've dismissed Calvin, I still can't help feeling like I'm not ready for such another giant step so soon. I keep telling myself that I'm not in love with him but I dreamed about him two nights ago, and when I woke up, I was so horny I had to jump up and get in the shower and pray for strength.

Now here I go again, setting myself up. Something tells me that this may be a big mistake. But, oh well, at least I'm trying to have some fun.

Jeffrey Jackson

I was out on the balcony chillin', smoking some herb, daydreaming and listening to Coltrane and trying to write a song. Jazz music always puts me in the mood to create. Which is what I was trying to do to keep from thinking about how lonely I've been since I moved here. I haven't made very many friends other than Benny. The guys I work with are pretty cool and they always invite me over to their homes to watch a game or come over for a barbecue but I've always made it a rule not to get too involved with the people I work with. I try and keep it as impersonal as possible at my workplace. Which is why the fat cats up in the Chicago office hated me. I was one of their top employees and that's all they knew about me. It drove their nosy white asses crazy.

I don't really kick it with my relatives either because I can only take so much of them stuck up niggahs. They no longer fascinate me like they did when I was a kid; they get on my nerves. So that leaves me alone most of the time.

Anyway, so while I'm out on the balcony chillin' feeling sorry for myself the phone rang and it was Celia. I lit up like a Christmas tree when I heard her voice. And then I chastised myself for getting so excited. I have never felt or acted this way about *any* woman, with the exception of my first love that is, and it's trippin' me out. And then when she asked me over to her crib for dinner, I was shocked. Of course I immediately thought about that shit Miles told me. And because I was smokin' a fat ass blunt, I began to really trip. I started to wonder if I was already under some kind of spell. I mean I think about that woman day and night - night and damn day.

I said yes of course but I've been nervous about it ever since. I'm not sure

COFFEE-COLORED DREAMS

what to expect from her. She's so sometimey and she can be just a little bit stand-offish. I can tell she's interested though, she's just tryin' like hell not to be. I really believe she's still in love with that niggah she just left, but I ain't trippin'. I'll give her some space. But, I bet after tonight… she's not gonna want any…

Celia DuBois

As soon as I opened the door, the phone rang. I smiled and waved him in. I knew who it was on the phone before I even answered it.

"Hey, girl, is he there yet?" Maria whispered.

"Yes."

"Does he look good, girl?"

"Yes."

"Does he smell good?"

"Yes."

"Can you tell if he got a big dick?"

I laughed. She always has to be so nasty.

"Do you want me to let you go?"

"Duhh? Yeah."

Maria laughed. "Okay, girl have a good time. And if you give up the pussy you betta' make sure you call me and give some details. Have fun."

"Don't stay up too long waiting for *that* phone call."

When I turned around he was staring at me like I was lunch and he hadn't eaten all day. Damn, this man is fine! "Are those for me?" I asked. He had a bouquet of roses in his hand.

"Yep. And this time you get all six." He smiled.

"Thanks. Have a seat. I'll just go check on dinner."

"It smells good in here. What are you cookin'? I hope you cooked a whole lot of whatever it is. A brotha' is starvin' and I haven't had a home cooked meal since I moved here. I eat all my meals at the café. And if I eat one more poboy and another bowl of jambalaya I'm'a scream."

Damn.

I knew I should've made Etouffee' instead. That's what I get for listening to Maria. Talkin' bout, "Girl don't you cook that man nothin' with no red gravy. You know how men feel 'bout that. That Niggah gone think you tryin' to trap him." Her and her damn voodoo wives tales. It's not that I haven't heard about women who used to cook their men a red gravy dish during their "time of the month" and put a drop of her blood in the food in order to ensure that her man would be true to her forever. But I really don't think women do that nasty shit anymore. At least I hope not. My Mudear told me that old wives tale a long time ago and some people really believe that it works. But I'll be damn if I would do something as sick as that and I doubt it would have crossed Jeff's mind.

pamela davis-noland

"Oh oh, we may have a lil' problem?" I giggled.

"Oh no, don't tell me we're having poboys?"

"Nope. But we're for damn sure havin' jambalaya. And I thought I was fixing to impress you. I could make something else real fast to go with the fish though."

"No, that's quite alright. I'm sure I'm gonna love it. I'm just tired of eating at Benny's that's all. You need some help in the kitchen?"

"No. I got it. Just make yourself at home."

"Okay. Where's the bedroom?"

"What?!" I yelled.

"I'm just joking Celia. You know you really ought to loosen up a lil' bit. Hey, come here and sit down with me for a minute."

He grabbed my hand and I followed. We sat down on the couch. He stared at me, like he always does, and I blushed, like I always do.

"Look Celia, I just want you to know that I really like you and if I make you uncomfortable at any time tonight, just let me know. I know you just been through some shit and you're probably at that 'I don't trust a niggah' stage, but believe me, I'm not the one. I'm not gonna sit here and tell you that I'm not interested but I will tell you that I'm not about to put any pressure on you. None. Okay? So just chill, man. I mean I just went through some shit myself. But that doesn't mean I'm going to be leery of every woman I meet. Hell, I haven't pursued a woman in so long, I don't even know how to do it anymore. So right now, all I want is a friend. Someone to talk to other than Benny. I mean, he's my boy and all but I can't chill like this with Benny, youknowwhatImean? A brotha' needs some female companionship every once and a while. And by that I mean a woman to talk to, laugh with, and enjoy sharing my thoughts with. And right now, there is no woman I would rather do that with except you. So just chill, man, I ain't no dog brotha', I just look like one." He smiled that heavenly smile and I melted like ice.

"Thanks Jeff, I needed to hear that. I'm not really uptight, just a little nervous." *Nervous as hell, but that's because I don't trust myself, not you.* "I got some herb. Look in that leather bag and roll us one. I'm just going to put these in water."

"Hey Celia," He said as I was heading for the kitchen, "you look beautiful. I wanted to tell you that as soon as I walked in."

"Thank you Jeff. You look nice yourself. I'll be right back." Now that's what I call a gentleman. And to think, I thought that there weren't any left.

He has definitely got a big appetite. Only thing is, I don't know if it's because he has the munchies or if my food is really good. He did everything but lick my plate. I love a man with a good appetite, though. My Mudear says that's the sign of a good lover. I don't know how right she is, but if it's true, Lord help the next woman he sleeps with. My Mudear knows so much about men. I wonder if she was a 'ho back in her day?

COFFEE-COLORED DREAMS

After we ate, he wanted to go out to the balcony and chill. I warned him about the mosquitoes but he didn't seem to mind. He seemed more interested in me telling him my whole life story. He even made me tell him what my book is about. Even after I specifically told him I did not talk about my writings. He said,

"Writing is a gift, Celia, it's supposed to be shared. What if people wrote songs and didn't sing them. What the hell would that do for anybody?"

"Well I share my writings after they're published. I have this superstitious habit of not sharing before just in case it turns out to be a piece of junk."

"What kind of crap is that?" He laughed.

"What do you mean crap? I'm serious."

"Yeah I know. But I still don't get it. So what's your book about?"

"Okay Jeff, I'll tell you what my book is about but you have to keep it a secret okay." I pointed my index finger at him and he grabbed and shook it.

"Okay." He grinned and rolled his eyes.

"It's a love story. But it's not your ordinary love story. My novel is about a young woman who grew up as the blacksheep of the family. It's about her journey in finding herself. You see she always searched outside herself for love and acceptance. You know…she was…um… always trying to be what someone else thought of her. She would get so caught up in that that she was unable to achieve her goals and dreams in life. Then one day she comes out of her cocoon and realizes what a wonderful person she really is and then she begins to blossom. She's finally able to make her dreams come true without the added pressure of trying to please everyone. Anyway, it's the story of her life and how she learned to love herself."

Jeff stared at me and didn't say one word. I tried to read his thoughts but I couldn't.

"What?" I asked.

Jeff didn't answer. He just stared at me like he didn't know what to say.

"Jeff, what do you think about my book?" I shook his arm to try and get some kind of reaction.

Jeff hugged me and smiled. "Sounds like a wonderful book, Celia. What's the name of it?"

"Papillion Jolie Noir." I announced with pride.

"Is that her name?"

"No. It means beautiful black butterfly in French."

"Man Celia. And you manage to keep all of this to yourself, huh? You haven't told anyone else about your book?"

"My agent. But that's about it. And now you." I smiled and winked at him and *he* blushed this time.

"Well thank you very much for sharing that with me, Celia. I can't wait to read it. I'm sure I'm going to love it." He hugged me once more and kissed my forehead.

pamela davis-noland

It was very exhilarating to share my book with Jeff. I had never shared that part of myself with any man. But Jeff has a way of asking that's more of a demand and I love it. He reminds me of this sexy, chocolate, fine ass brotha' named Randy that I used to date. Nothing ever became of Randy and I because he moved back to Ville Platte and we didn't keep in touch after he left. But I'll never forget how turned on I was by his authoritative demeanor. I just hope and pray I'm a little stronger than I was back then. There wasn't too much that Randy could've asked me without me falling at his feet ready to please.

I walked over to the edge of the balcony to watch the commotion that was going on in the street. Jeff stood behind me and placed his hands on my shoulders. He leaned in towards my back and placed his nose against my neck and took a long steady whiff that sent chills up my spine.

"Thanks for inviting me over tonight, Celia. I almost gave up. I stopped calling you because I figured you might need some more time getting over what's his name and the last thing I wanted to do was to come across as desperate. I mean, it's not that I wasn't gonna call you again. I just didn't want to feel like I was imposing on you."

I just stood there not wanting to say the wrong thing, so I said nothing.

"So, have you?" He asked.

"Have I what?"

"Have you gotten over what's his name? Because I would love it if we could spend some more time together if you have. I don't know what it is about you Celia. But I haven't felt this way about a woman in years, if at all. Hell, I didn't even feel this way about my ex-wife. She was more of a sister or best friend. I mean I've always loved her but not the kind of passionate love that a man is supposed to feel for his wife. Anyway, I can't help but feel drawn to you. It's not even about your looks. Hell, you fine, that's for sure, but it has more to do with the way you carry yourself. You have this special aura. I'm sure this isn't the first time you've heard that. You know Celia, I'm thirty-four years old and I can honestly say that I've never really pursued a woman. I've only had a handful of real girlfriends. My luck with women is not all that good, believe it or not. Sometimes I think I have a crazy magnet attached to my ass, 'cause I always get caught up with some possessive chick that's afraid to let me out of her sight. My ex-wife was the only woman who knew me well enough to know that I was always a one woman man. She's known me all of her life, so she pretty much knows what kind of man I am. And as far as the other women I dated, that was just for convenience purposes only. If you knowwhatImean? They used me for my body; I used them for theirs. And that was about it. I can honestly say that I've never really been head over hills in love with anyone. You know when I was married, I felt as though I was drowning and I had no one to save me. And then I moved here, met Benny and now you. I know you're probably thinking that I sound just like all the other lying men but believe me when I tell you that I'm just as surprised as you are about the way I feel about you. It's not just a 'man I wanna hit it' feel-

COFFEE-COLORED DREAMS

ing, it's more of a 'man I want to know everything there is to know about this woman' feeling. And I do. I want to know your favorite color. I want to know your favorite foods. If you look like your mother or your father, if you like kids. I want to know everything from A to Z. And it's not the wine or the herb talking either. I am very sincere when I say that if you let me, I can make you very happy. I'm really one of the good guys. I promise. So will you help a drowning man? Huh?" He turned me around and lifted my chin until our lips met. He kissed me with all the passion he could muster and the tears, I was holding back ever since he said he wanted to spend more time with me, came pouring out.

"Will you Celia," he whispered between kisses, "will you help this drowning man feel alive again?"

"Yes Jeff." The words came out of my mouth faster than I could even think about it. We kissed some more until I felt the bulge. I backed away and turned around.

He whispered in my ear, "Don't worry, I have control over him, he doesn't control me. I would never ever put any pressure like that on you. So don't think you have to run away every time he pops up. I am human, Celia, and you know damn well you fine." He winked at me.

We walked back into the living room. I pressed the remote control button and the sweet sounds of Maxwell crooned through my apartment. He sang "Fortunate"; I felt it. I pulled Jeff by the hand and we danced. He sang the words to me just like I hoped he would. I buried my head in his chest, closed my eyes and thanked the Lord. And for some reason I thanked Benny, too. I have a feeling that he's been talking to his connections at prayer time.

I am so amazed that Jeff showed up in my life when I wasn't even looking. Now this can be one of two things: a test from God or a temptation from the devil. Whichever one it is I am going to make sure I stay prayed up. A few more nights like this and I'll be back where I started. And I ain't hardly going back there. But I am going to trust this man. At least I know he's not going to pressure me. And I honestly believe that he's sincere in all that he says. And that, my friends, is a welcome belief. I thought I'd lost all faith in men.

After we danced for what seemed like hours, I walked him down to his car and we said our goodnights. We kissed and hugged neither wanting to let go.

It was prayer time, as Benny calls it, and this time I actually got down on my knees and prayed instead of saying them just before I doze off. "Thank you Lord for sending someone so special into my life. I have no idea what's going to happen but it sure gives me a good feeling to know that even if nothing happens, I can honestly say I've met a wonderful man. Amen."

pamela davis-noland

Jeffrey Jackson

Benny Thibodeaux is one wise old dude. Case in point… I went to the Place for dinner (again) later that evening after the phone call and dinner invitation from Celia. I was sitting in my favorite corner booth with my back to everyone thinking about our upcoming dinner date and how I was going to let her know just how interested I am in getting to know her. I was really hopin' I wouldn't give the impression that I'm just tryin' to hit it. I mean I would love to hit it, but I don't just want to hit it one time. I want to get to know this woman but she has a wall up for real. A brick one! I'm too rusty at this datin' shit to be tryin' to figure out what's a good move and what's a bad one. *Damn!*

I was wolfing down my second bowl of jambalaya and my first half of a shrimp poboy when Benny walked up behind me out of nowhere, like he always does. For a slow moving old dude, he sure can sneak up on a brotha. He sat across the table from me and smiled that all-loving, all-knowing Benny smile of his. He then proceeded to tell me a story about the first time he met and fell in love with his beloved, now deceased wife. I mean he just started holding conversation as if I had asked him a question about the subject.

"I met Mamie right'chere in Nawlins. Rainy day in Septemba or Novemba, not zactly sho no mo. But I memba it wuz rainin' cuz Mamie face was wet and she borroyed my hand'chiff to wipe it. She wuz wit some of my good friends I ain't seent in a while and when I walk up to greet them, I jest handed hu my hand'chiff and she jest took it. We ain't even said no words." Benny paused and looked down at his hands where he was twirling a "hand'chiff" (that I did not see when he first sat down, mind you) around his big fingers and smiling. "Lord ha'mercy, I ain't never in my bo'n days seen a woman so beautiful. Just beautiful. She ain't know it though." Benny shook his head dramatically. "She ain't know jest how beautiful she wuz. I could tell by the way she tried so hard not to like me she wuz 'fraid of a man like me. You know. On the road all the time and all sangin' in juke joints wit lots a pretty women in'em. I fin'ly ax hu one day why she come to see me all the time but nev'r want to talk. She say it's cuz she wanna make sho my heart is true furst cuz she don't know why I want to be wit a woman like hu'self. Dat's when I figure it out boy. I figure she didn't even know she wuz beautiful, inside and outside. So from dat day on, I made sho she knew." He looked off into space and smiled like he had just gotten the most wonderful vision of his beloved Mamie. Then he looked back at me and frowned. "A woman gotta know yo heart is true boy, make sho you memba dat."

He slowly lifted himself up and shuffled and swaggered, at the same time, back to the kitchen leaving me shaking my head again in wonderment of how this lil' white-haired, bow-legged old man seems to keep reading my life. I haven't even shared my feelings about Celia to him except to tell him I think she's fine.

"And how the hell did I not hear you walk up behind me old man!" I shouted as he swung open the kitchen door.

I took his advice though. I don't care how he knew.

WHAT'S SHAKIN'?

Celia DuBois

Jeff and I have been jogging together just about every Saturday. I'm still a little nervous around him so I try and limit our time together. We usually meet in a public place. I figure if we're doing some physical activity, I might stand a chance of keeping my vow, 'cause God knows I would love to break it for Jeff. He's an incredibly understanding brotha'. I know he feels the same way but we both try our best to ignore it or at least I do. I'm feeling especially weak today so I decided to wait for him downstairs so that he wouldn't have to even come in.

I hopped up and sat on the hood of my jeep and a very familiar car pulled up right next to me. I looked over at my friend with her bruised eye and swollen lip and shook my head. I hadn't seen her in about five months and even then she looked just about the same way. She looked over at me and smiled her best fake smile.

I jumped down, opened her car door and took inventory. Just as I thought, four little girls, two suitcases, a bag of groceries, and all the toys that would fit. The same as the last time I saw her.

"Hi Cee, what's shakin'?" She asked. It's been our greeting for each other ever since we were kids.

"Bacon." I replied "What's shakin' with you?"

"Steaks, you got one for my eye?"

We both laughed although the sad truth was that this was not the first time she had to reply that way.

Deniece LaFleur has four girls. The three youngest, Hope, Scoie and Jasmine were asleep in the back seat and her oldest, Brandi, was sitting next to her looking like the exact replica of her mother long ago. She smiled when she saw me, but I could see the sadness in her eyes. This is not the first time she had to pretend to be the strong, unbreakable child that Deniece claims she is. She's only eleven years old but Deniece treats her as if she's a lot older.

pamela davis-noland

We carried the little ones to my bed and I quickly tried to call Jeff and cancel our date. I called him but he didn't answer so I figured he was on his way. I'll just have to explain it to him when he gets here 'cause there's no way I'm going to be able to leave now.

When I walked back into the living room, Deniece was brushing Brandi's hair and reassuring her that everything would be okay. I got a lump in my throat.

"Hey, would you two like some breakfast? I'm in the mood to cook."

"What in the world were you doin' outside at this time of the mornin'? You was goin' somewhere?" Deniece asked.

"Yeah, I was gonna go for a little run."

"Well, go'head and run. We'll be okay. I just stopped by to call Daddy 'cause we 'gon stay with him for a few days. I didn't want to just drop in, ya know? We 'gon sit right here 'til you get back."

"No." I ordered. "I didn't wanna go runnin' anyway. I just wanted to hang out with Jeff. He's a new one, girl. As a matter of fact, he should be here any minute. Brandi can you let him in when he gets here, baby. Come on Deniece lets go put some ice on that eye." I grabbed her by the waist and she followed suit. We hugged all the way to the kitchen, her head on my shoulder.

I heard the knock on the door. "That's him." I whispered to Deniece. "Wait till you see him, girl."

"He here!" Brandy yelled from the living room.

"Hey, I'm back here in the kitchen." I yelled back.

He walked in slowly and stopped in his tracks when he saw the ice pack in my hand attached to a very bruised woman's face. He tried to disguise the shock and he would have gotten away with it, but the size of his eyes said it all. He smiled and stuck his hand out to her. "Jeffrey Jackson." He simply replied.

"Hi, nice to meet you Jeffrey Jackson. Deniece LaFleur." She shook his hand and looked at me nodding her head in approval. I read her mind and nodded back as I gave her the ice pack and grabbed Jeff's hand and tried to save him. I led him to my bedroom so that I could explain. The look on his face when he saw the other three little girls asleep on my bed told me I'd better hurry up.

"Man, is this a bad time or what?" He whispered so he would not wake the girls.

"Yeah, well a lil' bit. As you can see, there's some drama going on with my friend. I'm gonna have to go runnin' another time."

"That's alright, man. Handle up. We can go running tomorrow if you feel like it. Man, your girlfriend looks like she just got hit by a Mack truck."

"More like a Mack fist. She's married to an asshole that's mad at the world so he takes it out on his wife. I don't have a clue as to why she sticks around, but you know you can't tell a woman who to love."

I just wish that Deniece loved herself more. This is not the first brotha' in her life who's treated her like his own personal, living, breathing punching bag. And for the life of me, I can't figure out why she allows it. I don't know what happened

COFFEE-COLORED DREAMS

to that little girl I grew up with. It's like someone has stolen her very soul.

Deniece had good parents, went to one of the best private Catholic schools in New Orleans and her family is very well off financially and socially. I don't know how and when she took such a turn in her life. Her four daughters have three different daddies. Anthony, the sorry black bastard who beats her, is the father of the last two. He is a complete bum, far worse than the other two. I can't understand how she manages to get mixed up with the same type of guy over and over again. I do recall reading an article in Essence about women who tend to date or marry men who were like their fathers. But I have never heard of women who date or marry the exact opposite. Her father has never raised his voice to her mother, much less beat her. He is one of the kindest, gentlest men I know.

Sometimes I think that the fact that she's the "black sheep" of the family and she grew up being treated like shit, her self-esteem is not all that great. Her snobby-ass mother, rest her soul, and her two sisters, who are both passin' for white, treated Deniece differently as a child and even more so now that she's an adult. I don't know why, though. She's just as pretty as them, has the same color, same hair texture and same petite figure. It's not like my situation where I'm the darkest and tiniest. I guess that maybe they treat her differently because she is different. Especially when it comes to the men she dates and people that she chooses to befriend. Every man that she has ever dated was black as night. That girl know she love her some black men. And believe me, they love her Creole ass right back. Her family wanted to die when she bought Brandi's father over to a family gathering and announced that she was pregnant. Hell, I don't think her grandmother has spoken to her since. Dear old Grandma is definitely from the old school. Definitely a "How dare her mess up the color line" type. She's been pretty much an outsider ever since that day and now the only person she has left is her father. The rest of her family still belongs to that very private clan who is prejudice against their own people. People who are still concerned about skin color and hair texture. People who think that the lighter your skin, the more prestige you have in the community. The very same people who smiled in my face whenever I was with Deniece but would ask behind my back why she, "hung out with so many black people?" Deniece decided at a very young age that they were wrong. Which I still think is the very reason she befriended me almost instantly. 'Cause Lord knows I have been a militant for as long as I can remember. I had to be. It helped to ease the pain of being teased.

Deniece seemed to be fascinated by someone as proud of being a beautiful dark skin girl as I was. She was brought up to believe that we all wished we looked like her. The sad part is that she wished she could be as proud of her skin color as I was of mine. And what's even sadder is that, although I hid it from her, my family and all my other friends, when I was a little girl there were days when I would have given anything to look like Deniece or even three shades lighter than I am. Just for a day. Just so that I could walk pass Ray LaRue and his friends and not be called "charcoal" or "blacky" or any of those dark names they'd call me daily.

"You think she really love that niggah? How can anybody love someone and beat the shit out of 'em all at the same time? How long has this been going on?" He asked concerned.

"Ever since he lost his job. I guess about two years ago. He gets a little job here and there but not enough to take care of his family. Every once and a while he'll get depressed and get sloppy drunk and commence to beatin' her. Like it's her fault he can't keep a damn job."

"Does she work?"

"She can't. Whenever he starts trippin' she has to call in sick 'cause she doesn't want anyone to see the bruises. Eventually, her employer will dismiss her. It's been a never-ending pattern."

"Man, I don't know Celia. I can't understand brothas like that. How in the hell can a man beat his woman and then have to lay in the bed and sleep with her and think everything's all right? How can they beat the woman who has to take care of their offspring? When is the brothas going to realize that blaming the white man and the black woman for our problems is just a cop out. We control our own destiny. God gives us that freely, man. Sure the white man enslaved us and tried to keep us down; but slavery is of the mind now. If a brotha' chooses to let them, they'll keep you down. That's why we as a people have to take care of our own. Start treating our women with respect. What happened to our people, man? That shit trips me out sometimes?"

I have never seen Jeff so emotional. He's a conscious brotha. Definitely my kind of man.

"I don't know, Jeff. I don't know what happened. But the question is when are we going to do our part in making a change? I feel so helpless sometimes. We have to make a change for the next generation, if not for ourselves. Hey, you go ahead. I'll get back with you later, okay?"

"Is that a promise?"

"It's a promise."

We kissed passionately and he turned and walked away without saying another word. I ran out to the balcony and waved goodbye. Deniece walked up behind me.

"Got yo'self a fine one, chile. Maria didn't see him first, huh?"

We laughed. "Ain't that the truth," I said. "Hell, I wouldn't have stood a chance. But he's not even her type anyway."

"Got class, huh?" She laughed. "So Miss Lady Writer, how's your book coming along?

I ignored her question. "Deniece when are you gonna put a stop to this? If not for you, then do it for those four little girls in there. How would you like it if Brandi grows up and starts dating men who beat her? Hell, she's been seein' this for so long she probably thinks it's normal. And what if he goes too far and kills you, Deniece. I mean damn! What then? Who's gonna raise them girls? Him? His poor ass excuse of a mama? If that bitch had any sense, she would call the cops on his ass instead of always takin' up for him. Deniece look at you. You used to be so beautiful. You remember how all the guys would ask you for your phone number everywhere we went. I would be so jealous. They used to call me your lil' black friend. Girl, that shit used to piss me off. Most of them color-struck fools were blacker than me. But they was sure crazy 'bout you with your yellow behind."

"Girl, sometimes I forget about those days. I hate the way I look now."

"You still got that knot on your lip, huh?"

"Yeah, it's a scar now. Lipstick'll hide it though. I hate my hair." She walked back into my apartment. I followed.

She went into my bedroom and studied her face in my cheval mirror. Her eyes teared up when she looked at her face that was getting bluer by the second. She touched it gently and then continued her conversation as if it didn't bother her, "I need to get this hair done. It is way too long. I just been so busy with these babies, girl. Hope just turned five the other day."

"Oh yeah, how's she doing? Is she talkin' yet?"

"No, not yet. She communicates so well that sometimes we forget. She's a big help with the little ones, too."

"How old are they now?"

"Scoie's two and a half and Jasmine's fifteen months."

"So what does the doctors say about Hope?"

"That they love her name." She smiled and stared off into space. "Anyway girl, I didn't come over here just to discuss me. Tell me about the brotha'. Who is he and where did you find him? I wanna know details. And don't think I'm gonna let you slide with the questions about your book. You gon' finally tell somebody about that thang?"

"I've already told somebody about 'that thang'." I mimicked her.

"Oh yeah. Oh let me guess. You shared it with Mr. fine as wine Jeff?"

"Yep."

"Ooohh… Celia done found the one, *sha*."

"Well I don't know about all that. But I do care for him a lot. I'll tell you all about him and my book okay, but how about some breakfast first? I'm starvin' and then after we eat we can walk to the park across the street and let the 'lil ones play."

Jeffrey Jackson

After meeting Celia's friend Deniece and seeing her black eye I started thinking about Laura for some reason. I guess it's because I was no better a husband to her than that sorry punk niggah is who hit Celia's friend. I never physically or verbally abused Laura but I did abuse her emotionally and maybe even a little

pamela davis-noland

mentally. I never showed her the love and attention that a man is suppose to show his wife and for that I am truly ashamed. I never really tried, really.

I picked up the phone and dialed her cell number hoping it hadn't changed. I've only called her on her cell maybe once or twice. And that's only because I couldn't find something I was looking for and I needed her help. I've never called just to say hello. I'm surprised I even remember the number.

She picked up on the first ring. "Hello." She barked.

"Damn. Did I catch you at a bad time?"

"Jeff?"

"Hey L. Whassup?"

"Hey you. What made you decide to pick up the phone and call me? On my cell at that? Hold on baby."

I could hear her yelling at some poor soul at the top of her lungs. I was always surprised at how mean Laura can be when she's angry or upset. And what's even scarier is that sometimes it's hard to tell if she's upset or angry. I've seen her stab people in the back looking at somebody square in the eyes with a genuine smile on her face.

"Sorry about that. I'm back. So what's up with you?"

"Nothin'. I didn't want anything. I was just thinkin' about you, that's all. You doin' okay?"

"Yes Jeff, I'm fine. But really, what's up?"

"Can't I just pick up the phone and call just because."

"Yeah I guess so. So how's *Naawwwlins*?" She exaggerated the name of my new home just as she always does. "You ready to come back home yet?"

"Laura. For the last time, and be sure and pass this on to Miles. I'm not moving back to Chicago. I'll visit but this is my home now. So when are you guys gonna come to the realization?"

"Do you miss me Jeff?"

"Yeah Laura I do miss you. But you know we did the right thing."

Silence.

"Hey? You there?"

"Oh I'm sorry. I was reading something. So are you seeing anyone yet? Or is that none of my business?"

"Yes."

"You are?"

"Yes it's none of your business." I laughed but Laura didn't. "Hey...um...obviously I've caught you at a bad time. Why don't I just try you again later when you're not so busy."

"Yeah. You're right. This is a bad time. I'll talk to you later baby goodbye." And she hung up before I could even get another word out.

Women – I swear I don't understand them sometimes. I mean just take for instance Celia, that woman is harder to figure out than Chinese math. We've been kickin' it on a regular and I swear I've been every bit of the gentleman my uncles

COFFEE-COLORED DREAMS

raised me to be. But I'll be damned if that girl don't still have her guards up. Now if I was a dog niggah like old girl's husband, she'd probably be all up on me twenty-four seven, covering my ass like blanket. What is it with women who like to be treated like shit? *Laura* – now that's a prime example of a woman who likes it rough. With the exception of maybe me, and one other dude, all of her so-called boyfriends were some dog-ass niggahs that she could not, and if she could – would not take home to mama and daddy. She was just fascinated by that bad boy image.

I think Celia is afraid of her own feelings. I can tell she's feelin' me, though. I haven't really pressured her into sleeping with me yet, well at least not verbally. But a brotha is tryin' his damnedest to get her to pressure me. I'd be more than happy to oblige. We've only talked about sex once and that's the night she, out of the clear blue, informed me that she had never had a venereal disease, can't stand the sight of a needle, and she's a firm believer in practicing safe sex. I was like okay… that's a different type of booty call. But then she said, "I'm not really ready to have a relationship like that with anyone right now. I just wanted to let you know."

The other night we were at my crib coolin' it and watching "Imitation of Life" for the third time. (It's her favorite movie too.) So she's lying between my legs with her head on my chest right. And she's smelling all good despite the fact that we had just smoked some herb. So I'm human right? I mean I'm lying here with a fine sista between my legs. She felt my jimmy responding to the softness of her body and her intoxicating scent and she did what she always does – sit up, look at her watch, yawn and then says it's late and it's time for her to go. But right before she heads out the door, she always gives me a long wet passionate kiss full in the mouth. I ain't trippin' though, I really believe she is sweatin' me the same way I'm sweatin' her. She's just not ready. I can respect that, though. I can wait as long as she can.

Celia DuBois

I pushed Deniece on one of the large swings, just like we used to do when we were little girls. We talked about the good old days while Brandi and Hope made sure that the little ones didn't get too dirty. Deniece wanted them to look pretty for their grandfather.

"We used to have so much fun, huh Cee?"

"Yeah we did, Deniece but what about now? You can still have fun now. Don't you wanna be happy? Don't you want those girls to see a genuine smile? I'm not saying divorce the man, Dee, just get out of the situation until he decides to get some damn help! How long are you gonna stay at your daddies'?"

"As long as it takes to let Anthony cool off. He trips so hard sometimes. But it's not as bad as it looks girl. Believe me he is feelin' like shit."

pamela davis-noland

"And so he should. But is that enough for you? Is that gonna take away the pain and humiliation? Damn! Is that all you need?"

"No. What I need to do is leave him. But where in the hell am I gonna go Celia? Who in the hell is willin' to take in a woman with fo' kids and no job? Hell, when my sistas find out I'm stayin' at daddies', they 'gon start all kinda' shit. I ain't 'gon be able to stay there too long."

"What about a women's shelter. Hell, if I had enough room for everybody, y'all could stay here."

Deniece looked at me painfully. She has no intentions of staying away from Anthony and I know it. It just hurts so badly and I feel so helpless. Deniece is going to have to make up her mind when she's had enough. All I can do is be here for her and continue loving her.

"You know Celia, if it wasn't for those girls I don't know what I'd do. They keep me alive, 'cause I swear I would've blown my brains out long time ago." Deniece was staring off into space again with tears in her eyes.

This is why I'm so angry with black men. Angry at men like Anthony, with his punk ass, who beat his woman to the point where she no longer loves him or herself. Men like Stephen, who was so insecure with his own manhood he could never accept me for my strength. Men like Joe a/k/a "Mr. Alphabetical Order", who is so full of himself that he tries to change every woman he meets. Men like Calvin who seems to find it so hard to love just one woman at a time. And even men like Jeff, who can talk a whole lotta shit about our people but what he is doing to educate? I'm damn near mad at the whole black male population right now. I just can't figure out how men that were born to fight; lay down their shields and just die.

"Don't worry Deniece, we'll get you some help. There's no need for you to give up just because Anthony did. Everything 'gon work out girl, and I'm sure your daddy's gonna let you stay as long as you have to."

"Well, we better get goin' before they get too dirty. Daddy gone spoil 'em rotten, girl, just like he always do. They love it over there."

I bet they do.

We put the girls in the car and made sure everyone was strapped in. Deniece hugged me so long that I could no longer hold back the tears. I was doing so well up until now. We cried for each other. We black women have such a cross to bear.

"I'm going to do everything I have to Deniece. Just promise me you won't give up, okay?"

"Lata' chick." She said.

"Is that a promise?"

Tears rolled down my face freely as I watched her drive off. I said a silent prayer for Deniece and her girls. And I said another one for Anthony and the entire black male population.

QUALITY TIME

Jeffrey Jackson

Every since the day I went over to Celia's crib and her girl was there all bruised up, things between Celia and I have changed a little. She's been trippin' for real. Our time together has just about slowed down to a complete halt. And when we do spend time together or talk on the phone, our main topic of conversation is her girl, Deniece, and the shit she's going through.

    Don't get me wrong, I'm not cold or heartless but I really don't want to get involved in that woman's business. I mean she even said it herself, "You can't tell a woman who to love." Now that statement alone should help her to back off and let her girl work out her own problems.

    Celia reminds me of my grandmother, my mother's mother, Mama Ella. Mama Ella moved in with us when my pops died to help our mother raise us. All the women in the neighborhood would come to our house to talk with Mama Ella when they had a problem of any kind. And Mama would do her damnedest to solve it, even if the person only wanted her to listen. Mama Ella lost a whole lot of friends for that very reason. She got too involved.

    I tried telling this to Celia but she didn't seem interested in what I had to say. I told her she should just be there for her girl, let her cry on her shoulder and walk away. And that should be the extent of it.

    Trying to lighten the mood a little, and merely to make friendly conversation, I opened my big mouth and told her that a brotha I work with owns some duplexes and had just completed renovating them. She got so excited and all carried away and begged me to talk to him and ask him to hold one for Deniece. So of course I did. Old boy said he had one left and that he'd hold it for her. But her girl didn't even want to move. She went back to her old man. Just like I tried to tell Celia she would.

    Celia was pissed and for some reason, shocked. And she got even madder when I said, "I told you, man. Look, it's not that easy for some women to just walk away from relationships, especially if they are really in love. But that's not your problem, it's hers. I mean you said yourself that you can't tell a woman who to love. If you were a real friend, you'd leave her alone." Maaan... I hit a nerve

pamela davis-noland

for real. She went off. I think her last words to me before she slammed the phone down in my ear were, "… and kiss my ass." Thus, our first argument…

Celia DuBois

Benny's is especially quiet this evening. And that's just fine with me. I have too much on my mind anyway. One of my closest friends is going through hell and I just have to sit back and watch her.

I talked to Jeff about it and he tried his best to be helpful, although I felt like the "I told you so," wasn't necessary. But he did inform me about a guy that he works with at the accounting firm who owns some duplexes. He said he'd talk to him and see if he had one available and he did. He explained Deniece's situation to him and he offered to let her and the girls move into one of them. He even offered Deniece a housekeeping job. His only stipulation was that she not bring her problems with her. He has evicted people for domestic violence before. It isn't something that he allows or tolerates from any of his tenants.

I called Deniece and told her about it and all she said was that she'd have to think about it. Think about it? I went off, "Now what in the hell is there to think about?" I asked her. Hell, she's getting her ass beat on every day that ends with "y" and she still has to think about it? I can't even see it! If someone offered me a way out I'd take it with no questions asked.

And then Jeff had to go and get personal on me and bring up the fact that I was so able to walk away from Calvin so easily. The nerve of him, he doesn't even know the entire story. Jeff reminded me that Anthony is her husband and that it's just harder for some people to just walk away from a relationship. This pissed me off. I cussed him out and slammed the phone down in his ear. I feel so bad. This is our first argument. So here I am sitting here fuming mad trying to collect my thoughts.

I noticed Benny sitting on the other side of the café' smiling at me. I'm really not in the mood for conversation but that never stopped Benny before.

"I haven't seen you look this sad in months, Doll. You wanna tell Ol' Benny what's on your mind?" He asked.

"Jeff and I had our first argument, Benny."

"Hmmm, well, where is that boy? Why he ain't sittin' here nex' ta' ya' tryin' to work this here thing out?"

"He's probably still at work. Besides, I'm not ready to talk to him, Benny. He doesn't even understand why I'm so angry."

"Well, did you 'splain it to the boy?"

"No, not really. I just think that he could have been a little more sensitive to the way I was feeling at that particular moment."

"Honey, let ole' Benny give you some advice. A man don't understand' sensitive. We wasn't born to. We only know what you tell us. You see when God made woman he made her from the man rib. Now my daddy once tol' me that God musta' took a piece'a man heart, too. A big part, too. And he left him wit' the smaller part. 'Cause sometimes women know how to love big. But y'all gotta be careful 'cause sometimes that big ole' heart can get you in trouble. 'Cause when you love big, you hurt big, Doll. Men don't understand' that we gotta be careful when dealin' with women folk and they big hearts. Only way we knows is if you tell us."

"So you're saying that I should tell Jeff how he hurt my feelings?"

"That's right. 'Cause he prob'bly sittin' somewhere wonderin' where he went wrong. He don't have no idea, Doll. So I say, if you love 'em, tell 'em."

"I don't recall telling you that I loved Jeff, Benny."

"You don't have to tell me. If you didn't love 'em you wouldn't be sittin' here lookin' so sad 'cause y'all had you first argument." Benny winked.

Of course Benny was right as usual. He always knows what to say. I reached over and kissed him on the cheek. "Thank you, Benny."

"Anytime Doll. 'Sides that boy and me got a song ta' work on this evenin' and I don't want him mopin' 'round me. He's been in a good mood lately and that's the way I'd like him to stay."

"So Jeff's been in a good mood lately, Benny?"

"You tell me honey. You see him more than I do." He winked and rocked away calling out over his shoulder, "Benny gonna go back here and make you a sammich. You just sit tight 'til I get back."

"I'm not hungry, Benny."

"I'll be right back, Doll." He yelled as he pushed open the kitchen door.

As usual he won that argument. He was going to bring that sandwich rather I wanted it or not.

I had just finished my second glass of iced tea when Jeff walked in. I pretended not to see him. He walked over to Benny and the two of them spoke quietly for a few minutes. I saw Benny push him and nod my way and Jeff smiled and walked over to me.

"Hi. I'm glad to see you here. I thought I wasn't going to see you for a while."

"Why do you say that?" I asked. *I bet you think that just because I was able to walk away from Calvin without thinking twice about it, that I'll do the same thing to you. I hope you realize that that's two totally different situations, baby. It would take a whole lot more than this.*

"May I sit?" He ask sheepishly.

"Sure."

"Look, Celia, I'm very sorry about the other day. I didn't mean to sound so insensitive. I was just tryin' to help you understand what your friend might be going through. That's all. I mean I know it must be pretty sad to have a friend who you care about more than she cares about herself."

"I'm sorry too, Jeff. I'm just really torn up inside, ya' know? I'm tired of seeing her go through this hell. I know Anthony is her husband. I never told her to divorce him, I just said that she should walk away from the situation until he gets some help."

"So, you forgive me for hurting your feelings?" He looked at me with child-like innocence and my big heart melted.

"Yes Jeff, I forgive you. Do you forgive me for going off the way that I did?"

"You had every right to. But yes, I forgive you. So you want to kiss and make up?" He asked.

"I would love to." I replied, grinning from ear to ear.

Just as our lips touched Benny yelled out from the other side of the café, "Now you two go and save that for lata'. We got some practicin' to do boy. You know Benny ain't got much time left and I still got a lot to teach ya'. Now hurry up."

"Oh please Benny," I pleaded, "can I just have one kiss from my man? Just one?"

My man. Those words came out so fast I shocked myself. And from the smile on Jeff's face, I could tell that he was as proud as a peacock to be considered my man. I just hope "my man" doesn't expect nothing else no time soon, 'cause I'm still not giving in. He may be "my man" but he's not my fiancé.

We kissed and he went to practice with Benny just as he was told to.

Jeffrey Jackson

Her man - you see what I mean. We had our first real argument, I piss her off, she cusses me out and then three days later - I'm her man. If I had of known that that's all it would take, I'd have pissed her off a long time ago. But man oh man it's hard to be mad at Celia DuBois for any reason except the fact that she's trying so hard not to feel the same way about me as I'm feelin' for her.

I woke up this morning with the revelation knowledge that I am a man in love. I love her. I love everything about this woman and if I'm not mistaken I think I fell in love with her the first time I laid eyes on her. I love her eyes, her smile, her walk, her talk (that well-educated Cajun accent) and that sassy southern attitude. But what makes me fall in love with her more every day is how she keeps her soft heart carefully protected by her hard exterior. I can tell she's been through a whole lot of bullshit in her life. I just want to be the brotha to show her that we ain't all the same. There's a few of us good ones left. It would be my pleasure to show her that.

To be honest, I don't really know if she loves me the same way. But I do know…no…I have a gut feeling that she'll come around. It's only a matter of time…

COFFEE-COLORED DREAMS

Celia DuBois

The song was beautiful. It was about a mother and her child and it reminded me of Deniece and her daughters. Tears welled in the corners of my eyes as I listened.

"Well, how did you like it?" Jeff asked.

"Beautiful Jeff, just beautiful. I sure would love it if Deniece could hear it. Maybe I'll bring her with me the night you sing it. What's the name of it?"

"No name yet. It's one I wrote myself a long time ago. I never dreamed I'd be singing it though. It was originally written for a woman to sing. But you know Benny. The first time he heard it he insisted that I sing it myself. But I still wish I could get a woman to sing it. You sing?"

"Hell no. Not at all." I laughed.

"I had a friend back home who was suppose to sing it but right before we were ready to do a demo she got a big recording contract and my little song wasn't very important to her anymore. She hauled ass."

"Well, you sing it just fine. Hell it's your song anyway. Who better to sing it then you?"

"Yeah, I guess you're right. So, I'm finished practicin'. What do you say we go to my place and spend some quality time together?" He looked at me lustfully.

Oh shit. I knew I shouldn't have called you my man.

I need to tell him about the vow but I don't want to scare him away. I mean what if he can't wait? What if he decides to start seeing someone else who will give up the drawls? He hasn't pressured me so far but how long is that suppose to last? He is every bit of a man. I know he expects it sooner or later.

Maria still thinks I'm crazy for even making this vow. And she doesn't waste any time telling me so. She says that even if something becomes of us and we plan to get married or something, how am I going to know what to expect on my honeymoon? I informed her that I'd already made up my mind that I'm going to sleep with Jeff. And quickly added before she got too excited, "As soon as we decide that we are going to be man and wife and there's a ring on my finger to say it is so. And not a minute before, Black! And if we don't make it that far because he only wants the milk and not the whole cow, oh well. I'll just move on. But the next brotha' gonna get the same thing. This is not some fad for me Maria. It's now my way of life. I am celibate. I am no longer giving my body over to any man other than the one I intend to spend the rest of my life with. And that's that."

So caught up I was in my thoughts that I didn't hear a word that Jeff was saying. He tugged on my arm to get my attention. "Hey baby, you ready to go?"

"Um, okay I guess so. Just let me go say goodbye to Benny." I said

pamela davis-noland

nervously.

When we arrived at his apartment I sat in my jeep for a few minutes smiling to myself because I feel like I'm finally free of Calvin. I am a little nervous about my feelings for Jeff but I can't deny that I really enjoy being around him. He makes me feel pretty the way that he stares at me and the way that he kisses me like he never felt something so good in his life. I'm loving every minute of it too but I do think that it's time for me to tell him about my vow. I can honestly say that I love Jeff. Benny knows I love him, too. Hell, Benny knows everything! But I guess it shows. I have been in such a good mood lately. And I haven't even thought about Calvin or any other man for that matter. He's all I think about.

"You're a sweetheart, Jeff. I sure hope I'm not setting myself up for another disappointment. I sure hope you can deal with my decision." I whispered as I locked my doors and ran to catch up with him.

Jeff asked me to sit and make myself comfortable while he showered. He turned on some music and told me to put my feet up. He propped my head on a pillow, kissed me gently on the lips and dashed up the stairs two at a time.

I tried to read a magazine but my eyes kept getting heavy and I nodded off a few times. I hadn't got much sleep in the past few days. I totally immersed myself in my book instead of thinking about Jeff *or* Deniece. And whenever I wasn't doing that I was on the phone with Maria until the wee hours of the morning listening to her go on and on about her construction worker. So, needless to say, all those sleepless nights had finally caught up with me and I fell asleep.

When I woke up, Jeff was lifting me off of the couch and carefully balancing me in his arms. He proceeded to walk up the stairs before I opened my eyes and looked at him like he was crazy.

"What are you doing?" I asked as if I didn't already know.

"I thought you might be more comfortable in the bed. Don't worry I won't drop you. I'm stronger than I look." He smiled.

By the time he laid me in the bed I had begun to shake and it scared the hell out of me. Was I shaking because I was scared? Was I excited? Was my mind playing tricks on me or was I really going through this again? My thoughts were going through my brain faster than I could keep up with them and all I could think about was how stupid of me to not tell Jeff about my vow and think this day wouldn't come. I didn't know what to say but the familiar feelings of self-worth had found its way back into my life. That grateful feeling that has caused me to be so blinded by a man's true intentions. Those men who had me fooled into thinking that I was special. I immediately became angry with Jeff for not being any different from all the others. "What are you doing, Jeff!" I yelled.

"I already told you what I was doing. I'm making you more comfortable. What do you think I'm doing?" He yelled back.

I jumped up and walked to the other side of the loft with my arms folded and my best sista girl look on my face. I did everything but roll my neck and snap my fingers.

COFFEE-COLORED DREAMS

He just stood there looking at me like I had lost my mind and he's not too far from being right. I think I finally know what people mean when they plead temporary insanity. My anger toward all the men in my past had so taken over that I felt like a mad woman. I had no idea just how angry I was with men and I felt bad for taking out all my anger and pain on Jeff. But I had to get it across to him that I wasn't ready for what he thought he was about to get.

"If you wanted to make me more comfortable, you could have brought me a blanket or something. You didn't have to carry me to your bed. I don't know what your used to, but…"

Jeff interrupted me before I could finish making a fool of myself, "No, I don't know what *you're* used too! Look Celia, I wasn't doing what you think I was doing, all right. I'm not the type of brotha' who has to take nothing! You think I would just force myself on you. Damn! Who do you take me for? Damn, baby, what kind of men you been fuckin' with? And whoever they are, don't even put me in that category. Have I ever tried to force anything on you, Celia? Huh? No. I have patiently waited for everything that you've given me so far. And I think I've been doing a damn good job. Do I want you so bad I can taste it? Hell yeah I do. Am I going to try and take it or trick you into giving it to me? Hell, no! Come on man, you don't know me yet? What a brotha' gotta do, man? I don't know what happened with you and that last brotha' you were with but if you don't take that big ass chip off of your shoulder, you are going to find yourself by yourself! I'm about to run out of patience, baby." He threw his hands up and pounded down the stairs mumbling to himself.

Damn!

I sat on the bed feeling like the biggest fool. All my life I've waited for my prince charming and I'll be damned if I'm not going to run him off! My Mudear used to always tell me that you might find what you're looking for just when you give up looking for it. And that seems to be exactly what has happened with Jeff. Just as I made up my mind to stop searching for Mr. Right, here he comes. And he's right. He *has* been very understanding. I guess I shouldn't really be worried about telling him the truth. I think.

I walked down to the bottom of the stairs and watched him as he typed furiously on his laptop. My mind raced with every step…

I have to apologize…again. This is my second time going off on him for no really good reason and if I don't stop acting like such a fool, it might not be so easy for him to forgive me… hell, maybe I'm just not ready for this right now… especially since I've made such a major decision in my life… maybe I'm just fooling myself…I can't even handle this shit! Jeff is such a wonderful man… the same man I told God I wanted when I was just a little girl and my mama told me that if I prayed hard enough, one day I was going to find the man of my dreams. I want a man just like my daddy… they've been happy all of my life and that's all I ever wanted for myself… if I don't screw it up too much, this may very well be the one…

pamela davis-noland

I walked up behind him and rubbed his shoulders to try and ease some of the tension. I could feel the heat coming from his body. "I'm so sorry, Jeff." I whispered to him. "I'm so sorry I jumped to conclusions. It's just that you caught me off guard that's all. I mean what was I to think? You were carrying me… Look, Jeff, all I can say is that I am very sorry. You have no idea how stupid I feel right now. I guess I have been seriously burned by some of my past relationships. I'm just trying not to make the same mistakes with you. I really care a lot about what happens with us and I'm scared of setting myself up for another disappointment. But if you'll be a little patient with me, I promise I'll calm down. Or at least I'll try to. Please forgive me, Jeff?"

He grabbed my hands and kissed them. He stood up, turned to face me and looked me straight in the eyes. "I'm going to tell you something that you can choose to believe or not, okay?" He smiled and continued before I could answer. "I've never loved a woman as much as I love you. I've never been with a woman who made me feel so good inside. I love everything about you. I love your smile, your walk, your sassiness, your creativity, and even your bad breath when we go running early in the morning." He laughed. "I can't tell you why I love you so much. But if I could then that would mean I could tell you the reasons I don't love you and there aren't any. I don't know if you love me the same way. And what's even sadder is that I don't know if you are capable of loving me the same way or can even allow yourself to be loved this much. I fell in love with you the first time I saw you at Benny's and you were so concerned with little Angel. But I didn't pressure you that day or the next time I saw you. I didn't pressure you the first night you came over here or the first time you finally invited me over to your place. I didn't pressure you the many nights that we spent at the movies or the evenings we spent sitting on your balcony smoking ganja or any other time for that matter. I haven't pressured you or even asked you. If all I wanted was just sex, I could get that, no problem. But I've had that. I've had enough meaningless sex to last me a lifetime, Celia. Hell, even in my marriage. That's not what I want from you whether you believe it or not. I'm looking for someone to share my dreams with. To share my thoughts with. This is the first time in my life that I'm living my life exactly the way I want to. All I want is someone to share it with, but if I'm pressuring you too much, maybe we should slow down, baby. Wait until you're ready to handle this. I'm sorry that you haven't experienced true love yet." He kissed me on the forehead and turned me around so that I was facing the door. "Go ahead and go home baby. I'll call you in the morning." He kissed me on the cheek and went upstairs.

Jeffrey Jackson

As bad as I hate to admit it, I'm gonna have to give Celia some space. She's giving a brotha too many mixed signals. I mean just a few hours ago I was her man

COFFEE-COLORED DREAMS

and she was lovin' me and shit. Now she thinks I'm some kind of dog niggah who's gonna just take want he wants.

Now a brotha will admit; when I saw her lying on the couch asleep I was tempted to wake her by kissing her in a few tender places hoping she would wake up as horny as I was standing there looking down at her. But I would have never tried to take it. Damn! That ain't even my style. I've never had to take shit! I've hardly ever been refused, turned down or asked to wait a little longer. I've hardly ever heard the words stop, quit, don't or later when it comes to getting the drawls. That always drives Miles crazy. He doesn't understand why I'm not running around taking full advantage of that. At one time I did but I've changed quite a bit since then. I want a woman in my life like Celia. I want a strong woman. Miles can have them weak-ass skeezas he bed-hops with.

Damn this woman is driving me crazy!

Celia DuBois

Shit! Shit! Shit! You are not like any other man I've ever dated. Hell, you may not even be human. You don't care if we sleep together or not? You love me just the way I want to be loved and I'm about to walk away? Am I a fool or what?

I stood there for what seemed like an eternity debating on whether to beat my head against the wall or fake a seizure in hopes that he'd come running back down the stairs to save me from myself but he didn't come back.

I grabbed my purse and keys and headed for the door. I stopped in my tracks and debated with myself rather I should go back up and try and explain. Or at least tell him about the vow. But I couldn't muster the nerve so I just sat at the end of the stairs and cried. Lord knows I love Jeff and I would give anything to run up those stairs and give him some of the best lovin' he ever had in his entire life. But to jeopardize my new feeling of self-worth that I am trying to accomplish without a man is something I can't do right now. My book is coming along beautifully and I have such a strong sense of power for being able to keep it first on my list of priorities whether Jeff and I are doing okay are not. For once in my life I actually feel like I'm in control of my own destiny.

"No Jeff. I'm sorry. I need just a little more time." I whispered as I walked out of the door.

THE TRUTH SHALL SET YOU FREE ("LET THE CHURCH SAY MEN.")

Jeffrey Jackson

I watched Celia wrestle with herself at the bottom of the staircase. She was crying. I don't know why she's trippin' so hard this time and I'm almost afraid to ask. I know she cares about me because all of the signs are pointing in that direction. Maybe she'll think about what I said. I haven't pressured her at all. I've been as cool as a freakin' fan. Can't a brotha get some props for that at least! She seems to still have me in that same dog-niggah category that so many sistas put us in after a bad relationship. I laid in my bed staring at the ceiling waiting for her to come running back up the stairs and apologize to me for going off on me the way she did. After about ten minutes or so I finally tiptoed to the edge of the stairs when I didn't hear her leave. That's when I saw her crying. I wanted to go back down those stairs and grab her and maybe shake some sense into her head but I quickly changed my mind. A brotha has to have some pride. I can't keep letting this woman play with my emotions the way she has since day one. I can't figure her out to save my life but I have a very good feeling that it has something to do with that last niggah she was with. That brotha messed that woman up and she can't seem to let it go.

    I wish there was something else I could do to convince her to trust me, man. Hell, I thought I was doing something by not putting any pressure on her. I mean she told me in the beginning that she wasn't ready for a sexual relationship but damn, that was in the beginning. We've been together for months now. I would love to get pass second base. Hell, what brotha' wouldn't. But I'm not going to force her and I thought she would have realized that by now. I bet if I was one of those dog-niggahs sistas seem to like so much these days, I would have that woman wrapped around my little finger.

    Women!

It's been two days and I still haven't heard from her. But I'll be damned if I pick up that phone and call her. I didn't do anything wrong. I can actually look myself in the mirror and say that, man. I didn't do nothing but try and be a damn gentleman. That same gentleman women swear don't exist anymore. And what do I

COFFEE-COLORED DREAMS

get - accusations and attitude. So hey, I figure two can play that little game. From here on out, if Celia DuBois wants me to be her man, she's gonna have to stop trippin'. I, on the other hand, am going to give her a taste of her own medicine. I'm going to be as stubborn as she is. I've been as open and honest as I can be about my feelings for her. Now it's her turn to be honest with me… and herself. In the meantime, I'm going to concentrate on my singing and make myself as unavailable as possible. No more Mr. Nice Guy. That shit doesn't seem to work anyway.

I was in the middle of writing an "I hate love" song when the phone rang. I was too lazy to get up and walk across the room to answer it so I let the answering machine pick up the call.

Beep....

"Hi Jeff." She spoke softly.

I put my pen and pad down and moved closer to the phone so that I could hear what she had to say.

"Jeff. I know you can't figure me out and I'm sorry. That's my fault. I haven't exactly been totally honest with you. And as sweet and patient as you have been, I think it's only fair that I let you know the whole truth."

I turned up the volume on the answering machine, grabbed my beer and braced myself.

"Jeff." She paused and took a deep breath. "Jeff, before I met you I made a life changing decision that I've been avoiding telling you about. I've been avoiding it for two reasons. One - I didn't think we'd get this far in our relationship and two - well, I guess I was afraid that I'd run you away."

Damn! I hope my girl is not about to tell me that she's into women. I finished my beer in one long steady gulp, hoping to quickly numb myself.

"You see Jeff, all of my life I prayed that God would send someone like you into my life. You're the man I used to dream about many years ago before I gave up all hopes that there really was such a man. After this last jacked-up relationship I was in, I decided that love was not in the cards for me. I began to feel as though maybe my future is my career as a writer and that's it. So after this last breakup, I totally immersed myself in that and it has now become more important to me. Now I guess you're asking yourself what does that have to do with us? Well Jeff, it has a lot to do with us. You see, I've always allowed the man in my life to overtake my thoughts. Therefore, my book would get placed on the back burner whenever I considered myself a woman in love. And then we'd break up and I would pick it back up again. It became more of my therapy than my gift. And then someone else would come along and then back on the shelf it would go. Jeff, I can no longer do that. I'm as close to making my dream come true as I've ever been and it feels so good. So that's one of the reasons why I've been so distant with you. Secondly Jeff, throughout most of my adult life, I've made some bad choices in men. I've finally come to the realization of why that is. It's because I never carefully chose the men I became intimate with. I allowed myself to be chosen. And I never thought enough about myself to say no. No, you are not good enough for me. No, you don't meet my standards of what my man is suppose to be. No, you cannot have my body after you treated me like shit. I just said yes. I said yes out of sheer gratitude that any of them felt as though I was pretty or smart or fine or whatever lie they told me to make me feel special..."

Lie? Baby you are all of that.

"...And then I'd lay with them thinking we are actually in love and one day we'd get married, have babies and live happily ever after. Jeff, I am thirty years old, going on thirty-one and I'm still living in fantasy land waiting for a man to come riding up on some white horse. Well, I was. Now I'm not. My common sense has finally kicked in. Now, about my life-changing decision."

I sat upright and stared at the answering machine. My heart was pounding, man.

"I've taken a vow of celibacy, Jeff."

DAMN!

"I'm no longer having sex until I feel a sense of security that my partner and I are truly making love. In other words, no more premarital sex for me."

Damn.

"I know I should have told you right from the start, Jeff, but I was afraid. To be really honest with you, I didn't think you'd stick around this long." She laughed. "I really didn't think I was your...umm...type."

Oh baby, if you only knew.

"Baby, I hope you understand. I have to do this for me. I really care about you a lot Jeff. A whole lot. More than you know and definitely more than I have shown you. If you can't handle this, I understand. I just hope we can remain friends." She paused and let out a long sigh. "Well, that's it. That's all I have to say. Hopefully, I'll talk to you soon. Peace." She hung up.

Damn! She's celibate. No sex? None? Damn! No wonder she jumps up and runs every time that we... well I'll be damn. And here I was thinking that she just didn't want to be with me. Whew! I can handle that. As long as I've gone without a woman, hell, I could almost consider myself celibate too. She's trippin' for nothin'. If she think she's gonna get rid of me for that she can just think again. Besides, she said she just wants to be absolutely sure that the next man she lays with is going to be someone who really loves her. Well the only man I know of that loves her right now is me. I just have to convince her to trust that.

Celia DuBois

The knock on the door startled me. I was just about to get in the bathtub. I had my candles lit, a new Essence magazine, a glass of Merlot, my ganja and Anita Baker singing softly on the stereo. I was ready to sooth my soul and the last thing

COFFEE-COLORED DREAMS

I needed was an interruption. I threw on my bathrobe and ran to the door because whoever it was wasn't being very patient. The knocking kept getting louder and louder.

I looked through the peephole and smiled so big, I thought my face would crack in half. Standing there looking as fine as hell was Jeffrey Jackson in all of his rhapsodic glory. He had a huge bouquet of flowers in one hand and a bottle of wine in the other.

I took a quick glance in the mirror and took inventory of just how bad I really looked – sky blue, terry cloth, dingy-ass robe, dried up Noxzema on my face, unbrushed teeth and damn…ashy feet! I opened the door and let him in and quickly jogged back to my bedroom to do something with myself. Or at least my feet!

"Make yourself comfortable." I yelled. "I'll be right out. The flowers are beautiful."

"Don't run and hide." He yelled back. "Come back here so I can see you in your natural habitat."

"I'll be out in a minute." I yelled. "And you don't want to even see me in my natural habitat." I laughed.

"Well don't come back without putting some lotion on those feet!"

"Oh forget'choo. Sit down and make yourself comfortable. I have a bottle of wine already opened in the fridge. Grab you a glass." *Damn. Of all days to be sittin' 'round here lookin' like shit.*

I was brushing my teeth when he came up behind me and stood in the doorway, grinning from ear to ear.

"Well it's a good thing I'm decent. Don't be walkin' in on me like that, you." I pretended to be angry.

"Well I was just going to talk to you through the door. But since you're dressed, may I come in?"

"You're already in. And don't be grinnin'. I know I look like shit."

He walked up to me, grabbed me around the waist and kissed my neck gently. "No you don't. You look beautiful. You are beautiful. And I feel like the luckiest man on earth to be standing here holding you." He looked down and grinned. "Ashy feet and all."

"Get outta my bath…!"

"I'm crazy about you Celia." He said just before he kissed me gently on the lips.

"Jeff, I'm sorry I didn't explain everything to you right away. I just…"

"Shhh…" He interrupted me and then kissed me with all the passion of a knight in shining armor. I felt like Jell-O in his hands.

He grabbed me by the hand and we walked back to the living room.

"Jeff can I explain?"

"Explain what baby? You already explained. And you have no idea how relieved I am."

pamela davis-noland

"Relieved?!"

"Yeah. Relieved. The way you started the conversation, talkin' about you've made a life-changing decision, hell I thought you were about to tell me that you are…umm...you know…" He giggled.

"You thought I was about to tell you what?!"

Jeff laughed.

"What Jeff? You thought I was…" I put my hand over my mouth in shock when I realized how I must have sounded.

Jeff doubled over with laughter. "Well hell, I had no idea what you were going to say. Now you know why I used the word relieved."

I took one of my throw pillows and hit him across the head. "Gay?! You thought I was about to tell you that I was gay?!"

He tried to shield the blows to his head as he laughed uncontrollably. He finally grabbed the pillow and tossed it across the room, grabbed me and threw me back on the couch, all in one big swoop of a movement. He then began tickling me until I cried out for mercy. "Okay, okay, okay. I quit!" I begged.

Jeff and I sat up, both of us panting from exhaustion. His facial expression then changed to a more serious one. I cried out for mercy again, but this time in my mind when he stroked my face and stared me deeply in the eyes and then he whispered, "I'm going to show you what true love is."

Mercy!

A SUMMER TO REMEMBER...

Celia DuBois

I waited impatiently as Brianna's new secretary Tonique placed me on hold again. She accidentally hung up on me the first time I called. I couldn't wait to tell Brianna my wonderful news. Last night, after two non-stop weeks of lonely nights without hanging out with Jeff, no phone conversations with Maria about her sex life, a diet consisting of take-out food and no pot, I finally finished my book.

I decided the first few weeks of the summer would be a perfect time so I willed myself to do it and it worked. I let everyone know that I would be out of commission for the next few weeks and they all respected me. Even Maria! I just finished reading the entire manuscript for the second time and am well pleased.

Tonique picked up the line again. "Miss DuBois, Miss Walker is on another call. May I please take a message for her or would you like her voice mail?"

"I'll leave a message with you." I tried to contain my disappointment. "Can you please tell her that Celia says mission completed."

"Mission completed? Will that be all?"

"Yep. That's all." Mission completed. Those two words engulfed my whole being with gratitude. I hung up the phone and cried tears of joy. It is such an accomplishment and one I've been waiting to happen for a long time.

I called my mother and told her the good news. She promised to pass it on. (As if I was worried about her not passing it on. Mama talks about me as if I'm a superstar. And this is only my first novel.) I called Maria and left a message on her machine informing her of the good news. Deniece wasn't home either but I didn't leave a message because I didn't think she'd get it anyway. My brother grunted, "It's about time." And my sister said, "That's good girl. I'm so happy for you. Girl, did I tell you what the baby did the other day? Chiiille… she is a mess. She…"

I tuned her out after ten minutes or so and did my obligatory "yeah's" and "no kidding's" until I couldn't take it anymore.

And then I called Jeff. His reaction made up for all the sorry ones.

"Get dressed." He demanded.

pamela davis-noland

"Get dressed? Why? And where am I going, sir?"
"Somewhere special to celebrate your accomplishment, baby."
"Ooh...how should I dress?"
"Dress for success, baby, 'cause it's well on its way."
"Aww...thank you Jeff. That makes me feel so good."
"Good. Now get dressed. I'll be there at eight. Be ready."
"Okay I'll be ready. Bye."
"Bye." He paused. "Hey?"
"Yeah."
"I missed you."
I blushed. "I missed you too."

I was on the phone telling Brianna my good news when I heard a car horn blaring outside my balcony. I tried to ignore it but then I heard someone shouting and it sounded like they were shouting my name. I put the phone down and ran to the balcony and there he was, lookin' fine as hell dressed in a suit and tie, standing through the sunroof of a long black limousine with a bottle of champagne in one hand and a glass full in the other.

"Sorry it's not a white horse, baby! But I'm more of a long, black, sleek, motor vehicle type of brotha'!" He shouted. "Besides, I look too damn good to be ridin' a horse!"

"You are so crazy! All the neighbors can hear you!" I yelled back. "How much of that champagne you drank?"

"None yet! This is your glass! Now come on down here woman. I'm paying for this by the hour!"

I could hear my neighbors laughing and yelling at Jeff as I hurried back to the phone and said goodbye to Brianna and promised that my manuscript will be placed in the mail on tomorrow. I grabbed my purse and my keys, took a quick glance in the mirror to check my makeup, twirled around to look at my butt and dashed out the door and down the steps two at a time.

We rode around town and listened to Aaron Neville croon through the limousine speakers while we drank champagne and kissed and drank some more and kissed some more and… well, you get the picture. After about an hour, the driver drove us to Royal Street for dinner at Brennan's, a gorgeous 19th Century Building turned exquisite Creole restaurant. And the dinner *was* exquisite indeed. Jeff had sautéed fish covered in crabmeat and I had Oysters Rockefeller and seafood gumbo. We both cleaned our plates!

After the wonderful dinner, we decided to walk a little while. Well until my feet started hurting. Jeff flagged down one of the horse carriages and we rode through Jackson Square and enjoyed all the sights and sounds with my head resting on his shoulder. I'd drank too much champagne. But this was still romance at its purest form. Jeff held me so close I thought I would scream for all of those

COFFEE-COLORED DREAMS

familiar desires that kept creeping up. Especially with this buzz. So I took slow deep breaths, leaned my head against his shoulder, closed my eyes and prayed for strength and for time to stand still for just a moment because I didn't want the night to ever end.

Jeff caressed my shoulder and kissed the top of my head several times before he finally spoke, "I have something to ask you."

My eyes popped opened and I sat up and looked at him. "You have something to ask me?" I asked trying to sound nonchalant. I was screaming on the inside. *Ooh... ask me. Please ask me.*

"Yes. I do. But if you say no, I'll understand." He stared me in the eyes.

Say no? Brotha' please! As long as I've been waiting for this! "What is it baby?" I whispered, trying to control the tremor in my voice.

"Well... um...well, I'm going to Chicago and I umm..." He stopped. And so did my heart. "Well. I want you to come with me to visit. You know, meet my peeps, do some sightseeing. Hang out." He shrugged.

Damn! I hope my eyes don't look as big as they feel.

"Celia. Celia?" He shook my arm.

"Oh. I'm sorry Jeff. I was thinking about something I forgot to do." I lied. "So you're going to Chicago?"

"Well yeah. But I'd hoped that *we* could go to Chicago. Would you come with me?"

"Sure Jeff. Sure. I'd love to go to Chicago with you." I feel like such a fool. I know he saw the look on my face. "When?"

"Next weekend. That too soon?"

"Naw that's perfect." I smiled too big.

He hugged me and patted me on the back with appreciation. I rolled my eyes. Well at least I'm meeting his family. He still has not met mine and they live right here in the city. Oh well, that'll come in time. I ain't even tryin' to get my family all worked up. *Or myself!*

Jeffrey Jackson

It was my mother's idea for me to bring Celia with me to Chicago to visit. Lately she has been the only one that seems to be interested about my feelings for Celia. I quit talking to Miles about Celia. He always changes the subject anyway. I figured he'd be more interested if she were Creole with an available sister. And talking to Laura about my attraction to Celia is totally out of the question. My sisters don't have the time and my brother can give a damn. So that left dear old mom. We talk about Celia every time I call her. I told her all about Celia completing her book and she said that maybe she could use a vacation and why don't I bring her to Chicago with me. I was so thrilled by her suggestion. I think she has finally gotten over her deep seeded prejudice and has finally become that good Christian that she always claims she is.

I finally feel like I can tell my mother some things about me that she doesn't know. I told her how I felt when I was married to Laura and how I was head over heels in love with Lettie Smalls and that I'd never really gotten over her until now. Mom apologized. She said if she would have known I felt that way she would have never encouraged the relationship with Laura so much.

Although I had mom's approval of Celia, I still felt a little apprehensive. I begged her not to tell Laura or Miles I was coming to town. I figured I would just surprise Miles and show up alone at his crib late at night or something. I knew Laura was going to be out of town so I wouldn't have to worry about her showing up unannounced but I still didn't want mom to mention it to her. Laura likes to "pop up" and "surprise" me every chance she gets.

The trip was a blast. Celia and I had the time of our lives and everything was cool. Well that is until my mom and my sisters decided to trudge down memory lane. There are a few things about my life that I have chosen to keep to myself. I haven't shared everything with Celia yet and I didn't really appreciate them telling Celia things about me that I had no intention of sharing, like for instance, "church boy."

I hadn't heard that nickname in years and I don't miss it. I prayed a quick silent prayer that Celia didn't hear her but I was just a little too slow. "Church boy?" She'd asked. "Why'd you call him that?" And then they were off. They trudged up every memory they had about my private hell, or as some people call it – adolescence.

When I was nine years old I started to go to church at least four days out of the week with my mother. At first I went with her because I was afraid of letting her out of my sight. I was scared of losing another parent and it was a nightmare that stayed with me for years. So I went everywhere she went, even if that meant going to church four nights a week. But after a while I started to really enjoy going to church. I loved sittin' back listening to the elders and deacons try to out-preach one another. I gained so much knowledge listening to those old men and their words of spiritual wisdom. It became a part of my life and as natural as breathing. And my desire to spend as much time as I could in church increased the day Mama Ella told me that my pops was in heaven and if I ever wanted to see him again, I'd have to make it there. So I became a little boy with a mission. I had every intention to make it to heaven to see my pops. And I thought those little old wise men were going to help me get there.

My vision came to a complete halt when I started to get my ass whipped – daily. I was called "punk," "sissy," "mama's boy" and "church boy" just to name a few. After my eighth or ninth fight, I finally told one of the old men at church that I was tired of turning the other cheek. I'll never forget his response; "It's okay to turn the other cheek boy. As long as you comin' back with a left hook." I went to school the next day and did just that and I haven't lost a fight since. Everyone stopped calling me "sissy," "mama's boy" and "punk." But "church

COFFEE-COLORED DREAMS

boy" still remains my nickname to this day even though I stopped going to church years ago. I didn't think it still bothered me until I told Celia all about it. Celia understood how upset I was that they even brought up the subject. She told me all about her private hell too. I felt a little guilty listening to her tell her story about being teased about her skin color. I used to be one of those kids and then I realized I was only doing it to fit in. We spent hours talking about our childhood life after that and I shared things with Celia that I hadn't shared with anyone.

I haven't decided when or how I'm going to ask her but especially after the wonderful summer we had, I've decided I have found my soul mate and her name is Celia DuBois. I don't feel the need to rush into it or anything though. I just want to establish with her the fact that I fully intend on making her Mrs. Jeffrey Terrell Jackson one day. One day soon I hope.

Celia DuBois

I was scared to death on that airplane. I haven't been on a damn plane since I was 7 years old when my Uncle Gabriel died. I'll never forget it as long as I live. I peed in my pants the minute the plane was up in the air and I got a whippin' for not telling my mother I had to pee. I told her I was too scared to "walk in the sky," as I explained it but she just rolled her eyes at me and told me I was too big to still wet my pants. I hadn't been in a plane since, 'cause I was always afraid of heights and just the thought of wetting my pants as an adult sends chills up my spine. But I had never been to Chicago and Lord knows I wanted to go. I tell everyone that one day I'm going to be on Oprah's show but the fear of getting on a plane always superceded that vision. But Jeff was giving me my chance so I swallowed my fears and decided to board that plane and pray I didn't have to pee. We departed from Moisant Field at 7:05 a.m. the following Saturday and I couldn't have been any happier.

When the plane took off I immediately began to sweat. Jeff looked at me with sympathy because I had already told him the "pee" story. He grabbed my hand and kissed it lightly and told me not to worry. And that if I had to pee he would be more than happy to carry me to the bathroom so that I wouldn't have to "walk in the sky." I think he was just as worried as I was. But I made it through just fine, dry panties and all.

I was so excited to meet Jeff's mother. She is more beautiful in person than she is in her pictures. She kind of reminds me of Dorothy Dandridge in her later years. She has extremely dark hair and lashes, flawless skin and a classy updo. She has a timeless look about herself and she carries it well. She has a wonderful sense of humor as well and we hit it off almost instantly. She and Jeff's sisters told me stories about Jeff that he never told me. Like for instance, the little boys in his neighborhood used to tease him and call him "church boy." I had no idea that Jeff was so into the church at one time. He never talks about it and the

pamela davis-noland

few times I did ask him to go to church with me, he refused. Only saying, "Maybe next Sunday, baby." I assumed he didn't like church, so I quit asking him.

Jeff's mother told me stories about when she was in the band with his father and how much she enjoyed it. Now she "only sing for my heavenly father," as she so eloquently put it. Those were wonderful stories. She says that Jeff is just like his father, although everyone claims that he's his grandfather reincarnated. I saw pictures of his dad and it's scary how much he looks like him. His father was very, very handsome. Harry Belafonte handsome! This boy couldn't miss good looks if he would have tried with parents like his. And his siblings are just as attractive. And they are so affectionate. They kiss and hug each other with every greeting. I had never seen such closeness among relatives in all my life. My sorry ass family, ha! The women give those fake air kisses and the men squeeze you so hard it could be considered incest in some states. I haven't been kissed so much in my life and I loved every minute of it.

We went sightseeing every day. One night we went to Navy Pier and rode the Ferris wheel and talked about "church boy" and "blacky." It sure felt good to finally laugh about those days. We went to Oprah's Studio but it was closed so Jeff took a picture of me standing in front of it praying that one day I'd be back. We had dinner at Michael's restaurant, went to the roof of Sears Tower, went to a baseball game and we even went to the projects where "Good Times" was filmed. I had so much fun. I had always dreamed of going to Chicago and it was sure a nice surprise. We stayed for a week and I still didn't want to leave. We made a vow to go every summer as long as we're together. And that's another vow that I intend on keeping. I can honestly say that I saw a different side of Jeff and I fell in love with that side too.

It sure would be nice to become a part of his family. I've always wanted to be a part of a family that was happy for one another and not so backstabbin' and judgmental as mine. But I'm not gonna even go there right now. I love him and he loves me and I'm just trying to take it one day at a time.

As soon as I settled in from my trip, I went to see Benny to share with him all of my good news. I would have never met Jeff had it not been for Benny. And this would have been one the most boring summers of my life. But instead, it was one of the best I ever had! I so dread going back to work, but at least I'll be going back a helluvalot happier than I was last year. Just like Patti sang; "I got a new attitude!"

FOOLS AND OLD PEOPLE

Celia DuBois

I was hanging posters on the walls of my new classroom when Mr. Lee walked in grinning as usual. I tried my best to ignore him. But of course, he decided to strike up a friendly conversation.

"Well, how was your summer Ms. DuBois?" He sang.

"Just fine, Mr. Lee" I sang back, mimicking him, "and yours?"

"Hmmm, probably not as nice as yours. You seem to be in wonderful spirits Ms. DuBois. Care to share your little secret?"

"No secret. Just happy, that's all."

"So there is a new special someone in your life, I hear?"

That damn Miss Jenkins, with her big mouth! "Yes as a matter of fact there is. His name is Jeff."

"Well, well, this Jeff must consider himself a lucky man to have caught your eye. I wonder if he'd share his secret." He laughed.

"Well, I can tell you what his secret is, Mr. Lee. He treats me with the utmost respect, he's a very good dresser, he hates a lot of jewelry and he's a one-woman man. And not to mention he has a whole lot of class! Yep, that's his secret, alright, a whole lot of class." *Now get yo' nosy ass out of my face.*

His smile turned into a frown. "Well, I have to get back to work. Good luck this year and try and pass that good mood on to our students." He turned and left.

That's what he gets for tryin' to get all up in my business with his no-dressin' ass. Somebody ought to really tell him that men stopped wearing polyester shirts, two gold chains and a pinky ring on both little fingers a long time ago. He looks like John Travolta in "Saturday Night Fever".

My first day back at work went extremely well. Everyone seemed to be in a good mood. Their attitudes were superb. But then again, this was only their first day back. I was pleased to meet a new little girl named Lisa Davis. She reminds me so much of Jennifer. Lisa is a soft-spoken child with an incredible talent for writing poetry. I decided to make her my new protégé for the year. I pick one every year. She's a very gifted child who seems to love writing more than I do and we hit it off instantly. I'm going to really enjoy working with her.

pamela davis-noland

After work I decided to go to Benny's and unwind. I hadn't been in the last two weeks because I was so busy preparing for the new school year. Jeff told me that Benny hadn't been feeling too well, so I felt obligated to go and check on him. When I walked up to the doors, there was a Closed sign in the window. I peeked through only to see the chairs stacked up on the tables and not a soul in sight. I banged on the door expecting to see Benny "rocking" toward me from his back office but no one came so I left.

Jeffrey Jackson

When Big Man called this morning and told me Benny wasn't feeling well, I wasn't surprised. Benny had been moving kinda slow lately. Slower than normal for Benny that is. Anyway, I called my job and told them I wasn't going to make it in today. I cancelled all other plans I had for the day and headed straight for his crib and found Benny lying on the couch with his eyes closed looking like he was already dead. And by that smirk on his face, he looked like a *happy* dead man. I called his name out at least three times before he opened his eyes, looked over at me and grinned.

The way he looked, so peaceful, reminded me of my pops lying in his coffin. I was only eight years old but I remember that day as if it just happened yesterday. Pops had a traditional New Orleans funeral just like every other Jackson man. Complete with black horses pulling a black carriage with my pops' coffin lying in the middle of it surrounded by flowers. All the women wore black dresses and my mother looked like a death angel in all of that black lace with matching veil and gloves. We paraded, on foot, right down the middle of some rural back street of New Orleans from the church to the graveyard. That day was the saddest day of my life and I resent the fact that I've let another man get so close to me. Just the thought of having to attend Benny's funeral sends chills through me. I shook when I saw him.

After thirty minutes of persuading Benny, he finally agreed to let me take him to the hospital just to be on the safe side. Me and Big Man helped him shuffle his way to my car and I drove like a bat outta hell through rush hour morning traffic while Benny sat on the passenger's side with his head resting against the headrest, eyes closed and that same half-smile on his face.

"What are you grinnin' at old man?" I finally asked.

"I didn't know I wuz." He responded with his eyes still closed.

"Well you are. Why?"

"Jest tryin' to figure out what the big hurry iz? You ain't got to rush on my account boy."

"Well old man you sure are not getting any younger. It's not like we got a whole lot of time to waste."

"Time? Waste? Boy what'choo talkin' bout?" He finally opened his eyes and

COFFEE-COLORED DREAMS

looked over at me.

"Why you walk around acting like you could care less if you die tomorrow Benny? I mean what is that about? And why you over there smiling like you think this is the day? You don't think it bothers us to hear you talking about death so much?" I looked in my rear view mirror at Big Man for some kind of support or an Amen or something but he suddenly found the palms of his hands interesting and he acted like he didn't even hear me. Big Man is never one for saying much of nothin' about any subject.

"Look here boy. The only reason I'm going to this hospital is to ease yo' mind a little. I'm an old man. You cain't 'spect me to not have days when I don't feel a hunnerd percent. Today jest one of those days dat's all. You wait and see. Them doctors ain't gonna find nothin' wrong. Jest like deys always don't find nothin' wrong. Benny is an old man. But I am *far from* sick." He closed his eyes and leaned his head back against the headrest.

Celia DuBois

I drove straight to Jeff's house after I left the Quarters. He wasn't home so I left a note on his door to call me as soon as he got home and I briefly explained how surprised I was to find Benny's Place closed. This was definitely a first and I was just a little bit worried.

I was sitting on the balcony drinking a glass of iced tea, trying to cool off. It had been three hours since I had left the note on Jeff's door and I had still not heard from him. I even tried calling him on his cell phone but he didn't answer. So my mind is really racing now. I was just about to go in and call him again when the phone began to ring before I could get to it. I quickly picked it up and prepared myself for his excuse. "Hello." I said in a not too friendly manner.

"So how was your first day back? Them brats gave you hell, huh?"

Damn! "Oh hey, Black." I was disappointed.

"Damn! Well, hey to you, too. What's wrong wit'choo? You sound like shit."

"Oh, nothin' I just thought you were Jeff that's all."

"Like y'all don't see enough of each other anyway. Hell I don't ever hear from you since you and Mr. Dimples been hangin' out on a regular. I was beginning to think I had lost my best friend. You never call. And then when I call yo' ass, you got the nerve to be disappointed 'cause I ain't Jeff. Well ain't that some shit!"

"Yeah, ain't it? Now you know exactly how I feel when *you* meet a new man." I snapped.

"Uh, I guess this must be a bad time for ya' Celia. I'm'a talk to you later, chick." Maria was hurt.

"No, Black, I'm sorry. I didn't mean it. I'm just a little worried that's all. I left a note on Jeff's door three hours ago and I still haven't heard from him. And I'm worried about Benny, too. Jeff told me he hadn't been feeling too good lately so I went by to see him and the café was closed. My mind is just racing, that's all. So what's up wit'choo fool?" I tried to redeem myself. But I know Maria; she hates it when I'm rude to her.

"Whatever." She said.

"Look, I said I was sorry, Maria. Don't go catchin' no attitude with me, girl. Now what's up? What'cha doin'?"

She sighed. "Nothin'. So did you try and call that old man at home? Maybe he has that flu that's done swept the city. Girl, we been so busy at the hospital with all these old people and that damn flu. It ain't even funny."

"I don't have Benny's number at home."

"Well look it up in the phone book, dummy. You know where he live?"

"I tried. I couldn't find his name in the phone book. And information didn't have it either."

"Damn. As much as you been hangin' out with him, I would've thought you've at least got his phone number. I guess y'all not as close as you think, huh?"

Classic Maria. She can't stand for me to have other friends. Especially friends that she doesn't know. That's one of the reasons she can't stand Deniece. She says it's because Deniece is a "high-yellow snob." But I know she doesn't like her just because we are so close and Maria is just jealous of our friendship.

"Look Maria. I don't even have time for your smart-ass, alright. I'm really worried. So can you be a little more sympathetic? Please!" I begged.

"Alright. Damn, I was just kiddin'. So you want me to try and find his number for you?"

"Naw, that's alright. I'll just wait for Jeff. But thank you anyway. Hey do you mind if I call you back later? I was just about to try Jeff on his cell phone again."

"Fine. Don't mind me. I'm just your oldest friend that's all. I guess I better just wait until you have time for me, though. Call me when you have time." And with that she hung up.

I was tempted to call her and remind her spoiled-rotten ass of all the times she put me on the back burner for all her sorry-ass men but I didn't have the strength. Besides, she'll call back again tomorrow to find out what happened, anyway, with her nosy self.

Jeffrey Jackson

The doctors couldn't find a thing wrong with Benny. They did several tests and the only conclusion they could come up with is he just has a bad case of old age. They insisted that he stay overnight though. Just so that they could monitor what

COFFEE-COLORED DREAMS

they thought might be an irregular heartbeat.

While I was waiting for one of the doctors to come back to give me some more information, I decided to visit the chapel. I'm a grown man now and I still looked over my shoulder before I entered. I got a flashback of one of my childhood torturers calling me names and throwing rocks like they used to do when I was by myself. I was surprised that I still got that same peaceful feeling that I used to get everytime I'd step foot in church. I had to hang my head in shame at how I let those kids, and just about everyone else in my life, persuade me to do or not do what makes me happy. It felt good to be back. I knelt down and said the longest prayer I've ever said in my life. I have so much to be thankful for and so much I had to be forgiven for. But I mainly prayed that God would keep Benny alive a little while longer. *Just a little while longer, man. It feels good to have a father figure in my life. Especially now at this point in my life.*

After Benny went to sleep and I could hear him snoring, I decided to go over to see Celia. I needed to feel her next to me. I needed some kind of confirmation that I was now living my life according to my own terms. I needed to feel loved and accepted for who I am. I needed Celia DuBois. I needed her in more ways than one.

I drove like another bat outta hell to her crib. She would just have to forgive me for popping up so late.

Celia DuBois

I tried calling Jeff again but he still did not answer. I decided to watch a little television in my bedroom and had just dozed off when I heard a soft knock. I jumped up and ran to the door in just my T-shirt and panties.

"Who is it?" I asked as if I didn't already know.

"It's me baby." He said it so low I could barely hear him.

"Jeff, is that you?"

"Yeah, baby, it's me."

I could tell by the look on his face that something was wrong and my heart began to pound. I was afraid to ask so I just stared at him waiting for him to give me the bad news. He walked over to the sofa and placed his face in his hands. I suddenly felt guilty for being so angry with him. Because apparently my instincts are right. Something is definitely wrong.

"What's wrong baby?" I asked.

Jeff looked up at me and tried to smile but I could see right through it. He was really sad.

"I had to rush Benny to the emergency room, baby and..."

"What?!" I didn't even wait for him to finish. I jumped up and began pacing the floor. "What happened? Is he okay?"

"Come sit down, honey. I'll tell you the whole story."

pamela davis-noland

I sat down and braced myself for the worst.

"Big Man called me this morning and told me that he was worried about Benny because he was complaining last night about being dizzy. He said he tried to take him to the hospital last night but Benny wouldn't hear of it so he thought that maybe I should have a talk with him. When I got there he didn't look real bad but I could tell he was weak and his color was a little pale. He wasn't himself at all. I knew something was wrong. I called you on my way there but you had already left for work. Anyway, I had to practically beg him to let me take him to the hospital. He could barely sit up, he was so weak."

"So where is he? What's the matter with him?" I was trying not to get too upset but Jeff was making a short story long and it was driving me crazy.

"He's still in the hospital. The doctors are just running some test to see if they can find out what's going on. Man, we've been there all day and I still don't know what's wrong with him." His voice cracked a little.

I sat next to him and kissed him lightly on the cheek and tried to be strong for him. I could tell that he was about to choke up. "Are you hungry, baby?" I asked.

"Naw. I just came by to let you know what was going on, that's all. I wanted to tell you in person. I have to get back to the hospital. I'm gonna stay all night with him. Besides, I still haven't gotten the answers I want yet. Although one doctor said that he just thinks it's a case of old age. I'm still scared. I don't know how much time I'm gonna have left with him."

"Jeff don't talk like that. Benny will be just fine. You know the Lord takes good care of fools and old people. Don't worry baby. Hey, do you want me to go with you?"

"Naw. I know you're probably exhausted. How was your first day back at work, anyway?"

"Fine. I had a wonderful day. Now wait while I go and put some clothes on. I'll follow you and stay for just a little while. I want to see him for myself anyway. Just give me a minute." I jumped up and ran toward my bedroom.

"Hey!" Jeff yelled out.

"What?"

"The next time I come over here and you have that on. I ain't 'gon be held responsible, okay?" He looked at me seductively.

"Oh I'm sorry, Jeff. I wasn't thinkin'."

"Yeah, but you sure got me thinkin'. Go put some clothes on woman before I forget that I'm a gentleman." He laughed.

Room 412 was dark except for the white light directly above Benny's head. He looked so tranquil. The I.V. that was in each arm didn't even seem to be bothering him at all. He almost looked dead and it scared the hell out of me.

My Great-Granny died when I was 10 years old. She was lying in a hospital bed with IVs and tubes everywhere and she looked just as peaceful as Benny does right now. I'll never forget that night as long as I live. I actually witnessed

COFFEE-COLORED DREAMS

her death. It was by far the scariest thing I ever had to endure in my entire 10 years of life.

My Mudear and my mother were sitting by her side comforting her and she was smiling and talking with them about all the good times that she had in life. We were happy to see her smiling because she had been in a lot of pain since they had to amputate both of her legs. My mother said they had to cut her legs off because she had "sugar." I had no idea what that was at the time but I stopped eating candy and even though I know better now, I still don't eat too many sweets. That fear has stuck with me all these years.

We were only there for about 30 minutes when Great Granny closed her eyes for the last time. I'll never forget it as long as I live. My Mudear started screaming and crying and begging the Lord not to take her mama. My mother ran up to us and tried to shove us out of the room. I was so petrified, my feet would not move so I witnessed everything. I remember hearing the nurses screaming, "Code Blue, Code Blue!" I remember watching as they unsuccessfully tried to bring her back to life. I remember them covering her face and saying those god-awful words, "She's gone. But she's in a better place." Now I knew, even at the tender age of 10, that old woman may not have gone to a better place because she was the meanest old bitch I knew. She used to beat our ass with her cane just for looking at her the wrong way. I was ashamed for what I thought but I was glad she was gone.

I haven't thought about that in years. Standing here looking at Benny brought back that memory. I just pray that he doesn't close his eyes for the last time while I'm standing here because I don't think I can handle watching two people die in my lifetime.

Jeff stood next to Benny and caressed his hand. "Hang in there old man. Don't leave me yet." He whispered.

Jeff looked over at me and motioned for me to come closer but my damn feet wouldn't move. All I could think about was Great Granny. One minute she was smiling, the next she had closed her eyes forever. I'll be damned if I go through that again.

He walked over to me, "What's the matter baby?"

"Nothin'. I think I'm just gonna go on home. I just wanted to see for myself that he was okay."

"Well, why don't you stay a little longer. He might wake up. He'll be so happy to see you."

"Naw. That's okay. Will you walk me to my car?"

We walked through the parking lot in complete silence. I felt stupid for driving all the way to the hospital and only staying for five minutes but I had no idea that I was still afraid of hospital rooms.

"Hey, will you do me a favor?" Jeff asked.

"Sure. What?"

He pulled a piece of paper out of his pocket. "Will you call this number first thing tomorrow morning. It's Samuel's number, you know, the cook. Tell him about Benny. He's the only one who doesn't know what's going on yet."

"Sure. Hey, are you going to be okay?"

"You know Celia, I never really had the chance to really get to know my father or my grandfather. Benny is the only man that I can really consider a father figure and I'm not ready to lose him yet, baby." He lowered his head. I could see the tears welling up in the corner of his eyes.

"Oh, don't worry. Benny is strong. You know that. You just have to keep the faith that's all." I hugged him and tried to comfort him the best way I could.

He pulled away from me, looked me deeply in the eyes and kissed me so passionately that every hair on my body stood at attention and moisture formed between my thighs. My heart pounded and my body ached. I love this man with all my heart and soul and I want to feel him close to me so badly. And by the way he's squeezin' my ass I know he feels the exact same way. I'm not sure how much more of this I can take. And to be honest, I'm not sure that I'm gonna make it any farther. I want him *waaay* too much.

He stepped away from me and smiled.

Damn!

Now any other woman in the world, with the exception of my mama, would have given up the drawls 50 kisses and two grinds ago. But not me. I can't bear the thought of giving into my feelings and sleeping with him and then we just break up. Just like every other man that I wasted my time with. That would be devastating!

I am so sorry, Jeffrey Jackson. I want you baby but I have to be just a li'l bit more sure about us. Unlike all those other women in the world, with the exception of my mama, I finally learned from my mistakes. "Jeff, I….."

He placed his finger on my mouth. "Shh…whenever you ready, baby." He said. He winked at me, gave me one more "I-can-tear-that-ass-up" kiss and opened my car door for me. Just like the gentleman he is. He stood and watched me drive off, blew me a kiss and jogged his fine ass back to take care of his father figure.

I cried all the way home. It's a good thing the Lord takes care of fools like me and old people like Benny.

BEST FRIEND, WITH BENEFITS

Celia DuBois

It's amazing to me how strong Jeff is. I mean most men would have either tried to take it, said the hell with me, or had another woman anyway, so it didn't matter if I give 'em some or not. But Jeff doesn't fit any of those categories. Well, at least not yet. So far, so good. I'm definitely keeping my fingers crossed. But I ain't no fool. I'll do it if I absolutely have to. Like for instance if some other chick try and take him or somethin'. I just hope it doesn't have to come down to that. Then it would be spiteful and that's not what I picture when I dream about us making love for the first time. Naw, I picture roses and silk sheets and candles and champagne and both of us in total ecstasy. The entire scene is a softly lit silhouette in my mind, nothing raunchy at all. Now that scene alone makes it much easier for me to keep my vow. I have to be the "stubborn child" my mother always said I was and not settle for anything less. *Lord, help me.*

I picked up the phone and decided to call Jeff to see if he had slept okay. He picked up on the first ring. "Hey baby." He whispered.

"How'd you know it was me?"

"'Cause I been waitin' on your call all night, Sylvia." He said in his sexy, Billy Dee Williams' voice.

"Who??!!" I yelled.

Jeff burst into laughter. "Caller I.D., baby, I got Caller I.D. on my cell phone, remember? You so crazy, Celia."

"Why you always fuckin' wit'me, Jeff?" I laughed.

"Ha! I wish."

"Well, anyway. How'd you sleep?" I quickly changed the subject.

"I slept pretty good. Hold on."

I can hear Benny talking in the background and he sounds terrific.

"Yeah, I'm back. Benny says hello, baby."

"Tell him I said hello and that I'll be there in about an hour or two."

"Uh, don't you have to go to work?"

"Uh, don't you?"

pamela davis-noland

"Yeah, but I already let them know that there was an emergency in my family. They're not expecting me."

"Well, since I consider Benny my family too. I'm gonna have to let my job know the same thing. Besides, you need to at least go home and shower and change clothes. I can sit with Benny until you get back, okay."

"Uh, ain't this your second day back to work, Celia? Are you sure?"

"Sure, believe me it's okay. My class is strictly an elective. I only have four classes and they're very small. Believe me, I'll hardly be missed. Besides, when I'm not there I'll just leave a reading assignment for them. They're really good students. They have to be in order to get into the class. So I'll just let them know that a member of my family is in the hospital. It'll be fine."

"Okay. So what time you 'gon be here, sis?"

"I got your sis'! We ain't that kind'a family, Mr."

"Well that's a good thang. So what kind of family are we?"

I was at a complete loss for words. I hate when he does that shit to me.

"What kind?" He asked again.

"I don't know, Jeff. I guess a happy one."

"Yeah, I guess so. But do you ever think about us becoming a real family?"

"A real family?"

"Yeah."

"What exactly do you mean by that?" I asked. My palms were so wet I damn near dropped the phone.

"What exactly do you think?"

"Don't be answerin' my questions with a question!" I demanded.

"Hey, look, you know exactly what I'm sayin', baby. But look, I have to go. The nurse is here. I'll see you in a minute, right?"

"Right."

"Okay, I love you. Bye."

I fell back on my bed kicking and screaming like a mad woman. He loves me and he wants to marry me. "Hot damn! Hell just to be asked is enough for me. At least that's a sign. I may not be wasting my time after all. Will I marry you? Hell yeah!!!" I yelled.

I jumped up and ran to the living room, played my favorite CD and danced naked as I sang along with Alanis Morrisette as she wailed the words "You've already won me overrrr......." And that's exactly what he did. He's my best friend with benefits.

The phone rang as soon as I shoveled my first bite of Captain Crunch in my mouth. I grinned because I assumed that it just might be Maria. And I was right.

"Hey bitch." She snarled.

"Well good morning to you too." I said with my mouth full.

"Damn girl, you got a dick in ya' mouf? What the hell you doin'?"

"No I don't. I have Captain Crunch in my mouth. Most of us normal people

COFFEE-COLORED DREAMS

eat food for breakfast."

"I weep for the normal people." She replied. "So how's the old man? Did you ever catch up with Jeff?"

"Benny's fine. Thank you for being concerned Maria. Hey, and I'm sorry I hurt your feelings yesterday. I was just worried. Okay?"

"Yeah, whatever. Anyway, sorry for bein' a bitch. You know I just be trippin' sometimes, girl."

"That you do. Anyway, Benny's in the hospital Maria."

"What??! What happened?!" she yelled.

"Well, Jeff went over to his house yesterday and he was real weak. Jeff took him to the emergency room and they kept him so that they can run tests. The doctors say that he's just old that's all."

"Damn. I'm really sorry to hear that."

"Yeah, I know. I went to see him last night for a lil' while. I'm about to go back in a few minutes."

"You're not goin' to work?"

'No. I took the day off to go and relieve Jeff for a little while. He needs to go home and freshen up a little."

"Celia, you not 'gon start that shit again are you? You used to take off to spend time with Calvin and you see what happened with that relationship."

"Yes ma'am I do. But this is totally different. I'm not taking off just to hang out with Jeff. I'm really concerned about Benny and I want to be with him. Believe me girl, I've learned my lesson well. But even if I did decide to take off just to be with Jeff, don't worry, he is definitely worth it."

"Yeah and you thought the same shit about Calvin."

"Calvin was a mistake, Black. The whole damn affair with him was a total waste of my time. Believe me, I know. But I do believe I can say that Jeff truly loves me."

"And what makes us so sure of that?" Maria asked sarcastically.

"Well, Miss Ann, if you have to know, Jeff asked me to marry him."

"What??!!" Maria yelled in my ear.

"Quit yellin' girl! You heard what I said."

"Well damn, bitch! When were you gonna tell me?"

"Mais, he jes' ax me dis mornin', *sha*." I replied, mimicking my Mudear's thick Cajun accent.

"Well?"

"Well, what?"

"Well when is the damn date? And I better be yo' maid of honor, Cee. You betta not pick Deniece. You know she might show up wit'a black eye. And you bet'not ask one of yo' sorry ass cousins. You know they 'gon be trippin' and cryin' broke all the time. And not one of'em 'gon give you a bridal shower or nothin'. You betta pick me, Celia DuBois." Maria was all wound up.

"Slow down Maria, damn. I haven't even given him an answer yet."

pamela davis-noland

There was silence on the phone.

"Hello?" I asked.

"You have got to be one of the strangest women I know, Celia." She said, solemnly, "You know damn well there is a major shortage of good men in this hot ass lil' musty tourist town we call home. Now out of the sky blue you meet that fine ass motherfucker, who you ain't even givin' no pussy to mind you. He take you to meet his family all the way in Chicago, he treat yo' ass like a china doll and you haven't even given him a answer yet? Girl, you got issues."

"Well I'm gonna say yes, bitch. You think I'm stupid. I just want to tell him in person that's all."

"Whew! Girl, I thought you had lost yo' mind. I mean that vow thang is bad enough. I still can't believe you ain't gave 'em any. Hell, come to think about it, that shit must work, huh? He asked yo' ass to marry 'em, didn't he? Huh! I might have to try that shit."

"Yeah, right Maria." I laughed.

"Girl, you know I'm fulla shit, huh? Anyway, I'll let you go. Congratulations chick."

"Thanks. Hey, I might come by and see you after you get off. And then we can discuss whether or not you're gonna be my maid of honor."

"Whether or not? I betta be or I ain't goin'."

"Oh it's like that?"

"And that's the way it is. Bye, girl. I love you."

"Bye."

When I arrived at the hospital Jeff was standing in the doorway of Benny's room talking to a very attractive nurse who seemed to be enthralled by his every word. Her lil' giggles were sickening. And if she would've stepped up to him any closer, she would have been standing behind him.

Jeff finally looked up and saw me. He excused himself and pigeon-toed toward me grinnin' from ear to ear. I grinned right back.

He grabbed me around my waist and kissed me tenderly. "Good morning." He said.

"Hey. You look so tired. You ready to go get some rest?"

"Yeah, man. I didn't sleep too well. I had to get up and walk around just to keep my eyes open. I was just talkin' to Benny's nurse. She's nice. Come on, I'll introduce you."

Little did he know that sista' girl had already walked off. He didn't see her walk away when he grabbed and kissed me. But I did. And I also saw that look of disappointment she had. *Sorry sista, the boy is mine.*

"Oh well, I guess she had to get back to work. You'll meet her later. Anyway, Benny's asleep. Let's go in and sit with him."

"No. I'll go in and sit with him. You go home and get some rest. Now! Me and Benny'll be just fine."

"I kind of wanted to wait 'til he woke up."

COFFEE-COLORED DREAMS

"Well, I'll tell him that you went home to get some rest. He'll understand."

"Okay, baby. But if he wakes up and asks for me call me, okay?"

Jeff didn't mention anything about the proposal. Therefore, I didn't either. I guess he's just tired. Maybe we'll talk about it when he gets back.

I sat next to Benny for hours staring at him making sure that he was breathing. I swear I hope he doesn't die. I don't want him to die at all much less right now when I'm the only one in the room.

Sometimes I wonder if Benny is an angel. The bible does mention something about us entertaining angels, unaware. And after all the stories I've heard about him, not to mention my own personal experiences, I'm really starting to become a believer. I can't exactly put my finger on what he might be. But whatever he is, I'm sure glad I met him. I love this old man.

I pulled my chair closer to the bed and laid my head on his leg. I closed my eyes and said a silent prayer that the Lord would give us more time to be with him. He has been a father figure to me as well. Hell, my father and I don't even talk that much. And the only advice he's ever given me was when I went on my first job interview. I'll never forget that afternoon when he knocked on my door. I opened the door wearing only my slip and he closed it and told me to go put on a robe and open the door when I was dressed. I rolled my eyes at him and put my robe on. He came in, sat on my bed, and told me to sit next to him. He placed his hand on my knee, looked me straight in the eye and said, "Make sho' you polite. Shake the man hand. Always look'im straight in da' eye. And don't chew gum." He gave me a half-hearted hug and walked out. Later that day, I found out my mother made him come in there and give me some words of encouragement. And that's about as close as we've ever come to a real father/daughter talk.

I was startled when Benny spoke to me. "Well, what have we got here? Have I died and 'gon to heav'n?"

He didn't look sick at all, just a little pale. "Benny!" I stood up and kissed both sides of his face. I was so happy.

"Hi Doll, what'choo doin' here. Don'tcha have to be to work?"

"No. I'm exactly where I need to be. I took the day off to be with you. I hope you don't mind."

"Mind? Now why would I mind? It's always a pleasure to spend time wit' my fav'rit Doll. So you got any good news 'bout yo' book yet?"

"Not yet Benny. But I'm sure Brianna is still reading it. I'll keep you posted though. How you feelin' Benny?"

"Oh Doll. I'm fine. Just old and tired." His gray eyes twinkled. "Where's that boy?"

"He went home to get a little rest. So you'll have me all to yourself this morning."

"You know if that boy got in touch wit' Samuel?"

"Yes. I called him myself. He says he'll be right over after he gets off of work."

pamela davis-noland

"Good. Now I want you to do somethin' fo' me."

"Anything, Benny."

"Take care'a that boy fa'me when I'm gone."

"And just where do you think you're going Mr. Thibodeaux?"

He sat up slowly. "Well, I'm just about finished, Doll."

"Finished? What do you mean finished?"

Benny lowered himself back onto his pillow, closed his eyes and smiled. "You gonna promise me Doll." He said this as more of a command than a question.

"Yes Benny. I will. But you have to promise to do something for me."

"I'd be more than happy to."

"You have to promise me that you'll stop talking about dying. At least until you get out of here," I looked around the hospital room and all those memories of the day my Great Granny died came back. "It kind of makes me nervous."

"Dyin'?" Benny chuckled. "Okay Doll. Now I'm gonna git some mo' rest. As long as I know you 'gon do me that fava' I can sleep peacefully. I love that boy. Love'em as if he wuz my flesh and blood. He 'gon need some body to take care'a him, and I think you 'gon do jes' fine." He closed his eyes and went to sleep.

Don't worry Benny. I'll keep my promise. Forever, if he'll let me.

MISS YOU MUCH

Jeffrey Jackson

The phone rang just as I grabbed my keys and was headed toward the door. I started to ignore it but it crossed my mind that it may be Celia so I jogged back to answer it. "Hey baby." I had no doubt in my mind that it was her.

"Well hey to you too. So I'm "baby" again, huh? Or did you think I was someone else?" She tried to sound nonchalant.

I haven't told Laura all about Celia yet. I've sort of been avoiding the subject. Laura and I are divorced now and live in two different cities. So why am I hiding it? Maybe because of the track record Laura has with butting into my affairs with other women.

I ignored her question. "Hey Laura. What's going on?"

"I don't know. Why don't you tell me."

"Hey look, I'm on my way out of the door. I gotta meet some people. Can I call you back?"

"Meet who? Where are you guys going this early on a Saturday morning?"

"I'm going down to the Place. A few other guys and I are going to spruce it up a little for Benny. You know wash windows, put a fresh coat of paint on the walls. That kinda shit. We want it to look nice when Benny comes back to work. Anyway, I have to pick up some paint on my way there."

"So you work *there* now?"

"No. I help out *there* now."

"Oh."

Silence.

"So whose baby, Jeff?"

I was waiting for that question at least one more time. Who's baby? Well let's see. "Baby" is Celia DuBois and Celia DuBois is my future wife I hope. I don't really know because she hasn't even given a brotha' an answer yet. I mean I'll admit my proposal wasn't what you might call romantic but she could have at least acknowledged it. She hasn't even mentioned it. So I've been giving her some space because I feel like I may have gotten a lil' carried away and now I feel like a damn fool. So I've been busying myself at Benny's Place just to keep my mind off of it. I don't know what made me pop the question like that. I really didn't put much thought into it. I just opened my mouth and it flew out.

Benny is always telling me to brush up on my singing. Hell, I need to brush up on my romance skills. Brotha' is a lil' rusty.

"Laura, if you have a minute, I'd like to tell you who she is." I might as well get it all out now because there ain't no way in hell she's gonna let it die.

"I have a few minutes." She replied.

"Okay. There is someone I've been wanting to tell you about for a very long time."

"How long is a very long time?"

"Well not that long."

"Is this the same chick you came home with when I was conveniently out of town?"

Miles makes me sick!!!

"So why didn't you let Miles meet her?" She giggled. "Ashamed?"

"No. I have absolutely nothing to be ashamed of." My heart skipped a beat as soon as I said those words. I stood my ground anyway. "I'm in love with Celia, Laura." There I told her. I just hope like hell that I didn't make a big mistake.

"I figured as much. Why else would you bring her over to Mom's?"

Silence.

"So who's the new guy in your life?" I tried my best to lighten the mood. "I know you're seeing somebody."

"Nothing serious. Not really looking for anyone right now."

"Oh."

"Jeff?"

"Yeah?"

"I called because there is something that I need to talk over with you. It's pretty serious baby but I don't want to talk about it over the phone."

"What is it? Is everything okay?"

"Yeah, yeah. Everything's fine baby, don't worry. It's just something I need to talk over with someone and you know you're the only one who really understands me."

"So what are you saying? You want me to go there?"

"Well I don't know. I've been thinking about taking some time off. I might just pay you a visit."

"Oh now you're making me nervous. Why would you want to come here? You hate Louisiana."

"I don't hate Louisiana. I just would have never gotten a wild hair up my ass to move there."

"A wild hair? You really believe that's why I moved here? You think it's just some wild hair and that I'll get over it and move back home?"

"Well, we are hoping, Jeff."

"Who the hell is *we*?"

COFFEE-COLORED DREAMS

"Everyone baby. Me, Miles, Mom, your sisters, your brother, my parents, your friends, well… just about everyone I guess."

"Well how about you tell all of them that they can quit planning my welcome home party cuz it's not going to happen."

"Mama Ella used to say that a person should never say never."

"Who ever listened to Mama Ella besides the old busy bodies in the neighborhood? So you want me to go there or are you coming down here?"

"I don't know yet. Let me decide and I'll call you at around 6:00 or 7:00 this evening, okay?"

"So are you just going to leave a brotha' hangin' or are you going to at least give me a hint."

"Let's just say it's very personal and I don't want you to discuss it with anyone. Okay?"

"Who do you take me for, Miles? I don't talk baby."

"Okay. Well I'll call you back."

"A'right."

"Jeff?"

"Yeah?"

"I still love you."

"Laura, we're gonna always love each other right?"

"Bye, baby." She hung up.

Celia DuBois

I hadn't had a good night sleep in weeks. But last night I slept so hard I woke up dizzy. I normally don't get up so early on Saturdays but I promised Black that I would help her move. Again. That girl moves more than the law allows and every time she moves I have to help her. I would've said no but of course she laid that guilt trip on me about our friendship, again. She called me about two weeks ago and asked me to help her. Or as she put it, "I figure I betta make a appointment now since you been so busy helpin' everybody else. Hopefully you can find the time to squeeze me in." That girl knows she's a pain in my ass.

I must admit I do miss Maria, though. I've been so busy these days that I just haven't been keeping in touch with her as much as I used to. But between my writing, my job at school and helping everyone take care of Benny, I haven't had much time for anything else. Hell, I haven't even been spending time with Jeff. Well at least not alone. We spend a lot of time at the café helping out.

I heard the phone ring when I was in the shower. I knew it was Maria so I didn't even bother getting out to answer it. I know she's just calling to rush me like she always does. That girl let the phone ring until I finally got out and answered.

"What Maria?" I yelled into the receiver.

pamela davis-noland

"Now is that anyway to talk to ya' homey? You awake yet, girl?"

"Yeah I'm up. You?"

"Hell naw. I'm just rollin' over. I had me a hot one las' night."

"New victim, black widow?"

"Girl, I think I'm the victim. This brotha' here know he gotta gold one!" She laughed. "That niggah dick so big, I was scared the damn condom wouldn't fit."

"Maria, where in the hell do you meet all those Mandingo niggahs?"

"Now you know I can spot a big dick from across the room, girl. So what's up? What time you 'gon be here? You still comin' right?"

"In a little while. But look, seriously Black, when are you gonna stop sleepin' around so much? Girl you ain't 'gon never find a good man like that."

"Who says I'm lookin'? Girl, look. You only live once. I say live it up!"

"Well I hope you're prepared to suffer the consequences of livin' it up after it's all over with."

"Chile, you been hangin' round that old man too much. How's he doin' anyway?"

"Oh he's fine. He's comin' along real well. He's even been back to the café two or three times out of the week."

"That's good. How's Jeff?"

"Alright." I said dryly.

"Damn! Alright? Oh, oh. What's up with the lovebirds? Don't tell me there's trouble in paradise?"

"Girl, look! I'm standin' here butt-ass naked and I'm freezin'. I'll see you in a lil' while, okay?"

"So you 'gon tell me when you get here, right?"

"Yeah. Bye."

Now why did she have to go and ask about Jeff? I feel stupid enough. There's nothing wrong, really. I'm just a little jealous, that's all. He's so caught up in Benny and the café that we hardly even talk anymore. I've been tryin' to be the understanding, unselfish girlfriend but it's starting to take its toll on me. It's not like he's ignoring me or anything like that. He's just not as attentive. It's like he's starting to take me for granted. He just gives me a little dry ass peck on the lips when he sees me. And if he's busy at the café, he doesn't even stop what he's doing, he'll just wink and blow me a kiss. He hasn't even mentioned the "M" word again! He's probably too scared I'll say yes. Hell, I think he was just emotional when he asked me anyway. He was probably just scared thinking that Benny might die and he didn't want to be all alone. Or he might've been just horny after seeing me in just my panties the night before. Who knows?

I had a dream last night that he told me that he didn't want to see me anymore. That scared the hell outta me. He's been so patient but he's not celibate, *I* am. That could be the reason he's been so distant. Hell, we've been together over six months now and have never gone any further than heavy petting. Maybe he knows exactly what he's doing. He's probably got it all figured out. He's just

COFFEE-COLORED DREAMS

waiting to seduce me one night, knowing damn well I'll probably give in 'cause I miss him so much.

"Men!!" I yelled to the mirror.

When Maria opened the door, I could have screamed. This girl hadn't packed one box, taken one picture off the wall, or done anything remotely close to moving at all. And when I looked at her like she had lost her damn mind, she has the nerve to look at me with that guilt ridden, crooked smile and shrug her shoulders and try and hand me a lit joint. It's 10:30 in the morning and this girl is already high as a kite. Maria can be so triflin' sometimes.

"Black! You haven't done a thing!" I have had just about all I can take from Maria. I yanked the joint out of her hand and hit it hard.

"I know Cee. Don't be mad, girl." She poked me in the side and tried to tickle me.

"Get yo' hands off me, girl. I ain't one'a yo' tired ass men. That shit don't do nothin' for me." I pushed her away and stormed through the house to see if she had done anything at all. Nothing. The girl didn't even have a box! "You haven't so much as packed a dish! And where in the hell are the boxes!" I yelled.

"Damn Cee! Why you comin' up in here yellin' and shit. I don't have to be gone until next month anyway. I just wanted you to come over and help me pack some things. And maybe spend some time together and talk and shit. Hell, I ain't seen yo' black ass in weeks and I didn't know how else to get you here. Excuuuuuse the shit outta' me for missin' my friend!" She threw her hand up and rolled her eyes at me.

I hate it when she does this to me. Just when I think I know her, she does something to surprise me. I had no idea she really valued our friendship that much. I guess I just always see the selfish side of her. But she really does have a good heart and I know she truly loves me just as much as I love her.

I walked up to her and hugged her. "I'm sorry Blackie. I miss you, too."

"No you don't." She pouted.

"Yes I do."

"Really?" She said in her baby voice.

"Really. Now why didn't yo' lazy ass at least get some boxes?"

She laughed. "Come'on girl and sit back here while I put some clothes on. We gonna go to somebody's grocery sto' and get some. And we 'gon flirt with some'a them lil' fine ass boys that be workin' there." She giggled like a schoolgirl, grabbed my hand and practically dragged me to her room.

I really missed Maria. I missed her very much.

Lunchtime...

I've got the serious munchies. We've been packing all morning and haven't stopped to eat a thing. And, from the looks of the refrigerator and the box of pantry things, I won't have much luck finding anything in here to eat.

pamela davis-noland

"Girl, what in the hell do you eat around here? I'm starvin' and all you have to eat is smoked oysters, crackers and a can of whipped cream. Where's the damn food?!" I scolded.

"Now you know damn well I ain't into that cookin' shit, Celia. Why you think I go out on so many dates? And when I don't have a date, I can always count on Simone. That lil' Negro know he can cook. I'm sure 'gon miss him when I move."

"Simone?" I laughed. "I thought that fool's name was Simon?"

"Chile, he changed it to Simone. He tells all the tourists that he's French, girl. Got a fake French accent, too. He be rackin' up on tips at that restaurant."

"I gotta tip for his ass." I said sarcastically.

"Why you always gotta rag on my friend? You just don't like him 'cause he's gay." She spat.

"Black, I don't give'a damn about that man's sexual preference. I don't like him 'cause he's so freakin' obnoxious."

"Girl, ain't he?" She laughed. "I guess that's why I like him so much. He don't even know how obnoxious he is. And speakin' of sexual preference? You give up the drawls yet?"

"Don't even go there, Black." I demanded, "I really don't feel like talkin' about Jeff, okay."

"Aw, come on Cee. I been avoiding the subject hopin' you'd just tell me what's up. Y'all broke up?"

"No."

"Girl, he messin' around?"

"No."

"You messin' around?"

"Hell, no!"

"He tired'a yo' ass, huh?"

I shrugged my shoulders. Hell I'm scared to answer that one. He just might be.

"Is he gay?" Maria asked with just a hint of sarcasm.

"Maria!!" I shouted.

"Well, hell, I'm tryin'ta get yo' ass to talk. It's like pullin' teeth wit'choo."

"If I tell you Maria, you just 'gon think I'm being silly."

"No I won't. Just tell me, girl."

"Well, I think I'm jealous."

"Jealous? Of what? I thought you said he wasn't messin' around?"

"He's not. He just spends more time at the café than he does with me. And I'm getting kinda tired of it. And when we're together, all we talk about is Benny and the café', Big Man and the café, the people who work at the café', the bands …."

"At the café." She interrupted. "Yeah and what else? He want some huh?"

"Black, will you let me finish. Anyway, don't get me wrong, I love Benny

COFFEE-COLORED DREAMS

just as much as he does. And I love everybody else there. It's just that I wanna be first in Jeff's life. You understand? But I can't help but feel like this is as close as we're ever going to be if I don't give it up."

"Yeah. Well that goes without saying…duhh!" Maria rolled her eyes.

"I'm not going to do it Maria." My heart didn't skip a beat this time.

Maria shrugged her shoulders. "Whatever man. That's you. But me? If it was me?" She shook her head and laughed. " Anyway, you gon' have to just talk to him and see where his head at?" She turned to leave and then spun around and added, "Boff of 'em."

"Thanks a lot Maria. Now that really makes me feel a whole lot better." I flopped down on the sofa and placed my head in my hands.

Maria sat next to me and placed her arm around me. "I'm sorry Cee. I am so sorry to tell you that that man does not have a clue as to how you feel. And he won't ever have a clue if you don't say somethin'. I tell you what, I know I date around a lot but that's only because I'm lookin' for that man who wants to understand me. You knowwhatImean?"

"Hell no."

"Well let me put it to ya' this way. Until I find a man who knows what I'm all about, I'm just 'gon keep on dating. He has to know me inside and out. He has to know my innermost thoughts without me ever havin' to say a word. He gotta buy the right gifts, know the kinds of food I like and don't like, know the kind of movies I like, know what does and doesn't turn me on, know the right things to say to me. But above all, he has to want to take the time to find all these things out. I ain't settling for nothin' else. So in the meantime I'm just 'gon have me some fun tryin to find'em."

"That's exactly what I want and exactly what I feel I've found in Jeff. But I think he has cold feet or something. He's been so distant." I pouted like a three-year-old child.

"He might just be busy, Celia. I mean damn the brotha' does have a nine ta' five, too, don't he? What does he do?"

"He's an accountant. Benny's accountant, too. I just found that out recently."

"See, that explains it. He's just doin' his job, girl. It only makes sense for Benny to ask him to run thangs. Hell, from what I hear about all the other people who work there, I think he may have made a good choice." She said sarcastically.

I ignored her little comment. "Yeah. I guess you right. I just miss'em."

"You really not gon' give him none?"

"I don't know, Black. I would love to make love to Jeff. But this time I'm 'gon try and keep my priorities straight. Nothin' or no one is going to stop me from keeping this vow. I know you think I'm crazy but that's the way I feel." I threw my hand up to stop her from saying what I thought she was about to say, "Yeah. You do. You think I'm crazy as hell. But let me tell you something, I have given up my miss kitty to too many men who were not even worthy. I value my

pamela davis-noland

body, Maria. I don't just sleep with a man 'cause it feel good. I have to have some kind of feelings for him. Deep ones. And I would be so disappointed if I gave in and slept with Jeff and nothing ever becomes of us. I love Jeff, Black, and I don't want to make the same mistake I made with all those other niggahs. Besides I really don't think that's even something that's necessary for us. We have a deep almost spiritual love for one another. Not sexual, but sensual. It's hard to explain, Black, but believe me, I am very happy. I just miss being with him that's all. I'm just trippin'." I lied. I am very worried. And to be honest, I don't really know how he feels right now, because we hardly ever talk about us at all. Hopefully, I am just trippin.

"Damn, Celia. Why you gotta make everything so much bigger than it need to be. Just fuck the man. What's so hard about that? What's with all that 'make love' shit? Forget about all that 'what if I lose him' shit. And?! At least you can say he had some good dick or something. Girl, you are so strange."

"Oh kiss my strange ass." I turned and grabbed my purse. "I got the damn munchies. Lets go get something to eat."

Marie just laughed and shook her head. She walked up to me and stared into my eyes just like her crazy Aunt Mauchin does every time we go to visit her.

I backed away and closed my eyes. Sometimes I think Maria knows some of those damn spells she always claim she doesn't believe in. I hate it when she stares at me like that. "Look Maria, I don't expect you to understand me, okay. Just be my friend and help me through this. And as far as the sex thang, that's not even important to me right now. Being with Jeff forever is what I want to accomplish. Not just a simple fling."

She smiled and a twinge of envy hit me when I noticed how beautiful and happy she is. And how she makes life sound so simple. "Maria don't make nothin' complicated," she always says.

I, on the other hand, am the absolute, complete opposite.

She placed her hand on my shoulder and said in her always matter-of-fact way of explaining everything, "Have you ever stopped to think that that is Jeff's thoughts exactly?"

I didn't answer her. My mind was a million miles away… Jeff and I are on the beach in Jamaica making love in the sand.

"Hey. You listenin'?" Maria shook me.

"Yeah", I muttered. "Whatever. Let's go get something to eat."

6:05 p.m.

I ran straight to my answering machine. The light was blinking. I crossed my fingers and pressed the button. I smiled when I heard his voice.

"Hey baby. I'm still here at the Place. Call me when you get home."

There was a slight pause and then another message, "Hey baby. It's 4:30 and I'm at home now. I'm not going back to the Place until 7:15. Call me when you

COFFEE-COLORED DREAMS

get home. Peace."

I picked up the phone and speed-dialed his number. The phone rang four times and there was no answer. I was just about to hang up when he finally picked up.

"Hello. Hello."

"Hey baby, whazzup?" I sang.

"Hey sexy, I've been tryin' to call you. Where've you been all day? Apparently wherever you were, there wasn't a phone 'cause I know if there was one you would have called your man, right?"

I smiled. I love it when he flirts with me in his Barry White voice. "Well as a matter of fact there was one but I didn't want to call you from Maria's 'cause you know how she be trippin'. She would have got pissed off and said somethin' smart. You know her? Besides, I missed her and we had lots of fun. I helped her pack her things. She's moving."

"Oh. That's nice. Hey baby, can I call you back? I was on the other line."

"Oh I'm sorry. I didn't know." All of sudden I began to sweat. Not a good sign.

"Stay right by the phone. Don't move."

"Okay." I said cheerfully.

Now why in the hell did that just bother me the way that it did? All of sudden I pictured myself sitting on my Mudear's back porch getting my hair pressed when her next door neighbor came over and started telling my Mudear about how she knew her husband was cheating on her and that her "sixth sense" told her so. When she left, I asked my Mudear what a "sixth sense" was. She smiled and said, "Chile, soon as you fall in love wit' a man, you 'gon find out soon 'nuff." I had not thought about those words again until this very moment. Then again, it could be Maria's comment about both of Jeff's heads. *Ughhh!* I don't think Jeff is talking to Benny. I don't think I want to know who he's talking to, either.

I suddenly got the urge to straighten up my apartment. Just like I always do when I'm nervous. I choked on a blunt that Maria had given me and started coughing uncontrollably when the phone startled me. The phone rang six times before I could answer it.

"Hello." I gasped.

"Smokin' that shit again, huh? What took you so long to answer the phone?"

Niggah, don't be questioning' me! Who the hell were you talkin' to? "Hey whazzup? I was chokin'. Maria and her damn blunts! She smoke just like a thug. I hate these things." I coughed. "Anyway, what'cha doin'?"

"Chillin'. I'm so tired. I just woke up from a nap." He yawned. "I dreamed about you."

"Oh you did?" I said in my Eartha Kitt voice.

"Yes I did. But get your mind outta the gutter, Eartha. It wasn't that kinda dream. I keep those to myself." He laughed. "I just dreamed that you and Maria were at the Place watching me sing, that's all. I just kept staring at you while I sang and then everybody disappeared and it was just me and you. It was wild. You know how everybody disappeared and it was like I was making everybody leave because I wanted to be alone with you."

"And then what?"

"The phone rang and woke me up."

And who the hell was it? "Oh."

It was a friend from back home."

"Jeff, you didn't have to tell me that." I lied.

"Oh I know. I was just making conversation. So are you comin' tonight?"

Well wasn't that the easy way out. Blurt it out – Change the subject.

"Hey. You there?"

"Yeah. Yeah, I'll probably pop in for a little while if I'm not too tired. We packed all day. And I'm expecting a call from Brianna. We have to discuss revisions."

"Well just call me on my cell after you talk to Brianna. So why is Maria moving? She got busted with somebody else's man again?" He laughed.

"Jeff I should have never told you that story. Why you always gotta rag on my friend?" I laughed.

"'Cause baby, she has so much material to work with. And you know damn well your friend ain't nuttin' but a ho."

"Jeff!" I laughed. I knew he felt that way about Maria but I had never actually heard him say it.

"You know I'm tellin' the truth."

"Oh you so silly. Hey, if I don't show up tonight, I'll still see you tomorrow okay. I'm still going to help you paint."

"Alright. But if you're too tired tomorrow don't worry about it, okay? I didn't know you were going to have to help Maria today. I can handle it. Besides, I don't plan on staying very long anyway."

"Well, I still want to see you. It's not like we've been spending very much time together." I hoped he didn't hear me pout.

"I miss you too, baby. See? It's not hard to say. Just say it. I miss you Jeff. Why you always tryin' to be so hard?"

"I miss you, baby." I replied. *If you only knew how much I miss you.*

"Hey, look, I better get goin'. If I don't see you tonight, I'll see you tomorrow. I love you. Bye sexy." He hung up.

I plopped down on the sofa, hit the still-lit blunt as hard as I could without turning blue and sighed with a smile. "I miss you so much, Jeff." I said to the phone.

THE "EX" FACTOR

Jeffrey Jackson

I shouldn't have told Laura about Celia. Well at least not until we were already engaged and had set a date. I wish I was even able to tell her that we had discussed marriage. And I know damn well I should have said, *"We* are in love," instead of "I'm in love with her." That sounds more like an infatuation. An infatuation - the very same word Laura used when I told her that I loved Lettie Smalls.

"Oh Jeff," she said, "you do not love Lettie Smalls. You're just like your grandfather that's all. Now you know we heard all the stories about Papa Jackson and his infatuation with dark skinned women. And those same black women kept his ass in lots of trouble didn't they? But did he marry one of them? Hell no. He just liked sleeping with them."

But what I'm feeling for Celia DuBois is by far an infatuation and I'm almost positive that the feeling is mutual. Today I intend to find out. I've avoided the subject long enough. The least she can do is give a brotha' some insight. She's going to let me know today if in fact she's feelin' me the same way and if so, why hasn't she given me an answer.

I want to know if she lies awake at night and fantasizes about what our home will look like, how many rooms, two stories or one. I want to know if she ever stares at the pictures of us together and tries to imagine what our kids are going to look like. I want to know if she will be Mrs. Jeffrey Jackson and I want to know today. I've had enough of this game we playin'.

Celia's afraid. That much I do know. She's afraid to let anyone get that close to her again. I know how she feels though. Most of my life I've been afraid to let anyone get close to *me*. But she already has. She's penetrated a part of my heart that I swore I wasn't ever going to share with another human being after my pops died. If only I could make her see that it's more than physical what I'm feelin' for her. I mean I know the lovemaking will be off the chain but it's not top priority right now. And that is some scary-ass shit!

I've been beating my head against the wall trying to figure out what the hell Laura wants to talk about. I can't, nor do I even want to imagine. She still didn't give me any hints when she called me back yesterday. She just said she was still thinking about coming here and that she'd let me know. I guess she thinks I'm stupid. I know why she wants to come here. She wants to see Celia for herself. But I'm going to solve that. When she calls again, I'll just tell her that I've already taken some time off and I'll go there.

I'm not ready for Laura to meet Celia just yet. Not until I'm absolutely sure about us.

Celia DuBois

On the way to Benny's Place, I thought of several different ways to approach Jeff about the proposal we never talk about. The same proposal that I haven't even answered yet. I want to say something witty and cute and definitely try and not sound desperate. I looked in the rear view mirror and pretended that I was talking to Jeff, "So have you changed your mind about making me a part of your family?" Hell naw, that sounds stupid. I think I better just play it by ear.

I was relieved when I pulled up and his was the only car. Alone at last. He placed his paintbrush on the newspaper surrounding his feet and took long strides toward me, grinnin' from ear to ear. He picked me up, swung me around and then kissed me full in the mouth with his tongue searching mine hungrily. And all this before he even said hello.

"You're all alone." I panted.

"Not anymore." He smiled.

I felt faint. "So how does that make you feel?" I asked.

"Like the luckiest man on earth." He smiled and all my negative thoughts faded away.

"Ooh, flattery. One of my biggest weaknesses."

"Have I told you lately how beautiful you are? Have I told you how the sun rises when you walk in the room and how it sets whenever you leave? Have I told you....."

"Have I ever told you that you're fulla shit?" I laughed.

He kissed me again. "I sure miss that foul mouth."

"I really miss you too, Jeff. I love you." *There I said it. I miss you and I love your ass to death.*

"I know." He hugged me and kissed the top of my head. "I'm sorry I've been so busy. But don't think that one minute went by and I wasn't thinking about you. I've been wanting to spend time with you and chill like we used to. I want to talk, you know. I've just been so busy, man. But you know I wasn't tryin' to ignore you baby. Okay?"

"So you've been wanting to talk to me about something?" *Hell, why beat around the bush?*

"Yeah, I do. Let's go sit down. You want some tea?"

"Yeah. I'm sweating."

COFFEE-COLORED DREAMS

"You are? It's pretty cool in here to me."

"Yeah, but you don't have a sixth sense." I mumbled.

"What?" He yelled from across the room.

"Nothin' honey."

Now I know I'm not usually very easily shocked, but nothing on God's green earth could have prepared me for the words that came out of Jeff's mouth when he returned from the kitchen, iced tea in hand.

"I might have to go back home to take care of something. I'll only be gone for about a week, though. I'm not really certain just yet. I'll find out tomorrow."

What?! "Is that what the phone call was about?" I tried to stay as calm and cool as I could. I did not want him to see me act a fool.

"Yeah. But nothing's definite yet. I'll let you know for sure when I find out tomorrow, okay?"

"Okay. I guess we better get started then, huh?" Now in my past life, which was two men ago, I would have gone off! *What in the hell do you mean, you might have to go home for a week? For what?! What kind of business? And was I invited? Hell no! And still no answers about the mystery caller? Now let me get this shit straight: First - you come at me with a lame-ass-excuse-of-a proposal. Second - you tell me not to answer you. Third - you stay so busy all the time that you have not had time to talk to me about anything, much less about the proposal. And now all of a sudden you have to leave town?! What?! Is this the kind of shit I'm gonna have to go through if I don't give up the drawls. "You ain't givin' it to me, so I have to get it somewhere," Is that your attitude? And I'm not supposed to say shit, 'cause if I was really worried about that I would give you some? Oh hell no. I didn't even think about this. Well, at least not with you, Jeff. Anybody but my Jeff.*

I tried to shrug it off as well as I could and decided to just enjoy the moment because I didn't know how many more we were going to have now that I see him in a different light. I don't know. My mind is telling me to run like hell but my heart is saying, just wait. So in the meantime, I'm just going to enjoy him. And so far I'm having the time of my life...

He stood behind me and guided my hand and showed me how to properly stroke the brush while he kissed my neck. Then he'd stick his tongue in my ear until I'd double over with laughter. We did more hugging, kissing and grinding than painting and there was more paint on us than there was on the wall. The temptation to pull off the color-splattered clothes was getting unbearable. He is driving me crazy and he knows it.

He picked me up and propped me up on the bar while he stood between my legs. We were kissing when she walked in. I blinked twice when I saw her. I remembered her from the pictures at Jeff's mom's house. Jeff saw the look on my face and quickly turned around but the funny thing is; he didn't seem to be shocked at all.

She is gorgeous. She looks like she comes from old money, angelically dressed in a crispy, snow-white sleeveless shirt and matching snow-white Capri pants, ankle-strapped, white stiletto sandals and incredibly expensive, uniquely designed sterling silver jewelry with matching belt. Her ensemble probably costs more than my mother has spent on her entire wardrobe.

Her hair is the color of wet sand, long and flowing past her shoulders, all one length, straight as a board and it's hers - not a weave. Her eyes are some funny greenish-brown color and she has a pointy nose. The only thing about her that resembled a "sista" in any way, are her full lips, high cheekbones and protruding ass. Other than that, she could probably "pass."

All of a sudden all of my childhood insecurities I once had came rushing back to haunt me. I began to hear the voices of those mean kids – *"blacky, "tar baby", "mud", "black thang", "monkey", "ol' black bull", "midnight", "night-time", "darky"*... I used to have to hold my head up high when I walked down the halls of Our Lady of Immaculate Conception. I had to be a militant. It was the only way I'd survive. Never let them see you cry; that was my motto. And boy were there times when I had to run and hide for fear of being seen. Sort of like now.

The fact that Jeff didn't look surprised was more than a little devastating. When I saw the look on his face and he gave her the same beautiful smile that he gives me, I nearly jumped off of that bar and scratched her eyes out. But instead, I sat there and watched the man of my dreams walk up to another woman and kiss her on the cheek. My entire world was falling apart around me.

If that niggah introduces me as his good friend somebody 'gon die. And it ain't 'gon be me!

He ushered her over to me. "Baby, this is Laura. My ex-wife."

Baby. That's a good start. Now who am I?

"Laura, this is Celia."

Celia? Is that all?! "Hi." I could barely get the word out.

She extended her hand to me. "Hi Celia. It's nice to finally meet you. I've heard so much about you."

Oh shit! A fake bitch. "It's nice meeting you too."

I looked over at Jeff who all of sudden began to look guilty to me. I hoped that it was just my imagination. Is this the reason he might be going back to Chicago? Is he going back with her?

"I thought you were going to call tomorrow and let me know what your plans were?" Jeff asked Laura.

"Yes, I know. But there was a sudden change in plans. I called the airport and there was a flight leaving for New Orleans last night so I came. I tried to call you this morning but you were already gone. I hope you don't mind me popping up like this."

What?! Oh hell no.

"So how did you find me?" Jeff asked.

"Well you talk about Benny's so much and you mentioned having to paint

COFFEE-COLORED DREAMS

today, so I just took a cab straight here and here you are." She extended her arm like Vanna White and smiled even bigger. And then she placed her hand on her heart and added, "I'm sorry if I interrupted."

Yeah I bet you are. Jeff, you have some serious explaining to do. I sat there like a fool watching them go back and forth as if I was watching a tennis match.

"Naw, it's cool. I was just telling Celia that I thought I was going to have to go home for a little while but I wasn't sure." He looked at me with pleading eyes, begging me to give him a chance to explain.

I rolled my eyes at him. "So is this your first time in Naawlins?" I asked with my southern accent. Jeff knew I was being facetious.

"No, I've been here on several occasions. Mainly for business and some pleasure." She smiled at Jeff.

Ooh you Bitch! "Jeff says you're a buyer."

"Yes, I am. And you're a schoolteacher?"

"I'm a writer who teaches creative writing to gifted students." I didn't mean to sound so defensive but I had a flashback.

"A writer?" She nodded her approval. "That's wonderful. What do you write?"

"Celia has a novel coming out soon." Jeff intercepted. As if I needed him to.

"Well congratulations Celia." She sang.

Oh give it a rest, Barbie. "Thanks. So are you here on business now?"

"Well, sort of."

Jeff intercepted again. "So how about I go and get you a glass of iced tea? You want another glass too, Celia?"

"Yeah. Why don't I come and help you." If he thinks he's going to leave me alone with Malibu Barbie, he's got another think coming. I'm standing here covered in paint from head to toe with old torn up jeans on and looking tacky as hell. Is he crazy? I'm glad I kept my makeup on after church. At least I don't feel like too much of an ugly duckling.

As soon as we walked into the kitchen he started explaining. "Baby, I'm sorry. This was not the way you were supposed to find out about me going to Chicago. I wanted to wait for her phone call first. I should have known better. That's the way Laura's always been. Spontaneous. I wasn't even surprised when I saw her. But I should've explained it to you. I just didn't want to get you all upset before I knew what was going on. Laura called and said that she had something very important to talk to me about and she wouldn't tell me over the phone. I was worried because Laura has never been what you might call melodramatic. So I knew whatever it was, it must have been very important to ask me to come home. She said if I couldn't go there, she might come here but nothing was definite. I wanted to talk to you about it but first I had to find out the exact plan. You knowwhatImean? I'm sorry baby."

I folded my arms and glared at him. "So what does she want, Jeff?"

pamela davis-noland

"I don't know."

"You don't have a clue?"

"Believe me baby. I don't. I'm just as puzzled as you. You have no idea how puzzled. But baby, when I find out, you'll be the first to know."

I wanted so badly to believe him. He has never lied to me before. But there is a first time for everything. *Damn, I need a joint!* "Well, I think I'll just leave you two alone to discuss what obviously is so damn important. Call me later. I'll be home."

"Wait, baby. You don't have to leave. I can talk to her later. We haven't been alone in weeks. I miss you."

"I miss you too. But I'd rather you two talk here and not at your apartment. Does she know where you live or is she going to have to sniff you out again?"

"She knows my address but she's never been to my house."

"And what else does she know? Does she know that I'm your woman and not just Celia?" That jumped out of my mouth faster than I could stop it.

Jeff hugged me and whispered in my ear, "She knows that I'm in love with you and that I'm happier than I've ever been."

I closed my eyes and breathed in every word. It was music to my soul. "I'll leave you two alone. Call me when she's gone."

"When am I going to be able to spend time with you without anybody wanting something from me? We haven't been alone in so long, man."

I walked up to him and gave him the wettest, sloppiest, nastiest kiss I could and whispered in his ear, "It's a good thing," winked and walked out the back door and left.

I cried all the way home.

11:00 p.m....

I have still not heard from Jeff. I must be out of my mind for leaving him with that woman with a hard-on! Knowing damn well men think with their smallest head. I'm gonna give his ass thirty more minutes and then I'm gonna call him and leave a nasty message on the machine. Out of habit, I picked up the phone and called Maria. Her answering machine picked up and I listened to her speaking over Adina Howard in the background singing "T-shirt and My Panties On."

"Hey you, this is me. Whassup? Kinda busy at the moment (seductive laugh) leave me a sweet message." Beep.

Maria is so nasty. "Hey girl. Just callin'. Talk to you la..."

"Hey chick." She picked up the phone and it screeched in my ear.

"Hey Black, you busy? I was just about to hang up."

"Naw, I wuz just walkin' in. Whassup?"

"Girl, you got time to talk?"

"Girl puuhleez! Now when haven't I had time to talk? Hold on let me sit my ass down. Whew! Alright shoot. Whassup?"

COFFEE-COLORED DREAMS

"Black, you are not going to believe what happened to me today." I sighed and my eyes watered.

"What, girl? You alright?"

"Oh fine. Just dandy." I said sarcastically.

"Girl, you betta start talkin'. What the hell is wrong wit'choo?"

"I met Laura."

Silence.

"So who the fuck is Laura?!" She yelled.

"Laura is Jeff's ex."

"Ex what?"

"Wife."

"Girl. Where you met her?!" Maria shouted.

"Jeff and I were at Benny's painting when she just walked in."

"What? She just walked in? What the hell you mean she just walked in? Like how in the hell did she know where to find him? Apparently this was not her first time. That motherfucka' two timin' you Celia? I knew it. I knew that pretty motherfucka' wouldn't no good. I told you girl."

"Bitch, I know *you* trippin'! Out of all them sorry ass niggahs you call boyfriends who ended up breakin' your heart, how many times have I said I told you so? Huh? None. Not one. You got way too much nerve Maria. And to answer your question. No. He is not fuckin' her. She still lives in Chicago."

"Well what is she doin' here?"

"I don't know yet."

"Girl, what she look like?"

"Hmmm, let's see, how can I describe her? How about perfect!"

"Whaaatt! She pretty girl?"

"Like Miss fuckin' America. Perfect size 6, 'bout 5'7, long flowing hair that she didn't have to buy, cat eyes, high yellow. You know, the kind in all the rap videos yo' ass like to watch so much."

"Vanessa Williams, huh? Well so fuckin' what! He's with you now, not her. You are definitely a beautiful sista, so don't even start trippin'. Them lil' kids that used to tease us didn't know any betta, girl. But you know damn well you are pleased when you look into a mirror. Besides girl, you know we're in this season." She laughed.

"Yeah." My mind was a million miles away.

"So what she want?" Maria asked.

"I told you. I have no idea. All I know is Jeff had just told me about 4 hours earlier that he was going to Chicago for about a week. Then if that wasn't bad enough, *Miss Thang* walks her ass in Benny's lookin' like a damn Maybelline commercial."

"Hold up! He just told you he was going to Chicago? Today?"

"Yeah."

"What the hell for?"

pamela davis-noland

"Well, all he told me was that she called him and said that she needed to talk to him. She said she might be taking some days off and she wanted him to go there. Nothing was definite though. He was waiting for her to call back before he told me about it."

"That was his story? Ha!"

"Why you say it like that?" I snarled.

"Girl, how you know that she wasn't suppose to come here all along. He pro'bly told you that so that he could spend time with her and you'd think he was out of town. You bought that shit?"

Why in the hell did I call Maria? I don't need her confirming all of my fears. I have enough shit on my mind as it is. "Well Maria, all I know is that Jeff has never lied to me so far. I just have to trust him. But I don't trust that ex-wife of his at all. I have a feelin' that conniving' lil' witch knew exactly what she was doing. Poppin' up the way she did, talkin' about, 'Sorry if I interrupted anything,' Yeah, right."

"It ain't always the woman's fault."

"I know Black. But he called me "baby" right in front of her and begged me not to leave."

"You left?!" She yelled.

"Girl, stop yellin' in my ear! Yeah I left!"

"You mean'ta tell me you left that man alone with somebody he done slept with? When you know damn well you ain't givin' up *no* drawls? That's it. You done loss yo' mind." She laughed.

"I trust him Maria. I have never trusted anyone as much as I do him. Don't ask me why. Like I told you before, there is something so deep with us that sex comes second. I know that that is more than your sick little one track mind can handle, but it's the truth." I spat.

"Chile, I hope for your sake that that line of bullshit that just came outta your mouf is true." She giggled.

"Fuck you Black."

"Aww, come on girl. You know I'm just fuckin' wit'choo. Anyway, what did that bitch want?"

"I don't know. I haven't talked to him yet."

"What?! What time did you leave them alone?"

"About five, I guess."

"Uh, it's 11:30, Cee."

"I'm well aware of the time Maria. I'm givin' him fifteen more minutes and I'm calling him."

"Fifteen more minutes? You shoulda called his ass five hours ago. You always talkin' 'bout not losing him, but I'll be damn if you ain't 'gon hand him over on a silver platter. You can keep trustin' him if you want to, but you betta make that Niggah give you some answers."

"Yeah, I will. Hey, look, I gotta go. I'll call you tomorrow."

COFFEE-COLORED DREAMS

"You can call me back tonight if you want to."

"Okay bye."

I hung up the phone and took a deep breath. I counted to ten and picked up the phone again and dialed Jeff's number. The phone rang three times. No answer. Five more times. Still no answer. I slammed the phone on its hook and went to bed. I had about all I could handle for one day.

Jeffrey Jackson

"No." That was my first, last and only reply.

Maaan...Laura never ceases to amaze me. Here we are well into our thirties now, have been married, are now divorced and live in two different cities and she's still determined to be involved in my life. Funny thing is; I don't know if she's trippin' because she loves me or she's just used to pulling my strings. She's gonna have to let it die whatever it is. And she knows damn well it would never work anyway. Hell we tried didn't we?

We left the Place about fifteen minutes after Celia did. I felt funny being there with her. It felt like Laura was trespassing. So against Celia's wishes I asked her to ride back with me to my crib so that I could shower and change clothes. And then we'd come back to the Quarters and grab a bite to eat.

I was surprised that Laura actually behaved herself. Maybe because she was pissed, seeing Celia and I all up on one another the way she did. Who knows? Who cares? I was just glad she didn't try anything because believe me, she's not above it.

I parked my car on Canal Street and Laura and I walked down Bourbon all the way to Dumaine. I don't care how many times I do it; I still enjoy walking through the Quarters at night, checking out all the tourists, mimes and street musicians. And it seems to be what Laura likes to do most too. Although I don't appreciate her showin' up the way that she did, I had to admit that I was happy to see her. We grabbed the first horse and buggy to Jackson Square and then back to St. Peter. Laura wanted to grab a bite to eat at Pat O'Briens. I didn't have much of an appetite so I nibbled on fried crawfish and watched her eat a fat shrimp poboy and drain two Hurricanes like a pro. And she kept talkin' about something but I couldn't figure it out. After about an hour I finally asked her to stop beating around the bush. "Alright Laura, come on. You jumped on the midnight plane to Louisiana to say what? Talk to me."

She proceeded to make more small talk about her life and how lonely she had been the last past year or so and how she yearns for someone to share it with and blah, blah, blah….

I was thinking, *"Oh shit, I hope she's not proposing. Again! Why does she always do this shit when I meet someone I really care about?"* But the question that came out of her mouth shocked me even though I thought she could never

pamela davis-noland

do it.

"Jeff, I've decided that I want to be a mother. Will you be the father of my child?"

And my reply was "No." I didn't blink, flinch or clear my throat. I didn't put my finger to my mouth, look up at the ceiling and say, "hmmm." I didn't even take a breath, I just said, "No."

She sat there and stared at me like I wasn't even speaking English. And then that other vindictive, mean side of her kicked in. She looked like she wanted to scratch my eyes out. "You promised Mama Ella. You promised Mama Ella that you wouldn't be like your grandfather and try and bring no nappy head children in the family. *We* promised her before she died that *we* were going to have a baby one day Jeff!" She clinched her teeth with every word.

"No." I stood my ground.

"What the hell is it with you, Jeff?" She asked.

I shrugged my shoulders and got as close to her face as I could and looked her in the eyes. "Whatever it is, I'm no longer ashamed of it." I announced.

We sat there for twenty minutes in total silence. I finally stood up, placed money on the table and we left. I didn't say two words to her on the walk to The Bienville House, the hotel where Laura was staying. There really wasn't much to say besides no. I can't believe that woman still thinks she can bring up Mama Ella's name and think I'm gonna shiver. I walked her to the front doors of the hotel, kissed her on the cheek and said goodnight.

I can't believe Laura still manages to stay one up on me. It pisses me off how she jumped on that plane without calling first. I should have known she had an ulterior motive for asking me about my every move for the next two days. And then she pops up. I wasn't even surprised really. She was just being true to her nature, man.

I wanted to call Celia as soon as I left the restaurant but I had to clear my head, first. Decide exactly how I'm going to explain all of this to her because I know she's going to have a thousand questions for a brotha. *Damn!*

Celia DuBois

12:20 a.m.

I jumped so high when the phone rang, I damn near gave myself whiplash. I looked over at the clock and picked up the phone on the fourth ring.

"Hi." I grunted.

"I'm sorry to call so late."

Silence.

"We ended up talking more than I anticipated."

Silence.

COFFEE-COLORED DREAMS

"You're just getting back from Benny's?" I finally asked.

"No. I came home to shower and change right after you left. Laura and I had dinner and then I went to the Riverwalk to hang out for a minute. I just walked in about twenty minutes ago."

"You took her to your apartment?"

"Yeah, but only so I could shower and change. Look baby, I know you're upset. And I don't blame you at all, man. I had no idea Laura was going to pop up like this. I mean she's done some shit like this before but you gotta believe me, if I would have known she was in town I would have told you."

"Look, I already heard all about Miss Spontaneous okay. What the hell did she want?"

"To talk to me about something that she's going through. Something very personal. Baby, first of all, I want you to understand something. Although Laura and I are no longer married, she's still very much a part of my family and has been for quite some time now so we do keep in touch. She's my friend baby. Always has been. I'm there for her when she needs to talk and she would do the same for me. And that's it. Can you accept that?"

"Do I have a damn choice?"

"That's the wrong attitude, baby. You don't trust me?"

"It's not you I'm worried about."

"Well you don't have to worry about Laura either. I can handle her. Anyway, it's getting late baby. Meet me tomorrow at 4:30 at Benny's. We can talk all about it then. Get some sleep, baby. I love you."

"Do you?"

"More than you know, apparently. Good night." He hung up.

Next day...

I could not concentrate today at all. I kept thinking about the erotic dream I had about Jeff last night. I have only had about one or two wet dreams in my entire life, but this one was slammin'. Brotha' had it goin' on. When I woke up, every inch of my body was soaking wet including Miss Kitty. I had to pray for strength.

Driving to the French Quarters during rush hour traffic is horrific. I thought I was doing good by just avoiding Canal, but I ended up stuck behind a huge tourist bus who was picking up and dropping off a thousand lil' bald head men all dressed in different shades of blue. When I finally maneuvered my way around them, I ended up on Chartreuse where things looked even more bleak; college students on vacation drunker than Scooter Brown. All of them had huge cups in their hands and more Mardi Gras beads than their scrawny lil' necks could handle. I could just scream. I couldn't get to Benny's fast enough. Jeff has some more explaining to do and I can't wait a minute longer to hear what he has to say.

I was surprised when I walked in the café and saw Jeff sitting at the piano singing. I had a vision of the first time I had stepped foot in here and saw Benny playing the saxophone.

He stopped singing when he saw me. "Hey baby, come here." He said.

I walked as far as the front of the dais and stopped.

"I mean here." He patted his knee.

"Jeff, isn't there something we have to talk about?" I placed my backpack on the nearest table and folded my arms, hoping he would get the hint that I was not here to play with his ass.

"Yes. But does that mean I can't have a kiss first?"

Why men always gotta try a woman's patience? Here I've spent the entire day playing scenario after scenario over in my mind trying to figure out what the hell is going on and he wanna just act like this is no big deal.

I stared at him like he had just loss his mind.

"Okay, okay. Here have a seat. I'll explain the whole thing."

Just as I sat down, Big Man walked in from the kitchen. "You need me to do some'n else, Jeff'ry?" He spoke in his usual dry manner.

"Naw. I can't think of anything. You going over to Benny's house?"

He nodded yes as he walked out the doors.

"Okay. Tell Benny I'll see him later." Jeff yelled out.

We watched how the people parted like the Red Sea as Big Man made his way through the crowded sidewalk. When he was no longer in sight, I turned and glared at Jeff, my eyes demanding him to start talking.

"Celia, before I tell you. You have to promise me that you'll hear me all the way out. *Before* you get upset. Okay?"

As soon as he said those words, my Mudear's voice started ringing in my ear, *"Chile, soon as you fall in love wit' a man, you 'gon find out soon 'nuff."* My sixth sense kicked in and I began to sweat and my bottom lip quivered. "Okay, I promise." I whispered.

"Celia, you remember me telling you that Laura and I grew up together and that our families have always been very close, right?"

"Yes." My heart was beating ninety miles per hour.

"Well let me explain it like this. I had this crazy ass grandmother right. We, well just about everyone who knew her, called her Mama Ella. Anyway Mama Ella ran everything and everybody. Do you remember me telling you the story about how everyone said that Laura and I was going to get married one day? Well, it was Mama Ella who started that rumor as soon as Laura was born I think. Anyway because no one ever doubted her words, she was a self-proclaimed prophet, that shit stuck with us." He took a deep breath. "And sometimes it seems like Mama Ella still has her hand in my life."

"Jeff. Are you going to get to the point?"

"Yeah. Look Laura is going through some issues right now and I'm the only one she can really talk to and she's made this big decision and she wanted to talk it over with me."

COFFEE-COLORED DREAMS

"So what's the big decision?" I could just scream. *Why is he torturing me like this, Lord?*

Jeff lowered his head and mumbled, "She, uh, wants to have a baby."

"She wants to have a baby?!"

"Yes."

"She jumped on the first plane heading for New Orleans to tell you that she wants to have a baby? Oh. Okay." I paused, waiting for his next bit of news. "And?!"

"She wants me to be the father." He muttered.

"What did you say, Jeff?" My head is pounding.

"She wants me to be the father." He repeated.

"What?!" I yelled so loud, I scared myself. "You were married to her for six years and now she decides she wants to have your child?!" My lips quivered uncontrollably.

I stood up, grabbed my purse and headed for the door. Jeff grabbed my arm and I pulled away.

"Get your hands off'a me, Jeff!" I shouted. "Miss Beauty Queen just waltzes her ass on an airplane, comes to New Orleans, without letting you know mind you, tells you that she wants to have your baby and you don't want me to get upset?! Well, too late. I was upset when the bitch walked in the door." I turned and stormed away and he grabbed me again.

"Celia, just let me explain. Please." He begged.

I pulled away again and stared at him as if daring him to touch me again. He got the message. I turned and walked out the door praying that the tears, that had suddenly blinded my vision, would not fall.

As soon as I turned the doorknob to my apartment, the tears flowed. The room was spinning and my head was light as a feather.

I walked into the bathroom and stared at my reflection. "What am I doing wrong?" I asked the woman in the mirror. She didn't answer.

I ran back to the living room, grabbed my keys and my purse. I hopped the streetcar to St. Charles Avenue to talk to my friend and mentor, Benny. I needed to talk to him about all of this and fast.

NOT SO RUDE AWAKENINGS

Celia DuBois

"These mansions stand in the center of large grounds and rise, garlanded with roses out of the midst of swelling masses of shining green foliage and many-colored blossoms. No houses could well be in better harmony with their surroundings, or more pleasing to the eye."

Mark Twain

Mr. Twain was speaking of the Garden District. And he couldn't have been more accurate in his well-versed description. The Garden District is so beautiful. And even more so at this time of year when every flower has bloomed to its full potential. I've always adored the architecture and brilliant tapestry of the homes here and I plan on moving somewhere on Magazine Street or Louisiana Street or Jackson Street or some street in between as soon as the deal is done and they hand me my advance check for my book. *If the Lord says the same.* And I'm planting a garden of my own in this beautifully rich, garden-ready dirt.

    I decided to take a long walk and think about things and before I knew it, I was sitting on the very first seat of the streetcar headed here. I've made quite a few decisions about my life walking along these streets. I remember praying about my decision to become a nun while standing in front of the George Washington Cable house. And thanking the Lord that I was wrong in the very same spot a month or so later. I remember visiting the Henry Sullivan Buckner House the day before I made the vow to be celibate and here I am again. Only this time I'm not here to change my mind like I did about being a nun. Today I stand here to see if I could get that same feeling back. That unbreakable feeling of self-assuredness that I had that day that enabled me to make such a huge decision. Lately I've been feeling a little weak.

    I was digging in my backpack looking for my shades when I bumped into a priest. He was on a tour with about six or seven young boys all dressed in white buttoned-down shirts, black chinos and shiny black shoes. He tipped his head to me and announced a solemn, *"Bon jour."* I smiled and quickly crossed the street.

COFFEE-COLORED DREAMS

I was also walking along somewhere in the Garden District when I made the decision to no longer practice Catholicism. That pious look on that priest's face reminded of the lecture I got from Monsignor John Paul when I confessed to him that I had been thinking about joining a full gospel church. The Monsignor wasn't too pleased with me that day and he almost lost his "religion." I left the church in tears but I stood my ground and followed my heart.

There are two main reasons I left the Catholic Church and number one on my list is Confession. I never understood the concept of Confession when all I ever heard from all of the nuns and priest was God is everywhere. So I figure if God is everywhere, he knows what I'm doing so I'm sure it's not going to be a shock to him when he "finds out" what I've been doing. I can hardly believe that the "formula" (two Hail Mary's, three Our Father's and one Act of Contrition) is supposed to keep me from Hell's gate. I remember when I was in the third or fourth grade; I would write elaborate stories of a mischievous little girl and recite them to the priest behind the black screen where all I could see was his hands making the sign of the cross. I would cross my fingers to ward off any bad luck as I confessed to the priest a made up sin or two. But my biggest confession was one I never told *him*, "Lord please forgive me for lying to Father John. I really ain't done nothin' wrong since *last* Saturday." I confessed *that one* to God a lot. I knew he could hear me. They were sadly misinformed.

I guess number two on my list would be because of the docile reverence that was placed on a man to the point where we trust him with our darkest secrets. That never set right with me. That among other things (mainly boredom) made me seek other alternatives for worshipping God. I now belong to Abundant Christian Chapel. And when asked what my religion is my reply is none.

The dictionary says that religion is *any* organized system that serves God *or* the supernatural. For some strange reason, after I read that, I didn't quite feel right inside about the way I served God. And I for damn sure didn't like to be placed in the same category with people that have anything to do with the supernatural. And many Catholics do. Take Maria's Aunt Mauchin for instance. That woman is a devout Catholic who runs around with rosary beads in one pocket and chicken bones and feathers in the other one. Aunt Mauchin is known for whipping' them rosary beads out at any given moment and begin mumbling' the rosary. Or sometimes she'll just take them out and kiss Jesus' feet, make the sign of the cross and put them back in her purse. Maria says she does this whenever she feels a bad spirit. Aunt Mauchin is a stone trip. And rumor has it that she moonlights as a voodoo priestess.

I was already church hoppin' and tiptoeing around leaving the church altogether when sixteen year old Dion Keyes, one of my students who had a very bright future, was found dead in his bedroom. He committed suicide because a secret that he had kept hidden for years was about to be revealed and he was too ashamed to face it. Monsignor Paul Delahoussye was found guilty on eight counts of child molestation and all eight were alter boys. Dion was one of them.

pamela davis-noland

He strangled himself with a belt in his closet. Two days after his funeral, I came here to deal with my anger and my decision to join the full gospel church that I so enjoyed.

After crossing the street and turning right, I could no longer see the priest or the boys so I pushed the memories into the back of my mind so that I could concentrate on why I came here today. I came today to pray for strength and to thank God for the journey he's taken me through and for the one ahead. The journey I'm about to begin as an up and coming, black, female novelist.

Brianna called last night to tell me that my book is all the rave at two publishing houses that have made very substantial offers. Brianna also informed me to celebrate because I have arrived. Both publishers want me to sign multiple book deals. Brianna is still in negotiations. She wants to feel both of them out first to make sure I get a good editor who really loves my work.

I was ecstatic after the phone call. I screamed and yelled and called everybody to tell them the good news and then Maria and I went to Margaritaville Café and danced the night away. We had so much fun. But when I woke up this morning I realized that something, or should I say someone, was missing.

I haven't talked to Jeff in over a month now. He called me later that night after I left him at Benny's and we had a terrible argument. He told me that I was stubborn and bullheaded and he was tired of my temper tantrums. I told him to kiss my bull-headed ass and he wouldn't have to ever deal with my temper tantrums and me ever again. He slammed the phone down in my ear and when I tried to call him back to cuss him out and tell him exactly what I thought of him and his bitch of an ex-wife, he wouldn't answer. He hasn't tried to call me back since but that's cool. To be honest, I haven't even really been too worried about it. I've been at peace with the whole thing really. I think it has a lot to do with the fact that we have no soul ties. We've never slept together so at least I didn't give up my body in vain. That alone helped me to cope those first two weeks. But now I can't seem to get him off of my mind. I miss him so much. Deep down inside I feel like we'll eventually work things out. I really don't believe Jeff is stupid enough to get that woman pregnant, but I just don't like the way he acts around her. I still think he loves her. But I know he loves me too. I mean he did ask me to marry him, as lame of a proposal as it was. And he stayed with me even after I wouldn't give it up. But I should have known that as soon as the opportunity would present itself, he'd turn out to be just like all the rest. Oh he was lovin' me and shit, but as soon as some other chick comes along and offers him something that he's not getting from me (And definitely not getting after this shit.) off he goes. And he hasn't even tried to call me. *Ugh!*

I went to see Benny about a week ago and I was hoping to at least run into him but he wasn't there. I had gone by to ask Benny for some advice and oddly enough, he didn't have any. All he said was that he'd pray for me.

"What exactly are you going to pray for Benny? Do you think I can't live without Jeff?" I asked.

COFFEE-COLORED DREAMS

"No Doll." He said. "I don't think you cain't live wit'out Jeff." He stood and patted my hand. "I *know*s you won't."

So that's been on my mind ever since, although I'm tryin' real hard not to get my hopes up.

Well, at least I'm not sweatin' or regrettin' the relationship Jeff and I had. I just feel as though I've just awakened from a wonderful dream. That's all.

Jeffrey Jackson

I just completed my letter of resignation. Man, that was the hardest thing I ever had to write in my life. Not that I had a hard time finding the right words, I just couldn't believe that I was actually writing it. I knew this day would eventually come but I was still a little unsure of myself. Every time I'd start to write it, I'd think about my pops and how I wish he was here to give me some advice. You know, let me know if it's a good idea to quit such a secure job to start my own business with only three clients to start with. And hell, one of them is Benny. I don't even charge Benny.

I've been planning to do this for years but I just kept putting it off. Mainly because I didn't think I could afford to do it and pay bills too. But now that I'm living here and my expenses have been practically cut in half, I feel like I can do it. Hell, now that I've moved here away from everybody and their opinions, I feel like I can do anything I set my mind to. It's hard for a brotha to start his own business, I don't care how good he is at what he does. I'm an excellent accountant. I know this. And the big wigs at Rubenstein, Crandle & Associates know it too. And they are going to shit a brick when they find out that I'll be leaving them in two weeks to start my own business.

Benny suggested that I continue using his office at The Place as my office until I find one. "Why don't you just use dat office boy. Ain't really usin' it myself. You spen' mo' time back 'dere than I do anyway." He'd said. And I took him up on that offer with the quickness. Brotha' can't really afford to pay rent at some high rise building just yet anyway. And besides that, I can help Benny out, work on my music and do my accounting work all in the same place. It couldn't have worked out any better if I'd planned it that way.

I finally made the decision to start my own business after Celia and I broke up. She inspired me. She doesn't know she inspired me but she has. I admire her for stickin' to her guns the way she has with her book and her celibacy thang. She's a strong sista. A lil' *too* strong for her own good sometimes, but I love that about her. She's taught me a lot about perseverance. Which is exactly what I plan on doing. With or without her, I'm going to persevere. I'm taking care of my business and doing what I have to do. Even if I have to go broke doing it. At least I can say that I gave it a try. And it sure as hell beats the hell outta working my ass off to make some white fat-cat rich.

pamela davis-noland

I haven't talked to Celia since the day I told her what Laura wanted and she stormed out on me before I could even tell her that I said no. I'm not calling her, though. She owes *me* an apology. She was wrong for going off without even hearing me out first. I didn't mean to slam the phone down in her ear like that but she pissed me off. I've done nothin' but sweat this woman ever since I laid eyes on her and all I keep getting in return is attitude. And as patient as I've been with her, I don't really think I deserve that. I mean, how many brothas would stick around this long without at least a lil' "leg?" Not *very* many. That's how many. But I have. I even asked her to marry me. But did I even get an answer to that? Hell no. She never mentioned it, so hell, I didn't either. I guess she's not ready for somebody like me yet. Man, I'm not even surprised that she hasn't called me. That's pretty much her character anyway. That is one stubborn sista.

I saw her about a week ago. I was in the back office doing some paperwork when my stomach started growling. I was on my way to the kitchen when I saw her sitting at her favorite table talkin' with Benny. She didn't see me. My first instinct was to go up to her and say hello but my male pride kicked in and I went back to the office, grabbed a pencil and tried to look busy because I was sure that she'd come and say hello or somethin', man. I wasn't even going to look up when she walked in. My plan was to pretend like I was too busy for her. I waited forty-five minutes at that desk with that pencil in my hand – ready. When the door finally opened, Benny walked in and announced, "Doll says fo' me to tell you hello, boy. She gone on home." All I could do was shake my head and laugh. That's Celia all right. Always being true to her nature.

I don't know why I just didn't follow my first mind and just ask her why she hadn't given me an answer to the marriage question first that day? I could have told her about that baby issue later. But there are times, when Celia's eyes speak louder than her words. And those big beautiful eyes were yellin' at a niggah. They were telling me that she wanted an explanation about Laura first and foremost. So, contrary to what I had practiced, I did just that. I just wished she would have at least heard me out before she stormed out the way that she did. But how the hell was she supposed to react? Especially after the way I explained it to her. And now she's not even talking to me. I imagine I've now been added to her long list of sorry-ass men.

Laura called the other day to apologize. And just like always, I forgave her. I am glad she called though. We were able to talk things out. And by the end of the conversation we were sharing stories and laughing about Mama Ella and her prophecies and how pissed off she must be at me right now. It felt so good to laugh about it all. I felt a big old weight lift and I felt as free as a bird. The sound of Laura's laughter makes me believe she's finally free too. Or at least I hope so.

I told her how upset Celia is about the whole thing and she offered to talk to her and explain the whole story but I said hell no. There is no way I want Laura to explain *shit* on my behalf. This is all her fault anyway. Poppin' in the way she did. Naw… I don't need anybody to do anything for me as far as Celia DuBois

COFFEE-COLORED DREAMS

is concerned. I got this. I'm just givin' her time to think that's all.

Benny walked up behind me and scared the shit outta me. Even after all this time, he's still able to do that. I don't *ever* see him coming.

"What'cha writin' dere boy? New song?" He asked.

"Naw Benny, man. This here is written proof that I am a black man on a mission. It's my letter of resignation. You know the one I've been puttin' off writing for far too long. I was just headin' to the back to type it up. I'm givin' it to my supervisor tomorrow. Well tomorrow or maybe Monday. Man I don't know Benny, man. I wanna do this and I don't want to. I mean I know I got what it takes but what if I fall flat on my face? I work for a pretty big firm Benny. And maybe one day I'll move up into management or something like that, but I ain't feelin' that Benny. It's not what I want."

"So what's the pro'lem boy? Whatcha' cryin' bout? If it ain't what'choo want, den why you doin' it er'day?"

"Because I'm a black man. And you know a brotha' gotta work ten times harder to make it. Man a brotha gotta go through hell to get money to start up a business but a white man can do it everyday like it ain't shit. We have to work harder for everything we get. And then we get the attitude of 'Niggah, you should be happy you're getting that.' So what's a brotha' to do?"

"First of all boy, er'body knows dat a black man gotta work harda'. Dat ain't nuttin' but da' truf. But, dat ain't the pro'lem. Dat ain't it at all."

"Well what *is* the problem old man?"

"Da pro'lem boy iz dat brothas. Iz dat what we callin' ou'sef now? Brothas?"

I laughed. "Yeah Benny. Brothas." I patted my chest.

"'Cause you know we change our name a lot. 'Dis here one new 'ta me. Brothas. Okay. Now what wuz I sayin' boy?"

"You were about to tell me what the problem is?"

"Yeah. Da pro'lem iz dat we gots dis knowledge. You know… dat we gotta work harda'. But what we don't realize iz we also equip wit da solution. We got it. *We* got it boy. You get it."

I was puzzled as hell. "Naw man. I don't get this one." I shook my head and laughed.

"God already equip us wit a bigga' portion of strenf, energy, stamina and drive to do it wit. He jest gave the white man'a head start to be fair. Soon's black folk figa dat out, betta off we all 'gon be."

I leaned back in my chair, folded my hands behind my head and smiled. Benny was right as usual. And his answer made my pride go up a notch. *Hell yeah I can do this. Who's going to stop me?*

"You're one wise old dude Benny? I hope I'm as wise as you when I turn a hundred or so." I laughed.

Benny chuckled a little and then cleared his throat and looked me square in the eyes. "Speakin' of Doll…"

pamela davis-noland

"Wait. Hold up." I threw up my hand. I'm in no mood to talk about Celia. "Ain't nobody at this table mentioned Doll."

"Well now we have. Wake up boy! Stop walkin' round here daydreamin'."

"O believe me, man, I'm awake big time."

"So when the two's y'all gon' stop playin' dis silly game? Call dat woman boy. Go see her. Take'a some flowers boy, or somethin'. What'choo waitin' fo?"

"Benny man, I ain't hardly 'bout to go there with that woman again. A brotha' gotta have some pride, man. I don't want to come off like some punk. She stormed out on me. Remember? Naw man, she's gonna have to come to me." I stood up and left him this time.

But you know he had to have the last word. "Don't 'spect her to change if you don't give her a reason to, boy." He yelled.

MY BAD

Celia DuBois

I am so glad that this week is over. The high I had two weeks ago from the news Brianna gave me is slowly taking a downward spin. I just hope my students haven't noticed just how miserable I've been all week. I try not to bring my personal life to work but I miss Jeff so much. I could just crawl up into a big old ball and die. I've been really trying to take Benny's advice, "Let go'the hurts of the past, Doll, give true love a chance to prove itself," he said. And Lord knows I've tried that. But so far I have not succeeded. I get more depressed every day.

I have never been in love with a man as much as I love Jeff. I love the way he makes me feel so beautiful. I'm mean, he is exceptionally attractive, he can have any woman he wants and he wants me. I hate that I still look in the mirror sometimes and still see that ugly little girl who was teased almost daily. Although I know that I've grown to be attractive, those feelings of inadequacy still haunt me at times. Those are probably the hurts of the past that Benny is talking about. I don't think I even know what true love is, really. I seemed to equate love with a physical feeling. I've never known this kind of love that is so spiritual.

I keep telling myself to stop being such a damn fool and call him but I am so stubborn. And I'm still pissed off anyway. If he thinks I'm just gonna to accept her in his life he got a whole'notha think comin'! Sista girl has got to go. I don't give a damn how long they've been friends or if she's so-called family or not! I pray every night that I'd either hurry up and get over him or that we'd hurry up and work this thing out.

The knock on the door interrupted my thoughts and I dropped the eraser on my black pants. *Shit.* When I turned around, Mr. Lee was staring at me like the wolf he is.

"Oh I'm sorry I startled you, Miss DuBois."

"It's alright. Can I help you?" I asked as if I really wanted to.

"Someone is here to see you. I took the liberty of walking her to your class." He grinned.

She walked in and smiled at her announcer. My mouth fell open as we stared awkwardly at each other. I turned around and continued erasing the blackboard.

"Well, I'll just leave you two ladies alone." He said nervously. He waited for me to respond and quickly left when I didn't.

pamela davis-noland

"I'm sorry for popping up on you like this, Celia, but I felt that the least I could do was apologize." Laura explained.

First of all, bitch, how in the hell did you find me? "Well, popping up seems to be your specialty." I grunted. If she thinks I'm going to try and be civil with her, she can just think again.

"I know I deserve this reaction from you, Celia. Jeff did tell me that you two were pretty serious. I don't know what I was thinking about when I put him on the spot the way that I did. It's just that Jeff has always been there for me. I didn't even consider the fact that I would be interfering. I've always been first in Jeff's life. Even if he was dating someone else, she was never as important as me. I guess you can say that I'm spoiled."

I finally turned around and looked at her. "Rotten." I replied.

"Celia, please try and understand this if you don't understand anything else. Jeff has never said the word "no" to me. Not in our entire lives. He even agreed to the divorce when I suggested it. He would do anything to make me happy." She paused. "Well…he used to." She stared off into space and smiled. "Well, anyway, girl, so you know what that means, huh? It means that someone else is more important to him. He loves you Celia. He loves you more than any woman he's ever known. Including me. He didn't hesitate, he didn't ponder the question, he didn't even say that he would get back with me. He simply said, "No." And you know what? I didn't even have to ask him why. It was written all over his face."

She looked at me as if waiting for me to respond, but I still did not say a word. I've known her kind all of my life. Standing here like she's satisfied that she lost.

Yeah right! Don't even think we about to become friends so that you can still be in Jeff's life. I don't think so sista. I do feel bad, but not for you. I gotta get to my baby as soon as you get your ass out of my class.

"So I guess you're wondering how I found you?"

"Did Jeff send you?"

"No. As a matter of fact, I'd hoped that we could keep this little visit between us."

"So how'd you find out where I worked?"

"When I was here the last time, Jeff and I drove right pass here and he mentioned that this is where you worked. I figured you'd still be here at this time of the day."

"Oh."

"Well, I have a plane to catch. I'm headed to Houston. I just made the stop in to talk with you. Again, I am very sorry if I caused any trouble. I talked to Jeff the other night and he is miserable. I thought that the least I could do was try and help him. He's always been there for me."

"What about the baby?"

"I think I'm going to wait and rethink that. My biological clock is just tick-

COFFEE-COLORED DREAMS

ing, that's all. I'm sure it'll pass. But anyway, I gotta go. It was nice seeing you again, Celia."

Yeah right. I gave her my fake smile.

She tossed her long flowing wet sand looking hair and slithered out of my class. The same way she came in.

Jeffrey Jackson

I turned in my letter of resignation today and I feel like a load has been lifted off of my shoulders, man. The good old boys didn't seem to be surprised by it at all. They probably noticed my "I could care less about this job" attitude right from the start. And rumors of me leaving to pursue a singing career has been flying around the office ever since some of the guys came by to check me out one night. They went back to work and told everybody that my days there were probably numbered 'cause a brotha got skills. I must admit, I did like all the attention, but I didn't particularly like the fact that they put it out there like that before I even made up my mind what I wanted to do. I mean I knew I was going to quit eventually, but they kind of forced my hand a little.

Just about everyone in the office has come by The Place to hear me sing and a few of them have even become regulars, which I think is cool. I sure can use the support and Benny can sure use the money. Hell, *I* do Benny's books and I'm still baffled. I don't know how he manages to pay two full-time cooks, pay the bands that perform, pay all the expenses of runnin' a café' and pay Big Man, too. Big Man works 'round the clock. But he's never late on anything. Benny doesn't even sell liquor, only Coke, tea and coffee, but his place is still packed on Friday night and even some Saturdays. But hey, what else can I expect from Benny? Miracles just happen around that brotha'.

Some of the fellas wanted me to hang out after work today to celebrate me starting my own business but I didn't feel up to it, man. I much rather celebrate with Celia. I picked up the phone three times to dial her number and froze each time. I'm not scared or nothin' like that. I'm just pissed. Damn! How can a woman be so stubborn?

Benny's words keep playin' over and over in my mind. *"Don't 'spect her to change if you don't give her a reason to, boy."* But damn, haven't I given her enough reason? Am I not the niggah who asked for her to marry me? How can she just skip out like that? Just like she did with that other brotha. I wonder if she even stopped to think that *she* might be the problem. Her and her not trustin' a niggah. I mean, does she really think I would've gotten Laura pregnant? I mean, damn! That's why I'm so pissed off. For her to even think of me that way after I respected her the way I did. Well man, I give up. At least I can say I did absolutely nothin' wrong except fall in love with a sista who doesn't believe that there really are some good brothas left.

pamela davis-noland

I stared at our picture on the nightstand. I picked it up and smiled when I thought about all the good times we had together. And to think, none of them involved sex. That shit still trips me out. You know - that I ain't even trippin'. I mean I'm human that's for *sure*! But I ain't sweatin' it. That'll come in time. But if I have to hold out and wait until we get married, well so be it. I'd rather do that now anyway. I told her that I wanted to be the man to show her that we not all alike and I meant that. And if we never get back together because her ass is so stubborn, oh well. At least she can say I was true to my word. I took one more look at the picture and was getting lost in my thoughts when I heard somebody pounding at my door. I jumped up, threw the picture in my nightstand drawer and slammed it shut. "I'm going to get over you Celia DuBois. I ain't gon' be trippin' like this for long!" I said to the drawer.

The knocking got louder. *Damn man!* "Hold up!" I yelled.

I looked through the peephole. *Oops, my bad.*

Celia DuBois

I knocked softly on his door at first hoping and praying that I would say the right words. I practiced all the way here but nothing sounded good enough. He didn't answer and I know he's home because I saw his car. I knocked harder and then I heard him yell, "Hold up!"

I heard his heavy breathing. I became nervous and almost ran. I feel so stupid.

He opened the door wearing nothing but a worn out pair of blue jeans and a serious five o'clock shadow. He smiled so big that my heart leaped for joy.

"Jeff, I'm sorry…" I began to hurry and explain.

"Come in baby." He grabbed me around my waist and kissed me gently.

"Baby please let me finish." I insisted. I grabbed his hand and walked him over to the sofa. "I'm sorry I stormed out the way that I did. I didn't even hear you out and I promised I would. I didn't even give you a chance to tell me that you told her no."

"And how did you find out I said no?" He asked.

"Laura came to my classroom a little while ago."

"What?!" He shook his head, stood and began pacing the floor.

"Yep. She popped up. Again!"

"That Laura, *maannn*…I swear. Well, I hope you know that I didn't send her."

"Yeah. She asked me not to tell you." *I don't know what the hell made her think I wouldn't. Yeah right!* I rolled my eyes and he laughed. "I'm sorry I jumped to conclusions. I should have known better."

"Yeah, but I should've told you the whole story from the beginning. That would have killed all that confusion."

"So do you forgive me?"

COFFEE-COLORED DREAMS

"I don't know, man. What if Laura wouldn't have showed up at your job? Just how long was it going to take you to come to me?"

I lowered my head. I didn't know how to answer that. I guess I probably would have eventually. I don't really know. I guess I just assumed he would come to me. "Well why didn't you come to me Jeff? You could have at least called me and told me that you said no."

"So you really thought that I was going to do it baby?"

"No. It's not that. I really didn't think you would but…"

"But what?"

"But she was offering you something that you are not getting from me." I whispered.

Jeff sat next to me and placed his hand under my chin. He lifted my head. "Look at me." He demanded. "She was offering me a chance to bring a child into this world with only one parent. Do you know what it's like to be raised without a father in the home? We have enough black fatherless children runnin' round here. I don't know what Laura was smokin' on when it even entered her mind to ask me to do some dumb shit like that. And I thought you knew me better than that, Celia. I mean come on, baby."

"Well I thought I did too. And I was right. But damn. I mean how would you feel if you were in my shoes? Be real."

He looked away. "I guess I would have tripped too." He mumbled.

"Uh… *heelllooo*… I can't hear you. What'd you say?"

"I said I guess I would have tripped a lil' bit myself. But I would have at least given you a chance to explain."

"So I'm sorry for being so bullheaded, okay. I really am Jeff. Will you ever forgive me." He stood up and started pacing again. No answer. *I must have really pissed him off.*

He walked up to the stereo pushed the play button and Miles' hypnotic trumpet filled the room. He walked back toward me, stood in front of me, looked around and folded his arms. "Only on one condition."

"What?" I asked looking around at his very messy apartment. "I hope I don't have to clean *this* shit."

He laughed. "Naw, man. I'm gonna clean up this mess tomorrow."

"Okay. Then what?"

Jeff knelt down on one knee in front of me. He grabbed my hand and looked deeply into my eyes. "Celia, baby, why haven't you answered my question?" he asked.

"Jeff." I breathed in and out very slowly for fear of hyperventilation or passin' out. Or both! "Are you talking about the question I think you're talking about?"

"Yeah. Well, at least I hope so."

"Jeff, you never mentioned it again so I thought you'd changed your mind."

"What? Changed my mind? Why would you think that? I was waiting for you to answer me and you never did. So I thought the answer must have been no. I thought maybe I had put too much pressure on you, so I decided to give you some space."

"Are you serious?" I laughed. And I laughed even harder when I saw the look on his face.

"What's so damn funny?"

"Oh, baby, if you only knew." I reached over and kissed him. "I love you, Jeff, and I would love it if we became a real family."

He nodded his head in approval. He smiled and stood up and ushered me into his arms where I stayed for as long as the tears kept pouring from my eyes when he whispered, "Thank you, baby."

I began daydreaming about us making love. Our bodies entwined as one. Our sporadic breathing and the movements of our bodies in unison. I listened to his heart pound and wondered if he was thinking the same thing I was. He pushed away from me a little. Just enough so that he could see my face. He stared at me so deeply, my instincts kicked in and I began unbuttoning my blouse. Jeff watched my hands as they moved ever so slowly. He placed his hands over mine. "Celia, I have the rest of my life to know your body." He said staring into my eyes. "The most important thing to me right now is to know your soul. And I want you to know mine. Making love does not have to necessarily be sex, baby. And I didn't know that until I met you."

I hung my head in shame. Now any other brotha' would have already had his dick in me talkin' 'bout, "Who's is it?" But not my baby. He just keeps on surprising me. "I just thought…"

"I know what you thought, baby." He interrupted. "I've already told you, Celia. I'm not like all the others. Haven't you figured that out yet?"

"Yes Jeff. You are definitely one of a kind. I love you so much."

"I love you too. I told you baby, you my dream lady. " He said.

We kissed passionately. I had a hard time controlling myself, but I figure if he can, so can I.

YOU LOOK LIKE
A FRIEND OF MINE

Celia DuBois

I was so excited when Deniece accepted my invitation to lunch. I hadn't seen her since that early morning she and the girls came over. We had talked on the phone a few times when I'd called her to tell her the good news about my book but that's about it. I'm still a little upset about her staying with that jerk of a husband. But we don't even talk about that. She pissed me off. How can she not want any help? Everytime I made some type of suggestion, she would have some lame ass excuse as to why she couldn't leave. I don't have any patience for silly women who don't think they deserve better.

I was so afraid to call and ask her to meet me. Our conversations have been brief and somewhat strained. But she's still my friend and I love her. I want to tell her about the engagement but I felt as though I owed her a formal apology in person first. I should never have taken her decision so personally.

I looked at my watch for the twentieth time. I had only been waiting about fifteen minutes but it felt like forever. I wanted Deniece to get here first so I could break the news that Maria was joining us. The two of them act like cats when they're together.

I was staring out of the window watching the *Mississippi Queen* make its daily route up and down the Mississippi River far off in the distance, when I felt a light tap on my shoulder. I turned around and could not believe my eyes. It was the old Deniece. She had come back to life and she was beautiful.

She was wearing a very well tailored two-piece black suit with an embroidered silk blouse. Her hair was pulled back into a chignon and she was wearing a rather very expensive set of pearl earrings. Her makeup was flawless and she even managed to disguise the knot on her lip.

I stared at her with my mouth open, stood up and hugged her. It was all I could do to not cry. "Oh, Deniece." I whispered.

"Yeah it's me. What's shakin'?"

"Yo' fine ass. That's what's shakin'. Girl, look at'choo!"

She twirled around. "Heeeyyy!"

"Girl, you look so good."

pamela davis-noland

"Thanks. Now we 'gon sit down and order somethin' or stand here and look at me? I need a drink girl. What'choo drinkin'?"

"A glass of Merlot."

"Oh that sounds nice." She waved to the waiter. "Double shot of crown on the rocks." She demanded.

"Damn." I laughed. "Okay, start talkin'. Whassup? I want to know everything that's happened since the last time I saw you. Don't tell me Anthony finally gotta damn job."

"Chile, hell no. That deadbeat husband of mine is behind bars."

"What?!" I felt like jumping up and clicking my heels.

"You heard me. I finally had enough of his ass, Celia. I stood by his sorry ass through the good and bad times. I was there for him when he was down. I washed his dirty drawls, fed him, gave him two beautiful children, and even gave him some lovin' whenever he wanted it. I was too good to that niggah. Even when he treated me like his personal punchin' bag." She giggled, psychotically. "I stayed right there. I firmly believe in standin' by man. I mean our brothas have so much to deal with. So many battles to fight. But you know what? The battle in their minds is the biggest one of all."

"Amen." I agreed.

"I would do anything for Anthony, Celia. But I'll be goddamned if I let that motherfucka' hurt one'a my babies."

"Girl, he started hittin' on the girls?"

"No Celia. Anthony touched Brandi."

I placed my hand over my mouth. I had no idea how to respond. I wasn't expecting to hear that at all.

"I caught him." She sighed. "Brandi was starting to act very strange and she never wanted to stay home by herself. I knew something was wrong right then, 'cause Brandi love to stay home and talk on the phone and read them damn magazines, girl. So anyway, I had a flashback of my Uncle Pierre. You remember the one I told you about who used to try and touch my sisters and me. We used to hate it when my mama would make us go there for the summer. We used to take turns sleeping 'cause he wouldn't mess with us if we were awake. He used to like to come and touch us when were asleep and then pretend he was just tucking us in. That motherfucka' was crazy, girl.

So one day, I told Brandi to stay home and watch the girls until I went to the store. She begged me to let them go but I told her to stay because Hope was asleep. It was almost time for Anthony to get home from work so I parked the car on the other block and stood outside in the backyard. When I heard him pull up and the screen door slam shut, I creeped around the side of the house to the porch and peeked in. Anthony walked up behind Brandi and kissed her on the cheek. She pulled away from him and turned around. Celia, I saw the fear in her eyes. The same fear I had when Uncle Pierre would come into our room at night. Just as she was about to walk away from him, he grabbed her arm and put his

COFFEE-COLORED DREAMS

hand on her ass. Girrrll, the next thing I knew, I was runnin' at him like a mad woman. I jumped on his ass like a cat. I tore that niggah up. I broke a lamp over his head and Brandi beat him with the phone. I don't know where my strength came from or what was even happenin'. All I knew was that I wanted that sonuvabitch dead! Girl, when we finished beatin' his ass he was bleedin' everywhere but the bottom of his feet." She laughed, took a long sip of her double crown on the rocks and didn't even flinch.

"Deniece, he didn't even try and fight back?"

"Girl, Anthony ain't nuttin' butta bitch if he ain't drinkin'. Besides, he was too guilty to fight back. I called the cops and told them that I had caught him in the act of child molestation and they carted his charcoal black ass off to jail where I hope he stays for a very long ass time." She gulped her drink until it was all gone.

"Why didn't she tell you what was going on, Deniece?"

"I guess for the same reason we never told on my Uncle Pierre. You feel so ashamed. As if it's your fault. But I take total blame for it. I let Anthony treat me so bad for so long. She said she was scared she was going to get me in trouble. She was trying to protect me by not protecting herself. You believe that? I was just as much at fault as Anthony was. I love my daughters, Celia. I'm going to make it all up to them somehow. They are never going to see their mother weak again."

"So what did you do girl? You look so good!"

"Well, for starters, I went back home. Daddy is so glad that we're there. He's been so depressed since Mama died. He needs the company."

"Okay, so what else?"

"I decided to live again. And I have you to thank for that. I admire you so much Cee. And girl, before I forget to say it, congratulations again on your book. Girl, I am so proud of you."

"Thanks Deniece. I'm really happy. Chile, you of all people know how I've been strugglin' with this book. You have no idea how many times I wanted to pick up that phone and call you. I was catchin' hell tryin' to finish that book. But we can talk about me later. So doesn't it feel wonderful when you make up your mind and stick to it."

"Hell yeah. And you know what Cee? If I didn't make the decision to do better, my girls were going to have to watch their mama die. I just couldn't let that happen, Celia. Brandi is blossoming into a very pretty young lady and you know them lil' boys after her. How am I suppose to teach her to respect herself if I don't respect myself. So I sent my resume to a few places, lucked up and got a job at a doctor's office through a friend of my daddy's and went on a shopping spree and spent three thousand dollars of daddy's money that he insisted on giving me. I went crazy, girl. I bought the girls dresses. Bought me some of the finest shoes. A couple of these nice suits and even joined a spa. I am so happy, Cee."

pamela davis-noland

"Well, you sure look like it. I'm sorry about being a bitch toward you, Dee. I was just so angry with you. I hated to see you letting yourself go the way you were. You, of all people. As beautiful as you are, you can have any man that you want. I couldn't understand the thing with Anthony's black ass."

"Well, there ain't no need to apologize. You played a very big part in this. Your words to me played over and over in my head every day. I began to see things as they really were. I just couldn't think of a way to get out, so I prayed and asked the Lord to help me. And He did. I was very concerned about Brandi at first, but she's a'right. She's so strong. She reminds me of the old me. I told Daddy what happened and he put her in Karate so she can learn how to protect herself."

"Well, how are the other girls?"

"Scoie is getting bigger by the minute and Jasmine is talkin' up a storm. Daddy and I talked it over and we decided to place Hope in a special school. She 'gon start next fall. In the meantime, Daddy spends all of his spare time teaching her. She's learning so much. She can say "mama" now. And she is so pretty, Celia. She looks just like Tina."

"Uhn! Speakin' of Tina. I know she trippin' 'bout you livin' at your daddies."

"Naw, not really. She knows what happened. She's not as bad as she used to be. She all happy and shit now. Her new husband is a chiropractor and he has his own business and shit. My big sista is livin' in style girl. I talked to her yesterday. She called to see if I got the check she sent me."

"She sent you a check?" I was shocked. Tina a/k/a "The wicked bitch of the north" wasn't too keen on helping her baby sister. She hasn't really spoken to her in years.

"Yeah, girl. I can't keep livin' with Daddy. He doesn't want us to leave but I have to Celia. I have to prove to my girls that I can take care of them. So I asked Tina to borrow some money to get an apartment. The apartment is right around the corner from my job and it's in a good neighborhood, too. Brandi will be able to go to a good school."

"Oh, Deniece, I am so happy for you."

"Thank you Cee. I knew you would be. I wanted to tell you on the phone, but every time you called, you didn't really sound like you wanted to talk. I've been wantin' to call you but I was afraid you wouldn't talk to me."

"Now, Deniece, you trippin'. You know I would've talked to you. I thought you were mad at *me*. I used the good news about my book to break the ice, but then you wouldn't say anything else so I figured you didn't have much to say to me."

"So how's that coming along? Got that big check yet?"

"Not yet. Still going through the formalities."

"So what's the big secret you couldn't tell me over the phone?"

"Well, I have some more good news."

COFFEE-COLORED DREAMS

Just as I was about to tell Deniece about Jeff, Maria walked up. "Hey. Y'all ain't ordered no food yet?" She asked, waving at the waiter.

Deniece glared at me and all I could do was shrug my shoulders. After I saw how good she looked, I was so excited that I forgot to tell her about Maria.

"Hey Deniece. Whassup? You finely left that bum husband, huh? You look good girl." She flopped down in her chair and lit a cigarette.

"As a matter-a-fact, I did. I was too good for him. He has the one quality you look for in a man though - *available*."

"Well, we won't talk about the qualities of the men we choose now will we Miss Thang." Maria hissed.

"Alright Fluffy and Kitty. Don't y'all start! How y'all 'gon help me plan my wedding if you two 'gon fight all the time?"

They both stared at me with the same look on their faces. I bust out laughing. "What ch'all starin' at. You heard me."

Silence.

"Celia, you didn't tell me that y'all had worked everything out." Maria finally said. "The last time I talked to you, you said you left him 'cause that bitch wanna have his baby."

"What!!" Deniece shouted. "Baby? What woman? What the hell she talkin' 'bout, Celia?"

"Well," Maria began, "Jeff's ex-wife came to town tryin' to get him back, girl. Talkin' 'bout she wanna have his baby. He told her to come down here, right. So they can talk it over. Then he told Celia that he was going outta town for a week."

"What?!" Deniece yelled so loud, people were beginning to stare.

"Shhh. Damn girl, keep it down. You know Maria fulla shit. You know how she like to exaggerate. That's not what happened. Jeff's ex did come to town but he did not invite her. She came without even telling him. She told him that she had something very important to talk with him about. They went out to supper, and that's when she asked him to be the father of her baby. No strings attached. He told her no. He didn't even hesitate. He said no, flat out."

"Well, how you know he said no right away? How you know he didn't say yes and then realized that you wouldn't 'gon go for that shit, so he hurry up and changed his mind?" Maria asked.

"Yeah, Cee? How can you be so sure?" Deniece asked.

Both of them were nodding their heads like two old church ladies.

"Well, Laura, his ex, came by my job to see me. She came by to tell me that she was sorry for popping up the way that she did. And she told me that Jeff had told her no. And that he couldn't do that 'cause he is in love with me. She thought the least she should do is come by and apologize."

"I don't know Cee." Maria said. " How you know he didn't put her up to it."

"Yeah." Deniece agreed. "How do you know that they didn't sleep together while she was here and now she's in Chicago carrying his child?"

pamela davis-noland

"Look you two. I trust Jeff, okay. If he said nothin' happened, nothin' happened!"

"Well all I gotta say is don't be surprised if she come back in 10 months talkin' 'bout child support." Maria said.

"Oh shut up Maria." Deniece scolded. "Cee ain't no fool. Unlike some'a us, she gotta good head on her shoulder. If she trust him, he must be trustworthy. Right."

"Thank you Deniece." I agreed.

"Well look Miss Thang, you been around the block a few times. Have you ever met a man that will say no to some pussy wit' no strings attached? Especially, especially if he ain't gettin' no pussy from his own woman."

"Why you always all up in my bizness, Black!" I shouted.

"Shhh. Girl, calm down. You know Maria always tryin'ta fuck wit' somebody." Deniece glared at Maria. "Girl, grow up. We used to tease virgins in high school. Celia is a grown woman. If she chooses to be celibate, that's her choice. Not to mention, a very smart choice this day and age."

"Thank you Deniece. This bitch know she been gettin' on my nerves. She wants me to sleep with Jeff more than I want to."

"Well, I don't care if you ever fuck'em to be honest. I just don't see what the big deal is that's all. Hell, y'all been together, what? Six or seven months, now. He's not seeing anyone else. You not seein' anyone. What's the damn big deal."

Deniece nodded. "I hate to admit it, but Maria has a point. Why won't you sleep with him?"

Maria jumped in before I could give my testimony. "Chile, have you seen'em? That Niggah fine. I still don't know how she can keep her hands off of him this long."

"I saw him. Girl, did you see them dimples?"

"No girl, did you see that ass? Celia you lucky you saw him first."

"Not as lucky as Jeff." Deniece choked on her second double. We burst into laughter.

"Well y'all can laugh if y'all want to, but that man's number would have definitely been in my lil' black book."

"At least until he had it changed." Deniece added. We high-fived. Maria hates to be the brunt of a joke. And Deniece and me love double-teamin her. She thinks she's all that *AND* a bag'a chips. But no matter how hard we laughed, Maria just kept right on talkin' cash shit.

"You know the first time we met he was checkin' me out, girl." She said.

"Uhn, Uhn, Black, now you lyin'. Now you know damn well Jeff totally ignored you. No, no, he totally dismissed yo' ass. He didn't give you a second look."

"Not while you was lookin', honey."

Maria pisses me off but I don't even feel like going there with her today. If

COFFEE-COLORED DREAMS

Deniece wouldn't have patted my knee and shook her head I swear I was going to cuss Maria out. I know it's not worth it though.

We both looked at Maria who was puffing seductively on her cigarette, proud as a peacock as if she had just won the argument. We shook our heads and giggled.

"Y'all ready to order?" Deniece asked.

We sat for two hours eating and talking about my wedding plans at first and then ended up talking about the good old days. We talked about old boyfriends, old lovers, old friends and getting old. We had a wonderful time. Even Maria and Deniece seemed to be getting along. We acted like three schoolgirls and it was very refreshing.

Just as we were about to tally up the bill, a very tall, very white, gentleman walked over and picked up the blue slip of paper and said in a wonderful version of the King's English, "I would be happy to pay for your meal, ladies."

Maria and I looked at each other and then at Deniece, who was grinning from ear to ear. Apparently she knows who this man is.

I finally spoke up because it didn't seem like anyone else wanted to. "Excuse me sir, but I think we can pay for our own meal. Thanks anyway." I held out my hand so that he could place the bill back in my hand.

Maria poked me in my side. "Now Celia, don't be rude. If the nice gentleman wants to pay for our meal, I don't see why we shouldn't let him." She crossed her legs and smiled at him.

Maria is such a whore. I poked her back. "We can pay for it ourselves." I insisted. I wasn't about to let this total stranger pay for my meal.

Deniece, who, couldn't stop grinning, finally acknowledged him. "How long have you been here?" She asked.

"Not very long. I have to meet with a very important client. I wanted to come over and speak sooner but you ladies seemed to have been having a wonderful time, so I thought better of it."

What?!

I am totally shocked. These two are actually flirting. I have never seen Deniece act that friendly with any white folks. She can't stand white folks! Especially white men. I've seen her cuss white men out just for looking at her too hard. Hell, she'd cuss out any man who would mistake her for being anything other than the "pro-black" sista she is. That girl know she love her black men. Even sorry ass men like Anthony. She even had an excuse for him; he was going through a slump. She believed that as soon as he would get over it, his true strengths would come shining through. Ha! She's still waiting.

"Well if we are going to let you pay for our meal, we should at least know your name." Maria interrupted their conversation. "You look familiar but I can't seem to place your name."

Deniece looked at me and we rolled our eyes in unison. If I had a dollar for every time I heard that girl say that shit, I'd be filthy rich. She really needs to get

pamela davis-noland

a new line.

"How about placing your share of the bill on the damn table Maria. It's time to go. I have a hair appointment in twenty minutes." I scolded.

He extended his hand out to her. "Jonathan Sinclair. It is so very nice to meet you."

Maria grabbed the tips of his fingers. "Nice meeting you too. I'm Maria."

He extended his hand to me. "And you are?"

"Celia DuBois. Thanks for the offer, but we'll pay for our meal." I put my hand out and he placed the bill in my hand.

"*Par don*. I did not mean to offend you, Ms. DuBois. I was just being friendly." He patted Deniece on the shoulder and winked. "See you later, Dee Dee?"

"Yeah. Bye, bye." She sang.

"Dee Dee?" Maria whispered. "Alright chick, start talkin'." She demanded.

"What time is your hair appointment, Celia?" Deniece totally ignored her.

"In about ten minutes. Let's go."

"Uhn, Uhn. Hell Naw! Y'all ain't goin' nowhere until Miss Dee Dee here spills the beans on the great white hope." Maria insisted.

"Girl, come on here with yo' nosy self. If Deniece wanted us to know who he is, she would have introduced him herself. Can't you respect anybody's privacy, Black. Damn!"

"Thank you Celia. I always did appreciate your ability to respect one's privacy."

"Yeah, yeah, whatever. Let's go." I said impatiently. I hate being late for a hair appointment. It's not that I didn't want to know who he is myself, I just don't have the time. And besides Deniece has always been very private so it's best to just wait until she's ready to talk.

We said our good-byes in the parking lot and agreed that we should try and get together more often.

I watched them as they drove off and thanked the Lord for my two wacky friends. And I prayed that Clara wouldn't be mad when I showed up. I was definitely late.

I
GOTTA NEW ATTITUDE

Jeffrey Jackson

I called everyone back home, who I thought cared and told them about the engagement. And just about everyone except Miles and a few of my relatives who love Laura were happy for me. Miles, of course, had more than a few comments about my decision but swore he'd never talk to me again if I didn't ask him to be my best man. I haven't told Laura yet. I figure Miles is going to tell her anyway and I'd rather her hear it second hand. I'm not about to let her try and play any more mind games with me. I don't care to hear her opinion. And it sure felt good to tell Miles exactly what I felt about him and his.

He started this long drawn out conversation about how a man should choose a woman and how he should choose his wife. He said something like, "I mean, you gotta take into consideration a lot of things, man, like what you want your kids to look like. I mean it's okay to have, you know, a certain kind of sista to kick it with, but you gotta pick the *right* wife. I mean, come on man, why did you and Laura break up anyway? I mean if you guys would have just tried a little harder. Or should I say if *you* would have tried a little harder. Man, you two are perfect for one another. Everybody knows it too. And the children man... you know y'all would make some pretty ass babies. You could at least think about the promise you made, niggah."

I could have reached through the phone and rung his neck. How in the hell is he going to tell me shit about keeping a promise? Miles has never kept a promise in his life. Just ask all the wanna be divas who are still waiting for that phone call from Miles, the great producer, who's going to make them all rich and famous.

At that very moment I decided that I'd had enough of everyone and their opinions about my life. I've tried to get as far away from them and their opinions as possible. But, until I tell them all exactly what the hell they can do with their opinions, this is going to be a never-ending cycle. And they're not going to change, so I'm going to have to.

"Miles, my brotha, let me tell you something," I paused and sighed dramatically, "You are the most conceited, self-centered, color-struck, niggah I know. And how is it that you are such an expert on my relationships when yo' ass don't know jack shit about women? Besides how to lay'em. And from the rumors I've heard, you need to quit braggin' so much." I laughed. "Hoes, Miles - those are the one's who give it up when they think they're about to get something in return; they're called hoes. You ain't bangin' all them babes cuz you're Don Juan my brotha. But maybe one day you'll stop focusing so hard on me and my women and get one of your own. Then maybe we can have this discussion again, niggah."

Miles didn't say anything. I thought he had hung up until I heard him breathing real heavy. After about two minutes, he said, "Niggah I *can* fuck. Forget'choo! So when is the date?"

"I'll let you know, niggah."

"A'right. I'm the best man, right?"

"Yeah, Miles."

"A'right niggah. Peace!"

"Peace, Miles."

Well, at least I finally got it off my chest. One down, more to go. The next time someone gives me their negative opinion concerning me and mine, they are going to get the same attitude.

Celia DuBois

I did it. I took my braids out and cut my hair. I figured it was time for a new look. I'm getting too old to be walkin' 'round here lookin' like Brandy. I needed a more sophisticated look for my book jacket. So after much consultation from Clara, I finally decided to wear it short and natural. I wanted a totally different look. I was blessed with my daddy's "decent" hair, like my mother says, so with the help of a good deep conditioning and some gel, it looks healthy and quite sophisticated. I look more like a Nubian princess than I did before.

I smiled at myself in the mirror. I was very pleased. I just hope Jeff is as pleased. I told him that I had taken my braids out, but I didn't mention how short my hair is. He did seem to like playing in my braids. I just hope he ain't one of those brothas who are stuck on long hair.

We're supposed to meet at seven o'clock but I'm running late as usual. It took me forever to find the right outfit. I settled on a sexy earthy look and it works well with my haircut - light brown, linen halter with matching mini-skirt, African jewelry, and high-heeled leather sandals. I hadn't worn my nose ring in years, so I decided to wear it for extra effect. I gotta new attitude and I love it!

It's a Saturday night and I expected Benny's to be jam-packed. I stood at the door looking around for Jeff but I could barely see through the crowd. I managed to squeeze my way through a very narrow path and had just about made it to the kitchen when I felt a tug at my arm. I smiled thinking it was Jeff and was shocked when I turned around and saw the face of my old fiancé. I had not seen Stephen

COFFEE-COLORED DREAMS

in almost two years and this is the last place I ever expected to see him.

"Hello, Celia." He said.

"Hello, Stephen. How are you?" We hugged lightly and he kissed me on the cheek.

"How've you been?"

"Wonderful. And yourself?"

"Pretty good." He reached over to the woman standing next to him. I hadn't even noticed her. But by the way she was glaring at me, I could tell that she wasn't too keen on meeting me. "Celia, this is my wife, Tracy."

Wife? Oh, Lord!

Now why I all of sudden got this sharp pain in my temples, I have no idea. I cannot even justify this feeling I'm having right now. I don't know whether to be happy or sad. He had caused me so much pain in our relationship. I should be happy that that's not me standing next to him but I can't help but feel a little envious. Why the hell didn't he marry *me*? She isn't very pretty and from what I can see, she doesn't seem to have a very pleasant disposition, either.

I reached my hand out to her and faked an incredibly large smile, "Hi Tracy. It's nice meeting you." I lied.

"Nice to meet you too." She said. And she didn't even have the common courtesy to fake a smile. She still had the same "ooh somethin' stink" look on her face.

"Well it was nice seeing you again, Stephen, I have to go. I'm meeting someone and I'm runnin' late."

"Okay. And by the way, I love your hair."

"Thank you." I smiled again at Miss Angry and walked away. Suddenly a feeling of relief came over me. I am so glad that I'm here to meet Jeff and not him.

I can say one thing about the two of them; they're a match made in heaven. I giggled when I turned around and saw them two fools arguing. Apparently, Stephen hadn't changed a bit. *Angry ass!*

I finally made it to the kitchen but there is still no sign of Jeff or Benny. I saw Samuel, the cook, and his wife Hattie busy cookin' up a storm. "Hey y'all. Have you seen Jeff?"

"Celia? Is that you?" Hattie asked, wiping her hands on her apron and walking toward me to get a better look. "Chile, look at'choo. Yo' hair is slammin'!"

"Do you like it?"

"Girl, yeah. I wish I had the nerve to do somethin' like that. Samuel, you see Celia?"

"Yep. Looks good girl. I think I saw Jeff in the office. Check 'dere." He said.

"Hey guys, you think Jeff 'gon like my hair?" I shyly asked.

"Chile, dat man'll like it if you dyed it three diff'rent colors. I ain't never seen no man so crazy 'bout a woman in all my days. He been axin' fa' you all night. E'ry damn five minutes he axin', "Y'all seen Celia?", he 'bout to drive me

pamela davis-noland

crazy. Please go find dat man, girl, so he can sit hiz behind don somewhere."

I laughed. "Okay. You sure I look okay?"

"Girl, 'gon now. You know where the office iz." She said impatiently.

I kissed her on the cheek. "Thanks."

"Hey!" she called out, "You 'gon knock 'em dead, *sha*."

I winked at her and headed for the office feeling like a million bucks. So far, so good. I just hope Jeff has the same reaction.

I knocked softly on the door and placed my ear to it but I didn't hear anything. I was about to knock again when he wrapped his arms around my waist and blew in my ear. I grinned from ear to ear. "Excuse me sir, but do you make it a habit of walking up behind women and blowing in their ears?" I asked. I turned around slowly and looked him in the eyes.

He didn't say anything. He reached behind me and opened the door to the office and guided me back with his pelvis. When we made it inside, he turned on the lamp, lifted me up on the desk and began kissing me passionately and uncontrollably and every part of my body yearned to be touched by him. All those familiar feelings enveloped me. I remember how I loved making love to a man that I cared so deeply for.

I felt as though I had two little people on each shoulder, an angel and a devil. The little devil resembled Maria and the little angel was me. Maria's look-a-like kept saying, "Go for it girl. Get some." My look-a-like reminded me of the times that I went for it in the past, only to face a lot of heartache and disappointment.

I had just gained some of my strength back when Jeff placed his hands under my butt and lifted me up again so that my legs were around his waist. He walked over to the sofa and laid me down. I didn't say a word, although I wanted to scream, "Hurry up before I change my mind!" He stood over me and stared at me as if it was his first time ever seeing a woman. I had never seen him look so impassioned.

"You're beautiful." He whispered.

I reached out my hand to him and he gently laid on top of me. I felt his excitement and mine grew even more. I placed my hand on his crotch and he moaned. He put his hand under my skirt and was just about to put his hand in my panties, when the overhead light came on. We froze.

"Hey, you two. Dere's plenty time for that lat'a." Benny said. "It's time ta' go introduce the first band, boy."

"Uh, okay Benny. Be there in a minute." Jeff didn't even look up. He was staring at me and trying not to laugh. He could tell how embarrassed I was.

"Hey 'dere, Doll. How you doin' this evenin'? I saw you when you came in but I wasn't sure if it wuz you. How you like her hair, boy?"

"I think she looks incredibly sexy, Benny. What do you think?" He said, still looking into my eyes.

"Yep. Now come on here. I'll meet you on stage. Ole' Benny 'gon talk to ya' lata, Doll."

COFFEE-COLORED DREAMS

"Okay." I answered like a five-year-old child who just got caught with my hand in a cookie jar.

As soon as he closed the door Jeff and I burst out laughing. "How in the hell does he do that?" I asked.

"Do what baby?" Jeff jumped up and hurriedly fixed his clothes.

"It's like he appears out of nowhere. I didn't even hear the doorknob. Did you? And how did he know we were in here? It's almost like he knew exactly what we were doing. I bet he did."

"He did what?" Jeff was so busy trying to adjust himself that he didn't hear a word I said.

"Jeff, are you listening to me?"

"Yeah, baby, I'm listenin'." He kissed me on the forehead and headed for the door.

"*Jeeefff.*" I whined.

He walked back over to me and sat down. "Look baby. Benny is right. We do have plenty of time. Hopefully, the rest of our lives. But right now, I have to go introduce the band." He pleaded.

"That's not what I'm talkin' about, Jeff!"

"Oh. Okay, what? I'm all ears."

"Don't you sometimes feel like you have a guardian angel?"

"Yeah, sometimes. A black beret wearing, saxophone playin', death lovin', wise old bowlegged one." He kissed me on the cheek and pounced out the door.

"I'm serious Jeff!" I yelled.

"Me too!" He yelled back.

I sat in the back of the café and watched Benny work the crowd. It's hard to believe that he was just in the hospital a couple of months ago looking like he was two or three breaths away from his last. I can't seem to keep my eyes off of him. I can't recall ever meeting someone who brings such happiness to so many people.

The bands dedicated all of their songs to Benny. One band by the name of "Presumption", played an instrumental simply titled "Benny". It was one of the most beautiful instrumentals I'd ever heard. So appropriate it was for someone as beautiful in spirit as Benny Thibodeaux.

Jeff had been introducing the bands all night. He finally came and sat with me. "Are you enjoying yourself, baby?"

"Oh yeah. I loved Presumption. Wasn't that a pretty song?"

"Well, if you liked that, check this out." He pointed to the stage just as Samuel's wife, Hattie sat at the piano.

"Oohh Jeff, can she sing?"

"Shh. Just listen." He whispered.

I couldn't believe my ears. Could she sing! What in the hell is she doing working at this café serving up poboys? She has an incredibly unique sound. Sort of a cross between Anita Baker and Lauren Hill. That slow naturally blues-y voice. She sang "Killing Me Softly" and Jeff informed me that Roberta Flack was one of Benny's favorite artists.

I especially liked it because that song she was singing so beautifully reminded me of the first time I heard Jeff sing. He was definitely "singing' my life with his words." I looked over at Jeff who seemed to be mesmerized. "Jeff." I whispered.

"Yeah, baby?"

"Jeff, I love you. I'm ready to set a date."

"Okay, when?" He asked, still staring at Hattie.

"Tomorrow. I want to marry you tomorrow."

Jeff laughed. "Okay, baby. Tomorrow it is."

"Are you serious?"

"Are you?"

"Well, I really would love to have a church wedding so that I can invite my whole family but I don't think I can wait much longer."

"Okay. I tell you what. Tomorrow, you call your mother, your sister, your girlfriends and anybody else you can think of and you guys get together and plan that church wedding you always wanted to have. In the meantime, I promise not to put anymore pressure on you."

"What'choo mean, pressure?"

"I know I got a little carried away in the office earlier and I'm sorry. It's just that when I saw you walk in the door tonight you looked so beautiful. Every man in the café was staring at you, man. And then I saw you hug this dude and …"

I started laughing.

"What?" He asked.

"Nothin'. Hey I know what you're talkin' about. I got a little carried away myself."

"So do you agree that we should spend less time alone together and more time planning this wedding?"

"Yes. And I'll get on it first thing tomorrow."

He touched my face and smiled. "I love you." He winked and left me alone again.

THAT'S WHAT FRIENDS ARE FOR

Celia DuBois

Four weeks later...

"Hey, Cee, how you like this dress?" Maria asked.

We have been shopping all day and I'm am getting tired. Not to mention, Maria is in some kind of funny mood. She's not her normal talkative self and when I offered her a joint back at my house, she said no. I knew right then that something was up. I can tell she has something on her mind but I'm just waiting for her to talk.

"It's kinda short. Don't you think?" I asked.

"Hell yeah. That's what I like about it. I'm gonna knock Mark's socks off tonight!"

"Who the hell is Mark?"

"Oh, he's this incredible hunk of 'a man I met about a month ago. Celia, this time I think I found the one, girl."

I opened my eyes wide and imitated Buck Wheat, "Oh no, Alpalpa! Not 'da one?"

Maria laughed. "Fuck you bitch. I know you done heard me say this a few times before. This time I ain't trippin'."

"A few times before?" I rolled my eyes and grabbed the tiny lil' black dress out of her hand and placed it back on the rack.

"Look Miss Thang, just because you finally lucked up and landed you a man, don't mean you can go 'round judgin' other folks." She snapped. "I mean who that make you, Queen Motha' or some shit?" She yanked the tiny lil' black dress off of the rack and stormed towards the dressing room.

Now I'm am not sure what to make of Maria. She seems to have just a little more attitude than normal. Normal for Maria, that is. I walked up to the dressing room and tapped on the door. "Maria?" I said softly.

"What?"

"Can I come in?"

She opened the door and turned her back to me. I zipped up the little dress for her.

pamela davis-noland

"So what'cha think?" She twirled around.

"Girl, how do you stay so thin?"

Maria didn't answer. She just kept on admiring herself in the mirror.

"What? No smart ass reply? Alright Maria, out with it. What the hell wrong wit'choo?"

She sat next to me, not saying anything for a moment as if contemplating her words. She grabbed my hands and looked at me in the eyes. "Cee, I need some serious advice, girl." She begged. "First of all, Mark and I have only been datin' for about a month but I really like him a whole lot. I mean he so different from all the other one's, girl. Cee, he treats me so special. And he like me for me, you know. We talk all the time. He call me at work and we see each other all the time. We go for long walks, we talk about life, our beliefs and our disappointments. Cee, he even cried in front of me. We were talkin' 'bout our families and he started talkin'bout how his mother battled breast cancer and died. We sat there and cried together. Celia, he's a beautiful person and I'm crazy 'bout him."

I have never heard Maria sound so sincere. I'm not sure where she's going with this speech, but it sure was a nice change from, "Girl, that man gotta gold dick!"

"So what seems to be the problem, Black?"

She stood up and began admiring herself in the mirror again. "I'm eight weeks pregnant." She blurted out. And then sighed with relief as if she had been holding her breath too long.

"Oh, Maria. What did Mark say when you told'em?"

She jerked her head and glared at me out of the corner of her eyes. "I said I was eight weeks pregnant. You get it? *Eight* weeks."

It took me a minute, but I finally caught on. *Damn! Not even his.* "So the baby…"

"Is not his." She finished my sentence.

"Oh Maria."

"Girl, will you please stop sayin' that shit! I don't need yo' pity, I need some damn advice!" She scolded.

"And who the hell do I look like? Fuckin' Dear Abby? I don't know what to tell ya'!"

"I've been thinkin' bout havin' an abortion."

"No Black!" I shouted.

The little nosy-ass salesgirl tapped on the door, "Everything okay ladies?" She sang.

"Yeah. Everything's fine." I answered.

"I don't like this dress. Come'on, let's get outta here. We'll talk about it over a big fat greasy muffuletta. I'm starvin'."

We ate in silence. I didn't have much to say to her. I was too busy trying to figure out how women get themselves in these kind of predicaments.

"So?" Maria asked.

COFFEE-COLORED DREAMS

"So what?" I asked as if I didn't know.

"So, I know you have somethin' to say, Celia. So say it."

"Black. How did this happen?"

"Chile, you been celibate *waaaay* too long. I slipped and fell on a hard dick. How you think it happened?!"

"Look Miss Smart-ass, if you were really smart you wouldn't be sittin' here tellin' me you pregnant!" I scolded. "What I mean is how can you just sleep with a man, break up with him and just move on like ain't shit happened. I mean do you actually love these men?"

"Chile, will you please wake up? I never realized just how naïve you are. Celia, this is the nineties, we damn near in the next millenium. Women don't sit 'round and wait for Mr. Prince Charmin' to come ridin' up on no fuckin' white horse no more. We go lookin'. So just get out of that lil' fantasy world you livin' in, okay."

"Well Miss Nineties Woman. If livin' in my fantasy world is what helped me to meet Jeff, *my* Prince Charming, well I just think I'll stay right here in it, thank you very much." I snarled. *Now take that Bitch!*

Maria smacked her lips and rolled her eyes. I think she's speechless. I mean she knows I'm right. Not only is my Prince Charming incredibly handsome and talented, he is also willing to accept the fact that I'm not going to sleep with him until we say I do.

"Look, Black." I continued. "I'm not judging you, okay. Please don't misunderstand me. I'm just curious, that's all."

"Curious about what? How and why I date so many men? How I jump from one relationship to another. Do I love these niggahs? What?"

"All of the above." I demanded.

"Look Celia. I would love to go into detail 'bout the why and how's of my relationships but right now there's somethin' more important on my mind. You knowwhatImean?"

"Yeah I know. So. Can I ask you a question?"

"The construction worker." She answered.

"Oh."

"Oh? Is that all you have to say? Oh?"

"Well, did you tell him?"

"No. He moved to Detroit to find a better job. His uncle offered him a job with his construction company over there. He said he would call when he got settled."

"Well how long ago was that?"

"Eight weeks ago." She laughed. "We had a helluva farewell dinner."

"I should say."

"Yeah, well, we got caught up in the heat'a the moment and I didn't bother to stop and put my diaphragm in. I don't know what the hell I wuz thinkin' bout, man."

"Well, there's no use in tryin' to figure it out now. The damage has been done."

"Cee, I don't know if I'm ready for this shit."

"Strange how you wouldn't thinkin' bout that eight weeks ago."

"Look Celia, I know a'right. I was stupid. Do you have to keep rubbin' it in?"

"Maria, please don't have an abortion. I mean there's other alternatives. Have you thought about giving it up for adoption? I mean there are so many couples out there who would love to have children and can't. What about that girl you work with? Tina. Her and her husband been trying to have a baby how long? Six or seven years? Maria, you can't have an abortion. It's just sounds so cruel to me."

"I know, Cee. I feel the same way. It sounds selfish, huh? I mean why take it out on the chile just cuz his mama is stupid. I'm just 'gon have to sit down and call Fisher."

"Fisher?"

"Yeah. The baby daddy. Fisher Waters."

"Fisher Waters?" I laughed. "What the hell kind of name is that?"

"Girl, I know." She joined me in my laughter. "That's that niggah name, girl. But you should see that brotha'. Ooh, Chile! He put the "F" in fine. And talk about got some good dick. We ain't ever had what you might consider a commitment or anything. We just enjoyed each other, sexually. You knowwhatImean?"

"No I don't."

"Well it happens, Celia. Some people don't want a commitment. They just want somebody to hold every once and a while."

"Yeah, well, what'choo think he gonna say when he find out about the baby?"

"I don't know. I'm kinda scared. I have his uncle's phone number."

"Where'd you get his uncle's phone number?"

"From one of his homeboys. He datin' TaLisa, one of the girls I work with. He came in the office the other day and I asked him if he had heard from Fisher. He said yeah. The next day he brought me his uncle's phone number."

"So why haven't you called him yet?"

"Because I'm scared. Celia, be with me when I call'em. Please. Just for moral support."

"When are you gonna call?"

"What time is it?"

"Two fifteen."

"Okay. If it's two fifteen here, then it's three fifteen in Detroit. We can call in about two more hours. That'll give us plenty time to shop some more."

"You sure you wanna do this today?"

"Yeah, I guess there's no time like the present. Let's go back to that lil' dress shop. I wanna get you somethin' sexy to wear on your honeymoon."

"Chile, as long as I've waited, I don't plan on wearin' much of nothin' that night."

"Ooh, you go girl! Hey and when we finish, let's go the French Market. I saw a painting the other day at one of the shops that will be perfect for you and Jeff."

Jeffrey Jackson

"So when is the date?" She asked. I was waiting on this phone call. I'm surprised it took this long. She must have been out of town again. "Miles says that he's the best man, but he doesn't know. Moms and everyone else is being very evasive so I guess that leaves no one else to ask but you. Even though you didn't have the common courtesy to call and tell me yourself. I mean I know I'm your ex-wife but have you forgotten I'm also your closest friend?"

"No Laura, I haven't forgotten, baby. It's just that I didn't want to hear any more negative opinions."

"So whose been giving you negative opinions? Why can't they just be concerns from people who know and love you? You didn't have to be so mean to Miles, you know."

"I wasn't mean to Miles. What are you talking about?"

"He said he was trying to give you some advice and you blew him off and started talking about rumors that you'd heard about him. And you said he only dates whores. Miles cares about you Jeff."

Yeah okay. "Well that's nice to know. I care about him too. Which is why I thought he oughta know the truth. Anyway Laura, whazzup? I really don't feel like talkin' about Miles and his aversion toward relationships."

"Miles is happy being single."

"Yeah. So he says."

"Moms says she's happy for you but she's sad for the family. She says she wonders if Mama Ella is sad too."

"Why can't everyone just be happy because I'm happy?"

"Are you Jeff?"

"Yes. I am."

"Well. Then I'm happy too. So am I invited?"

"What?"

"To the wedding? Am I invited?"

"Laura, why on earth would you want to come to my wedding?"

"Because I've met Celia and I like her. And I would like it if we could all be friends since I see how happy she's made you."

"Don't you think that would be awkward?"

"For whom?"

"You. Celia. Me. Hell everybody!"

"No I don't. I think that in this day and age it would be very trendy. Besides, she's knows I'm family anyway. We've always been and we are definitely friends. And if you are going to celebrate a joyous occasion, I should be there. That's what friends are for. Right?"

"Well, let me just…"

"I know." She interrupted. "Talk it over with Celia first. I'll understand if she feels a little threatened or something."

Threatened about what? "Yeah, okay, I'll ummm… mention it to her."

"Okay."

"Bye Laura."

"Jeff?"

"Yeah."

Silence.

"Yeah L., what's up?"

"I'm happy for you."

"Thank you Laura. You don't know how good it feels to hear you say that."

Celia DuBois

5:30 p.m.

"Black, look at the time. We betta get goin so you can make your call."

"Oh shit. Let's go find a pay phone."

"Maria! I hardly think a pay phone is an appropriate place to call the father of your child and break this kinda news. Besides, it's too noisy out here anyway. Here comes a streetcar. Come on. Let's go to my apartment. It's close. We can call him from there."

I went into the bedroom so that I could listen on the other phone. I wasn't sure why Maria wanted me to do this. But if it helped keep her mind off of the abortion, then this is a'right with me.

The phone rang four times. Just as I was about to tell her to hang up, a man with an extremely deep voice answered. "Hello." He barked.

"Yes hello. Is this the Waters residence?" Maria's voice was shaking.

"Yes it is. May I help you?"

"Well I hope so. I'm tryin' to get in touch with Fisher Waters. I was told that he could be reached at this number."

"Yes. I believe he's still outside. Shall I tell him who's calling?"

"No sir. I kinda want to surprise him."

"Sure. Please hold."

"Cee, are you there?" Maria whispered.

"Yeah." I whispered back.

COFFEE-COLORED DREAMS

After about five minutes, Fisher Waters finally came to the phone. "Hello." He barked just like his uncle.

"Fisher?"

"Yeah."

"Fisher, it's me baby. Maria. Whassup?"

"Hey, Sweet Black. Whassup? Whatcha' doin' callin' me up here in Detroit? You miss Big Daddy? Can't find nobody to do it like I do, huh?"

Damn, Maria you sure know how to pick'em. Where in the hell did you find this sorry ass conceited niggah?

"I thought you said you was 'gon call when you got settled?"

"I meant when I got my own crib, baby. You know, so you can fly up here and give me some'a that sweet stuff. Damn I sho' do miss it, girl. You savin' some'a that shit fa' me ain'tcha'?"

Oh Lord, I think I'm gonna puke. Why on earth did Maria want me to listen to this shit? This jackass didn't put the "F" in fine. He put the "No" in "Class".

"Yeah, baby. But look, there's somethin' more important we need to talk about, okay."

"Whassup?"

"Fisher. Do you remember the last night we was together?"

"Baby, I still dream about it. We had that kitchen cookin'."

I made a mental note to never eat in Maria's kitchen again.

"Well, we got so carried away that I didn't take my lil' trip to the bathroom. You knowwhatImean? And you didn't pull out your wallet and get yo' lil' faithful friend."

"So what you sayin'? You pregnant and shit?" He spat the words out like they left a nasty taste in his mouth. I cringed.

"Yes. That's exactly what I'm sayin'."

"Damn! Every time a brotha' try and get on his feet, somethin' gotta always get in the way. You sho' it's mine?"

Now unlike Maria, from what I could gather from her reaction, I was waiting for this question.

"Yes it's yours!" She yelled. "I ain't been with nobody else!"

"Well how the hell I'm suppose to know that? I'm all the way up here in Detroit and shit. How I know you just ain't tryin' to put it on me cuz I don't know any betta'?"

"Look you sorry bastard! If I just wanted to put it on somebody, I think I'd have betta' sense than to put it on some sorry ass niggah who don't have a pot to piss in or a window to throw it out of." Maria's voice squeaked. I could tell she wanted to cry.

"Well I wasn't a sorry bastard when I had yo' ass hollerin' all up in that kitchen now was I?"

Maria slammed the phone down.

"Silly bitch." He said before he slammed his phone down.

pamela davis-noland

My ears were ringing. I ran to the living room to find Maria sobbing with her head buried in her lap. I stroked her hair while she cried. There was nothing I could say. Maria had made her bed and now she's gonna have to lie in it. She looked up at me with pleading eyes.

"We'll get through this, Black. I'll help you in every way I can, you hear me. You're not going to go through this alone. I promise."

PRIDE AND STUPIDITY

Celia DuBois

"How's dem weddin' plans comin' Doll?" Benny walked up behind me so quietly, I didn't even hear him coming. My mind was a million miles away. I had just spoken to Maria again, and she was still pretty upset. I decided to come to Benny's for a little peace and quiet. Besides, anytime I need to figure something out, Benny's is always the right place to do it. It's getting harder and harder to convince Maria not to have an abortion and I'm about at my wits end.

"Hi, Benny, how you feelin'?" I asked.

"Ole' Benny jest fine, Doll. Jest havin' a hard time keepin' that boy mind focused. He got other things on hiz mind, you know?"

I blushed. "Yeah, I know."

"You mind if I sit down wit'choo for a spell?"

"Of course I don't mind. Here, sit down."

"I was jest in the back talkin' to Samuel 'bout Hattie. Deys havin' some pro'lems. Boy I tell ya' what. When dat gal sets her mind to somethin', there ain't no stoppin' her. She as stubborn as a mule. Found that out furst time I laid eyes on'a. Gals been dat way all her life, too. She got so much potential. So much talent. Head jest hard as a rock, dat's all."

"What's goin' on with them, Benny?"

"Well, it's somethin' kinda personal, Doll. Promised I woodn't go 'round tellin' no body. But I can tell ya' dis. She ax me for some advice and when I try and give it to her, she gets mad. Jest like she always do." He giggled. "Yep. Jest like when we I furst talked to her right fo' she and Samuel got married. She was a lil' ol' pregnant gal wit' a whole lotta anger inside. Mad at the world she was. Mad at Samuel too. I sat her down and had me a long talk wit' her. It took her a while, but she finally came 'round. She jest needed someone to tell her jest how sweet life can be if you let it. If you sit 'round mopin' bout your problems, that's all you 'gon 'complish. Sometimes we gotta stop bein' so selfish, walkin' 'round cryin' about poor lil' ole' me, and do what we can to betta ourselves and help others." He stared off into space for a little while, smiled at me, stood up and "rocked" away.

pamela davis-noland

I sat there with my mouth open. He did it again. I didn't have time to figure out how he knew. I had to get home and call Maria. And fast! She needs to be given the same advice because Lord knows, she's been walking around moping long enough.

When I pulled up to my apartment, Jeff was backing out. I blew my horn to get his attention, pointed towards my house, parked and dashed up the stairs. I didn't have time to wait. By the time he walked in I was already on the phone with Maria.

"Hey, Black. You gotta minute? I need to talk to you." I could tell that by the way she'd answered the phone, she had been crying again.

"What is it, Cee?" She asked pitifully.

"Look Maria! I've had just about enough of this pity party of yours, okay!" I shouted. "I mean enough is enough. Stop bein' so damn selfish. So you got mixed up with a jerk. You ain't the first woman and you for damn sure won't be the last. So what'choo 'gon do? Stop livin? There's another human being who might just want a chance to experience this thing called life, you know? And just because he has two stupid ass parents who didn't take any precautionary measures doesn't mean he has to suffer the consequences. You are not alone in this world Maria, so quit actin' like you are. What about your mother? What about Mark? If he is as nice as you say he is, he may just understand. Hell, this happened before y'all met anyway. And what about me? Haven't I been there for you through thick and thin? I told you I'd help. We'll go through this together. We'll find you a good O.B., sign up for some natural childbirth classes, and shop for baby things and whatever else it takes. Just stop feeling sorry for yourself! Please!" I begged.

Jeff walked in from the kitchen and handed me a glass of iced tea. He stood behind me and massaged my shoulders. His touch made me feel less tense. I loosened the tight muscles in my neck and sipped my tea. I had said all that I was gonna say so I just sat there and waited for her response.

"So what makes you so damn sure I'm havin' a boy? What's with all the "he" shit!" She snapped. "I have you know, I want a girl."

Yes!!

It worked. She was going to keep the baby. I looked up at Jeff, who was looking down at me like he was a proud parent.

"So do you need anything?"

"No. Mark is about to come over. We going to a crawfish boil at one of his homeboys house. I was plannin' on breakin' it off with him, but I think I'll take your advice and explain everything."

"I think that's a wonderful idea. You gonna call me tonight and let me know how everything turns out?"

"Yeah. I'll call you."

"And Maria, please don't get upset if he doesn't understand right away,

COFFEE-COLORED DREAMS

okay. This might come as a complete shock to him so be prepared for the worse. And if he doesn't understand, don't worry 'bout it. Jeff and I will be here for you." I looked at Jeff for his approval and he nodded in agreement.

"Okay. Look, he here. I'll call you. I love you, Cee."

"I love you too, Black. And don't eat too many crawfish. You know they make you breakout if you eat too many. You gotta take betta care of yourself now Maria."

"Uh… yes ma'am." She laughed. "But do you think I can have one beer? Can't eat crawfish without beer."

"You betta not even think about it!"

"I'm playin' girl. I'm take care of myself, Cee. I promise."

"Good. Call me when you get back. Bye bye." I hung up the phone and turned and hugged Jeff as hard as I could. It is such a relief to have a wonderful man like him.

"Ooh. What did I do to deserve this?" He asked.

"You were born."

"So is she gonna be okay?"

"I think so."

"Good. So how are comin' along with your guest list?"

"Pretty good, what about you? Yours ready?"

"Yep. Here it is." He handed me a piece of paper with a total of twelve names on it.

"Is this it?! Is this all the people you want to invite?"

"This doesn't include my immediate family. Hell, you know they comin' anyway. This is the names of people who I know will come down here. New Orleans is a pretty far distance from Chicago, baby."

"Yeah, I guess you're right. It would be kind of last minute for them to just jump on a plane and come, huh?"

"Celia?"

"Yeah?"

"Never mind."

Oh god. I hate it when he does that. "What Jeff?"

"Well, there is someone else that I'd like to invite but I'm not sure how you'd feel about it. I mean it might be kind of awkward."

"Who?" I asked, as if I didn't already know.

"Laura. And before you say no baby, please understand that she's more than my ex-wife, she's my friend and I would love for her to be there."

I walked out to the balcony. I suddenly felt the need to get some fresh air. Jeff followed. I was tryin' to figure out a way to tell him that there's not a woman in the world who would be comfortable about this. Besides, I'm still pissed off at her for asking Jeff to father her child, *after* he already told her he was in love with me. But how can I say no to him after he's been so understanding with me throughout our entire relationship.

pamela davis-noland

"Jeff, baby, I know that Laura's your friend and I wouldn't mind havin' her over for dinner or something like that. But does she have to come to our wedding?! I mean this is going to be the most special day of my entire life. I want everything to be perfect. I'm gonna be nervous enough. Her presence there might make me just a lil' uneasy. And what about her? What makes you think that she would even want to come?"

"She does."

"And how do you know this?!"

"She called me the other day to see how I was doing. I told her that you and I are getting married next month and she asked me if she could come. I told her that I had to talk it over with you, first."

"Why in the hell did you tell her that? If she doesn't get an invitation, she's gonna know why! Thanks a lot Jeff." I stormed back into the apartment. He followed me.

"Well why don't you call her and explain to her how uncomfortable this would make you. I'm sure she'll understand."

I gave him a look that I could serve a life sentence for.

"Okay, okay. Maybe that's not a good idea. I'll call her myself."

"Jeff, can I ask you a question?"

"Yeah, baby."

"How often does she call you? I mean you never talk about her but I get the feelin' that the two of you talk quite a bit."

"Well we don't. And there is no reason for you to feel threatened by Laura. She has no intention of trying to split us up. I promise."

"And the fact that she wanted you to father her child should not make me jealous, right?"

"Baby, she didn't know how serious it was between us."

"Didn't you tell her ass over the telephone that you were in love with me? I don't know if the words "in love" means anything where she comes from, but where I come from, it means a whole lot. That alone should have made her high yellow ass stay home!"

"There's no need to call her names, baby."

"And why are you always defending' her?! What's that shit all about? That's another reason I feel so threatened. She can't do shit wrong in your eyes!" He tried to put his arms around me and I pushed him away. "I can't marry a man who's still in love with his wife, Jeff!"

"Now where the hell did that come from?! Celia, you trippin'! Who the hell says that I'm still in love with my *ex-* wife?! Who the hell said I was ever in love with my *ex-*wife! I've known her all my life, Celia!" Jeff shouted.

"Yeah, I know! You keep reminding' me."

Jeff threw his hands up in the air, grabbed his keys and headed toward the door.

"Where you goin'?"

COFFEE-COLORED DREAMS

"Home. I'll talk to you when you're a little less emotional." He walked out and slammed the door.

Two things stopped me from running after him: Pride and Stupidity.

DREAM WEAVER

Jeffrey Jackson

> Life is too short for
> Lonely nights
> Papier-mâché loves
> And silly fights
> I've dreamed all of my life about
> Someone like you
> And now I can die
> Knowing my love was true
> You've stolen my heart and
> Brightened my days
> What can I say, baby, to make you stay?

"That a new song, boy?" Benny yelled out.

"I guess you can say that. How long have you been standing there? I thought you were gone old man?"

Benny put the broom down that I guess he was sweeping with and wobbled over to where I was. "Long enough to feel yo' pain, boy." He sat next to me on the piano bench. "its called jitters, boy. Every woman go through it."

"What are you talking about now, old man?"

"Well, it's obvious, boy. I can hear it in yo' voice. Those words come from the heart. I rememba' when Mamie and I decided to get married. 'Dat woman give me the blues from the day I proposed 'til the honeymoon night. I thought dat woman had done gone mad. She broke up wit' me at least sev'n times before the weddin' day."

"So how did you deal with it old man? Was she as emotional as Celia is? That girl be trippin', man. She told me she couldn't marry a man who was still in love with his ex-wife. After all I went through to get her to even notice me. Benny, man, I fell in love with that woman the first time I saw her. And just for the record, I was never in love with Laura. I've always cared about her, but I

COFFEE-COLORED DREAMS

should have never married her. I should have never put her or myself through that. The only good thing was that we were friends. So many people marry someone that they can't be friends with. At least I can say we were friends and I guess we'll always be. Man, I don't know."

"Is that why you want her to come to the wedding?"

"Have you been talking to Celia, old man?"

"No."

"Then how'd you know that? As a matter of fact, how do you know any of the things you always seem to know? You psychic or somethin'?"

"Psychic?" Benny threw his head back and laughed.

"Yeah psychic."

He patted me on the shoulder, "No, boy. I ain't no psychic. I done told' ya' I got me some good connections." He looked up at the ceiling.

I looked up too. "So can you ask your connection if me and Celia gonna get through this, man. I would really like to know what to expect next."

Benny waddled away, calling out, "Dreams come true here, boy. Whenever you step foot in dis'here place, all yo' dreams come true..."

> Life is too short for
> Sad good-byes
> Un-mended hearts
> And midnight cries.
> Say that you'll stay
> For an eternity
> Make may dreams
> Come true, baby
> Stay with me.

Celia DuBois

12:00 a.m.

He still hasn't returned any of my calls yet. I know he probably worked late but damn, it's midnight. I know he got at least one of my messages.

The phone rang and interrupted my anger. I looked over at the caller I.D. and smiled. "Hello." I whispered.

"I love you, baby."

"I love you too, Jeff."

"Please say you're still marry me?"

"Please say you still want me too." I begged.

"Were you asleep?"

"No. Actually, I was lying here prayin' you'd call me back."

pamela davis-noland

"Now what makes you think I wouldn't call you back?"

"Because I was stupid. I should have never blown up the way I did. I mean as patient and understandin' as you've been, I had no right to act like that. I should've just put my silly lil' hang-ups aside for once and just told you that yes she can come."

"Naw, that's a'right, it's just gonna make you uncomfortable."

"I'll be alright. Hell, ain't nothin' or nobody gonna stop me from going down that aisle. Absolutely nothing! Hey?"

"Yeah?"

"I got some good news."

"Oh yeah?"

"Yep. Brianna called. We're gonna go with Karane Publishers. Brianna overnighted the contract. It should be here in the morning."

"Oh baby, that's wonderful. Congratulations! Is my baby about to get broke off?"

"Your baby sure is."

"No shit! Hey now! You deserve it baby. You worked so hard. So how much you gonna give Big Daddy?" He laughed.

"How much Big Daddy want?" I purred.

"All Big Daddy wants… he about to get when you say I do, baby."

"*Awww*… thank you baby. So how do you feel about moving to the Garden District?"

"If that's where you wanna live baby, that's fine with me."

"I can't wait to be Mrs. Jeffrey Jackson."

"I can't wait for the honeymoon." Jeff said in his Barry White voice.

"You can't wait?!"

We giggled like two teenagers.

"I love you, Celia DuBois and I can't wait to make you my wife."

"I love you, too."

"Goodnight, baby."

"Goodnight, Jeff."

……….Benny was at home kneeling on the side of his bed, smiling. "Yep. Dreams come true at our place. Don't they?"

Big Man closed the door to give him some privacy.

I
CAN SEE CLEARLY NOW

Celia DuBois

"What colors do you want? Pinks and Blues or somethin' a lil' more sophisticated." Maria asked, thumbing through the bridal shower invitations.
"Pinks and blues? I'm not pregnant, you are." I giggled and patted her stomach that had already began to form a little pouch.
"Ooh, please, don't remind me. If I throw up one more mornin', I swear I'm 'gon jump off'a building'."
"Rough, huh?"
"Chile, I mean to tell ya'. The other day Mark brought me a big ass box'a saltines. He said when his lil' sista was pregnant, his mama told her to eat one every time she felt nauseated and it worked."
"So how y'all doin', anyway? Has he accepted the pregnancy?"
"Cee, this man is so wonderful. Not only did he accept the pregnancy, he said that he hoped that just because I was pregnant, I wouldn't let that stop me from going out wit'em."
"You see, Black. You go girl. He may just be the one." I poked her in the arm and she blushed.
"Quit trippin'. I'm just glad to have somebody to talk to when I'm feelin' lonely."
"I thought you said you was crazy about him?"
"Yeah, but I don't know. I've been thinkin' 'bout Fisher a lot. Maybe cuz I'm carryin' his chile."
"Maybe it's because you're a glutton for punishment, Black! If you let Mark slip through your fingers, you're gonna regret it. You hear me? I'm tellin' ya'. If you think that Fisher gives a damn about you, much less that baby you carryin', you are sadly mistaken. I don't know what you heard. But when I was listenin' to him on the phone, he sounded like he was more interested in when he was going to lay you again."
"Yeah, girl, that's just his way of tellin' me he miss me."
This girl can be so dense sometimes. All I could do was stare at her, and try to decipher whether she was serious or not...

pamela davis-noland

She was.

"What'choo starin' at me like that fo'?"

"Nothin'. Let's go over to Victoria's Secret, girl. I want to buy some new bras and panties. I want everything to be new when I get married." I changed the subject. There was no need to continue *that* conversation.

We were walking, talking and laughing and just about to turn the corner when my eyes met his. My heart pounded like a drum. I uncontrollably stopped dead in my tracks. Maria hadn't even noticed that I had stopped until she looked over and didn't see me by her side anymore. She looked at me and then at him. She placed her hand on her hip and walked toward him. "Well, well, well, if it ain't Mr. Calvin." She reached out and shook his hand. "Long time, no see. So where you been? Hibernating'? I hear snakes do that too."

"Hello Maria, still as beautiful and outspoken as ever I see. And if anyone should know 'bout hibernating', it should be you as much as you like to sleep." He stepped back a little and looked at her stomach. He tilted his head to the side and smiled. "Or is that sleep around?"

Maria threw up her middle finger, gave him a fake smile and walked off. "Cee, I'm'a be in Victoria's Secret. Meet me in there when you finish tellin' this motherfucka' off." She yelled out.

"Hey, Cee Cee. You look beautiful. I love your hair." He kissed me on the cheek.

"Thank you. You look nice too. When did you decide to grow a beard?"

"Well, I just got back from a lil' vacation. I just haven't shaved yet."

"Oh."

"So what made you decide to cut all of your hair off? I can't get over how good you look."

"I needed a change."

"How've you been, Celia?" He asked somberly.

"I'm doing great, Calvin." *Damn, it sure feels good to say these words and mean them.*

"Celia, I've been wantin' to call you. I still think about you all the time. I remember how we would just sit and watch TV and have the time of our lives. I miss you, baby."

Niggah, please! For the first time, I can see right through him. He is so good at what he does. He knows how to make women fall in love with his ass. He had no intentions of ever dating me exclusively. He was just playin' a game. I looked at him and smiled. "So are you dating anyone?"

"Naw, I'm not dating anyone. I mean I go out on dates every once and a while. But as far as anything serious, no, I'm single and free."

"So which one of them thinks that you're hers exclusively?"

"What?"

"I mean which one are you watching' TV with? Taking the day off to be with? Walking down the street hand in hand with? Sleepin' until noon with?

COFFEE-COLORED DREAMS

Eatin' out of the same plate with? Sending' roses to? Which one?"

"Look Celia, I realize I made a mistake. You're right, okay. I guess I had no right to let you think that I wasn't seeing anyone else. I just didn't think you would want to hear about that. That's all. But I see things differently now. I'm ready to settle down with one woman now."

"Oh you are?"

"Yes. I am. And I would love it if you would give me one more chance. I still haven't given up on us."

Does this brotha' take me for some kind'a fool or what? "Save the drama, Calvin. I'm getting married in less than three weeks." I informed him.

"What? Getting married? To who? That brotha' who kept breakin' up with you?"

"No, I'm happy to say that he's making someone else's life miserable. Well, it was nice seeing you again Calvin." I lied. "I gotta go."

"Wait, Celia. I mean, is there any chance that we can just sit and talk before you get married? You know, have lunch or somethin'?"

Just as I was about to tell him to kiss my ass, a very leggy, light-skinned woman tapped him on his shoulder. "Hey, there you are. I told you I'd be taking my lunch break in a few minutes. You were suppose to wait by the phone booths." She said.

"Oh I was just walkin' around." He said nervously.

I smiled at her. "Hi. I'm Celia. Calvin's *friend*." I exaggerated.

"Hi." She frowned and looked at him.

"Sooo... you must be the one."

"What? The one, what?" She asked Calvin. "Is this your girlfriend?" She turned and looked back at me, "Look honey, I just met him in the boutique where I work, okay. He asked me to lunch. I ain't even tryin' to mess with yo' man."

"No, *honey*, he ain't my man. Not by a long shot. But take my advice, sista, go to lunch by yourself. Men like this come a dime a dozen." I snarled. I walked away beaming.

Later that evening...

I can't sleep worth a damn. I'm just laying here trying to sort out these feelings I've been having all day. My heart pounds every time I think about the encounter with Calvin today. And it just keeps playing over and over in my head every time I close my eyes.

I'm ashamed to say he still hypnotizes me. And I have the nerve to talk about Maria? I wonder what that's all about? Sometimes we women act like we don't like it unless it's rough. He's just so damn cute, though. Not nearly as intriguing as Jeff, but I can't help but remember how he rescued me from a severe case of loneliness. Or maybe it's the way he treated me like a goddess. Then again, maybe it's because I'd made love to him countless times. Maybe that's the one

pamela davis-noland

thing that separates him and Jeff.

I wonder why Jeff has never tried a little harder? Am I not attractive enough for him? Maybe he's never made the first move before. As fine as he is, he probably never had to. Maybe he still has Laura on the brain. I gotta quit smokin' this shit. I know damn well that it has nothing to do with her. I'm trippin'. But what if we make love and I hate it? Do I love him enough to get past that? What if we're not compatible? What if he's impotent? That could be a possibility. No man can go that long without it? Naw, a lot of men do. Maybe he's not attracted to me sexually. Oh, god, what if we make love and he hates it. I put my pillow over my head and screamed, "Why oh why am I having all these negative thoughts?!" I reached over and grabbed the phone and speed dialed his number.

"Hello." He mumbled.

"Hey, baby, did I wake you?"

"Yep. You did, baby. Somethin' wrong?"

Suddenly, I felt silly. "No, Jeff, I just wanted to say goodnight. That's all."

"That's sweet. Good night, baby."

"Good night." I hung up the phone and then picked it right back up again. I hit the redial button.

"Yeah baby?" he asked.

"Jeff?"

"Yeah."

"Jeff, are you sexually attracted to me?"

"Got cold feet, huh baby?"

"No. I just wanna know."

"Celia, baby, I promise. No, I guarantee you that on our wedding night, you'll know just how sexually attracted I am to you. Not only that, I also guarantee you that you won't be the least bit disappointed. Now, why don't you close your eyes and dream about me lovin' you like no brotha has ever loved you before. Because, baby when I get through with you, you are going to forget about every tired brotha' who *thought* he knew how to make love to you. And believe me baby, I'm a man of my word. Goodnight."

"Good night, Jeff." I whispered. I reached over and turned off the lamp. "Calvin, who?!" I screamed.

SISTA TO SISTA

Celia DuBois

I was shocked when I opened the door and saw Deniece standing there smiling, looking happier than ever, "Hey, girl, what'choo doin' up so early in the morning?" I asked, cheerfully.
"Jones'n for a good strong cup'a black coffee. You got one?"
"No, not yet, but I can, come on in." I was so excited to see her. She always looks so happy lately. Just like the lil' girl I grew up with. I couldn't help but giggle when she used the term, "Jones'n." I don't know where we got that from but Deniece and me have been using it for a long time. Whenever we want something real bad, we're "Jones'n." I hadn't heard that in years. To hear it from her brought back a thousand memories.
I went to the kitchen to get the coffee started and when I walked back into the room, Deniece was whispering on the phone, pager in hand. I could have sworn I heard her say, "I love you too."
"You sure look happy, girl," I said, "Who you whisperin' to like that?" I asked.
"Where's my coffee, chick?"
"Brewing. Why you disregarding my question? Or is it none of my bizness?"
"No. As a matter-of-fact it's not! But it is the reason I'm here." She giggled. "Girl, we have got to talk. I have so much to tell you."
I jumped up and threw the pillows on the floor. I moved the coffee table and sat, "Indian style" on the floor among the pillows. This was a ritual that dated back to our high school days whenever one of us had something juicy to tell. I patted the pillow next to me and Deniece sat on it and placed her pinky finger in the air. I locked my pinky finger around hers, which meant whatever she said was not supposed to leave this room.
"Oh girl, I'm so excited. It's a secret?" I asked just like a schoolgirl.
"Yes ma'am. And you betta not tell a soul. Especially not that nosy-ass Maria! But first! I heard about that check Miss Thang! You movin' to your fantasy home in the Garden District now?"

pamela davis-noland

"Yep. How'd you find out? I wanted to be the one to tell you."

"Nosy-ass Maria. How else?" She laughed. "So you gonna go meet Anne Rice and all the other famous folk, huh? Well you go girl, you deserve it."

"Thanks Deniece. You know how long I've been saving to move in that district. Hell, I would have settled for a nice apartment, but Jeff and I saw a house for sale the other day that would fit our price range perfectly. Girl, I'm so excited."

"Doesn't it feel good to have a man like Jeff in your life Cee?" Deniece stared off into space, grinning.

Oh oh. Now I know what the big secret is. I'm sure it has something to do with that white man who tried to pay for our meal. "So what's your big secret Dee?"

"Okay, I'ma tell ya'. But you bet'not tell Maria. I don't want anybody to know 'bout this yet. Okay?"

"Okay." I lied. Now Deniece knows damn well I tell Maria everything. I don't even know why she always makes me tell her that lie.

"By the way, how is she? The pregnancy comin' along okay?"

"Yeah. Now come on girl! Start talkin'. I have to meet my mama at eleven o'clock to pick up some more invitations."

"Okay, okay. Celia remember the day we met for lunch?"

"Yeah."

"And there was a certain gentleman there who wanted to pay for our meal."

"Yeah. A very white gentleman, if my memory is correct."

"Oh yeah."

"Oh yeah?" I asked, surprised. "What you mean, oh yeah? What? You forgot he was white?"

"No, course not. I guess I just don't think about it."

"You don't what? Deniece you trippin'. Is that who you was talkin' too? The "Great White Hope?" You told *him* that you loved him? Oh, girl, did you have to go there? I mean I know Anthony put you through hell and shit. I can understand you being a lil' upset with the black male population for letting you down again, but damn Deniece, a lily-white, arrogant white man?! I mean you can see his whiteness a million miles away. Girl, don't he have blue eyes?"

"Yeah. And?"

"I mean he just look straight up white. You could have at least found one who look a lil' foreign or somethin'."

"And that would have made a big ass difference, right?"

"No, I guess not. It's just that…" I couldn't exactly think of the words to say but by the look on Deniece's face, I have a feeling I'd better be careful not to say anything any more judgmental than I already have.

"Just that what, Cee?! I mean damn, can't you at least hear me out before you go off, Miss Pro Black!"

"Okay. I'm sorry, Dee, I just can't imagine you, of all people, with a white man. Maria maybe, but not you."

COFFEE-COLORED DREAMS

"Yeah I know this comes as a big shock but Mr. Jonathan Sinclair is no ordinary white man, Cee. He's incredible! Can I tell you how we met?"

"Chile, that's the first thing I wanna know."

"Okay, I'll tell ya'. One of my co-workers invited me over to her house for a dinner party, right. I didn't want to go at first because I knew that there was 'gon be a whole lotta white folks there."

"Why? She white?"

"No. She a sista. Only in looks, though. She's a pretty, dark-skinned chick. I think she said she's from Kentucky or somewhere up near there. She kinda reminds me'a you, Cee. She got strong features and some big ass eyes." She giggled. "Anyway, girlfriend is dating this French, Canadian doctor. And girrrlll, talk about fine. I ain't never seen a white man that sexy in all my life. And girl you know how much I love me a French speakin' man."

"Yeah, yeah, yeah, so you went to the party. And then what?"

"Yeah I went. I was so nervous. I didn't even know how to ack in front'a those people. And girl, Santanna pissed me off right from the start."

"Santanna?"

"Yeah, girl. Santanna. Chile, I think that girl gave herself that name."

I laughed. "Why you say that?"

"'Cause. Some lady called one day and ax'd to speak to somebody name Mildred. I told her we didn't have a Mildred workin' in this particular department, and she said, "Oh I mean, Santanna. May I please speak to Santanna?" Girl, I laughed my ass off. Anyway, as soon as I got to the party, she grabbed me by my arm and led me to a multi-cultural group of people and said, 'Okay, you guys, let's see which one of you can guess what nationality this beauty is.' I was so embarrassed."

I burst into laughter.

"Girl, that shit ain't funny." Deniece giggled. "Only one'a them motherfuckers said, black."

I laughed uncontrollably. Deniece rolled her eyes at me and pushed me off of my pillow.

"Aww, come on, girl. You know that shit is funny. It's not as if you've never been mistaken before."

"Yeah, but for her to just point it out like that, Cee. She gets on my nerves, man. She likes to brag about all of her foreign friends and shit. And she seems to be especially partial to people who are mixed. I think that's why she latched on to me so quick. She thought I was a "half-breed" or somethin'. That bitch is strange."

"So what was Mr. Jonathan Sinclair, with his lily-white ass, doin' there? You can't mistake him for being nothin' else but white."

"He's a friend of Jean, Santanna's boyfriend. He just moved here from New York and the dinner party was in honor of his new law practice that he just started here. Anyway, girl, to make a long story short, I was very uncomfortable.

pamela davis-noland

Everybody there was fucked up on somethin'. They was passin' around coke and weed like crazy. I know you would've had a good time. Not with the coke, though, I mean the weed." She laughed. "I got tired of talkin' 'bout my Creole ancestry to all of them white folks from up north, so I tipped out through the back door. Just as I was about to put the key in the door, Jonathan walked up behind me and scared the shit outta me. He said he was standing in the back yard smokin' a cigarette when he saw me sneaking away. He hated the scene in there too, but he couldn't leave because he was the guest of honor. So he asked me if I wanted to join him in the gazebo for a lil' intelligent conversation. And you know normally I would've said hell no, but I was feelin' so lonely and he was so gentle and soft spoken so I just decided, what the hell. Celia, we talked 'til four in the mornin'. By the time I left, I had told this man my whole life story. I mean I told this man shit I ain't never told you!"

"What?! You told some white man some shit that you haven't told me?"

"Yeah. And I don't even know why. Jonathan just has this way about himself. He is such a good listener. And a damn good lawyer too. I've heard him win cases over the phone just by his power of persuasion."

"Hmph. That I can believe! He persuaded yo' ass to go out wit'em. So what? You two fell in love instantly or something?"

"No. No we didn't at first but we did move pretty fast. I can't even tell you how it happened. He just makes me feel so beautiful, Cee."

"You *are* beautiful, Deniece. And you don't need some white man to tell you that. What about the girls? Do they know?"

"Yeah. Jonathan has a beautiful home in Metarie and he invited the girls and me to spend the weekend there about two weeks ago. He has horses, too, and he let the girls ride. We had so much fun! I was scared Brandi might feel uncomfortable but I think she had the most fun. Jonathan even taught her how to ride by herself. Now she wants to take ridin' lessons."

"Are you going to let her?"

"Yeah. She really enjoyed it."

"Okay, so what else makes this man so incredible, Dee?" I stood up and walked to the kitchen to get our coffee. Deniece followed.

"Everything from the way he talks to the way he walks, and everything else in between, girl." Deniece bragged.

"So I take it y'all two have slept together?"

"No honey, we've done more than sleep." Deniece laughed and lifted her hand for a high-five but I turned away, shakin' my head.

Deniece grabbed me from behind, "Don't hate me, Cee. I haven't changed. I promise I'm still the strong black sista you've grown to love. But you know what, Cee. I'm tired. I'm tired of trying to hold up my black brothas. I'm tired of being the outlet for all their anger. I understand their anger but I don't wanna bear the cross anymore. You knowwhatImean? Do you know what it's like to have a man treasure you? To make you feel that you a queen and the whole world is

COFFEE-COLORED DREAMS

yours if you so desire. Who, if he had a bad day on the job, he don't take it out on you but looks to you for just a lil' moral support and occasionally just a hug? Celia, I ain't never in all my thirty years, felt so loved. I didn't know love could be so sweet. I been through hell with the brothas, Celia, and you of all people know this." She turned me around to face her. "Say you understand, Cee. Please."

I hugged her. "I do understand, Deniece. I understand that every woman; black, white, or otherwise want to feel like you do. But there's something wrong with this picture, Deniece. We're suppose to be queens and our men are suppose to be kings and we are suppose to treat each other accordingly. But that doesn't apply for a whole lot of us. Sad to say. But let me ask you a question, Deniece. Why does it seem that our race gives up on each other so easily? So you made some bad choices with the brothas you were with. Does that make all brothas bad? Deniece, Jeff makes me feel just like you feel when you're with Jonathan and he's every bit of a strong black man. And you know that I've been through a lil' bit'a hell my damn self."

"Not nearly as much as me, Cee."

"Yeah, but I chose those men. Just like you chose the one's you were with. And if you wouldn't have been tryin' so hard to pick a brotha' solely on how much pigment he has in his skin, you might have done a lil' betta."

Deniece turned and walked out of the kitchen. I continued to fix our cups of coffee. Black, for Deniece and lots of warm sweetened condensed milk in mine. I walked back into the living room to find Deniece picking up the pillows and straightening the coffee table.

"Does this mean our talk is over?" I asked.

Deniece ignored me.

"Look, I'm sorry if I offended you, Deniece." I said solemnly.

"It's okay, Cee, I deserved that. But you know I've always had an identity problem. I mean you don't know what it's like to have to prove you're blackness. You know the majority of the men that I was with only wanted me because of my light skin. I'm the closest thing a niggah can get to a white girl, I guess. You know how some'a our black men think that that proves their self-worth or some-thin'."

"Not all black men, Deniece. And how do you know that Mr. Jonathan Sinclair doesn't like you for your light skin? I mean, he can reap the benefits of havin' a black woman without havin' to deal with all the criticism from people who don't know that you're black. 'Cause you know white men fantasize about havin' a black woman in their bed at least once. I guess it's a sense of power for them."

"But me and Jonathan never talk about race."

"I guess not. Why should he, y'all look just alike." I giggled.

"Yo' ass, Celia." She giggled right along with me. She knew I was telling the truth.

pamela davis-noland

We sat and drank our coffee in total silence before I finally decided to break the ice. "Deniece, do you remember what we used'ta say whenever we saw a brotha' with a white woman?"

"Sellout!" We said in unison.

"You think I'm a sellout, Cee?"

I contemplated a while before I answered her. I didn't want to say anything else too negative to her so I chose my words very carefully, "No Deniece. You're not a sellout. If ever I met a sista who cared as much about her race, it's you. I just wish you wouldn't have given up. I'm sure this man does treat you like a queen. And if anybody deserves it, you do. But I'd be a whole lot happier if he was black. But if you're happy, then I'm happy. You deserve to be happy, Dee. And sista to sista, I say keep your head up. And please, whatever you do, just don't forget who you are and promise me you'll continue to educate the girls about Black pride."

"I promise."

"So, this white man makes you happy, huh?"

"Yes. But Cee, can you call him Jonathan and not that white man."

I laughed. "Give me time, girl. This shit ain't sunk in just yet."

We spent the next hour sharing our views about interracial relationships, Black men, Black pride and "bearing the cross". I still can't help but wonder how Deniece, of all people, could get herself mixed up in something like this, but at the same time, I can't help but share in her happiness. She has and always will be one of my closest friends and no Jonathan Sinclair or any other man is going to ever change that.

We are sistas for life.

THE EX (PART 2)

Jeffrey Jackson

It is two days before my wedding day and I was just about to thank my lucky stars that everything was going perfect... and then the phone rang. It was Laura informing me that she was on a plane that would be landing in "Naaawwlins" at one o'clock. She begged me to pick her up.

"I thought you were flying in on Saturday with Miles?"

"I was. But then I decided I'd arrive a couple of days early so that I could get some rest. I plan on getting pampered while I'm here. You know, get a facial, a massage, and the works. And then I plan on doing some shopping."

"So why do you want me to pick you up if you have all these things planned for yourself?" I asked.

"Oh, I'm going to do those things tomorrow. Today I want to spend the day with my best friend. Or should I say I would love it if I could spend the day with my best friend? You know, hang out and do nothing but talk and laugh. Just like we used to do. You know, like when we were younger and things weren't as complicated between us like they are now. This may be the last time were able to, you know."

"Well, I..."

"Just think about it." She interrupted, "If you don't show up, I'll know you couldn't and I'll just take a cab to my hotel. That's all. I'll be at Gate 12." She hung up.

The last statement she made hit a nerve. I can hardly remember a time when Laura wasn't a part of my life. She's right. This *may* be the last time. There's not a snowball's chance in hell that Celia is going to put up with Laura and I remaining friends. Not that I'd want to anyway, I think the time has come for Laura and I to sever the ties. It's time for us to part ways and not just in mileage.

I figure one last day wouldn't hurt so here I am at Gate 12 waiting for her although the lil' flight attendant dude with the tight shorts informed me that I am at the wrong gate. I was just about to head over to the information desk when I felt a light tap on my shoulder. I turn around to see her standing there looking as angelic as ever.

pamela davis-noland

"Hey."

"Hey to you too. Why am I at Gate 12? This is the wrong gate."

"No it's not. It's the right gate. I told you to meet me at Gate 12 didn't I?" She leaned into me and gave me a hug with her entire body. Just like the kind she used to give me when she'd come home from a long trip. "I'm glad you came."

"Why'd you hang up before I could tell you whether I was coming or not?"

"Because I wanted to be surprised. Come on, let's go get my bags." She locked her arm in mine and kept it there, looking up at me every ten steps or so, grinning from ear to ear until we made it to Baggage Claim.

Laura wasn't very talkative on the drive to the hotel so I made small talk to ease some of the tension. The silence was loud and very uncomfortable. Laura's mood had changed from when she first greeted me. I mean it's like she just shut down. I tried ignoring it but it was too obvious so I just decided to ask her, "Hey, is everything okay, L?"

She looked over at me and smiled. At least I think it was a smile. It was the sort of smile that someone gives you when they're about to give you some bad news. I braced myself.

"Everything's fine." She sighed. "It's a beautiful day and I'm about to spend it with my favorite guy and my best friend." And then she looked away and added, "For the last time."

I tried to lighten the mood, "Well then, we better have a good time then, huh?"

No comment - she just stared out of the window. I tried a little more small talk and then gave up. I didn't feel up to faking it. And it sure felt good not to have to. Laura's not my woman anymore so I don't have to try so hard to please her like I used to.

"So after we drop my bags off, you wanna go grab a bite to eat? I'm starved." Her mood had swung back to that giddy woman who tapped me on the shoulder at the airport.

"Yeah sure. What do you feel like eating?"

"Well seafood of course, silly. What the hell else am I going to eat in Naawwllins?"

I hate the way she says that. I know she thinks she's dissin' me on the sly. But I could really care less what she thinks about my move here. "Okay seafood, huh? Okay. How about we go to..."

"Bennys!" She interrupted.

"Bennys?"

"Yeah. Oh please Jeff. I've been thinking about that jambalaya, ever since the first time I tried it. That was the highlight of that fucked up weekend with Miles and that skeezer he brought with him. Or should I say *bought* with him. And I didn't get a chance to get any the last time I was here. Please baby."

You know, man, the mind of a woman has to be the most complex thing that God has ever created. I bet sometimes he sits back on his throne and has himself

COFFEE-COLORED DREAMS

a good laugh at us men. I bet he's gigglin' at me right now. Men - we are not quite adequate enough to deduce the female's ulterior motives. Or better yet – we are gullible enough to think that we are the stronger sex. Yeah right. Physically maybe but that's about it. Women have the upper hand on everything else and they know it.

Now I know Laura has an ulterior motive for wanting to go to Benny's. I just have no idea what it is. What is she trying to prove? And to whom is she trying to prove it to? Herself? I don't really think anybody else here cares. Everyone knows how crazy I am about Celia DuBois. They'd probably just assume she's family. And in a way, she is. But Laura has *something* up her sleeve. I know it. I just hope, like hell, she doesn't think that I'm stupid enough to let her ruin another one of my relationships. "We're going to have to walk in the rain if we go to Benny's."

"I would love to walk in the rain with you." She gave me that pitiful smile again.

"Yeah. Okay. But to be honest with you, I'd much rather we'd go somewhere else to eat besides The Place. I'm going later at about 7:30 or so. How about I pick you up some jambalaya and bring it back to your room later. I eat there everyday anyway. I'm a little burnt out."

"Is that the only reason you don't want to go to Benny's? You're not ashamed to be seen with your "ex" are you?" She gave me a playful grin and poked me in the side but I know deep down inside she is pissed. This is one of those times when, if you didn't know Laura, you'd think she was actually happy with you.

"Well, L. I am getting married in two days. Don't you think people will find it a little odd for me to walk in with my ex-wife?"

"Oh. So you *do* care what people think about you?" She hissed.

"No I don't. And don't think for one minute that I don't know exactly what that comment is about. As far as *that* is concerned, I don't give a damn. Does that answer both of your questions?"

She repositioned herself in her seat so that she was facing me and folded her arms and rolled her eyes. "You don't give a damn about what?"

"I don't give a damn about having this conversation with you. I thought we were suppose to be having a good time?"

She did a Dr. Jekyll and Mr. Hyde on me again and smiled. "Look, I'm sorry. Really I am." She patted my thigh. "Forgive me?"

I quickly said yes hoping that she would remove her hand because I knew what she was doing. It's worked many times before. She didn't move it. She kept it there until I looked down at it and then gave her a look that told her I knew what she was thinking.

She quickly removed it and then repositioned herself back toward the window where she stayed until we got to her hotel.

pamela davis-noland

Celia DuBois

"So what are we gonna do after the rehearsal dinner tomorrow night." Maria asked.

"Well, I thought maybe we could go to Jimmy's Club over on Carrolton. I would love to go before I get married just for old time sake. What'choo think?"

"Girl, I ain't even tryin' to go to Jimmy's with this belly. Who the hell 'gon ax me to dance? Uhn, Uhn, I don't think so."

"Maria, your belly isn't even that big. Besides, you don't have to dance. We can just sit and laugh and talk about people. You know, like we used to."

"Yeah, but that was a long time ago. The only reason why women go to Jimmy's is to pick up a man. And neither you nor me is in any position to do that. Why don't we just have a party?"

"A party? Where?"

"I don't know."

"Okay, I'll tell you what, I'm'a call Deniece and see what she thinks. Maybe she has some kinda idea."

"Hmph! Miss High and Mighty might try and talk us into goin' to some white folks hang out. Girl, don't ax her!"

"Black, now you know Deniece ain't changed that much. Besides, I think the whole thing with Jonathan Sinclair is just a phase anyway. Well, at least I hope it is."

"I don't know, girl. She did talk about him a lot at your bridal shower. She was getting on my damn nerves. Jonathan, this. Jonathan, that. Like we give a damn about her and that white man."

"Down, fluffy. From what I can remember, you talked a lot about Mark too."

"Yeah, but at least Mark is Black!"

"And?"

"And, I wouldn't go around braggin' to everybody *and* they mammy that I was in love wit'a white man that's all. I mean it's not that I *couldn't* fall in love wit' one, especially somebody with as much money as Mr. Sinclair, but I wouldn't go 'round tellin' the whole damn world."

Maria has always and always will be fulla shit! She had a crush on a white boy in high school and everybody and they mammy knew about it. "Yeah, right Maria."

"Girl, I ain't lyin'. I wouldn't tell nobody."

I laughed. Maria's memory is starting to fail her. "Well, let me call Deniece. Im'a call you back later, okay?"

"Alright. But I'm tellin' you now, if she pick some country club or some shit like that, I ain't even goin'!"

"Oh, as if! I'll call you back."

COFFEE-COLORED DREAMS

Jeffrey Jackson

How does the saying go? "A leopard never changes its spots" or is it "a leopard's spots never change? Or maybe it's… oh what the hell; Laura hasn't changed one bit. Not one damn bit. But I must admit she's gotten a little better with age. She didn't beat around the bush at all like she used to. She was very straightforward when she looked me in the eyes from across the table at Dookey Chase's, after gulping down her second glass of Chablis, and said, "I don't think you should marry her Jeff."

I leaned my chair back on its hind legs, folded my arms and shook my head in amazement. I wasn't amazed at what she had just said or the nerve of it, I was amazed that I was staring at the face of the same little seven year old girl who begged me, with tears in her eyes, not to play with any of the Jones' girls. There was about seven or eight of those Jones girls on our block. She said that they all liked me and wanted to be my girlfriend. I was staring at the same young woman who at the age of sixteen begged me to take her virginity despite the fact that I was in love with Lettie Smalls. The *same* young woman who looked me in my eyes and swore that she did not ruin my relationship with the first, and only up until now, woman that I loved. This is the *same* woman who claims that she loves me as if I was her brother. Family don't do the shit I've allowed Laura to do and say to me. The things I've allowed her to do and say to me for the sake of family. She's always taken full advantage of my kindness and genuine love for her. And not once has she given anything back to me except to keep reminding me about something my grandmother prophesied over thirty years ago. I wish she loved me enough to let it go.

After about three minutes of total silence, only because I was trying my best to refrain from calling Laura something other than her birth name, I finally cleared my head and my throat and told her just how I felt.

"Laura baby, can I ask you a question? No wait, better yet, can I make a statement or two?" She was about to reply but I put my hand up to her face and shook my head. "No need to reply right now because, I'm going to make them anyway. L, I want you to listen to me and listen clearly okay. There is absolutely nothing that you, Miles, Mama, your parents, all my dead uncles and relatives can do or say to make this wedding not take place on Saturday night. So you and whatever bag of tricks you packed with your luggage can take the next flight back to Chicago if that's what you came here for. It's not going down like that L. And before you think about trying anything with Celia, you better take a minute and think about it.

Now, I'm going to say it once more, and you can either take it or leave it; if we intend on having our last day together, let's make it a pleasant one. We can talk about the wedding but we are not talking about my relationship with Celia. So… it's your call. If you don't feel up to hangin' with me anymore, I fully understand. But I'd much rather we kick it for a little while because baby," I placed my hand on hers and stared into her eyes so that she'd know that I meant every word, "this *is* the last time. You gotta let it go baby. Free yourself. I know how much you worshipped Mama Ella, but the woman was not right about everything."

She let a teardrop fall and when I attempted to wipe it away she stopped me. She quickly recovered and wiped it herself. "So what do you want to do next?" She asked, not even acknowledging any word, phrase or syllable I said. "I wanna go to the antique shops over on Chartreuse."

"Okay fine then. The antique shops it is."

Celia DuBois

I looked up at the clock. It was 9:45 and I still hadn't heard from Jeff yet. He said he had to take care of some last minute details for the wedding but I wonder what in the hell is taking him so long.

I decided to call Benny to see if he knew where Jeff was. The phone rang five times before someone finally answered. I was shocked to hear Jeff's voice, "Hello, Benny's Place." He said.

"Hey. What are you doing over there? I thought you were coming over tonight?"

"Yeah, I am baby but I got a little side tracked. What time is it anyway?"

"About 9:45. Where's Benny?"

"He's at home. I'm just doing some paperwork. I didn't realize how late it is."

I don't know if it's my imagination or not but Jeff sure doesn't sound like himself. And why all of a sudden I began to worry, is beyond me. I hate this sixth sense shit. I wish Mudear wouldn't have ever told me that.

"So how long are you gonna be there?" I asked, trying not to sound pissed off.

"I'm about to leave now. I'll be right over. Okay?"

"Okay."

The one thing I can say that I've learned from my experiences with men is recognizing the half-truth. And that's exactly what I think I heard from Jeff. But who knows? He may just have a wonderful surprise for me. Or something. I'm not about to start trippin'.

I picked up the phone and dialed Deniece's number. Brandi answered on the first ring, "Hello." She said.

"Hi Brandy. How you doin' baby? Your mama home?"

"No Miss Cee, she ain't here. She went to the gro'shree sto'."

"At this time of night?"

"Yeah. They went to go get us some ice cream. Mr. John brought us some movies to watch. You wanna come over? We havin' fun! Wait hole'on Miss Cee."

I couldn't help but smile. That Jonathan Sinclair isn't so bad after all. He sure seems to be making the girls happy too.

"Okay, Miss Cee, I'm back. I had to go open the door up for Papaw."

"Oh, how is your grandfather doing?"

"He fine. You wanna talk to 'em?"

"No. Tell him I said hi and tell your mama I called. Ask her to give me a call back tomorrow."

"Okay, bye Miss Cee."

Jeffrey Jackson

I was in the office trying to do some paperwork, but I couldn't concentrate because all I can do is think about Laura. I started feeling guilty about the way that I jumped down her throat and didn't give her a chance to even explain why she thought I shouldn't marry Celia. As if I didn't already know. I picked up the phone and dialed her hotel and had no idea what I was going to say, but I felt the need to say something. She didn't answer so I decided I'd just bring her some jambalaya like I'd promised, even though I had already decided I wasn't going back to her hotel.

I was heading for the kitchen and just happened to look toward the door when I saw her standing there with a bag in her hand talking to Big Man. She was handing him a piece of paper. I called out her name and she looked at me and blushed. "I guess you caught me." She said.

"What are you doing here? You didn't think I was going to bring you the jambalaya?"

"Well, I was just trying to save you a trip. I was just leaving you this letter." She smiled at Big Man and he handed me the note on cue.

I took it from him and grabbed Laura by the arm, "Hey come with me to the office to get my jacket. I'll walk you back to your room."

Once we made it to the office, she started explaining. "You weren't supposed to see me." She grinned and shrugged her shoulders.

"Then why'd you come up in here?" I snapped. I didn't mean to sound so mean but Laura is playing her games again.

"Well I just came it to get the jambalaya. I'll go. You don't have to walk me to my room."

She tried to walk out but I grabbed her arm again and stopped her. "Look L, I'm sorry for being a little agitated. I just have a lot on my mind that's all."

"Yeah. I guess so." She pouted. "You've been biting my head off all day. Why don't you just read the letter, I'll just see my way out."

I walked up to her and hugged her because this time she really looked hurt.

pamela davis-noland

She laid her head on my chest. I smelled her. We stayed that way for a minute and then the phone rang and I damn near shoved her to other side of the room, it scared me so much. It was Celia. I tried my best to keep my composure. I wasn't doing a thing wrong but I swear I felt as guilty as a whore in church. I *hurried up* and told her that I'd see her in a little while and hung up before I gave myself away.

I found my jacket under a pile of bills and slid the letter in the inside pocket, grabbed Laura by the arm and we walked out of the office and out of The Place in total silence.

We were about a block from the Crown Plaza when she finally decided to talk. "I really didn't want a divorce." She confessed.

"Then why'd you ask me for one?"

"I was testing you."

"Testing me?"

"Well. You had started to become so distant. And it was so obvious that you were just going through the motions. But I was hoping I was wrong never the less. The only way that I could think of finding out was to just come out and ask you."

"So you ask me for a divorce? And it was just a test?"

"If you would have said no, then…" She shrugged her shoulders, "But anyway, all that doesn't even matter. Let's just say that my instincts were almost right."

"Almost?"

"Yeah. I thought you were having an affair."

"Oh. Well, you'll be happy to know that I didn't sleep with anybody while we were married. I was faithful to you Laura. I'm sorry you thought that, man."

"You weren't very attentive toward me. What was I supposed to think?"

"Yeah. I know. I was just unhappy, L." I stopped walking and grabbed her arm and pulled her close to me. I placed my hand under her chin so that she'd look me in my eyes. "Weren't you?"

"Yeah. Yeah, I guess so. Sometimes. But I was unhappy because I couldn't make you happy no matter how hard I tried."

"You make me the happiest when you're my friend. We're family baby. I'll always love you. You know that don't you?"

"Yes Jeff. I know that."

When we arrived at her hotel, she leaned her whole body into me again and kissed me in the mouth and once on each cheek. She closed her eyes and tears started flowing down her face. She let me wipe them this time. "I just have one more favor to ask."

"What is it?" *I'm almost afraid to ask.*

"I want to hear you sing for the last time."

"Tomorrow night at The Place?"

"Yes. And I give you my word that I won't start any trouble. I just want to

COFFEE-COLORED DREAMS

see you up there fulfilling your dream that's all. You won't even know I'm there."

"Sure L." *Damn!*

On the way back to The Place, I pulled the letter out of my jacket pocket and read it.

> *Well, Jeffy. Remember when I used to call you that? Jeffy? I loved me some Jeffy when I was a little girl didn't I? You were my Jeffy, my protector, my big brother, my daddy and hell my sanity for the most part. I love you so much for always being there for me. I thought long and hard about what you said about Mama Ella. I agree that she was a little eccentric, but Mama Ella was special to me Jeff. You know how much she adored me. And I loved her right back. I sometimes forgot that she wasn't my real grandmother. And she taught me so much.*
>
> *Anyway, I'm writing this letter hoping you'll get it before you come back to my hotel. I already have my jambalaya.*
>
> *Jeff, I won't be attending the wedding. I've decided that it may not be a good idea after all. Besides, my gift to you is not to show up. (smile) I know now just how happy you are and that makes me happy.*
>
> *I've let go, Jeffy... I love you*
>
> *L.*

By the time I finally made it to my car I was damn near blinded by my tears. I let them fall as soon as I closed the door and turned the key. I guess they were tears of joy with a touch of sadness. But mostly joy, man. Mostly joy.

Benny's words played over in my head, "Dreams come true at my place boy. When you step foot in dis'here place, all yo' dreams come true..." It was like an echo in my head.

Celia DuBois

I damn near fell off of the sofa when Jeff knocked. I don't even remember falling asleep. I looked up at the clock. I was pissed off when I saw that it was eleven thirty and he was just getting here. I opened the door and glared at him and I immediately didn't like what I saw. He had what looked like pale pink lipstick on his right cheek. And if my nose wasn't misleading me, I could swear I smelled a hint of Coco Chanel. I stepped to one side and he walked in slowly. I closed the door, stood there and counted to ten and blurted it out, "I take it Laura decided to pop up a couple of days early, huh?" I snarled. I remember that same scent the last time she was here. I remember that same smell lingering long after she had left my classroom.

pamela davis-noland

"Yeah, she did. And Celia, I had no idea…"

I waved my hand in the air, "Yeah, yeah, I know Jeff. She called the airport to see if there was a flight to New Orleans and just decided to come early to surprise you. Right? So what does she want now? For you to call off the wedding and marry her again instead?"

"Look, baby. I know you upset but why is it that you never give a brotha' a chance to explain himself before you start jumpin' to conclusions and shit. Damn! You ain't learned your lesson yet?"

"Learned my lesson?! What the hell is that suppose to mean?"

"I mean, come on baby you did this to me the last time Laura came to town. Why can't you just hear me out first, huh? Why do you always have to start trippin' and shit like you just waitin' for me to fuck up? Why you can't just trust me, man? And why in the hell are you always putting me on the defense?!" He shouted.

Oh we're angry are we? Well I'll just be damned. Is this the man I want to spend the rest of my life with? A man who gets angry and yells at me whenever he's guilty? I don't think so. "Who in the hell are you yellin' at, Jeffrey Jackson?!" I shouted.

"Look woman, you can be angry with me for being late. *That* I'm guilty of. But nothing else, okay? You ain't puttin' me on the defense this time. Now sit down and let me explain."

I looked at him and rolled my eyes.

"Sit down Celia!" He shouted.

I sat. I was fuming mad but I wanted to hear what he had to say. "Start talkin'." I demanded.

Jeff sat next to me and kissed me on the forehead. "Look, baby, I'm sorry for yellin' at you like that. It's just that it's only two days from our wedding day and I don't want anything or anyone to get in the way of it happening. Not even you." Jeff paused and took a deep breath. "No I did not know Laura was coming two days early. And if I would have known, I would've told you. I've learned *my* lesson from the last time. I didn't want to tell you when you called Benny's because I knew by the time I would've gotten here you would've convinced yourself that I was a sorry sonovabitch and you wasn't gonna marry me."

"Was she at Benny's with you?"

"Yes. Her hotel is just a few blocks from The Place. She walked over to pickup an order of jambalaya."

"Oh how convenient for her hotel to be within walking distance of Benny's."

"Celia, will you please just listen? I saw her earlier today for a little while okay. But I left her at about 5:00. She came by The Place to get her food that's all. I was in the office working. I was on my way to the kitchen when I saw her standing at the door talking to Big Man. She was headed out with her food." Jeff stood and walked around the room. I could tell he had something more to tell me so I stood and walked toward him. He reached out his arms for me and I laid my

COFFEE-COLORED DREAMS

head on his chest. I could smell her. I pulled away from him and glared into his eyes, hoping they would tell me that I was wrong for what I was thinking. He doesn't look guilty. But why is her perfume all over him?

"You smell like her." I muttered.

"What?"

"I said. You smell like her!" I said it loud. I wanted to make sure he heard every damn word.

"I walked her back to her hotel. I wanted to make sure she got back safely. She hugged me before I left her at the door."

"And when did the kiss come in?" I asked, wiping his cheek with the back of my hand.

"Right before I walked away from her. She was just sayin' goodnight, baby. She's been doin' that since we were kids. She wasn't tryin' to push up on me."

"Yeah, I know. She would never do anything like that." I rolled my eyes. "And why didn't she call you before she left Chicago to tell you that she was comin'?"

"She wanted to surprise me." We said it at the same time.

You know, I'm beginning to think that Jeff is just a little naïve when it comes to women. That lil' hussy is sneaky and my baby doesn't even have a clue. "So what is she gonna do for the next couple'a days? She doesn't know anybody here but you. And she oughta know you're gonna be too busy to hang out with her."

"Well she said she has plans."

"Oh I see."

"She did ask if she could come to the rehearsal dinner tomorrow and hear me sing though."

"Oh I see."

"Why you keep sayin' that? If you got somethin' on your mind, just say it."

"Did she ask about me?"

"Of course she did, baby. And she told me to thank you for the invitation."

"Why do I get the feelin' she would've come anyway. She just *loves* to surprise you."

"Baby, believe me, there is no reason at all for you to feel threatened. I'm in love with *you* not Laura. And her being here shouldn't affect you at all. She's my friend. That's it."

"I know you're not in love with her Jeff. But I wish I could say the same thing for her. I think sista girl is the one feelin' threatened."

"Now here you go! It ain't like that at all, Celia. Laura was never in love with me."

"Why do you say that? Because you were not in love with her?"

"Baby. I already told you the whole story. Laura is like a sister to me. Why do I have to keep repeatin' myself."

"I know Jeff. I'm sorry. I know you're innocent, baby. But I have a gut feelin' that Laura is not as innocent as you think. Somethin' tells me that she's a very smart woman. I think your lil' sista has grown up dear."

"What the hell is all that 'spose to mean?"

"Nothin' baby. Are you gonna spend the night?"

He looked at me as though he was truly puzzled. I don't know if he's just pretending or if this man really doesn't have a clue about his so-called sister.

He hugged me and kissed my forehead, "If I stay, you gonna let me hold you all night?"

"Are you gonna be able to handle that?"

"Yep. You?"

"Well, we done come this far."

"I'll behave baby, I promise. I'm tired as hell anyway."

I looked over at Jeff, who was sound asleep with his mouth wide open. He still looked handsome even with that spit on the side of his face. "I know you love me, baby," I whispered in his ear, "and I know you're innocent. But Miss Laura, on the other hand, has got some serious explaining to do. I think I'm just 'gon have to pay her a little visit tomorrow."

Jeff opened one eye, "What are you doing awake, baby? Was I snorin'?" He asked.

"No baby. Go back to sleep. I was just turnin' over."

He kissed my cheek and dozed off just as fast as he had awakened.

THE BOY IS MINE

Celia DuBois

I called every hotel in the Quarters until I found her. She didn't seem to be surprised at all by my phone call. It was as if she was sitting by the phone waiting. I couldn't help but feel a little jittery while I talked with her. She was a little too damn calm for me. She invited me to meet her for drinks at the bar in the lobby of the Crown Plaza. We decided to meet at three.

On the way there, I rehearsed over and over exactly what I wanted to tell her. My plan is to get her to confess. She may have Jeff fooled with that innocent shit but my sixth sense tells me that Miss Thang got somethin' up her sleeve. "She's in love with you, baby," I said to the rear-view mirror, "and she don't know who she fuckin' with. I've waited this long for a husband and this bitch ain't even 'gon get in my way so she betta back the hell up."

I sat at the bar slowly sipping a glass of Merlot for fifteen or twenty minutes before she finally decided to show up. Lookin' just as immaculate with her angelic white, sleeveless mini-dress and white opened toe mules. Her hair is silky and shiny and her makeup is flawless. I guess that's what took her ass so long; tryin' to find just the right outfit to meet the "enemy." And wouldn't you know it, I'm all dressed in black.

She walked toward me smiling and gave me one of those fake ass hugs my family always give each other. Her entire body wreaked of Coco Chanel. I wanted to gag. This smell is starting to get on my nerves.

"Well, don't you look classy with your new haircut." She said. "Jeff told me how much more becoming you were with your hair like this. I like it."

Honey, save the flattery, okay. I'm here to set your ass straight, not become your friend. "Thank you. It took a while but I'm getting used to it. It sure is easy."

"I'll bet it is. I wish I had the nerve to do something like that. I've never even cut my hair past my shoulders. It's been this same length for as long as I can remember. So what are you drinking?"

"Merlot."

"Sounds good. I'll think I'll have the same."

"Why don't we have a seat at one of the booths?" I suggested. I needed some

pamela davis-noland

privacy.

"Okay, sure."

As we walked toward the back of the bar, I noticed two, overdressed brothas sitting in a corner staring at us. I tried my best to ignore them and said a silent prayer that they wouldn't bring their tired-lookin' asses over to our table and interrupt my little talk. I have it all planned and I don't need any interruptions.

"I was kind of surprised when you called this morning. I figured you'd be busy getting ready for the big day."

Yeah, you was probably hoping' I was too busy. "No actually everything is done. My mother is very good at organizing parties and weddings and stuff. I told her exactly what I wanted and she took it from there."

"Well it must be nice to have such a wonderful mother. My mother and I aren't what you might call, uh…close. She doesn't have very much time for anyone but herself. She and my father travel a lot these days so I rarely see them. Which is just fine with me." She smiled as if she were truly happy with that shit. "If Jeff wouldn't have been there for me, there's no tellin' where I'd be right now. He has always been there for me."

"Jeff is wonderful, isn't he?"

"Yeah. You got yourself a good catch, girl."

"So why did you two get a divorce?"

Laura hesitated a while. She played with the rim of her glass with her index finger and then licked her finger seductively. "It's a long story, Celia." She finally said. "Jeff and I got married because it was expected of us. My parents and his mother had had it all planned ever since we were kids. So we got caught up and did it."

"Oh I see." I heard the same story from Jeff but for some reason it sounds fishy coming from her. "So you two were never in love?" I asked.

"No." She said it so dryly that it made my heart skip a beat. She was lying through her teeth, as my Mudear would say.

"Hey, did you see the two in the corner?" She asked giggling.

I looked over my shoulder and one of them lifted his glass to me. I smiled and quickly turned around. "Yeah. I noticed them earlier. I hope they don't come over here and ask to join us. I would hate to be rude."

"I bet someone as pretty as you gets that attention all the time."

"Well, I'm sure you get more than your share of attention yourself."

"Yeah. Sometimes."

There was an uncomfortable silence for a few seconds and then I decided to cut to the chase. I had to hurry up and get home and change and then pick up Maria. We had to be at the church at five thirty for rehearsal and I don't want to be late.

"So Jeff tells me that *you* decided on the divorce. Were you unhappy with him?"

"No. I wasn't unhappy with Jeff. It's just that…" She paused and took

COFFEE-COLORED DREAMS

another sip of her wine. "Well, Celia, even if I tried to explain it, I don't think you'd fully understand."

"But *you* made the decision, right?"

"Well to be honest, I think it was more of a mutual thing."

"Oh I see. So do you have any regrets?"

"Any regrets?" She shook her head as if I was speaking Greek.

"Yeah. Do you regret divorcing Jeff?"

"Celia, what are you implying?"

Oh, this is going to be easier than I thought. "I'm not implying anything, Laura. I'm sorry if I offended you." I said innocently. I figure two can play her game.

"How about another glass of wine?" She asked.

Are we trying to change the subject? "Yeah, sure, I'd love a glass."

I watched the two brothas in the corner foam at the mouth when she stood and pranced across the room like a runway model, tossing her hair and licking her lips and anything else she could do to get their attention. She even stooped over and picked up a napkin that she "accidentally" dropped.

"You sure seem to have gotten their attention." I said when she sat down and smiled her million-dollar smile. "I think I saw one of'em drooling."

"Yeah, I guess." She said dryly.

"So Jeff tells me that you want to go to the rehearsal dinner and hear him sing?"

"Yes, I would really love to hear Jeff sing. He has such a nice voice. I remember when we were kids I used to write poetry and Jeff would put some of my poems in his songs. He is so gifted. I'm so glad he's doing what he always wanted to do. You have to admit, Jeff was born to sing."

I watched her face as she talked about Jeff. She seemed to glow every time she said his name. She looked more like a woman in love instead of a best friend who was there to see him get married.

"So were you in love with him then?" I didn't mean to blurt it out like that but I don't have time to play cat and mouse with this woman.

She looked genuinely shocked. "Celia, I told you Jeff and I were never in love."

"Yeah I know. That's what Jeff tells me too. And when he says it, I know he's telling the truth. But looking at you mention his name is almost like looking into a mirror. I glow when I talk about Jeff because I'm in love with him. And pardon me for being so straightforward Laura, but you seem to have the same look on your face."

"No, Celia, I'm afraid you're mistaken."

"Oh well, maybe I am. But I don't see how you wouldn't have fallen in love with him. I mean, if there was someone in my life that practically did everything in his power to be there for me. Made sure that I was safe all the time and who married me just because he thought it would make me and my whole family

pamela davis-noland

happy. I'd have a hard time *not* being in love with him. But then again, I'm just speaking for myself."

"Celia, do I make you feel threatened or something?" She asked, hand on heart.

"No Laura you don't. I know Jeff is in love with me. But I *am* a little concerned about your intentions."

"I have no intentions." She said. I noticed that she was not as friendly as she was when she first sat down. She had suddenly copped a serious attitude.

"Look, Laura, Jeff told me that when you called him he told you all about me. And he even told you that he was in love with me. But that didn't seem to stop you from jumping on the first plane headed South and come here and ask Jeff to father your child. So maybe that makes me wonder why you decided to come here two days before our wedding day. I mean Whassup?"

"Look Celia, I explained to you when I went to your job that I had no idea I was causing any conflict. It's just that......"

"It's just that what? Is it just that you realized that the only man you've ever loved was no longer yours to pull by a string? From what Jeff tells me, he married you because it was expected of him and he didn't want to let anyone down. So when did you realize that he was never gonna feel the same way for you that you felt for him? I guess what I'm tryin' to say, Laura is that I think I'm more of a threat to *you* than you are to me."

"No Celia, you are not a threat. Because if I wanted to, I could have Jeff packing his bags and on his way back to Chicago on the next flight out."

"Yeah, maybe. Maybe not. But sad thing about that is you'd have to scheme in order to get him. I, on the other hand, need only be myself. Jeff isn't marrying me because it's expected of him. Jeff is marrying me because he loves me. So back off, Laura. You may have Jeff fooled into thinkin' you Miss sweet and innocent and shit but you paper-thin. It took me a little while to see what you were up to but I think I know now."

"And what do you think you know?"

Now this is the time to call her bluff. Jeff never said what was bothering him last night but I could sense that there was more to the conversation than what he was telling me. I'm gonna try and get her to tell me.

"Jeff told me all about your conversation last night, Laura." I lied.

She stared at her glass and began fingering the rim again. She looked up at me and smiled. "Oh he did, did he?"

"There's not much that we keep from one another. Care to talk about it?"

"So is that the reason you called me today?"

"Yes. It is." I tried my best not to smile. This is going better than I'd planned.

She sighed. "Look, Celia, I didn't expect Jeff to agree to the divorce, okay. It was only supposed to have been a test. It had been so long since we, well you know. Anyway, I thought he was having an affair. But when he said yes and said that he thought it was best for the both of us because we were just fooling our-

COFFEE-COLORED DREAMS

selves; I had no choice but to let him go. I felt as though I was keeping him locked up or something. And I knew he was living a lie. He even thanked me for being the first one to admit that our marriage was a mistake. He didn't have the nerve."

"So you told him that you wished you two would have never gotten divorced?"

She stared at me for a few seconds before she whispered, "Yes."

"You know Laura, if you love Jeff as much as I think you do, you should try and understand something. Jeff spent most of his adolescent and adult life trying to make you happy. Don't you think it's your turn to return the favor? I mean, can't you put your own feelings aside and just be happy for him?"

"Look Celia, I don't expect you to understand. I have loved Jeff all of my life. It's not easy to just let go."

"Uh, excuse me, Laura, but you don't have much of a fuckin' choice." *This bitch is pissin' me off. The nerve of her to just waltz her lil' yellow ass to New Orleans two days before my wedding and start this shit.*

Laura stood and smiled at me and started to walk away. I grabbed her arm.

"Look, Laura, I don't know about those other women you managed to push away, but I ain't the one, okay. Don't fuck with me. There is nothing you can do to stop this wedding from happening so you might as well go yo' ass back to Chicago." I was having a hard time controlling my anger. I was about to start a scene.

Laura, on the other hand, was as cool as a cucumber. She looked down at my hand, jerked her arm away and walked off and left me standing there fuming and ready to pounce on her like a angry cat. I looked behind me and the two brothas in the corner were staring at me wide-eyed.

Two things kept me from running behind her and pulling out every single strand of dirty-sand lookin' hair out of her head: pride and common sense.

WHERE MY GIRLS AT?

Celia DuBois

"I know damn well you ain't 'gon let that lil' high yellow tramp get away with that shit!" Maria shouted with her hands on her ever-spreading hips.

I went straight to Maria's house after leaving the Crown Plaza. I needed some sound advice about how to handle this woman and Maria is definitely the one to talk to. She's been in so many catfights she could give lessons on how to handle bitches like Laura.

"No. I have no intentions on letting her get away with anything, Black. That heifer is lucky I didn't put my foot up her ass."

"So now what? Have you told Jeff, yet?"

"No. And I'm not gonna tell Jeff."

"What?!" Maria shouted. "And why not?!"

"Because Black, Jeff is so naïve when it comes to that woman. He's not going to believe she's up to no good."

"So what you 'gon do?"

"That's why I'm here. I need some advice. What should I do? I can't let this woman walk in my life and try and ruin it. Jeff is the best thing that's happened to me and I'm not about to let anyone take him away. The bitch had her chance. She betta step off!"

"Well, girl. I suggest you waltz your ass back to that hotel and leave one'a your shoes behind, if you know what I mean."

"What?" I was puzzled.

"Put yo' foot up her ass, girl! Women like that don't just disappear without a fight. You 'gon have to put a hurtin' on her Cee. And if I didn't have this baby in my stomach I'd do it for you."

"I know Black. Thank you. But I have to keep my cool with this one."

"Hey, girl, I thought we were going to rehearsal? You going like that?"

"No. We have to go back to my apartment so I can shower and change. I came straight here from the hotel."

"So do you think she 'gon show up tonight?" Maria asked.

"Yeah, probably so. But she betta not trip, Black. I kept my cool at the hotel but I'm'a beat her ass tonight if she start some shit."

COFFEE-COLORED DREAMS

The Rehearsal Dinner...

So far the evening is a complete success. Everyone is here, including Mr. Jonathan Sinclair who would have stuck out like a sore thumb but his magnetic personality and quick wit kept everyone laughing. He and Jeff spent most of the evening debating about the vast difference between Jazz, then and now. Mr. Sinclair is a fan of modern Jazz whereas Jeff prefers the classics. It was comical to see them arguing like two old roommates.

Deniece walked up behind me as I stood admiring the two of them from afar. She put her arm around me and kissed my cheek.

"What was that for?" I asked.

"Because you look so happy. And girl, if anybody deserve it you do."

"Well, you lookin' pretty damn happy yourself these days, Miss Thang. I'm sorry I judged Jonathan, Dee. Girl, you couldn't have asked for a betta man. Him and Jeff seem to be getting along well, huh?"

"Chile, Jonathan never meets a stranger. He'll strike up a conversation with a dead man. He talks my ears off, girl. Sometimes I just tune him out."

Jonathan and Jeff looked over at the two of us and smiled. I blew Jeff a kiss.

"You go girl!" Deniece said, poking me in the side. "I'm gonna get some punch. Want some?"

"No I'm fine. I'm gonna go talk to Black and see how she's doing."

As soon as I took a few steps, I looked up and saw her at the entrance huggin' on Big Man and then taking her jacket off ever so slowly while casing the room.

My legs feel weak and my stomach is queasy. The last time I felt like this is when I walked into Calvin's house and saw that woman. I was seeing red again. I looked over at Black who was staring at me with a "Is that her?" look on her face. I nodded my head and walked right up to her and stood directly in her path. We stood there for what seemed like hours and stared each other in the eyes. She gave me a half-hearted smile and attempted to walk past me but I grabbed her hand and squeezed it. She turned and glared me in the eyes.

"I would appreciate it if you would let go of my hand. I don't think you want to make a scene. But on the other hand if you do want to make a scene, I would be more than happy to oblige." She spoke softly, but I could hear the harshness in each word.

"No, Laura, I don't think a scene would be appropriate." I tried to maintain every ounce of self-control. "But I'm not above it. Now we can do one of two things. You can turn around and walk out the front door with me or we can stand here and hold hands all night because I'm not letting it go until you walk out with me. Now which shall it be?"

She yanked her hand away from mine and slowly walked toward the front door. I followed. I walked around to the back courtyard so that we could have

pamela davis-noland

some privacy. She followed. Once there, I didn't waste a second. "Let's cut to the chase, Laura. I know you're still in love with Jeff, okay. And I don't know what you think you're gonna do to stop this wedding or ruin our relationship in any way but before you follow up on those little wheels turnin' in your head, let me be the first to tell you that I'm also not above hangin' my left foot in yo' ass!"

"Well I guess that's to be expected, huh? I mean, considering that's the only way you probably know how to solve your problems."

"Look bitch! If you had any common sense, you'd take your lil' high yella ass back to Chicago while you still can. Before I show you what you're expecting!"

Laura stepped back and smiled. "Look, Celia. I did not come here to start anything okay. I was invited. Now if it'll make you feel threatened, I'll just go in and explain to Jeff why I can't stay."

"You don't have to explain shit to Jeff! Somebody done told you wrong chick. Your presence is no longer important to Jeff. 'Cause if you hadn't noticed by now, *I'm* his main concern. You may have been able to play these lil' games with other women but I ain't the one, honey. Jeff is in love with me. Which is a whole hell of a lot more than you could have ever said. And you were married to him! Ain't that some shit?"

Just as she was about to pounce back, Deniece and Maria walked up. "Hey, Cee, everything okay?" Maria asked while pulling her earrings out.

"Yeah everything a'right, Black. Put yo' earrings back on girl." I couldn't help but giggle at the sight of Black with her lil' round belly, ready to throw down for her girl.

There was an uncomfortable silence for a few seconds and then Laura proceeded to walk through us. Deniece and Maria closed the gap between them so that she couldn't get through.

"Hey Celia," Deniece said, "I think Jeff is looking for you. Why don't you take Black with you before she drops that baby sooner than she 'spose to."

"Don't worry 'bout me, girl!" Maria snapped. "This belly ain't 'gon get in my way!"

"Calm your nerves, Maria. You two go back in and tell Jeff that I'll be right there, okay."

Laura and I stood face to face glaring at one another. I could sense her fear and that was good enough for me. I started walking away from her when she grabbed my arm. I looked at her and quickly jerked it away.

"Look Celia, I'm not here to start any trouble. I know you find that hard to believe but I'm only here to hear Jeff sing."

I smiled. "You can save that innocent shit, sista. I've already met the real you. You're a spoiled lil' rich kid who is used to getting any and everything she wants by any means necessary. Even if it means ruining someone else's life. Look Laura, when it comes to you, Jeff is very naïve. Hell, you had me fooled for a minute. But face it sista, you lost. It's over. Jeff is madly in love with some-

COFFEE-COLORED DREAMS

one else. Someone who didn't have to play on his sympathy, lie, scheme or cheat. So you can do whatever you think you can do to take Jeff, okay. But let me be the first to tell you that his heart belongs to me. And that's something, my sista, you'll never have." And with that I walked off and left her standing there.

Jeff had just begun to sing when I walked back in. Big Man took me by the hand and walked me to the front of the dais. He sang so beautifully…

> The sun rises and sets with you
> The moon and the stars are my gifts to you
> The earth moves when I'm near you
> the rain-washes away my tears
> when I'm missing you
> I've waited for you
> All of my life
> To be my world, to be my wife…

Maria and Deniece came and stood next to me. Maria put her arm around me and whispered in my ear, "Girl, I don't know what good deed you did for the Lord to give you such a good man. But honey, you need to fall on your knees right here and thank him."

"I let you be my friend." I whispered.

"What?"

"That's my good deed. I let you be my friend. Hell, who else could put up with yo' crazy ass." I laughed.

Maria rolled her eyes. "I love you too, bitch." She said.

Deniece nudged me in the side and nodded her head toward the door. I turned around to see a defeated Laura kiss Big Man on the cheek and walk out of the door just as calm and cool as she had walked in.

"She was crying." Deniece whispered.

I felt a huge lump in my throat. If I were her, I'd be crying too.

HAPPILY EVER AFTER...

Jeffrey Jackson

"Hey old man, have you seen my wife?" I saw Benny coming toward me with a sly smile on his face. I was dying to utter the words "my wife" to somebody so I figure Benny was just the person to try it on. He giggled when I said it.

"So boy. I guess you finally did it, huh? 'Bout time, too. I ain't never seen a man take so long to git hisself a woman. Good thang she fin'ly gave in, boy, I wuz 'bout to git a lil' worried 'dere."

"Thanks Benny. I guess that's your way of saying congratulations."

Benny chuckled and gave me a long hug. "It is boy." He patted me on the back, "It is."

He pulled away from me and handed me a large, slightly torn, coffee-stained envelope that looks just as old as he is. "Well boy, dis'here my gift to you."

"What is it old man?" He placed it in my hand and then started to walk away. "Hey wait. Don't leave. Let me open it first."

"Okay. I guess you can." He patted my shoulder and smiled.

I opened the envelope and pulled out the slightly worn deed. It was the deed to The Place. I looked at him and scratched my head. "Uh... what is this about old man?"

"Well what does it look like boy?"

"It looks like the deed to Benny's Place."

He peeked at it. "Well I declare. It is."

"And why are you giving me the deed to Benny's Place?"

"'Cause I'ma need me somebody to take care of it, dat's why. You'll do."

"Benny." I shook my head and attempted to give it back to him, "I can't take this man."

"Consider it took. Sides you been takin' care'a it fo' me ever since you been here. Been lookin' for somebody to give it to who 'gon love and take care'a it jest like me. Sides boy, I think Ole Smoove would be happy to see hiz grandson foll'in in hiz footsteps." He handed me a business card with a lawyer's name on it. Benny pointed toward Jonathan Sinclair. "See dat man o'er dere. He gone help you out wit all the details."

COFFEE-COLORED DREAMS

Jonathan Sinclair was standing across the room from me lifting his glass of champagne to me and mouthing the words, "Congratulations." Then he grabbed Deniece by the arm and walked her over to the middle of the dance floor where he had no shame in showing his affection for her.

"But Benny…" I shook my head. Hell, I didn't know what to say.

"But nothin' boy. You make ole' Smoove Jackson proud now. You 'gon do jest fine. I promise." He gave me one more fatherly hug and shuffled away calling out over his shoulders, "I see yo' wife boy, she out here on the terrace."

I closed my eyes and said a silent prayer. *"Thank you Lord. I don't know what I did to deserve all of this but I sure thank you."*

I watched Benny as he stood and talked with the woman of my dreams.

Celia DuBois

I walked out on the terrace of the grand ballroom of the Pontchartrain Hotel to gather my thoughts. "I'm married." I had to come out here to say it aloud. I wanted to hear myself say it. And damn it feels good. The wedding was a success. My mother did a wonderful job as usual. This all feels like a wonderful dream I once had.

I caught a glimpse of my reflection in the window and smiled. *No it's not a dream, it's really true.* I told myself. *I am the author of a soon to be released novel and I am the wife of Mr. Jeffrey Terrell Jackson.* I pinched myself again anyway. Just as I did when I walked down the aisle, when Jeff and I kissed as man and wife and when I walked into the grand ballroom of this hotel and saw what a wonderful job my mother had done. Everything is so beautiful.

As I stood there and watched everyone through the window it dawned on me that Laura did not show up. I cased the room once more just to be sure but there was no sight of her anywhere. But I did catch Benny's eye and he started to "rock" my way.

"Hey dere, Doll. What'cha' doin' out here? That boy is lookin' all over the place for ya'. He 'bout to lose hiz mine." He said.

"Oh I was just out here taking it all in, Benny. I feel so overwhelmed."

"Well you go right'head Doll. Benny'll leave ya' to ya' thoughts." He turned and walked away.

"Benny." I called out.

"Yeah, Doll."

"Do you believe in divine intervention?"

Benny laughed. "Well I'm not sure what dat mean, Doll."

"Do you believe that God puts people or situations in our life to make us happy while we're here."

Benny laughed again. He laughed so hard it made me a little nervous. I didn't get the joke.

pamela davis-noland

"What's so funny, Benny?" I asked.

"Yeah, Doll I do." He said between giggles. "I do indeed." He kissed me on the cheek and "rocked" away, shaking his head and grinning from ear to ear.

The next morning...

I opened my eyes and immediately looked at my finger. It was there. I placed my hand over my heart and said a silent thank you that yesterday was real. I looked over at Jeff who was sleeping ever so peacefully. I closed my eyes again so that I could replay the night before in my head.

We had decided to spend the first few days of our honeymoon in Jeff's apartment, so we went to the store and bought everything that we'd need so we wouldn't have to go outside for at least two or three days. Our plans are to make love every minute of every hour that we're awake. And from what I experienced last night, my baby is more than capable to oblige me.

He had not only made me forget about every other brotha' who I thought knew how to rock my world, he made me forget that I had ever made love before. It was so perfect. The way he kissed and fondled me until I screamed. And when he entered me, he did it ever so slow and gentle as not to rush it or hurt me in any way. He made love to me as though it was his purpose in life. And when we yelled out in ecstasy together, he didn't roll over and fall asleep but instead rolled me on top of him and started the whole process all over again. I thought I'd died and gone to heaven.

I decided to get up and make a pot of coffee. As I stood there in the kitchen, a funny feeling came over me. I felt as though someone was standing behind me. But when I turned around, no one was there. I went back upstairs and Jeff was still sound asleep just as I had left him.

I knelt on the side of the bed and said my prayers. "Thank you Lord for divine intervention." I whispered.

Benny smiled. "My work is done." He whispered. He patted Big Man on the shoulder and they were off on their journey...